THE 4TH MERCENARY

No. 002

ALL MEN DIE...

   FEW EVER LIVE...

PREFACE

This is a story written about a certain level of international intrigue that goes on outside the purview of very interested parties like CNN and the CIA; but who knows what is going on and where it is going on. The names are purely fiction and any relation to actual living persons is just a random event of coincidence. Likewise, actual business names and places are mentioned as a matter of fact, but the events occurring there are pure fiction and do not reflect and are not indicative of any actual events that might take place there. This novel is pure fiction.

ACKNOWLEDGEMENTS

A very special thanks again must go to Lynn Wilkins of the Key West Business Center in Key West, Florida for her magnificent handling and processing of the manuscript. Without her highly efficient and accurate processing of the manuscript, this production would not be possible; her contribution was vital and continues to be on future novels.

Also, a special thanks goes to the artist Ekkarat Sridee of Chiang Mai, Thailand for his excellent work on the front and back covers.

A final point, this book was written in various locations around the world, principally: Burma, Thailand, Colombia, Congo and Yemen. A special thanks to those places for providing a few days of solitude. In fairness it was also composed in Cape Town, South Africa, Phnom Penh, Cambodia and Reykjavik, Iceland. A special thanks to them also.

GENERAL

The book is organized by short, numerous Chapters. The Chapters are set up to assist in the flow of the story. A list of the principle characters is contained in the front of the book for easy reference.

AUTHOR'S BIOGRAPHY

The author has had a career in military intelligence, military aviation, international finance and space systems research. He has traveled to 173 countries, traveling to 57 countries by the age of 24. His education includes a B.S. International Affairs, B.S. Mathematics, Masters in Business Administration (MBA) and Ph.D. Finance. He resides in a number of locations, including Cape Town, South Africa, Nassau, Bahamas, Island of Kauai, Hawaii, and Las Vegas.

KEY LOCATIONS: THE 4ᵗʰ MERCENARY NO. 002

1. Western Sudan
2. Eastern Chad
3. Nice, France
4. London
5. Dakar, Senegal
6. Monaco
7. Nassau, Bahamas
8. Havana, Cuba
9. Norman Cay, Bahamas
10. Rangoon, Burma
11. Cape Town, South Africa
12. Khartoum, Sudan
13. Beirut, Lebanon
14. Mae Sai, Thailand
15. Fang, Thailand
16. Libreville, Gabon
17. Stone Town, Zanzibar
18. Angola Highlands
19. Manhattan, New York
20. Eastern Congo
21. Muscat, Oman
22. Gibraltar
23. Monaco

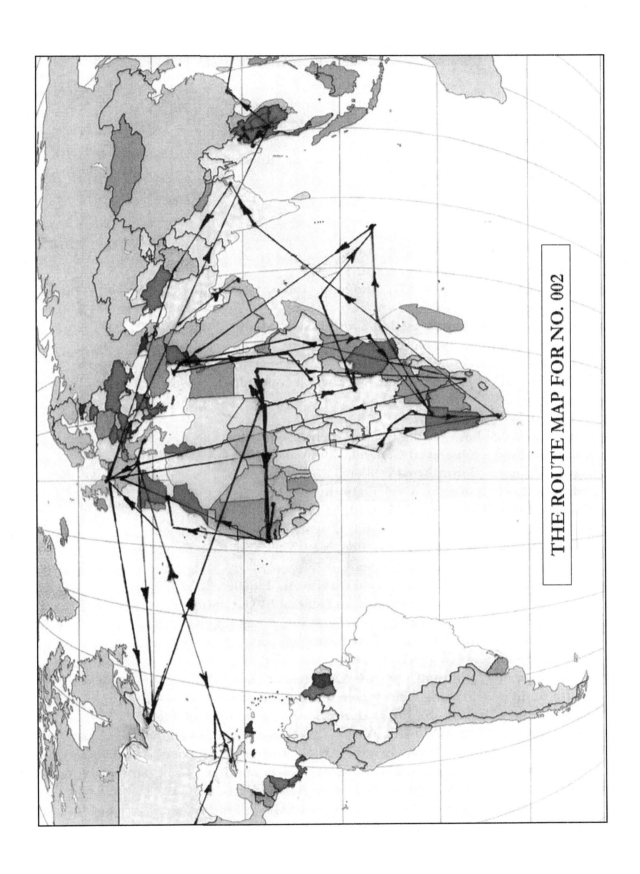

THE ROUTE MAP FOR NO. 002

PRINCIPAL CAST OF CHARACTERS:

The Principle Character comes with a number of names:

 <u>The 4th Mercenary:</u>
 Blake Anderson — Nice, France — Havana, Cuba
 Jason Stoner — Stoner/Franklin Investments, used in New York City
 Kent Benson — Name used with Lisa Aswanela
 Kent Weston — London with Kelly Grant
 Code 011 — Mission assigned name, Namibia, Russians
 Code 015 — Mission assigned name Code 037
 Code 017 — Namibia
 Code 057 — Western Sudan, Chad
 Code 087 — Mission assigned name
 Code 577 — Mission assigned name
 Code/Sierra 717 — Mission assigned name
 Conrad LaSalle — Code 037, Rangoon, India, South American name to the girls of
   Bogota
 Conrad LaSalle — Name used in South Beach, Miami
 Simon Greene — Rangoon, Burma, Khartoum, Sudan
 Mr. Stanley — Sahara Mission of The 4th Mercenary
 Kent, Suite 517 — Another name, used when convenient, mostly in Nassau, Bahamas

OTHER PRINCIPAL CAST:

 Farsi/Yassar Abbas — Arms Dealers, Beirut, Lebanon
 General Abdul — One-eyed General, Commander, Sudan Army Camp
 Ramy Abdula — Beirut Arms Dealer
 Ali Alawid — Syrian Arms Dealer, Brother of Said
 Said Alawid — Brother of Ali Alawid, 10 years younger
 Saif Alawid — Brother of Ali Alawid, 12 years younger
 Christy Alexander — Upper East Side, New York City Real Estate Agent
 Carlos Alvarez — Bogota Arms Dealer
 Hernando Alvarez — Havana Teacher, Havana Hustler, 32
 General Asamba — Congo Warlord for General Mosamba
 Lisa Aswanela — 18, Johannesburg — Sandton, young leggy escort,
  Operative South African/French Intelligence.
 General Bamamin — Uganda, High Commander
 Todd Blake — 47, Journalist, Partner with Jeremy Keeler
 Pierre Bodit — 24, Young actor for a part in the movie
 Abbey Bond — British, 20, Javier Henri LeCirac Studio Associate
 Trent Burton — Son of Winston Burton, 25-years-old, stationed in Congo, London
 Winston Burton — CEO, British Africa Executive Services, Specialized Security
  Company for Corporations, other Agencies, London / Cape Town / Hong Kong
 Frank Cramer — Photographer, Partner to Andy Morris, British
 Brandon Craig — British, 29, Writer, Head of Movie Production,   LeCirac Industries
 Eva Escobar — Havana, Cuba, 18, knows The 4th Mercenary

Didier Francois — French Intelligence
Patrice Guiot — French Intelligence
Pedro Gomez — Bogota Drug Lord
Alexis Gomez — Daughter to Pedro Gomez, 19
Kelly Grant — British, 20, Javier Henri LeCirac Studio Associate
Peter Hunt — British Mercenary, Congo
Erica Johnson — Hostess, Atlantis Resort, 21-years-old, Nassau, Bahamas
Winton Kigani — Retired Rwandan General, High Level Arms Dealer/Politician
Alex Kagamba — South African Arms Dealer, 33, Investment Banker
Jeremy Keeler — Journalist, mid-50's, South Africa
Ward Kent — Director, CFO, Kent and Martin LLC, New York
Wei Kyi — Burmese Arms Dealer
Pierre LaRue — Vice President, Finance/Technology to LeCirac
Javier Henri LeCirac — LeCirac Industries, 37, Producing movie on African Mercenaries,
    French Dealer, Arms/Finance/Autos/Jet-leasing/Jet Aircraft
Raja Majani — Calcutta, India Arms Dealer
Christina Mercedes Martinez — 19, Friend of Alexus Gomez
Andy Morris — 31, Journalist, Britain, Partner to Frank Cramer
General Mosamba — Ugandan Army, Western Forces, Congo Warlord
Bryan Norton — Former British SAS, Former Congo Mercenary
    Retired to Nassau, Bahamas, Executed in the Congo
Eric Olsen — 31, Special Projects LeCirac Industries, LSG, MBA
Pierre Patron — 27, French Air Force F-1B
Vanda Pntip — Head bodyguard, Chaya Ptorn
Chaya Ptorn — Thai Arms Dealer
Natasha Terrashova — Russian Translator, Namibian Base
General Simbas — Congo Warlord for Winston Burton

THE CREST OF THE 4TH MERCENARY

CHAPTER 1

Three p.m., Western Sudan, 23 miles from the Chad border in the massive Sahara Desert, North Africa.

The lone figure struggles to pull the rickety bicycle cart over the baked hard desert road. It is 121° with a five mph. wind out of the west. Tomorrow should be cooler . . . maybe 117° . . . if that lone figure can live that long. He has been walking four days but has covered only thirty-one miles. It may take three more days to reach the Chad border, as he is bone weary and slowing down. There is nothing alive here, lots of things that used to be alive were here, now they are skeletons scattered along the road. This lone figure actually tripped on a camel bone yesterday . . . it took him ten minutes to get up . . . just so tired.

The bike cart carried critical cargo, the last twenty gallons of water, seven protein biscuits, and straw piled up for some non-existent camel. It was his cover for his precious cargo.

In his head, buried there somewhere in the fog of heat and exhaustion, were six numbers. Tomorrow he would write them down, as his memory was disappearing into the vast heat waves and mirages of Western Sudan; yes, the mirages of the Western Sudan, his existence was becoming a mirage.

Leaving the Sudanese army base thirty miles to the east of the man was a Soviet-made Jeep with a 50-caliber machine gun mounted in the back. It headed west on the hard-baked road. It was in a hurry to go nowhere in particular.

The man traveled at high noon, only because nothing else moved then, and he could make a little progress. But night was better, and he would soon stop and hide in the sand dunes. Twenty gallons of water seems like a lot, but all would be needed in the next three days just to survive.

The Soviet-made military vehicle was hitting 60 mph. on the hard road. The three young soldiers were fully energized, they had rested for three days and were ready to just ride fast . . . and kill something. They were ready to patrol.

The man struggled on, draped in the traditional robes of the Sahara nomads. He didn't want to continue, he just wanted to rest . . . maybe forever.

In thirty minutes the military vehicle covered thirty miles, the struggling lone figure had covered just one quarter mile. Pulling the cart felt like he was pulling the military vehicle.

As the vehicle topped one of the desolate hills, they saw the figure. At first surprised to see anything at all, dead or alive, they then whooped with testosterone-laden joy. They would be on the figure in thirty to forty seconds. Just enough time to activate an AK-47.

The man faintly heard the vehicle, but in the wave of exhaustion and the waves of heat, it seemed surreal. He kept struggling; no energy to turn around.

The vehicle slowed to 25 mph . . . maybe it could help the man. No, not really.

The AK-47 was on semi-automatic; as the vehicle closed to within fifty yards, the man in the passenger side let loose with five rounds. Two were wide and three ripped into the back of the lone walking figure. As the vehicle rode by, the man was face down in the dirt, his back ripped up by the bullets, the swirling dust turning him into the most pathetic figure . . . a heap of rags lying in the sand.

The vehicle kept going, picking up speed, as the occupants yelped and fired more rounds into the air; the gunman still hanging out the open window. It roared away leaving a shattered body behind. The vehicle kept moving, but nothing else moved. The vehicle would go to the border, check with the guards, and return to base. It would take them a total of two hours, with drinks at the guard posts taking most of the time.

CHAPTER 2

When the soldiers did return, there was no dead man or his pitiful cart. Stunned, the young soldiers did a sideways, dust throwing stop. Maybe this was not the stop, not the place. They looked through their Ray Ban sunglasses looking for evidence, it didn't seem possible. Their manhood challenged, how could they not kill this pitiful creature? But no blood; maybe the robes soaked it up. . . slight signs of something going into the sand to a small dune north of the roads, about seventy yards away.

They gunned the Soviet jeep into the sand and, with full power, bulldozed through the sand to the base of the small dunes. They then got out of the jeep to be hit by the full force of the blistering heat. As young as they were, they still felt the blast and it made them dizzy and weak. Their sense of bravado vanished. All of a sudden they were not so keen to find their prey.

The dunes in front of them were only twenty yards high, but their energy had been drained, so it looked a hundred yards high. The young soldiers said nothing, each hoping the other would not spot their weakness.

By the time they got to the top of the hill they had no desire to find anything, dead or alive. After all, it was 121°.

They got to the top only to see the pitiful bike cart at the base of the dune . . . but nothing else. Well there were some rags covered by the sand ten yards from the cart, but that's all.

The three young soldiers really had lost interest in how they could kill a man and then he disappears. It was strange and confusing, but at 121° it all didn't seem to matter. They stood at the top of the dunes for a moment and then, without really thinking, slowly went down the dune to the cart. The wind had shifted the sand, so there were no real tracks, but without the intense glare and heat, they would have been able to see it . . . but they didn't.

. . . And it was too late.

Three bullets came out of the sand where the rags lay. A bullet hit each of the three soldiers, but no one was killed. So now we had four pitiful figures lying in the sand at 121° with the sun beating down; although the sun was not really hitting the rags buried in the sand, and that was a huge difference.

The three soldiers were hit and bleeding, but the blood caked and dried almost immediately. Each of the three had some residual energy for two to three minutes after being hit but were already fading fast just seven minutes after being hit. Their moaning and cursing had already stopped.

They needed water and shade desperately but had neither. The rags in the sand did not move. Soon the three soldiers just lay there under the searching 121° sun, each passing minute meant their ultimate condition was irreversible, they were going to die. Not tomorrow, not tonight, but just in an hour or so. It was too late to do anything already.

The slight wind continued to come out of the west, and the sun continued to scorch the earth. In the vast stretches of Western Sudan, nothing moved . . . and one lonely Soviet jeep sat there . . . you could cook hamburgers on the hood. And since the hood was big, you could have fried up some hash browns and pancakes for an afternoon snack.

It was now 3:30 p.m., a silent, scorching 3:30 p.m. in the Western Sudan, 23 miles from the border with the country of Chad. All of that meant nothing in the scheme of things to the four bodies lying there. Three wounded soldiers lay in the open desert, and one man laying two feet under the sand, under a pile of robes and rags, collecting more sand as each minute passed. The man in the sand was not going to move because it was so hot, and he was not going to move because pulling the trigger of a Beretta Px4 subcompact 9 mm had completely exhausted him. To save himself from the heat he had managed to take off the bulletproof vest he had been wearing. He was now laying on it two feet beneath the scorching sand, three water bottles were also buried with him, and they were the only reason he was alive, and he had not even been shot.

CHAPTER 3

The army camp thirty miles to the east of the lonely Soviet jeep was nominally a Sudanese army camp. But, in fact, there were only two hundred soldiers of the regular army there, the other three hundred men were a collection of rogue rebels whose trade was the raping and pillaging of the helpless towns and villages of the Western Sudan . . . the Darfur region. They live off the meager spoils of the nomads and traders of the region. As their raids took more resources from the people, they were ever more desperate to find new areas to pillage. They had become an ever more violent, desperate group.

"In charge" of this camp of five hundred men was a one star general, Abdul Atar. General Abdul had a Muslim name that went on with five separate names . . . so he was called General Abdul. General Abdul was the single army general in the region, and he had but a single eye. There was no dramatic tale behind the single eye, it had not been lost in a knife fight in Khartoum, it had not been lost to heavy combat on the Ethiopian Border; it had been lost to an infection when he was seventeen, that's it. But the eye patch did set a certain atmosphere in the camp, particularly given the backdrop of the three hundred rough and violent rogue warriors. They belonged to no one and had become more unstable with each passing day. A one-eyed general is what you would expect in this camp. It was kind of like the murderous Khmer Rouge general in Cambodia, Ta Mok. But General Ta Mok had both eyes and just one regular leg . . . and a wooden leg.

The general tried his best to keep these five hundred men under control but given the desolation and the nature of the desperation here, there was always a very violent unstable atmosphere in camp. Just a random unexpected event in camp would lead to a complete meltdown. The army men did not like the rogue warriors; the rogue warriors did not like anyone, even themselves, and everyone had guns and lots of ammunition. Thanks to the flights from Khartoum and the Bulgarian crews flying the old Soviet An-26 freight planes into camp, everyone had lots of ammunition and a little beer, a singularly bad combination.

But the camp also had more than just the Bulgarian flight crews to thank. They also had the Abbas brothers to thank; those wonderful fun-loving arms dealers out of Beirut, Lebanon. Farsi and Yassar were happy to supply their Muslim brothers, it was their calling to help the "cause," whatever that was, and the Abbas profits would help the cause as well. Well, the Abbas cause that is . . . Private jets, Rolls Royce's, suites in five-star hotels, the best wines and restaurants. Not for their families, of course, why be foolish. The wine flowed for the mistresses and, in particular, for one Lisa Aswanela; Lisa of Johannesburg, South Africa, you know, the one with the long legs, wild hair and the Audi R8. She would not be forever stunning, but she was now, and her hip hugger jeans barely stayed on her hips. A wild sight of toned, sex-fueled drama, and that was just her walk!

The pious Abbas brothers had been to Khartoum to seal the deals with their Muslim brothers and, to be sure, their pockets lined with tens of millions of dollars in profit. Those private jets don't fund and fuel themselves. And no matter what religion you are, Muslim, Christian, Hindu, Greek Orthodox or Tibetan Buddhist, there is always a higher power, and it is . . . money. All religions are subservient to money . . . money and more money . . . and the Abbas brothers were very religious, no matter how many mistresses they have. Offer any church $1.2 million and they will accept it, give them another $1.3 million the next day and they will take it. They likely would never say no.

They would walk over their religion for an extra dollar. There is God Almighty and then there is the Almighty Dollar . . . and the Almighty Dollar wins every time; yes, every time. God move aside, the Dollar is coming through. And so the Abbas brothers were very serious Muslims when they were home in Beirut and had no choice, but money and more money was the concept they truly worshipped, along with the next seven billion people on the face of the earth.

And the Abbas brothers had been in Khartoum, Sudan the last few days to accept the congratulations from the Sudanese government for bringing Sudan the key to the Sudanese way of life . . . ammunition for their AK-47's. Now that the newly formed South Sudan existed, the Abbas brothers would supply both sides with a gluttonous amount of money and weapons, money and weapons.

It wasn't just ammunition, of course. The five An-26 Soviet cargo aircraft parked on the ramp at Khartoum International were directly tied to the Abbas brothers. The load contained a complete buffet of arms, enough to keep the violence going in Western Sudan.

The weapons had been offloaded, and the arms were being distributed to the various Sudanese army camps; included in that distribution was the camp run by General Abdul. The weapons had arrived five days ago, carried by a string of seventeen trucks. The trucks had been built in China, and as each truck entered into the camp, they passed a string of subsistence vendors in ramshackle huts outside the camp. The weapons trucks had also passed by a man in ragged robes with his beat-up bicycle cart, selling small bottles of water.

The Abbas brothers were on the red carpet at the Khartoum Airport. The red carpet led to the infamous Abbas brothers' Dassault 900LX private tri-jet. All the Sudan VIP's were there to give the "Allah is Great" handshake to their arms dealing saviors. As the Abbas brothers were walking the red carpet, the tattered man was starting his slow walk with his bicycle cart. He would not return tomorrow to sell his water, but no one would miss him; they had never known he was actually there. Even if someone had seen him start his slow grueling march to the west they would not have taken note. He had been outside the camp for one week, but he did not exist.

Now the Abbas brothers were in their fourth day of wining and dining in Sandton, South Africa. The bicycle cart man was in a sand ditch sucking hot water through a straw, just lying there alive, but barely. The three bodies lying in the sand had not moved; they would never move again.

As the Abbas brothers were sipping a raspberry mojito and biting into a filet mignon in Mandela Square, Sandton, South Africa, the ragged man buried in the sand was biting into the second protein bar. With each bite he also got a nice little compliment of the hot gritty sand, washing it down with water naturally chilled to 117°.

The Abbas brothers were living, the man buried in the sand was merely alive.

The man in the sand had a route to survive, but he did not want to use it; it was not good for the mission. On his belt was a device with a red button, push and everything becomes dramatically different in a few minutes. But he did not want to push that button . . . at least not now.

CHAPTER 4

The border of Burma and Thailand is defined by two energetic rundown border towns. On the Burma side is Tachileik; on the Thailand side is Mae Sai. These two simple border towns have been the epicenter for drugs, arms, and international intrigue for over forty years; and it continues today.

As we note their existence, another epic series of events were going down.

Wei Kyi of Burma was in Thailand, but barely. He was only maybe forty yards across the small river that separates these two countries; a small river, which itself only spans thirty yards. But both sides of the river had been steeped in the drama and intrigue of not the United Nations, but the United Rogue Nations, of which Burma was a card-carrying member. So that thirty yards of river had a very big outsized role in the history of drugs, arms, and international intrigue.

Wei Kyi was in a small, cramped four-storied building. He was on the third story of the building in a room with a window facing the river. He was meeting with a Thai man named Chaya Ptorn; a key dealer who ensured the arms flowed to Burma and the drugs and money flowed through Thailand. Each man was the latest generation of "businessmen" who bobbed and weaved their way through the dark violent world that is the arms and drugs business in the Golden Triangle, the area named for the meeting of the borders of Laos, Burma and Thailand. And these two tried to span both worlds, a particularly dangerous game. But these men had a particularly strong religious base . . . you know, the one about the money . . . the worship of money, even as they have no clue what they will do with more.

As they sat and talked, two men sat on the Burmese side of the river with binoculars. The two men were not friends and did not know the other was watching the same window and were separated by only thirty-five yards in their hiding places.

Also, the Thai authorities and the U.S. DEA were monitoring the situation; they had been monitoring it for the last two years. They would watch for another ten years if allowed to; again, they needed the paycheck . . . they needed the money, not the mission.

As for the two men in the simple room, they were certainly a very intense center of attention.

The two men talked for twenty minutes, stood up, shook hands, and left the room. They went down the stairs and went separate ways. Chaya Ptorn went to a sleek Porsche SUV with three bodyguards. He was to be followed by two Porsche SUV's with an additional eight bodyguards. They roared off down the road toward Chiang Rai, Thailand. Mr. Wei Kyi simply walked thirty yards to the border post, then walked across the two-lane bridge for 150 yards, and got into an old British Land Rover on the Burmese side with two bodyguards. Before he rode off he bought a carton of Golden Triangle cigarettes for $3.00.

What is interesting is that Mr. Wei Kyi did not process any papers at the border, he simply walked into Thailand, and he simply walked back to Burma . . . maybe he owned both countries; he did not have a passport.

The next deal had been done, now the wheels would start turning. And the wheels were turning as Chaya Ptorn's Porsche convoy gently passed another Thai Border Police checkpoint on the way to Chiang Rai. No one had ever stopped him or his Porsche convoy. The checkpoints regularly got their shipment of Johnnie Walker Black Label, along with their Thai bank notes.

CHAPTER 5

On the fifth day the man was still buried in the sand of Western Sudan and his time was running out. He had used his last available water and the rest was ten yards away, but that was like ten miles to him. He had rested enough to have energy to think. The time had come.

So he pushed the red button twice. The first time sent the signal, and the second time sent the GPS coordinates. It was now 10 a.m., and the man felt he would not make 10 p.m.

Now he must use what little energy he had left to get out of the sand ditch and move to the bicycle cart. It would have to be timed; so he slowly, very slowly, propped himself up. He looked at his watch, yes it was a Bell & Ross and it was still working; it was a GMT version Bell & Ross, Limited edition of 500, get one at your local 7-11 store for $7,000.

He would have twenty minutes to move to the cart, and it would likely take that long, so he slowly rolled on the sand.

The Black Hawk helicopter was racing east to the GPS coordinates. It crossed into Sudan from Chad at fifty feet. The twenty-three miles passed quickly, and the cart and man were spotted, the man was still five yards from the cart. The helicopter had no markings at all, and the entire crew was in all black uniforms with no markings.

A team dragged the man to the helicopter in the swirling sand. He was immediately hooked up to an IV and the helicopter started up. One of the operatives had set fire to the straw in the cart as a distraction to the operation. Someone from afar would think the Sudanese army had an operation underway. Then the helicopter was gone, ripping across a blistering and barren landscape where nothing could live for very long . . . the Western Sudan.

The medics attending the man spoke in French. The two armed operatives also spoke a style of French and were right off the recruiting poster for the French Foreign Legion. "Welcome to Chad Mr. 057," one of them said to the man in French.

"Merci," the man replied. A slight sunbaked smile crossed his lips; then he closed his eyes. Code 057 had finished another day at the office, and it wasn't 11:00 a.m. yet. Mr. 057 was obviously keeping banking hours, no bonus for him. But he wasn't on a time card, he was on a contract; hours were not important, the mission was.

As the helicopter ripped away, the three bodies of the young Sudanese soldiers could be seen through the shifting sands. They had become black, and they had not moved an inch since being shot many days ago. Most of their bodies had simply dried up in three days of 120° heat, their skin now a very weathered black.

CHAPTER 6

And on that same fifth day Mr. Farsi Abbas rolled out of bed at his suite at the Michelangelo Hotel, Sandton, South Africa. As he went to the restroom he left the sexy figure of nineteen-year-old Lisa Aswanela still under the covers. She had come to know everything about him. It was not hard, these men are so predictable and full of themselves, and it would be hard to stop them from telling all. Lisa was singularly magnificent lying there, singularly clever; she had been there three days but had not had sex yet.

Mr. Abbas had taken his Dassault private jet from the red carpet of the Khartoum Airport to the red carpet awaiting him at Mandela Square, Michelangelo Hotel. His Rolls Royce car had taken him and Lisa everywhere, every day was opulent shopping and dinners, as the man labeled 057 lay cooked in the sand in Western Sudan. Had Lisa known she would not be happy; but she would never know.

CHAPTER 7

Nice, France is everything that is exotic and elegant about Europe; pristine clean with magnificent landscaping throughout the city, the narrow streets with date palms and many still of cobblestone, which just added to the mystique and glamour. The city was saturated with small restaurants that were elegant and charming, with an air of mystery. After all of this, Nice was also next door to the glamorous Monaco, the blue Mediterranean, and at the end of the day Nice was also in the "South of France;" a term for glamour, elegance and of course our old friend . . . money, lots of old money.

The tycoons of Europe must have a villa in the "South of France," just as American tycoons must have a place in Palm Beach. Actually, Bernie Madoff had residences in both the "South of France" and Palm Beach, so all is not what it seems. It never is. People are never as smart as they think they are, and certainly people are not as rich as they think they are. Self-delusion may be America's biggest export ever in the last fifty years. It certainly has been America's singular characteristic over the last fifty years. America has been so preoccupied with promoting little Johnnie's and little Mary's self-esteem that no one has noticed they are seventh grade honor students with the bumper stickers to prove it, but cannot write in complete sentences.

And their parents are so self-absorbed with the home, the nice car, nice clothes, and the private school tuition, that they must announce to everyone that they do not realize that they own nothing. They are just paying, they do not own. Pay, pay and then they die; they will likely never actually own anything. Only about 25% of Americans actually own their homes. Not a pretty sight.

On this beautiful, sunny day in a capital of the French Riviera, the other capitals being Cannes and St. Tropez, two identical silver limo Bentley's were weaving through the narrow back streets of Nice. They had emerged from a villa complex on the maze of narrow streets some five blocks from the sea. From the street it looked to be three separate townhouses. But an archway drive from the street led into a large circular courtyard with a center fountain that included two more townhouses off the public street. You could also use a road to exit in the back of the courtyard, should you need to escape. Would you need to escape?

The two Bentleys had come from this courtyard on Rue Lyon. The departing Bentley's had left two Ferrari's, two Maserati's, and a lone turbo Porsche in the complex's carriage house. This all meant one thing to the high priests of finance attached to the religion that is money; there was some serious money here, at least the "appearance" of serious money. Only a discrete, private bank on some back street of Zurich would know which applied here. But to have a carriage house versus a garage certainly puts one in a separate class. And to have a highly-trained house staff of eleven also carried a lot of weight, those are solid salaries that must be paid every month. The money must come from somewhere.

The man behind those salaries was a one Javier Henri LeCirac. He was from a wealthy French merchant family going back three generations. Three generations are a lot for a family business, and with Javier LeCirac they were going to make the fourth generation.

However, do not get excited, the magnificent Beretta family business of neighboring Italy goes back to 1526. Yes, that's right, the family business is closing in on five hundred years, and all the while maintaining a reputation for superior excellence in the manufacturing of arms and other industrial products; a family business that has lasted five hundred years, a stunning achievement never to be surpassed. If they folded tomorrow, it would likely take three hundred and fifty years to catch them in another family business.

Nonetheless, at thirty-seven years old Javier Henri LeCirac was very wealthy, and real money too, very accomplished. He had engineering and finance degrees from Paris, he spoke English and Arabic fluently, and he liked to design clothes and cars. He painted and liked sculptures. He loved reading about finance and military adventures and was involved in the maintenance and modification of military jetfighters as a subcontractor to large aerospace companies in Europe. He was a renaissance man who was unique among the brain dead and dimwitted masters of twitting and other thirty something's of his day.

He wore elegant custom-fit Tom Ford suits, Cartier watches, Hermes ties, and Bally shoes. He was a frequent visitor and treasured client for the shops along Savile Row, London and Madison Avenue - New York, as well as Salisbury Road - Hong Kong.

He was tall, slim, tanned and had a head of very long brown hair. It was often in a ponytail, but his personal barber had come this morning to trim it only two inches below his collar. He played high-level tennis, drove race cars, and had a polo team in Nice. If he were not so tall, he could be an F1 race driver. He certainly looked the part. Polo Ralph Lauren or Tom Ford would be so lucky to have him as their "go to" model. And at the end of all of this . . . he was single . . . never married. Life is not fair and Javier Henri LeCirac was living, breathing proof of it.

As the Bentley's wove through the streets of Nice the lead Bentley carried a driver, two bodyguards and a finance/technical Vice President to Javier, a young talented associate named Pierre LaRue. At thirty-five and single Pierre was almost a Javier but a bit shorter, and he was also lean with chiseled, model good looks. Think of the guy in the Davidoff cool water ads. Pierre and Javier were A-list playboys, if only they wanted to be. But they were not. They were low key polite guys who did like high-octane, high-powered toys, but kept everything low profile. No front cover of People magazine for them, no starlets, no playgirls. But they did like long-legged sultry blondes; the kind that are so hard to find.

In the second Bentley was Javier Henri LeCirac, along with his would-be assistant, a Kelly Grant from London. There was a driver and bodyguard in front.

Kelly Grant was beyond magnificent. She was five feet nine inches tall and Javier was six feet three, thank God. She was on the skinny side of svelte, but the long legs and arms were so well curved, if thin. She had high cheekbones, the pouting lips of an Angelina Jolie, a swan neck, crystal blue eyes, and long blonde hair that was constantly flying around. She was only twenty years old, but a very serious grounded twenty years old. She had entered British University at sixteen years old, finished at eighteen years old, and held a Master's Degree at nineteen. Javier "found" her at a government conference on defense that she was attending, and she had already had two years of employment with British MI6, British Intelligence, starting at a mere eighteen years old. She should have been on the cover of Vogue, but she was instead a serious, accomplished James Bond on the MI6 staff. Well, she was not a spy, but she knew one, well at least she thinks she might. She may have seen one at one time, not sure.

Javier pursued her professionally and would like to romantically, but she said it would be only professional and at twenty she only wanted to consider the professional angle. Javier offered her everything, three times her salary, the best of everything. As part of the interview process, Javier flew her on the family Gulfstream 650, costing $90 million outfitted, and gave her the five-star treatment. She was only twenty. The Bentley was waiting for her at the Nice airport.

Javier offered her a two bedroom apartment in the complex on Rue Lyon, an apartment worth $5 million market price. It would be decorated to her taste, and there would be an allowance for her clothes and the offer of a Porsche turbo. A twenty-year-old girl in a Ferrari is a bit much.

After three days of negotiating, she finally replied in her crisp British accent. Kelly never allowed for romance, and she did not smile much, so she became even sexier, more smoldering.

She would accept but she wanted to decorate and, most importantly, she wanted a separate private entrance going out the back of the complex, not onto Rue Lyon. The Porsche turbo was fine, and she smiled ever so faintly, but it was not necessary. Javier said no, she must take it; he wanted an excuse to shop again anyway and the carriage house could hold seven, "or 007 to Kelly," he teased. The Bentley's were always parked under the portals outside for ready use. Javier said she could use those as well.

He wished her to have an "assistant" her age and of her choosing to talk to, shop, or run errands and that assistant would have a studio apartment in the complex. Kelly's apartment would have a high-end full-service kitchen, but Kelly was free to use the complex's kitchen staff at any time every day. Just call the head chef with the requirements and the time needed. Kelly's head was beginning to swim.

While talking to Kelly, Javier LeCirac took the time to call his architect and interior designer to briefly discuss the upcoming project at the five-townhouse complex he controlled for the LeCirac family. Kelly was impressed, well actually overwhelmed. Javier hung up and said his staff would present options within a month.

She did accept but would not report for three weeks due to her notice requirements to British Intelligence, as well as other tasks. Javier gave her four weeks. Men give young sexy women the world, and the young sexy women take it.

The Bentley's were now heading to the airport. Javier Henri LeCirac would accompany Kelly Grant back to London, along with two VIP's waiting for him at the airport. He had other business in London. His personnel manager would also come to set up Kelly in her career move. It is likely no other twenty-year-old had ever been courted so aggressively with such salaries and perks.

However, it is unlikely any girl was ever as smart, low key, and quiet, while at the same time so physically spectacular. She was simply stunning, but not in a smiley, beauty pageant way. It was a sultry beauty that was so powerful with the hair, cheekbones, pouting lips, the very long legs, small round ass, and a sexual presence so strong as to stop the male just to watch . . . not to pursue. As sexy as she was, her quiet ways sent a message that she was unavailable by powers beyond any mortal male's capacity. Her physical presence was of a Greek goddess, or in this case, a British goddess, to be viewed but not courted or brought into this world. Even a powerful, sexy male like Javier was transfixed and mystified by her elegant, powerful sexual presence. He would not know how to begin to approach her as a male. She clearly would decide which male she would go to bed with. It seemed no male had come close to that yet.

CHAPTER 8

On the seventh day God may have rested, but Code 057 has a contract to complete. He told his medical handlers as much. He had quickly recovered from the heat and dehydration, and had slept some twenty hours a day for two days with an IV drip

Code 057 asked to see the other pilot. He had no idea where he was being kept, but it seemed like a bunker of some sort.

He requested a meal and was eating when a French man of forty-five came in. He was the other pilot.

He had been waiting but could not execute the mission without the six numbers, and Code 057 had the six numbers.

They talked in English and French back and forth for thirty minutes and then headed out.

They went up two flights of stairs in what looked to be a bunker, and it was. As Code 057 stepped outside he was first met by an overwhelming glare, Chad at 11 a.m. and searing heat again. Without the Polo Ralph Lauren aviator sunglasses Code 057 would be blind.

The top of the ground just showed a tin shed and that's all, so the entire complex was well underground. The tin shed was only fifty yards from a hard-baked dusty strip that would prove to be the runway. The strip ran north and south, and the French pilot led him toward a beat-up tent structure a hundred yards away to the north. Code 057 felt the heat take him down, and the glare seemed to be off an atomic explosion.

They stepped inside the tent structure to see the elegant beast that was there. A French Mirage F-1B made by Dassault Aviation of France. The air conditioning in the tent kept Code 057 from a heat relapse, but he said nothing of it.

The jetfighter was a raw flat black with no markings at all. It had two air-to-ground missiles and one large 500 lb. bomb slung under the belly, just as Code 057 had ordered. The 500 lb. bomb was napalm, Code 057 liked his napalm.

The pilots got into the plane to check the systems. Code 057 found it strange no one else was there, just the pilots. Code 057 saw the data entry area where his six numbers were to go, and he was satisfied.

The French pilot would be in front and Code 057 would fly from the back with the critical six numbers.

But nobody was going anywhere now. Code 057 set take off at 6:40 p.m. He wanted darkness and some cooler air to help this jet perform better.

The Mirage F-1B was a sleek and powerful single engine jet with a most distinctive landing gear. The main landing gears had two large wheels on each side. Thus the jet could take exactly the kind of runway he had in this "middle of a death vacuum," Chad. Well he hoped it would take it, this was one raw runway, but the plane had landed here so that was good. How do you get a powerful jetfighter to a beat-up tent in a scorched no man's land? There are people who do those things.

CHAPTER 9

As Code 057 and the French pilot exited the jet, a single ground staff came to them. He was not French, appeared to be Arab, maybe a tribe guy; he was dark, but who won't be in this fire pit called the Sahara.

The man came to Code 057 and asked if the six numbers had been put in. Code 057 said they had not. The man said rather forcefully that the numbers should be put in, maybe right now if possible.

The man had less than one minute to live. Actually, fifteen seconds.

Code 057 reached into his flight vest, pulled out his Beretta PX4 subcompact 9 mm and shot the man point blank in the throat. The man fell and Code 057 put one in his head.

The French pilot crumpled to the floor, and Code 057 was able to break his fall. The pilot had fainted from shock and the powerful sound shock of the Beretta.

CHAPTER 10

He immediately called a special number and the hangar was filled with French Foreign Legion guys in three minutes, as well as some French official. Code 057 said they needed full time security, as the Sudanese knew something, and the mission was moved up. It would leave as soon as the French pilot woke up. The six numbers were never to be known except by him, and he was not to enter them until after takeoff. He was going to kill anyone else who suggested otherwise, as he just did.

CHAPTER 11

As the opulent Gulfstream 650 of Javier Henri LeCirac was gently touching down in London with stunning Ms. Kelly Grant, Code 057 was roaring down the dirt runway in bleak crusted Chad, fully armed. When you hear the yelps of the African wild dogs starting to pack up for the hunt, then something is going to die. On this day, when you hear the singularly dramatic roar of the Mirage F-1B jetfighter ripping down a dirt runway and creating its own personal sandstorm, then you know someone is going to die. Not just someone, lots of someone's.

CHAPTER 12

In a perfect world, or even a stable world, these two pilots should not be flying a high-performance jet right now; no way, no how.

First, we have the French pilot in front who took off in a high-performance jet less than thirty minutes after he collapsed in shock. Second, the pilot in the back, Code 057, was only two days ago in a heatstroke induced coma.

Now they were ripping through the sky at 600+ mph, and the jet's air conditioning would never keep up with the high noon heat of Chad/Sudan; not to mention the cockpit canopy was just a big greenhouse trapping the sun's heat. On the plus side the dark flat black Mirage F-1B looked absolutely stunning against the crystal blue sky over the Sahara, raw black, but also sleek and today very deadly. It just was a very sleek, very powerful jetfighter; a raw sexiness like some nineteen-year-old long-legged French model striding down a Paris fashion runway in a tight mini dress. In a testosterone-fueled male world it did not get any better than a Mirage F-1B jet fighter ripping over the stark, bleak, scorching landscape on the border of Sudan and Chad.

And the Mirage F-1B was roaring. The entire mission would cover only one hundred and fifty miles, and they had fuel for five hundred miles. So they could be aggressive, if only the pilots had the strength to do it.

The jet flew due south only thirty miles, then a 3G turn to the left, and literally one minute later they crossed into Sudan. Five minutes later Code 057 entered the critical six numbers. A long and winding road had been travelled to finally use those six little numbers.

There were longitude degrees, minutes, seconds. There were latitude degrees, minutes, seconds. It was done. The pain and drama of being "on the ground," actually in front of the very door that leads to the massive Sudanese army weapons bunker in General Abdul's camp, was worth it only now. The GPS reading must be precise to the foot, as the missiles missing by six feet meant the storage bunker would be hit but not penetrated. "They" wanted the missiles through the front doors into the bunker by the main entrance. That meant going "on the ground" through a searing desert, through the camp of five hundred unstable soldiers, three hundred of which were psychopaths, then to be able to go to the very weapons storage doors, and then being able to stay there for about three minutes; all this without being shot and cut to pieces. It had been a difficult winding road for Code 057, and the three minutes at the storage door had seemed like three years. But it was necessary to check and recheck the precise coordinates with the satellite system. He had pulled that bicycle cart for a long time before and after getting those six little numbers. And he had killed a lot of people already over those six little numbers, but nothing on the scale of what was about to happen.

The Mirage F-1B then went into a 3G turn to the north. The mission was coming at high noon only because things had been compromised at the base, someone knew the mission, just not the base to be attacked, because only one man had the six numbers. Even the pilot in front had no clue where they were going. It was shut up and fly the plane for him . . . and he did.

Code 057 wanted this to occur at 7 p.m. in time for evening prayers so Allah's will could be done. But it was high noon and it didn't matter. Sudan had no real air defense, and all the MIG-23's of the Sudan Air Force were parked around Khartoum to give the bloated, self-absorbed politicians a sense of security. But parked MIG-23's give no security, flying ones do, but the Sudan MIG-23's mostly stayed parked.

CHAPTER 13

The first part of the mission was easy and safe; the second part not so much.

The first part happened five miles from the Sudan base. The two missiles were armed and the six numbers encoded, the missiles were ready for launch, and they were. In about fifteen seconds the results would be known, and they were, the missiles were launched.

The jet turned east and started a slow 360° turn to watch the show, and then the show started.

Two massive mushroom clouds emerged on the horizon, followed by three more massive mushroom clouds. The first two were the missiles, the last three the weapons stored in the bunker.

There was to be massive collateral damage, the base was leveled, including the poor sellers and their livestock.

The second part of this raid was for psychological reasons, just meltdown whatever was left.

The jet completed the 360° turn, and Code 057 took command and plunged the jet to 300 feet from 20,000 feet. They were coming in very hot from the south, and they were roasting in the cockpit.

The raw elegant jet was screaming across the bleak landscape at 630 mph. Without the computer Code 057 would have never known the release point. But holding steady at 630 mph and 300 feet the computer said "release now" and Code 057 pressed the button; 500 pounds of raw unguided napalm was tumbling toward the camp. And what in the best of times had been hell on earth, had turned into hell on earth times five. Now the napalm was coming, a signature end to the poster child for hell on earth, a searing liquid spray of fire at 1300° to a leveled and an already cooked camp. What was not vaporized was turned to a crusted black. The good people were melted down with the very bad people.

And General Abdul returning from a patrol with three accompanying vehicles was two miles to the east and saw the whole thing. He was just a bit late for the party. All were in total shock. General Abdul's one eye could not believe what it was seeing.

General Abdul had seen the black jet deliver the napalm after the missiles had leveled everything, and he heard the haunting roar of the departing jetfighter as the fighter continued at 700 feet into the desert. Then all was quiet, a deafening quiet from the extreme violence and noise of the explosions, then the raw signature roar of the departing jet, and then the eerie endless quiet of the bleak tortured desert landscape of the Western Sudan. And so it goes just after high noon . . . in the Western Sudan.

CHAPTER 14

The stark flat black jet roared on for five minutes, dropped to one hundred feet and did a 3G turn to the west; Code 057 pushed it to 700 mph. Now this was living, finally! The jet was actually kicking up small dust tornadoes over the taller sand dunes. It didn't last long, maybe four minutes. Then they went to 1,000 feet in order to land on the hard, dusty strip of land that passed for a runway. They pounded into the runway. They taxied to the tent, unbuckled and exited the cockpit, but only with the help of two ground staff . . . two for each pilot. They were exhausted and were carried to the crew bunker.

Three days later a man got on an Air Mali flight from Bamako, Mali to Dakar, Senegal. The next night a man sat in Air France seat 7A, Dakar to Paris. Tomorrow a meeting at 517 Rue Lorraine would take place, it would last thirty minutes. The funds would be transferred to Switzerland, and so it goes.

CHAPTER 15

Now a Blake Anderson, the same Code 057, was in a one bedroom suite on the water at the Majestic Palm Hotel . . . Nice, France. He would stay three days, and then take a helicopter to Monaco to stroll through the shops and casinos. He would shop for a new Bell & Ross GMT watch. He had destroyed his latest, likely from a massive slam to the steel side of the Mirage F-1B. It stopped somewhere along the way. And so it goes.

CHAPTER 16

Blake Anderson stayed four days in a one bedroom suite at the Palm Monaco, an elegant hotel near the harbor filled with 200-foot yachts and powerboats and 150-foot sailing yachts. A lot of wealth was always present in Monaco, a historic tax haven enclave.

His days were spent on quiet strolls through the city, with a 3 p.m. lunch at any outdoor café. They would find him. Each day at 3 p.m. he would dine at an outdoor café, no special routine, no special place, they would find him.

And on the fourth day, they found him. A tall 50'ish man in an impeccable Armani pinstripe suit came to sit with him. A very polite, very polished, very patient man came to him. He waited for Blake Anderson to finish his desert, a delicate carrot cake. The cake was excellent, likely a French recipe. Then they strolled along the harbor street until a jet black Bentley pulled alongside them and they got in. The man was the first person Blake (Code 057) had spoken to in seven days. Always alone, never lonely.

In quick order the car went to a powerboat, the powerboat to a 215-foot yacht, and they went up the yacht to a helipad. The helicopter took them to Nice International.

The helicopter landed fifty yards from the Dassault 7X, a private jet. A fantastic pearl white Gulfstream 650 with orange accents had just landed. As Blake Anderson walked the fifty yards to the Dassault, a one Javier Henri LeCirac had noticed the Dassault jet from his elegant pearl white leather seat on the Gulfstream. Javier had an artist eye and as a painter, he knew his colors. He had just returned from his London business trip and getting Kelly set to come to Nice.

The dark rich titanium gray of the Dassault was very striking; he had never seen that color before. Then as his plane taxied, he noticed the idling helicopter had the same titanium color. He had not seen that color before. Then he noticed the blood red accents, quite a dramatic touch. He did not notice the lone man walking to the Dassault, only the color scheme. Quite a striking color scheme, Javier noted, and he liked it.

As Javier deplaned with his staff from the Gulfstream, he stopped to watch the Dassault jet taxi. Keeping his limo waiting, Javier watched the Dassault line up and roar down the runway. The sunlight painted a beautiful mosaic of colors as it roared down the runway. The jet disappeared to the west. Javier got into the limo refreshed by the unusual light display and the new colors.

Blake Anderson enjoyed a pineapple juice in the Dassault . . . going somewhere . . . another day at the office.

CHAPTER 17

The Abbas brothers had returned to their dreary existence in Beirut, Lebanon. The deal in the Sudan had been worth $7 million to them, and they had managed to consume $1.1 million in eight days in a typical cascade of private jets, six-star suites, major liquor bills, major restaurant bills, Rolls Royce bills and, of course, the fee for Lisa Aswanela. But as usual Farsi Abbas, with his continuing obsession for Lisa, had handed over $200,000 and then they had sex. Lisa thought that was about the right price, given she would never have those eight days of her life back.

Farsi Abbas was the father of his fourth or fifth child, he had lost track, and because of Lisa he had lost interest. But still he fathered the children, mainly to keep his wife occupied. He only thought of Lisa. But even with all the time and money spent on Lisa, he was becoming a pain and an ever-distant memory for her . . . even as he took more of her time. It seems the dominant trait for the male to survive the disregard of the female was to have complete self-delusion, and Farsi was completely delusional.

Lisa had used the last $300,000 Farsi gave her to completely payoff her upscale townhouse in upscale Sandton, South Africa. This last $200,000 would be used by Lisa to obtain a personal goal of hers, to completely own an Aston-Martin DB9 with no payments while she was still a teenager! Men pay for beauty, women pay to be beautiful. Lisa did not have to pay to be beautiful, nature was still on her side.

And on Monday she was heading for Aston-Martin – Sandton to talk about the DB9. If she did not get a good price, she would buy a first class ticket on British Airways and head to Aston-Martin – Cape Town. If she bought it there, she would drive it home!

CHAPTER 18

And on that Monday Aston-Martin – Sandton had their ultimate treat, Lisa in her usual low-slung jeans and halter top. She didn't wear them to get a better price, she just wore them. They were especially provocative when they were cut one and half inches above the "triangle." She was as toned as ever, but over the last year had become even more quiet and worldly. The relentless pursuit by males of all stripes had become tiresome, but Lisa could handle it smoothly.

Monday at 11 a.m. at the Aston-Martin showroom was usually very quiet, and Lisa was banking on that. She wheeled her Audi R8 into the front parking spot. An eye-catcher in and of itself.

As she stepped out, the three salesmen got an MTV/Fashion Channel moment. Lisa's long legs came first, then the hips, then came the hair. As she got out, the hip huggers had slipped down the hips to show the ass checks. She pulled up the front of her jeans and left the rear unadjusted. Her slight sway as she walked into the showroom left the married, suburban males speechless. But then their fat, dimwitted suburban wives left them speechless as well, just in a very different way.

However, unusual for a Monday, there was one other customer in the showroom. From a distance he was the perfect match for a Lisa. He was tall and lean and impeccably dressed in Hugo Boss pants and mock long sleeve turtleneck. He had Polo Ralph Lauren aviator sunglasses propped on his head. Code 057 would be proud. The black boots were custom made at a small company in a back alley in Mayfair – London. The company was called Crane and Cable. For their expert services $3,000 will get you started.

He spoke to his salesman in an unusual accent, neither British nor South African, kind of a mixture. He had a light brown complexion, he was African, but from where? Actually, he was from Rwanda by way of Cape Town, his name was Alex Kagamba. Born in Kigali, Rwanda to teacher parents, he was evacuated eighteen years ago at the age of fifteen years to Cape Town as a result of the Rwandan genocide. His parents were killed and he was very, very lucky to go to Cape Town, a roll of the dice. Most refugees were merely shoved into the Eastern Congo . . . yes, that Eastern Congo. Alex Kagamba was a member of the Tutsi ethnic tribe. He was polite, well spoken, and had served five years in the South African military. The Tutsi of Rwanda were a traditional warrior tribe: smart, disciplined and unusually tall. Most men and women were six foot tall or more.

His business now was part traditional finance and part the financing of government military contracts and private military contracts. In short Alex was among other things a banker to mercenaries of Africa, and later he hoped of the Middle East and Southeast Asia. He was good at his job; his company was small but successful and professional and he had always appreciated the British military, particularly British Intelligence MI6. Thus, in homage to MI6, he was shopping for an Aston-Martin. It was as simple as that. What is good enough for James Bond is good enough for Alex Kagamba.

Alex certainly did notice the arrival of Lisa Aswanela; so intriguing and very young, very sexy, and very svelte coming into Aston-Martin . . . all by herself. No father, no sugar daddy, no girlfriends, just a young girl arriving by herself and driving an Audi R8 at that.

While he continued to look at the Aston-Martin and chat with the salesman, he was distracted by Lisa. It is just the way males are wired. So you go with Mother Nature, but there is no reason to let her win. The male goes from attraction to the need to conquer. And soon after you conquer, through the slight hand of nature, you find yourself waiting for her, waiting <u>on</u> her, and nodding agreement to a whole bunch of stuff that is her world not yours . . . except you are paying for it. Enjoy the scenery, enjoy the sex, and move on. Actually, nothing bad happens, the women always feel you don't know what you are missing; but you do know, there is nothing to be missed!

But all of this was above Alex's head. He noticed Lisa and then he stared at Lisa. Lisa noticed him but did not spend much time with it.

Predictably, Alex became interested in Aston-Martins ever closer to where Lisa was looking at Aston-Martins; funny how that is.

Finally, he was looking at the same car as she. Her sexual presence was always overpowering and today was no exception, the long-legged package was irresistible. A very strong package, well wrapped and at nineteen she was in full bloom, but oh so worldly. So the teenager lorded over any male, even ones in their forties, especially in their forties, except for that one guy who actually never wanted to obtain her. Where was that guy?

Alex was smooth and low key. That helped and he started the natural conversation about Aston-Martin's. Lisa was polite and five minutes into the conversation flashed the Lisa smile, and Alex was swept away. He kind of forgot why he was here, oh yes, the Aston-Martins.

And this was going to be his day. Lisa actually had done a lot of research online over the last year, yes starting at eighteen, so she knew that this car was here this day and she was going to buy it with cash straight up. She would "give" the Audi R8 to her close friend Sarah, who was her close friend in taking money from men. Sarah did not make as much money as Lisa, but she could afford this car since it was being given to her.

So as Alex and Lisa looked at the same car, and Alex made small talk he was hoping would turn into big talk, Lisa did actually look at the car.

They talked about what kind of car they were looking for, the colors, the leather, etc. Alex got questions in on where she lived, what she did, where she was from, etc. Lisa responded nicely. Alex was certainly above the usual male, he was handsome, polite and certainly not pushy, a nice young man.

Then Lisa decided enough time had passed. "What do you think of this car?" she asked Alex.

"It is spectacular, I love the deep green exterior color and the tan leather seats," he responded.

"Do you think you are going to buy it today?" she teased, a seductive smile emerged.

"Well, probably not today or tomorrow. I have been looking in Cape Town for some time, but just looking," Alex said and smiled back.

"So you are not going to buy this for me, today?" Lisa teased.

"Well, I would like to, but I don't know your last name. How would I register it?" he replied.

"My last name is Aswanela, now will you buy it?" and she laughed. He was a nice guy, and her charm was coming naturally.

"Well, I would like to sometime, but not today, maybe your birthday," he continued.

"My birthday is too far away and I so want this car," she smiled, pretending to pout. The salesmen were in heaven, a stunning girl who was also flirting. A rare moment in nature.

"Well, I would like to sometime, but can I just buy you lunch today instead?" Alex replied.

He was so nice, but so predictable. Lisa had become so accustomed to it. Still, he was handsome and charming.

So Lisa responded, "Yes, you can buy me lunch, just as soon as I buy this car;" a great moment for her witnessed by a stranger, and a young handsome stranger at that, as well as three shocked wide-eyed salesmen. The Monday morning salesroom doesn't have to be boring. "It won't take long," she told the salesman, "I'm paying cash."

She turned to Alex and said, "In say ten minutes I can take you to lunch, then when I return to pick up this Aston-Martin, in say two hours, you can continue to shop, sorry to disturb you!"

Alex was floored, "You will never disturb me." He hesitated, he definitely needed to know this girl. Two hours at lunch with this girl would make the rest of his life disappear.

CHAPTER 19

As the world turned, Blake Anderson, Code 057, and to be accurate, Jason Stoner, Code 717, also turned. The titanium colored Dassault 7X he boarded at Nice, France touched down in Nassau, Bahamas.

He entered his suite at the British Colonial Hilton at 3 p.m. At 4:30 p.m. he was having a cold drink at the Atlantis Casino overlooking the yacht harbor with the young statuesque Erica Johnson. At 7 p.m. Erica was naked in the hotel suite with Blake Anderson. After a spirited sexual reunion, Erica was sleeping on Blake's chest. At 8 p.m. Erica was departing the hotel. She would be marrying in just six weeks and this was part of her bachelorette party. Blake Anderson was not her fiancé, but she was to mail him an invitation in two weeks. There was no Bryan Norton to watch this time; his shallow grave in the Eastern Congo was still undisturbed.

Two days later Blake Anderson (Code 057) was on a Soviet built Yak-40 plane of Cubaña Air, Flight 103 Nassau to Havana. He took a 1957 Plymouth taxi from the airport to the Floridita Hotel in Old Town Havana. He unpacked and went down to sit on the veranda of the very famous Floridita bar.

He just sat there thinking of nothing in particular, just letting life flow by him. And the life flowing by him had a uniqueness to it . . . this was Havana after all.

Havana had been trapped for some fifty-five years to the manic ego of one incredibly self-absorbed buffoon, and let's not forget this one man was a lawyer. The legendary and the legendarily incompetent, I give you Fidel Castro. Essentially Havana, and Cuba in general, has not laid a brick in those fifty-five years.

Cuba's one social contribution to the world has been the six-hour speech by that one gigantic buffoon, the one and only . . . Fidel Castro. Six hours of words being spoken, the sum total through a lifetime of speaking words, all of which mean nothing. The heart and soul of Cuba, sugar production, has been self-liquidated as the machines become so old that they could not run anymore, the industry and employment collapsed by sixty percent in five years. Fidel Castro answered this call to action with a six-hour speech signifying nothing.

It is hard to comprehend Havana, it is truly a unique place stuck in a time warp. Leading the world in the time warp, surreal world categories would have to be Rangoon, Pyongyang, Havana, and until 2008, Phnom Penh, Cambodia. Now there are just three, as Phnom Penh has somewhat joined the world. Until 2011 Harare, Zimbabwe was in a major time warp, but then they had to destroy their own currency so they could survive, and it worked. Well, there was Stone Town, Zanzibar as well.

In Havana the image to the world is the 1940's and 1950's car, and the American car at that, not a Soviet car or some revolutionary car by the revolutionary Cuba. The revolution in Cuba was that a country could subsist and scrap along for fifty-five years on written words and spoken words by one delusional man. From a historical perspective, poor Fidel has hurt his historical reputation simply by living too long. A young, vigorous delusional man is far better for ratings than a bent, shrunken delusional old man. Che Guerra was lucky, they killed him before he got old, so he is still on the t-shirts. The same for Osama Bin Laden (OBL), although OBL was pathetically forgettable, except in the commercial world of 24/7 television. They need a brand for everything, and cable television elected OBL just as other brands like Coke and Chevy are promoted.

Blake Anderson sat for two hours reading Granma, the Cuban paper, and having a drink, pineapple juice.

In the subsistence world that is Havana and Cuba, everyone on the street must hustle to survive. During Blake's two hours in Cuba there was no complete peace. One after another, guys on the street were offering deals; cigars, women, and later, cigars and women. Even the vaulted Cuban cigar industry had collapsed by seventy percent in recent years.

The hustlers came and went until a man in his thirties came, a man called Hernando Alvarez, a hustler, but a more pleasant educated hustler who spoke clear English. Is there any hustler in the world who does not speak clear English, from Moscow to Rangoon, From Saigon to Maputo, Mozambique? No clear English means no path to the hustle.

Hernando Alvarez was a nice guy. So Blake talked and decided to test him. Hernando taught 8th grade but school was out, so the hustle had to be in. As a teacher Hernando made eleven dollars per month, up from eight dollars per month two years ago. He was offering thirty Cuban cigars for one dollar, and Cuban girls for three dollars. Blake bought one of each, but Hernando would have to work for the girl.

He said Hernando must find five girls, and he would choose one. Hernando was gone only one half hour. Blake left the Floridita to walk down a narrow back street of old Havana. Many of the back streets of Havana were crumbling relics held up by wood supports crisscrossing the street. Those poor supports had been paid for by UNESCO, Cuba could not even afford the boards to hold up the walls. The "buses" to the areas outside Havana are flatbed 18-wheel trucks full of people. There were no buses. We are talking an industrial-strength time warp called Cuba.

Hernando led him into a small door off the narrow alley where there were five young girls, all eighteen to twenty years old whose only knowledge of the world was dilapidated Havana and the occasional customer that allowed them to eat. There were five girls, four of whom were nice and one hidden in the corner who was stunning; a tall long-legged, thin and perky-chested fashion model stuck in the never, never world of Havana. She seemed sort of shy, nineteen years old, and her name . . . Eva, Eva Escobar.

Blake spotted her and then without choosing anyone, took Hernando outside. He instructed Hernando to bring Eva to the Floridita for lunch in one hour. Blake would be with Eva for the next five days at seven dollars a day. She became relaxed after two days and they became special friends and lovers after five days. She became his Rin, the girl from Chiang Mai, Thailand. Blake liked her and she was innocent and stunning, a Cuban version of Lisa Aswanela of South Africa. She was thin with olive skin and light blue eyes, thanks to an Italian father. For his trouble and three hours' work Hernando got a month's salary, eleven dollars. Blake enjoyed Eva, they had fun and sex together. Blake would return to Havana, he would have to, but not only because of Eva.

CHAPTER 20

Blake, Code 057, Conrad, Code 717, the names always go on, met with a Cuban gentleman in his fifties each day at the Floridita; sometimes at Blake's suite, sometimes on the veranda, and sometimes they talked for one hour or more. They met for five straight days. The man actually wasn't Cuban. The man, a one Carlos Alvarez, yes that Carlos Alvarez of Bogota, Colombia, was a true businessman, even if his business was international arms smuggling.

And after sitting across from "Mr. Carlos" for five days, Blake had connected the dots and knew this man from his random sighting in Sandton, South Africa, the Peninsula party of Ward Kent in New York, and the Zona Rosa in Bogota. Thank God Mr. Carlos did not recognize Blake from anywhere; at least he didn't think he did, and Mr. Carlos would not place Blake as the man with Alexus in Bogota, nor would he meet or know of the tall slender nineteen-year-old Eva of Havana. If he knew of them, his mind could only wander to the two girls together and then . . . the male mind wandering. And that's why they go off the cliff so often. Oh well, nothing can be done about that.

For five days Blake (Code 717), (LaSalle 5) had met with Mr. Carlos of Bogota, they met in Havana. Just the mention of Bogota and Havana leaves men seeing long-legged, full lipped, big hair senoritas. Smoldering hot girls, and they would be right. They did exist, and you need to go no further than Alexus Gomez, Christina Martinez of Bogota and the latest, Eva Escobar of Havana.

Blake, on this contract, had been given a more delicate mission than just dropping seven hundred pounds of Napalm on some tattered muddy Congo rebel base, or slopping through a jungle or a desert just to shoot someone in the throat. For five days Blake talked at a one to two hours per day rate with Mr. Carlos. They spoke only that long because Mr. Carlos had to navigate the maze of Cuban officials and military men who wanted their cut. Blake's job was easy, he had the money, he knew exactly what he wanted in technical detail, and he knew where he wanted it delivered. His "people" had set up the Bahamas end of it, but each day was torture for Mr. Carlos and fun for Blake Anderson. When poor Mr. Carlos left the meeting with Blake, his work had just started. When Blake left the meeting, his fun had just started. He went to Eva who was wearing only a Cuban t-shirt, barefoot, and nothing else. Old Town Havana was the exotic backdrop to this intrigue, a great backdrop; secret meetings, shady figures, a paranoid police state, old colonial quarter, backdrop of 1940's/1950's cars, and one thin long-legged teenage girl with a sultry Spanish accent wearing only a t-shirt, and nothing else. And that's the way the world is supposed to be.

Blake and Carlos met openly because Carlos Alvarez had the full backing of the Cuban police state. They needed Carlos as the middleman so as not to connect any Cuban official with the deal. But the Cuban officials were watching every day, they even knew about Eva. They even watched her walk around in just a t-shirt in Blake's room. So Blake and Carlos were the two safest guys in Havana, protected by the full force of the Cuban police state. Why? Don't be silly, the Cuban state has no religion, but they still worship money. There is that word again, and this was certainly about money.

CHAPTER 21

On the fifth day that Blake was meeting with Mr. Carlos on the very specific requirement to acquire five very specific military subsystems from the bankrupt Cuban military, the Abbas brothers were heading from Beirut to Juba, South Sudan. The very Christian South Sudan needed weapons to go against the very Muslim North Sudan. But while the Abbas brothers were very Muslim and the people of Sudan were their brothers, they also worshipped on a higher plane than just Islam. They worshiped the almighty dollar over the almighty Allah. No disrespect, but to the Abbas brothers, dollars trumped everything.

Their sleek private jet looked very out of place in the very ragtag, desolate, dreary, scorched and tortured South Sudan. The runway they landed on was essentially the only paved runway in the country, and it became more like gravel every day.

The Abbas brothers had told their families they would be gone seventeen days on business, but that was not true. They had three days of business in South Sudan and fourteen days of pleasure in the company of Lisa and Sarah in Sandton, South Africa. Lisa would have her $200,000 Aston-Martin by then, the one paid for by Farsi Abbas, but he would never know of it or get a ride in it. And that is the way of the world.

CHAPTER 22

Javier Henri LeCirac of Nice, France had spent his time controlling the multitude of daily issues always present in a big company. They had some eleven product lines and $200 million plus in sales, most still made in France or Italy, but they did have one plant in China only fifteen miles north of Hong Kong. They had had it for only three years, but it had been successful. It was a precision machining center making high-end ball bearings and the circular collars to contain them. Their Chinese machinists were very good and very cheap.

These parts were of particular interest to Javier because they were part of a small but very intriguing area of his family business. It was a business Javier had started, and a business his father had let him continue in order to keep Javier in the family business. The business was small, maybe $7 million per year in sales, but demanding. It was the business of providing maintenance parts for French military jetfighters, and Javier loved the business because he liked the concept of military adventures, and particularly jetfighters.

He had always thought that without his upbringing and the family business he would have become a jetfighter pilot for the Armée de Air, the French Air Force. So to replace that dream he started the company so he could be around the jetfighters, visit the bases and meet the guys who fly them, try to get in the community. The business was seven years old and Javier had succeeded. He was a supplier to Dassault Aviation for selected airframe panels and parts for two Dassault-built jetfighters, the Mirage F-1B and Mirage F-2000D

The business made up less than three percent of the family's business empire, but it was the one area that kept Javier excited and eager. He loved his visits to the French airbases and still dreamed of having an excuse to visit a wild base in Africa, like in Djibouti or Chad or Gabon.

He had so many interests, but jetfighters always fit in. His artistic side had a marriage of architecture, art and beautiful women, all merged into a military adventure with Africa and the Middle East as a backdrop to intrigue and, of course, jetfighters. He thought he should produce a kind of movie or series that would be a cross between the movies "The Thomas Crown Affair" and "Blood Diamonds," with jetfighters thrown in. Elegance and intelligence paired with raw violence in even more raw places like Liberia, Mali and the Congo, maybe even Sudan.

For most young men this would be only a dream, as the money and resources would be beyond them, but not for Javier Henri LeCirac. He had everything he needed to do this on the money side, and he had a unique artistic and creative side to make the story interesting and unique. So he worked on this in addition to his business responsibilities. He was just that talented to do all of this at the same time. He even had his new assistant Kelly Grant slotted for a role. She was great for his company, but also his movie. The world must see and know this girl, even if for just one movie. So underneath his busy business executive persona he kept his energy going by drafting the storyline to his artistic dream.

His spare parts business for Dassault meant that on any day an unusual and intriguing military requirement might come up. It kept his pulse going, well that and beautiful art, beautiful girls, fast cars, and elegant food. This guy did have it all and he knew how to handle it, a most rare combination.

As it often happens, Javier's taste for adventure and jetfighters hit a lucky sweet spot. The Mirage F-1B jetfighter that Code 057 had used on the Sudan air strike had been damaged. Both Code 057 and his French pilot were so drained and weak upon their return to the desert air strip that they had buried the landing gear into some very hard dirt and rocks, and the resulting damage to the gears and under panels had been very significant. The plane had been parked for two weeks so Dassault could send some repair people. Word was the plane was grounded until the parts were available to repair the jet. Code 057 knew nothing of this, as he left the scene as soon as he was able to walk. He actually didn't remember how hard he landed the plane; he was barely able to sit in the cockpit. But the parts requirement came through the system to Javier's company.

On the sixth day that Blake (Code 057) was in Havana, a report went to Javier's company to supply critical panels and gear parts to a Mirage F-1B. Javier saw the report by chance and his pulse raced.

He knew his French jets by heart, except for this one. It seemed it had no number or registration, nor a stated location, a jetfighter without a passport. He had heard of this but didn't believe it . . . but now he did, and he finally realized there might be a whole separate world out there. He would love to know that world and to tell its story . . . with Kelly Grant as the secretive femme fatale. With all his other jobs his focus was on getting to Africa to actually see a Mirage F-1B in action, and this secret F-1B would be perfect. He would have to get that job done. He was excited.

CHAPTER 23

As Javier was scanning the parts order from Dassault in Nice, France, the man who had beat the Mirage F-1B into the ground was still in Havana. This contract had been the best, six days of rest so far and playing with Eva Escobar. The two hours a day he talked to Mr. Carlos Alvarez hardly counted as work, he had it easy. The Cuban Air Force had the subsystems and liked Blake Anderson's price, they just needed their hand held by Mr. Carlos. Should the Cuban Air Force generals be found out, maybe Fidel or Raul Castro would have them shot. Maybe the generals were trying to keep this from the Castro's, and maybe the generals were not trying to give the Castro's their cut.

In these rogue mafia countries the petty intrigue is endless, and the shallow dimwitted incompetence reaches legendary levels. It doesn't matter if you are talking about Libya, North Korea, Sudan, Zimbabwe, the Congo, Venezuela or the ever neurotic, ever incompetent Cuba. The United Rogue Nations has become smaller over the last ten years, but it is still just as entertaining. Self-absorbed buffoons pretending to run countries, except the countries are rundown family owned plantations. First you have the dictator. Then over time there are the sons, daughters, cousins and uncles who are put in to try to get to the next generation of the family to run the plantation; Hussein of Iraq, Gaddafi, Castro, Hun Sen of Cambodia, Mubarak of Egypt, Assad of Syria, Jung Il of North Korea, and on and on. They steal the money then become addicted to the power of running the plantation, even as the plantation becomes a desolate rundown joke. They will scramble to keep their place out of greed, but also out of fear. They are alive but they know the pack of African wild dogs is circling for the final kill.

African wild dogs are relentless, perfect killers. They do not ambush, they announce their hunt to the world through yelping as they pack up, sometimes reaching thirty dogs. Then they start running. Once they start running they will spot a herd. It doesn't matter which herd: zebras, wildebeest, antelope, or Cape buffalo. It doesn't matter because they will kill something virtually every time. Lions kill maybe fifty percent of the time, African wild dogs maybe ninety-eight percent of the time.

The dogs are patient, they run and they run. They run after their prey until one or more of the weak and sick reach exhaustion. It is going to happen because an African wild dog can run at a steady pace for maybe six hours, yes six hours. They have two percent body fat and their prey may last one hour, and the weak or sick less than that. So it is no contest, their prey is so exhausted that the dogs attack at will, and it is all over and the meal finished in less than ten minutes.

The Castro's have been running for fifty-five years, Mugabe of Zimbabwe for thirty-two years, Mubarak of Egypt for thirty plus years before the dogs caught him, Gaddafi for forty-two plus years before the dogs circled, Mobutu of the Congo for thirty-two years before the dogs killed him, Hussein of Iraq for twenty-four years before the pack descended, closed in and killed. But the dogs are always running, so the kill will come. The Castro's are like prey that has been running for three hours, but that is not long enough to avoid the kills. The pack dogs can run for six hours if they have to, so what looks like a long run for the Castro's is only the beginning for the pack dog killers. And the pack is vital, the pack has so many killers and their prey are only a handful. So it's always pack dog killers one and shallow incompetent dictators zero. And lately in the United Rogue Nations it seems they are hearing the yelps of the African wild dogs more and more, packing up to go on a kill. Who is next?

CHAPTER 24

So that is why Mr. Carlos has to spend so much time going between Blake Anderson and the Cuban generals. The generals are not sure if Blake Anderson is a sign of the pack dog killers. God knows the generals have been hearing the pack forming up for years.

Blake is happy to have this confusion. He sits on the veranda, strolls through Old Town Havana, takes Eva to bed at every opportunity, and then they go to a nice tourist restaurant for a quiet evening before he takes her to bed yet again. At nineteen she is lovely, quiet and quite ready after almost a week with Blake.

Often Blake will sit on his suite balcony and fantasize about a convention, a special convention.

The convention would have Alexus Gomez of Bogota, Christina Martinez of Bogota, Lisa Aswanela of Sandton, South Africa, Christy Alexander of New York City, Ashley from London, and now Eva Escobar of Havana. Okay, add in Eve of Bukavu – Congo, she needs the break.

Seven girls all dressed in loose fitting short shorts, thong underwear, loose fitting shirts, no bra. Just sitting and relaxing on a balcony under a big shade tree. Clean flowing hair, no makeup, no jewelry except hoop earrings, and everyone barefoot, just relaxing and giving the occasional slow sleepy smile. As the camera moves one to another, each is equally sexy, serene and enchanting.

Blake Anderson, Jason Stoner, Code 717, Code 057, Conrad, Kent, whoever he might be today, would like that. But he got no further in this fantasy because one of the parties in the fantasy, a one Eva Escobar had come from behind to open her shirt and put his head between two very perky, very toned, nineteen-year-old breasts. And his hand had slowly gone up between her very toned, very long, nineteen-year-old legs. Just another day at the office, he would return to Havana for sure, maybe by way of London, Sandton and Bogota.

CHAPTER 25

Then it happened. Mr. Carlos came to the Floridita Hotel, Suite 215 where Blake and Eva were staying. It was 1 a.m.

Blake came to the door and Mr. Carlos apologized repeatedly for the intrusion, but Blake must come immediately.

Blake, in an all-black paramilitary outfit, joined Mr. Carlos in the downstairs lobby. They both got into an old Soviet jeep of the Cuban military. There were two escort military jeeps, one in front and one in back. As they pulled away from the hotel, Havana was ghost quiet and dark. Havana was always dark, Cuba had virtually no electricity. Eva went back to sleep wearing just a t-shirt, legs thrown across the bed. Fifteen minutes had passed.

The jeeps drove one hour to the east of Havana to a Cuban Air Force base on the beautiful Caribbean coast.

They immediately went into a dilapidated rusting aircraft hangar. The hangar only had five light bulbs working, and those were not very bright; they cast a dim orange pall over the large hangar. The three jeeps drove in. So far the whole operation had been surreal. The quick wakeup in Old Havana, Eva ever sexy on the bed, the Soviet/Cuban jeeps in the dead of night, and now an old Air Force hangar bathed in orange light . . . Javier should capture this for his movie, a great movie set, but this was real life and Blake's real life . . . another day at the office.

To complete the movie set there were three Soviet-built jetfighters in the hangar. Two were MIG-29's and one MIG-23. None looked very air-worthy but the MIG-23 clearly had not flown in a long time, maybe to never fly again, likely not, as Cuba simply did not have jet fuel to fly them. Nothing works in this collective waste dump called Cuba. Nothing works except speeches to each other, signifying nothing.

Blake was led to the MIG-23 and specifically the nose landing gear. Blake did a technical inspection and referred to a technical book he had brought with him. His inspection took thirty minutes, and he noted that every time he looked up the assorted Cuban generals, there were three, were stressed and sweating. The Castro bothers had not been cut in on this deal.

Blake was generally satisfied. Blake told Mr. Carlos, his interpreter, that he would take six of these nose landing gears. He needed five but ordered six to be safe. The generals were relieved. They had five already stripped for shipping. Blake would look at these to set the deal. He asked the Cuban generals to strip the sixth from the standing MIG-23. Two personnel started immediately to strip the nose landing gear, a very visual sign of the Cuban decay, tearing apart the national defense structure on the spot for a few American dollars. Cuba had become a sort of auto salvage yard, but it actually had been an auto salvage yard for fifty-five years, led by that irrepressible carnival barker and rodeo clown, the one and only Fidel Castro. It was 3 a.m., a Cuban Air Base on the north coast of Cuba, only fifty miles from where Castro was sleeping tonight.

Blake went outside as the work was done on the MIG-23. He pulled out a satellite phone, dialed a number, spoke three minutes, and hung up. He dialed another number, spoke three minutes and hung up. He dialed one more number, spoke one minute and then hung up.

He returned to the hangar where the two airmen already had the nose gear off and the MIG-23 was propped up by a series of jury-rigged ladders, a truly sad sight. But they got the money, the supreme religion of the dictators, the democracies, the communists. The Cuban generals were getting American dollars.

CHAPTER 26

Blake watched as the boxed landing gears were loaded onto a trailer. The jeep took the boxes to a Cubana Air AN-26 with civilian markings.

Once loaded, Blake and Mr. Carlos and the three Cuban generals met under the wing. Blake gave Mr. Carlos the aluminum case he had brought with him, it had $100,000 dollars in $50 bills. The price was high; the whole plane was only worth $20,000 for scrap metal and parts. Actually, no one needed MIG-23 parts but Blake's contract needed them, and badly.

Everyone shook hands. Mr. Carlos and the generals headed back to the hangar. Blake climbed aboard the old Soviet AN-26, and he told the crew of three Russians to start the mission. The plane taxied to the runway and coughed down the runway, eventually taking off. The plane carried only Blake and the six boxes as cargo. It was 3:40 a.m., Havana was dark and quiet, Eva was sleeping peacefully, and the "civilian" Cubana Air plane was heading to . . . Nassau, Bahamas.

Fifteen minutes out over the sea Blake startled the crew by opening the rear door. The door was open for only ten seconds. Blake apologized to the crew quickly and went up front to sit with them. They were puzzled, but then didn't care. They had their mission . . . to get their money, to get their cigarettes, and to get their vodka. Their life was simple.

In those ten seconds Blake had thrown the $2,000 satellite phone into the sea. It had been wired to a MIG-23 part to get it to the bottom of the sea. Ironic.

Well, it was supposed to be Nassau, but at the last minute the plane would drop off the flight path and at two hundred feet altitude head for one Norman Cay. Norman Cay had an infamous landing strip built by a Colombian drug lord in the 1980's. It was rarely used now but was still there, and Blake was going to use it.

The plane landed thirty minutes later. Blake got off with the six boxes and sent the Russian crew merrily on their way. Nassau was less than thirty minutes away, the crew maybe sixty minutes away from their vodka. It was 7 a.m.

Mr. Carlos would see to Eva this day and settle Blake's hotel bill. Blake hoped to return to Havana to see Eva. Mr. Carlos did return to Bogota, he was seen at the Zona Rosa, Bogota the next day. This had been a small deal for him, but necessary to keep his Cuban customers happy. He did want another Congo deal though, those were so great. But his one contract with General Olongowe had somehow been wiped from the face of the earth. A dangerous business.

Blake Anderson was to wait on Norman Cay in an abandoned home for two days. He had five gallons of water and three protein bars, but this was five-star compared to Sudan when he was Code 057, or all those other times in some remote apocalypse. It was hot and humid, but so quiet; so Blake just relaxed, very alone, but quite content.

On the third day a Learjet 60 swooped into Norman's Cay. It was a light gray with orange accents. It taxied to Blake, two commandos appeared to load the six boxes. The plane landed with British registration; it took off with US registration.

An hour later a sleek, titanium colored Cigarette Powerboat took Blake to the British Colonial Hilton, Nassau. Two days later British Airways Flight 831, Nassau to London, had a gentleman dressed in all gray in Seat 4A. He wore Ralph Lauren aviator sunglasses, but the Bell & Ross was missing; he wore no watch.

CHAPTER 27

Kelly Grant had eleven days left in London before joining the Javier Henri LeCirac corporate staff. She would be highly paid, $200,000 per year for a twenty-year-old, a lot even for a stunningly sexy, educated and composed girl. She was to also be lavished with perks, chefs, drivers, helicopters and private jets, not to mention the turbo Porsche thrown in. She had agreed to it and had a specific employment contract, all she needed to know now is what exactly she was going to do for LeCirac Industrial Inc. of Nice, France.

She also needed to get her "assistant," someone to keep her company and help her as she needed. Without this part of the deal Kelly would not have gone. Being "bought" for $200,000 a year to move to Nice, France to be preyed upon by a rich man was a no go for her without a female companion to keep her company and be her assistant.

Javier did not seem the type, but you never ever know. Men and their sex drives, a perennial threat to the social order. Even the thousand-year-old social orders are threatened daily with the relentless destructive thrust of the male sex drive. Nothing is ever safe or stable from it, just ask the massive, repressive, all powerful Catholic Church.

But today with most of the moving and paperwork done, thanks to the staff at LeCirac Industries, Kelly was free to stroll through Hyde Park. She felt free today and just wanted to stroll; no headphones, no twitter, no Facebook, no cell phones, just to walk in the elegance of Hyde Park, London. It was a mild but somewhat chilly day, perfect for a walk. It was 1 p.m.

By 2 p.m. Kelly was so refreshed; she had enjoyed an hour of solitude and fresh air. Ever conscious of her sexual allure, given free to her by nature, she had worn loose floppy clothes and a scarf over her chin to block the last and most powerful of her sexual features, the dimple in her chin, so the untrained eye of the average internet male would not detect her long legs, tiny waist, raging blonde hair and light crystal blue eyes. She was a stunning girl of twenty years, who also happened to have a Master's Degree, as well as employment at MI6. So, as much as the girls from Bogota flaunted their immense sexuality, the young Kelly hid hers.

As she walked, she glanced and then she stopped, then she was stunned.

A quiet girl was reading an actual hardcover paper book. Like Kelly, no cell phone, no headphones, just reading an actual paper book. Equally stunning was her incredible sexual presence. Even Kelly felt a rush of sexual attraction, the girl was more than Kelly's equal. She should be at a Chelsea pub with ten of her best friends, laughing, flirting, and turning the place upside down with her scorching good looks. But she sat alone reading a paper book, no electronic device in sight, in a quiet corner of Hyde Park across from Lancaster Gate on Bayswater Road – London. It was 2:30 p.m.

For the first time Kelly felt the very difficult world of the male. She wanted to approach this girl but had not a clue how to do it just because of the girl's enormous sexuality, which this girl appeared not to have a clue about. She was so quiet and innocent.

The girl had the raging blonde curly hair of a Shakira, the Colombian singer, hazel blue eyes it appeared, and a small perky nose above luscious pouty lips. And what put her over the top, an ever-rare dimple in the chin. The tiny waist, tight ass and long legs were a given. Victoria's Secret was slipping, how was this girl loose!

Two beautiful scorching girls at the same location, each with a dimpled chin, an event as rare in nature as Haley's Comet passing. The only event to put this in the ultimately rare territory, a one in ten million occurrence in nature, was the two girls were actually sitting and talking together. Rare sensual beautiful girls do not mingle and socialize. It's just nature competing for the male, and winning is best done with the female one-on-one with the male. Then it is no contest, the female simply overwhelms the male. But two equally sexy girls means the male has somewhat of a choice, so the girls must expend energy to be the "one." Sexy girls don't want to go to that trouble, so they choose to hang out with girls less sexy, and their lives are much easier.

But this was different, each girl was purposely avoiding the sexy, young social female role. They were so hidden, so low profile as to be painful . . . if the young men knew they existed, they would be in relentless pursuit. Only rarely will equally beautiful girls ever become friends. No one wants to share the power, and it is power we are talking about here. Not an acquired power, but a power given by nature when you are a sexy young girl between seventeen and twenty-three years. Then the "wrong side of twenty-three" applies and you must fend for yourself.

CHAPTER 28

Thirty yards away a man sat in Hyde Park, Lancaster Gate, reading the Financial Times. He had come to London for a week to ten days to relax . . . and shop for a new Bell & Ross watch.

He had noticed the blonde in the loose-fitting clothes. She was as stunning a girl as he had ever seen, to include the "girls" of Bogota, as well as Lisa Aswanela of South Africa. His trained eye had gotten past the loose-fitting clothes and scarf. She was simply sensual, but a very quiet beauty that made it all the more powerful. He had not seen the other stunning girl. He kept reading his newspapers. He kept watching casually as the girl in the loose clothes had stopped.

If he had known about it, he would also have known this was the same neighborhood of London where the young Andy Morris and Frank Cramer had once lived. Two very talented journalists whose bones now lay exposed to the tropical rain on a hillside in the Eastern Congo. He would recognize them, as they had interviewed him. They had been very smart and also very earnest and pleasant; nice guys, but the wrong place at the wrong time and they were dead, executed by two faceless mercenaries.

But the man did not know any of this. He also did not know that he was the "4th" Mercenary" of their story. He was still the "4th Mercenary" of that story to the one person still alive who knew the story, Todd Blake of Johannesburg, South Africa.

The man on the bench knew none of this; he was a shadow in a world of shadow people. The people of the world's intelligence agencies live in the shadows, but organized stable shadows, and then there are the people living in the shadows of the intelligence agencies. Even the agencies do not know about them. To live in that ultimate shadow world you must travel fast, and thus you must travel alone. The man on the bench reading page five of the Financial Times did travel alone, but he was never lonely, never.

CHAPTER 29

Kelly continued to stroll very slowly, almost at a stop. Then she decided to go, and she veered off the main walk and took a small path to the bench under the tree where this magnificent girl sat.

The man watched her over the Financial Times page. It seemed like an innocent detour of the beautiful sexy girl, maybe to pick up a leaf. Then he saw her, he saw the other girl. She was likely more gorgeous than the first, should that be possible. He could tell they did not know each other, as the approaching girl was quite tentative. Then the man just dropped the newspaper in his lap to watch, not to stare, but to take a break from reading. He fully recognized the immense rarity of this event, one in ten million at least. Two sexy young girls, not tens, likely twelve's or thirteen's, meeting on their own, no cocktail parties, no functions. The man had to witness this fully; he was thirty yards away and fully into the background on this day, Hyde Park, Lancaster Gate, Bayswater Road – London.

The standing girl sat down on the bench after talking for ten minutes. They talked a further ten minutes and they both got up, they strolled and walked a quiet slow stroll, still talking. The man did not move and resumed "reading," but not really reading.

As the girls strolled out of his sight, he got up. He got to the main walk about the time they turned right to the gate out of Hyde Park onto Bayswater Road.

He quickened his pace. By the time he had gotten to the gate himself he saw the girls strolling on the opposite side of the road. He stayed on the park side.

They then turned into the elegant Black Swan Pub and sat down in the outdoor section. This was the rarest of events. Two smoking, sexy girls sitting quietly and they had only met.

One was of course Kelly Grant, soon to be of Nice, France and LeCirac Industries. The other would turn out to be one Abbey Bond, no not James's niece, just Abbey Bond.

The man kept strolling by; he had witnessed a true random rare event and did not in any way want to spoil it. He wanted to always remember, so he kept walking and left the girls to their talk. There is something to be said for just witnessing a very rare occurrence in nature, appreciating every minute of it and then just letting it go undisturbed. The man did that, the Blake Anderson of Havana, the Jason Stoner of Manhattan, New York City.

Had they known, it would have been sad. The Black Swan had been the "go to" pub of Andy and Frank. They had spent many an afternoon chatting about their young lives, their dreams and aspirations. They had met their nice stable girlfriends there and had gone there before leaving for the Eastern Congo.

Sad, but the two beautiful girls did not know their story and Blake Anderson did not know their story, even as he was a brief part of it. And life goes on.

CHAPTER 30

Directly across Hyde Park from Lancaster Gate is the Knightsbridge section of London; very upscale, very affluent, lots of very expensive real estate. The section is marked by many embassies around the world occupying five level British brownstone townhouses, any one of which is worth $20 million plus on the market.

Many of these embassies in turn are from dirt poor African countries. These countries had citizens who subsisted on $300 per year, while their dear Ambassador to Britain spent $200,000 per month, yes per month, to rent their embassy in London. Not to mention their chefs and the drivers, the Bentley, the assistants. It all seemed so obscene. The dirt poor country politicians had to save face, even as they kept their citizens' faces buried in that same dirt. And Sudan was one of those countries.

As the two gorgeous girls sat down at the Black Swan, a very large, very fat man was sitting down in the office of the Sudanese Ambassador to Britain. As the girls on Bayswater Road began to talk quietly and softly, the fat man began to talk loudly and rough. The man with the Financial Times continued to walk on Bayswater Road. He was going to shop for a new Bell & Ross watch now and knew nothing of this . . . yet.

As the young sexy girls continued to talk softly and adjust positions, the very large man continued to shout and also adjust positions, but it was difficult for him as the chair was too small and he breathed heavily. His name was Ali Alawid; the Ali Alawid of the People's Republic of Syria. He was a major arms dealer and Sudan was his territory. Or was until the Abbas brothers came waltzing in to take one of the largest arms contracts in Sudan's history.

As the Abbas brothers strolled through Mandela Square, South Africa with the massive arm candy, Lisa and her friend Sarah, Mr. Ali Alawid was about to have a stroke as he yelled and sweated. He would buy his young girls later, he did love them, but Mr. Alawid had things to say now.

Most of which had to do with the Abbas brothers. How did Sudan choose them, had he not sent enough money to the cabinet and prime minister? Every time he had provided them with the best when they were in London and when they were in Khartoum, the dusty capital of Sudan. "My God," he yelled, "is there no end to the greed!" Well, actually there isn't, you pray to Allah five times a day, but you think of money twenty-four hours a day, so it's money one, Allah zero, every day, all day long, till the end of time.

Poor Mr. Alawid, he busts his massive ass to end up with orders for AK-47's and bullets. The Abbas brothers swoop in to take a massive contract, only to have much of it vaporized by some rogue attack mission, so now the Abbas brothers will likely get another massive contract. And that is why one Mr. Alawid was here today in Knightsbridge, London, sitting in the opulent richly appointed office of the Sudanese Ambassador, drinking some great Sri Lankan tea in great gulps in some of the finest china on the face of the earth; all the while trying to sell arms so that some skinny teenage boys in the dust can shoot some skinny pathetic village people and have them fall into that same ever present Sudanese dust.

The Ambassador had had enough, and he politely excused himself from Mr. Alawid to go to the next engagement. The Ambassador went to his private quarters and turned on CNN, sat down and relaxed. That was his next appointment. To be an Ambassador takes massive skill, to smile in the face of an endless parade of buffoons. Mr. Ali Alawid was no buffoon, but just as disgusting. Foul, smelly, fat Mr. Alawid wanted his Dassault 7X private jet, and he was going to fight for it no matter how many dead bodies he had to step over.

CHAPTER 31

As the sexy young girls were concluding their talk, across Hyde Park Mr. Alawid was forced to end his.

As the girls rose to leave and head together toward Oxford Street, the picture of pristine beauty, Mr. Alawid was on the elevator down to Burton Street to his waiting Bentley limousine, the picture of obese sweating foulness.

Mr. Alawid's very sour attitude was helped a bit when a doorman came from nowhere to assist him to his car. His staff had been sent ahead.

As his door opened, Mr. Alawid noticed the front curtains pulled and his personal bodyguard absent. Oh well, he is likely in the front seat chatting with the driver; bodyguards were not allowed in the Embassy.

As the doorman held the door so the massive Alawid could squeeze in, he put his right hand in his long coat pocket. In one motion, as he helped Mr. Alawid wedge his head in, he put his right hand behind Mr. Alawid's ear and pulled the trigger.

Mr. Alawid slumped to the center of the car but no one saw it, the door had been closed quickly and loudly to mask the slight pop of the subcompact Ruger .22 LR. A tiny gun with a tiny bullet, but that tiny bullet lodged in your brain is just as effective as a Howitzer. Dead is dead.

The "doorman" went through the motions of telling the driver his passenger was ready. It was not Mr. Alawid's driver, but the man slumped next to the driver was Mr. Alawid's bodyguard, dead from a .22 LR bullet.

The Bentley drove off, but for only three miles, then it was parked and the driver got out and walked away.

The doorman walked casually down the street and made a cell phone call at the corner. The assassin looked British but spoke with a South African accent. In his $3,000 suite at the Michelangelo Hotel Farsi Abbas smiled and thanked the man. The man had done an excellent job, Farsi thought, and his work would help his business. Meanwhile, across the room, Lisa just raided the till but Mr. Farsi did not see it that way, at least not yet. Lisa was Farsi's goddess.

The evening came and the London girls decided to meet tomorrow, maybe Abbey would become Kelly's Assistant. And Blake Anderson returned to a special townhouse in Mayfair – London, he had looked but had not found a new Bell & Ross.

The Guardian newspaper would run the Alawid story in two days. Mr. Blake Anderson would read it as he sat again in a quiet corner of Hyde Park.

Said Alawid, Ali's brother and No. 2, also read about it. He was so sad and so furious, and so someone must pay. But he was also happy to be No. 1 now. And Said Alawid would move to Sudan to make sure the deals went his way.

CHAPTER 32

Javier Henri LeCirac couldn't wait for Kelly Grant to arrive, but that was still a week away. Her basic goods had arrived in Nice, but Javier would insist she use his interior decorator to fix her residence. She was only twenty, but well past the "dorm room" motif. He had not heard from her so he didn't know her frame of mind, nor whether she had found an "assistant."

He had been busy with the usual corporate stuff. All was going well business wise, but what kept his enthusiasm going was this lone Mirage F-1B. He needed this kind of intrigue.

He re-read the parts order from Dassault Aviation and it only increased his interest. Somewhere in this mundane parts order was an industrial-strength story of adventure, intrigue and international military relations, plus more he didn't know. It had the beginnings of the film script he had conceived three years ago, but he lacked the experience or details to flesh it out. It was to be fiction, but he wanted some real events to drive the story. He didn't know about the military adventures he wanted to film, but that just made it that much more interesting to him.

In the next two weeks he would personally take on the repair parts order for this lone Mirage F-1B jetfighter somewhere in Africa; the aircraft all alone without a "passport." It existed, it seemed, but no professional air force seemed to claim it. Yes, he would get involved himself; this is the reason he had started this military aircraft business. It was small but it got him into the parallel universe of military operations and adventures. Actually, Javier Henri had all the money, glamour, women, education, and cultivated interests when he was in his twenties. He had everything but random explosive adventure, thus his drive in this area, and now this small event for spare parts presented itself. And the young Mr. LeCirac knew it was much, much more than a single order for spare parts. The order form was like the opening page to the shadowy, dark, subtle, and likely deadly world of contract international military operations. Put simply, it seemed to be the foggy ghost-like world of the modern mercenary. In biblical times it was the image of the Four Horsemen of the Apocalypse riding in . . . in today's world maybe it is just the coming of the silent shadow that seems to be the modern mercenary.

Javier Henri LeCirac didn't know, but he was so happy to have this new challenge, this new dimension to his life. The idea that there might be mercenary pilots flying high-performance military jets in Africa seemed so over the top in his rather stale corporate world, but he knew it might exist. He could only hope.

CHAPTER 33

Wei Kyi, the Burmese arms dealer from Tachileik, Burma had been assembling the weapons to fill his order. The weapons were headed to Mindanao, Philippines via the Mekong River through Laos, Cambodia and Vietnam.

It was complicated in that the Mae Sai, Thailand meeting with Chaya Ptorn, the Thai dealer, had gone well but no money had changed hands. Mr. Wei Kyi was busy building a delivery order, but no money had come. Mr. Ptorn needed to get with him, as the money, there is that word again, had not come. Mr. Ptorn had the contacts, Wei Kyi had the weapons.

He wanted another meeting and hoped to bring some major cash back across the Thai-Burma border at Mae Sai. He knew Mr. Ptorn was making big money on this and Wei Kyi needed his, as he had used his own cash to build this stock of weapons. It seems that nobody likes to use their own cash, they want to hoard it to themselves just to throw it around on DeBeers diamonds, Las Vegas roulette tables, Aston-Martin 177's, $7,000 Armani or Ralph Lauren suits, maybe a $1,300 Hermes handbag, or a $217,000 Ulysses Nardin watch. Humans and their quest for these pieces of paper need to be studied, not just lightly, but by a whole international team of experts. It's not even paper anymore, just electronic bits in some bank's computer, but it consumes whole lifetimes.

Wei Kyi was restricted to Burma due to a long winding road of intrigue and sanctions, and Mr. Ptorn roamed the world. So without Mr. Ptorn's contacts, Wei Kyi was not in business, at least not now. There are always middlemen and Thailand was full of them, but so far Mr. Ptorn was the best.

But with the rogue nation of Burma Wei Kyi could get most everything from small arms to maybe a MIG-29, at least parts to a MIG-29. He reigned supreme in Burma but was blind outside of it. What he could not get in Burma he could smuggle from China.

At the time of their last meeting two covert operatives had watched the Wei Kyi/Chaya Ptorn meeting from the Burma side. One of the operatives was from the Burmese military. He was not there to build a case against Wei Kyi, but just to make sure Wei Kyi was working hard to move the arms in Burma to keep up the cash flow. For the Burmese military to buy Chinese or Russian weapons they needed US dollars, and to get US dollars they needed to trade through the Thai arms dealers. The Burmese were not only spying on Wei Kyi, they were doing an accounting audit to make sure they got their cut. It's the same dynamics as played out on the other side of the world in wretched little Cuba, or North Korea, or Congo, etc., etc.

And things were little different this time. The other operative spying on the same meeting, but unknown to the Burmese intelligence, was a young man "they" had recruited two years ago. The identity of "they" is always murky, it is always two or three agencies, then often just one, and always hidden under multiple layers, and then often in the open. Who knows.

But "they" needed five nice landing gears for a MIG-23, and Burma was one of a few possible sources to get these subsystems. "They" could have used Cuba again, but preferred to diversify and to keep the trail . . . murky.

CHAPTER 34

Two days after the story of Ali Alawid's assassination ran in the papers, one Blake Anderson was in Hyde Park again.

This time a tall slender British man sat down by him. They both read their respective papers for ten minutes, then the British gentleman in the Savile Row suit put his paper down and smoked a pipe for fifteen minutes, then got up and left. Blake Anderson had become Code 037 with the Code name Conrad.

Fifty yards away Kelly sat with Abbey Bond again. They both had again camouflaged their figures, hair and long legs, but they were noticeably warmer and happier. In the full bloom of youth two stunning young girls sat in the quiet elegance of Hyde Park. And a one Conrad, Code 037, was uniquely qualified to witness it, appreciate it and . . . ten minutes later he walked away, leaving the momentary perfection of nature to play itself out alone. Oh, to be young again. The warm glow of youth and beauty bathed the young women.

Abbey Bond was to be Kelly Grant's assistant. It is unlikely the world of Nice, France is even remotely ready. Should these girls "unveil" themselves they will take the male world by storm. Unlike the "Bogota" girls of Alexus, Carmen, et al, it was hard to calculate their sexual power; they had kept it so much under wraps. Maybe the Muslims were right to cover the women, it kept life simple and under control.

CHAPTER 35

Three days later . . .

Thai Airways Flight 175, Bangkok to Rangoon, Burma, touched down at 5:15 p.m. By 6:45 p.m. "Conrad" was in a suite at the old colonial hotel in Rangoon. It was called The Strand on Strand Road. Catchy, the PR guys never rest; actually, it was 113 Strand Road.

Rangoon and Havana should be the world's sister cities of the United Rogue Nations. On opposite sides of the world in distance and culture, they share so much. Things like no regular electricity, a rich treasure of colonial architecture that is falling apart, whole blocks of dilapidated apartment buildings; just sad, backward places that could be world class cities. It's not going to happen. On the upside there is not much noise, as there are very few vehicles on the road.

The city is a true representation of two concepts that often come up. First, at night it is a true city of ghosts, and second, it is a true Heart of Darkness.

The residents of the old Colonial Quarters in each city walk quietly amid the quiet dark. There is no electricity and, as said, there is very little traffic. What little there is only accents the ghostly figures of the residents moving silently about in a city that is quiet. No traffic, just the occasional Cyclo-bicycle taxi and beat up 1950's truck from China. They match the 1950's American cars in Havana.

And on each block are scenes of pure poverty and subsistence; pieces of humanity just acting as clutter to the ruling military elite, the ruling tribe. And so it goes in another "country," but the countries are just collections of tribes. Actually, without the military the Union of Myanmar, as it is formally known, would not exist. There are some one hundred plus tribes in Burma. From the ancient Pai tribe in their all black costumes, to the larger Wa tribes and Karen tribes who basically engage in an endless war with the central military government and run their own mini-states within Burma.

CHAPTER 36

And such as it was, Conrad found himself here only two weeks or so after serving in the same capacity in the sister city of ghosts, Havana, on the other side of the world. If the United Rogue Nations were to form, he could be its Secretary-General.

Apparently, the assorted contract agencies that employ him were giving him more gentle contracts for a period to let him recover from the Western Sudan missions. And they were right, those missions had drained him to the lowest level of survival.

So he needed to do the dangerous but more sedate jobs of negotiating to buy five MIG-29 nose landing gears on the black market from the assorted group of traitors, assassins, rogue mercenaries and armed con artists who populate this shadow world. But he had his world of shadows to help him survive. And the nice young man who had "sold" him a bag of pitiful apples, as Conrad strolled through the maze of ruins that was central Rangoon, was part of it. But in the bag of pitiful apples was a not so pitiful Beretta, a PX4 9mm was included with one hundred bullets, just in case. So the guys, whoever they were this time, were concerned for him; it sounded sweet, but it was just business.

His Rangoon contact was none other than the legendary, well legendary only inside Burma, Wei Kyi.

And on the way the clients had changed their minds. They didn't want MIG-23 landing gears, they wanted MIG-29 landing gears. Apparently, the next mission dealt with MIG-29s, and the success in getting the MIG-23 landing gears in Havana had led to a change in the landing gear order.

The money Conrad (Code 037) was offering was staggering; $1 million dollars even for just five nose landing gears for a MIG-29. You could probably get these for less than $100,000 on Ukrainian Ebay or the Bulgarian Black Market.com., so Conrad knew something else was in play here.

And what was in play was likely an attempt to identify every significant player in the black market arms business in Southeast Asia. That kind of stupid money surfaced every player, big or small, to come to the table. But likely the cleverest of the players would stay away, but that said a lot in itself.

And right in the middle they had put Conrad, Code 037. Maybe it wasn't dodging bullets and stepping over bodies in the wretched wet Congo and being baked to death under the Sudanese desert, but Conrad thought this might be quite dangerous also. Well, of course, why else contract with a mercenary, whether it's the first mercenary or The 4ᵗʰ Mercenary.

CHAPTER 37

On the second day, as Conrad stepped onto the street and walked fifty yards, a street hustler approached trying to sell some fake Channel sunglasses. As Conrad waved him off, the man gave him a small piece of paper. Conrad kept it in his hand but did not read it, he knew at least three Burmese intelligence operatives had been assigned to follow him. He continued to stroll but did not meet anyone. Just strolled, sat a bit, and strolled some more; when under surveillance it's best just to bore them to death.

So for two more days Conrad just walked through the dilapidated city and sat and observed. Too many people from all walks of life knew exactly that he was here in Rangoon.

Each day he was passed a note by some hustler or street vendor, it was the same meet me at Trader Hotel, 8 p.m., Wei Kyi. And for three days Conrad ignored it. Why? Because the Southeast Asia dealers had known "from the street" that he was here and was a serious buyer who wanted to spend $1 million dollars. With this much money he was the "man" and they could wait, like pigeons waiting in the park for someone to bring the popcorn. For what Conrad wanted, it was huge and so easy. The dealers couldn't wait. Greed leads to irrational greed.

On the fifth day it happened. A man in his thirties, dressed cleanly, came to him and said, "Swadi Kup," Thai for hello, and gave him a note. He then got into a black Camry and disappeared. Conrad put the note in his pocket and continued to walk. But the game was on, likely a one Chaya Ptorn was added to the game. Conrad would check the note later.

When he did check it later, it was Mr. Ptorn.

The next day a smartly dressed Indian joined Conrad for breakfast at the Strand. The man just sat down, said hello, and started talking; the man was Raja Majani of Calcutta, as in India. A new surprise player, but who he worked for was the staggering surprise, a one General Abdul of the Army of Sudan. It seems General Abdul, having survived Conrad's brutal air attack on the base, had done wonders for his career. Since the devastation was so great and General Abdul by Allah's will had survived, he had become a bit of a legend. The eye patch only added to the legend. He went from two stars to three stars and got an office in Khartoum and immediately went into the "business" of selling off what he could of the Sudanese military equipment. T

The best arms merchants are the generals and prime ministers.

Cambodia and its "generals," self-appointed generals but just greedy arms dealers, kept the Sri Lankan Tamil Tigers going for fifteen years. When caught red handed, Cambodia promised to stop publicly, but kept shipping. Sri Lanka finally put their army generals into Cambodia to make it stop. Less than two years after the Cambodian shipments stopped the Tamil Tigers imploded. A very strong guerilla military went to nothing when the shipments stopped.

So, here was the one-eyed General Abdul with his three stars about to deal with the very man who almost barbequed him just a few months ago. It's not ironic really, it's just business.

So Conrad was forced to listen to Raja Majani. Mr. Majani was actually staying at a suite at the Strand Hotel also. These guys had expense accounts to bypass the street people. The word got out quickly; the African wild dogs were packing up for the kill.

Conrad listened, excused himself and went to his suite. No strolls today, too many carnival barkers out there. Raja wanted Conrad's cell phone number and email address. Conrad said proudly,

"I don't have either actually, but if I need you I can call you." Conrad glanced at Raja's business card and excused himself. Another meeting called, Conrad said, but there was no meeting.

There is power to communicate and there is the larger power of not being willing to communicate. People did not call Conrad, he called them.

CHAPTER 38

The Abbas brothers were spending so much time in South Africa they might as well buy a home. They had become big players and the new Sudan business put them over the top, maybe $17 million in arms, with $51 million to come. Love the Sudan. The bigger they got, the bigger they wanted to be. Greed is good, Allah is great. Actually, Allah doesn't even show up in their world . . . his face is not on any currency . . . so how can he be important.

Lisa Aswanela had her Aston-Martin now, so she was the complete fantasy; long-legged teenage girl striding through Sandton, South Africa, as stunning as ever. The definition along her hips and stomach had become even sharper, so the low-slung jeans were pure erotic, beyond sexy, and now maybe an inch above the triangle. Sometimes there were no panties, so she was becoming ever more bold.

Not that Farsi Abba was touching any of it. Lisa had manipulated him into a warm mush, but he still took her time, and even with the latest $200,000 in cash he was getting irritating beyond her endurance.

On the spur of the moment she decided to wash the Aston-Martin, pack her clothes, swing by to pick up Sarah, and head to Cape Town. She asked Farsi for $11,000 for shopping in Cape Town, she got it. Maybe she would give a one Mr. Alex Kagamba a call. He was nice looking, charming and had been chasing her ever since they met at the Sandton Aston-Martin dealer.

She liked that plan, and with Sarah along she could keep her distance. Actually, Sarah and Alex should be the couple, they were the good match.

Lucky for Lisa the Abbas brothers were leaving the next day. Farsi insisted on taking her by private plane to Cape Town, but she said Sarah needed to see a sick relative so they would take her car. Farsi had never seen the Aston-Martin. So Farsi would spend this last night alone, and he already missed Lisa. Guys truly are pathetic.

With that Lisa kissed Farsi lightly on the cheek and was gone.

Fifty miles outside of Johannesburg Lisa called Alex. She was on the way to Cape Town for one week but had a day open if he was available. Alex basically passed out. He would do anything to see her.

Fifty miles later Lisa got a call. But not from Alex, from some guy named Kent, and Lisa basically passed out.

"Where are you and when are you coming?" Lisa shouted.

"Soon, I hope," is all Kent said.

Marooned and isolated in his suite in Rangoon he thought of people to call and thought of Lisa. She was so magnificent and who could forget those legs, particularly the way she would slightly spread them and look at him. James, bring the Bentley around, it's time to see Lisa. That is when he called her.

But right now he was mired in a growing web of intrigue; the bait put out was attracting every shape of arms dealer. Maybe he could get Lisa to help him; he knew she was an operative for a number of people; a little business, a lot of pleasure. How would he do this?

CHAPTER 39

Alex Kagamba was ecstatic. As soon as he put the phone down his mind began racing on where to take Lisa in Cape Town.

His business was growing and a new contact in the Sudan, helped by a Rwandan general, may be the big break. If his luck held, he would be invited to Khartoum in two to three weeks. With that potential ahead of him, the Lisa visit was that much more exciting.

He did not have his Aston-Martin, of course at thirty-three it would be at least five years before it could happen. So how did nineteen-year-old Lisa have one and paid for at that. It was just the way of the world, women may complain about having a tough time, but those women are not long-legged teenage sultry sex goddesses. Lisa stood out because she was clever, cool, and far smarter than the next ten nineteen-year-olds.

As Lisa was ripping across the African plains between Johannesburg and Cape Town, Alex was selecting the right wine, insuring his impeccable wardrobe was set, and trying to keep his energy under control. He couldn't wait to see Lisa.

Kent, as Lisa knew him, felt the events of the day in Rangoon, Burma were too chaotic and he felt vulnerable. Too many people knew he was here and what he was doing. That's not good. As he sat in his suite and watched the sparse traffic shuffle by, he would let things settle in his mind. Lisa was freewheeling across Southern Africa, and Kent was imprisoned in his elegant colonial suite. He wasn't really sure if "they," the agency or agencies who triggered this contract, really wanted to get the five MIG-29 nose landing gears. The contract and arrangements just completed in Havana would have been fine to actually get the landing gears quickly. The Cuban generals would sell the entire Air Force by next week.

But here he was surrounded by a carnival of con artists, middlemen and, very likely, a small army of small time gunmen just waiting to make their mark. Conrad (Kent) had in the space of two days gone from the "main man" with the money to the "target" with the money.

He would try one more simple thing today to measure the intensity of the situation. Then he would report back; this situation seemed to be going south quickly.

Too much money for too little hardware, too many carnival barkers, someone was using dear Conrad as bait. It was a dangerous game for Conrad, but it was always a dangerous game; just another day at the office.

CHAPTER 40

Kelly Grant and Abbey Bond touched down in a Gulfstream 650 at Nice International Airport, Nice, France. The jet belonged to LeCirac Industries and was bringing home a team of seven LeCirac managers from London.

The seven managers were stressed and overworked, but when they boarded the private jet at Northolt Airport outside of London that exhaustion evaporated. Already onboard and sitting quietly in the back were not one, but two of the most beautiful and yet sexy girls on the face of the earth. The girls were not interested in being sexy or beautiful, and they were girls of twenty that looked seventeen years old. What were they doing here? Their quiet controlled studious life was about to change. As Kelly, Abbey and the corporate "suits" settled in, the man in Rangoon had to move. No one told him to move, he just decided to move.

The African "wild dogs" smelled easy money and were ever more aggressively circling their prey. And this time . . . he was their prey.

Javier Henri LeCirac could not wait for his Gulfstream 650 to land in Nice. He was at his massive, high-ceilinged, very opulent corporate office overlooking the Nice harbor. His business mind was racing on four different levels, but he had two other less profitable situations that were actually much more exciting than making more money. First there was the imminent arrival of one Kelly Grant, the stunning girl from London with her light crisp British accent. Javier Henri had no idea that an even more stunning girl, Abbey Bond, was also on the plane.

And within a week he would have cleared his corporate schedule to get into what had become an intense exciting event; the existence of this lone, crippled, orphaned Dassault Mirage F-1B. A story on the surface so intriguing Javier Henri could not wait to get into it, but he was seven to eight days away from that.

Lisa Aswanela was speeding toward Cape Town, her long leg on the Aston-Martin pedal, her hair everywhere and oh so sexy.

Alex Kagamba had just finished a phone call with a former Rwandan general, one Winton Kigani. And the good General Winton Kigani had just the hour before finished a critical phone call from the global leader in arms financing and mercenary financing, the very powerful ex-British army general, Winston Burton of Mayfair – London. And Winston Burton had just finished his twice weekly call to his international finance source, the one Ward Kent, Kent/Martin Investments, Manhattan, New York City.

CHAPTER 41

In Rangoon the main man had decided to move. During the day Conrad had positioned himself for this option. He was alone and felt surrounded by the circling wild dogs. There was Wei Kyi who was rather stable compared to the increasingly erratic Mr. Chaya Ptorn. Then out of the blue comes this slick corporate hustler, Mr. Raja Majani out of Calcutta. God knows how many more might be forming up to descend on poor wretched Rangoon. It had become global central for this one small deal. What is happening? The arms business couldn't be this desperate. Whatever was happening, he was going to figure that out somewhere else. The wild dogs were packing up and this time he was the prey.

He went to the Strand Hotel lobby desk at 9 p.m. and said he was checking out tomorrow, so he wanted to clear his bill tonight. Once that was done he walked quietly to the back of the lobby. As he disappeared, the front desk manager quietly called to the Traders Hotel seven blocks away, and the man in the suite answered. He thanked the man and sent his assistant with $200 dollars. Mr. Chaya Ptorn was on a roll. It was 9:15 p.m.

As the call ended, Conrad (Code 037) was quietly walking out the back of the hotel down the dark and dirty alley. The Strand is a five-star hotel, but within twenty-five yards of it begins dirty and dilapidated Rangoon, a city of survival not elegance.

At the back street he walked three more dark wretched blocks and then caught a rickety cab. He just left like that, a shadow. His Beretta PX4 9 mm had gone into a sludge filled sewer of a canal.

That night Myanmar Airways left for Bangkok and later Cathay Pacific left for Hong Kong, he was in Seat 5A on both flights.

Also that night in Code 037's suite at the Strand a man with a Soviet K-57 pistol sat in the desk chair. He told Mr. Ptorn the man was absent, and Mr. Ptorn told him to wait. By the next afternoon Mr. Ptorn told him to come back. And on the next night Mr. Ptorn had a man killed, it was supposed to be Mr. Wei Kyi, but it was just his bodyguard. He was "0" for "2" and leaving Rangoon before someone took him out. The wild dogs were running in the night, but it was now confusing who were the hunters and who was the prey.

CHAPTER 42

Code 037 decided to resurface in Hong Kong as Jason Stoner, Investment Advisor, mid-town Manhattan, New York. He was at a suite at the Peninsula and had just ordered a suit to complete his new cover when the suite bell rang. The staff had a pristine note typed and sealed for him, no name on it.

The note simply said Nathan Road, 9:17 p.m. Jason looked at it and it seemed authentic. But his world is a world of shadows, so what is real and what is a mirage makes this the most difficult of professions. It was 8:07 p.m. Jason started his walk up Nathan Road at 9:05 p.m., they would find him, and they did. He was a Chinese man in his forties, a rough chain-smoking man. His English was heavily accented.

The conversation was brief; you are to return to Rangoon the day after tomorrow, he said between puffs. "Do you understand?" he sternly asked.

"Yes," Jason (Code 037) replied, the man walked away to the west.

Jason walked to the north, then ducked into a park off Nathan Road and sprinted to the west. He slowed as he approached the parallel street to Nathan Road and looked south. He saw the Chinese man strolling to the north and he waited. As the Chinese man stopped to light yet another cigarette, Jason stood ten feet away in the shadows. Jason quickly grabbed the man by the arm, and then the neck, pulled a Hawksbill knife from his side, and cut the man's throat. He laid him gently face down in the bushes. He then waited in the shadows, the urban rush dulling all sounds.

Within ten minutes a second man came to look for his associate. He walked slowly on the street and then into the park where he had seen his partner go. A shadow came, grabbed his mouth, pulled his head back and cut his throat; the Hawksbill knife is good for that. He was placed into the same bushes. The urban sounds never missed a beat

Jason then quickly went back east through the park to Nathan Road. He walked to the Hong Kong Hilton and booked a suite. As he stepped into the elevator, a man joined him. "Hong Kong Airport, private jet terminal, 9 a.m. tomorrow, clothes and accessories are in your suite. Have a nice evening."

And in Jason's Peninsula suite yet another "friend" sat at his desk. He had a SigSauer P250 with silencer. He waited but the "target" did not return. But at "turn down service" in the Peninsula suite a polite British man entered his suite. A little odd the man thought . . . and it was. The room attendant shot the man with a tranquilizer gun. Two other men came in, dragged the man to the laundry chute and dropped him head first. His body was covertly dropped on the other two in the Nathan Road park. He had a broken neck.

Apparently the Chinese triad had gotten tired of the drugs and prostitutes and was looking to expand into arms dealing. Great, just great, it's always something. But the man in the Peninsula suite did not belong to them, so who the hell was he? And the $1 million for five MIG-29 nose landing gears was so over the top they needed to act. The Chinese offer had been $100,000 to buy and to sell at $500,000. Who the hell would <u>buy</u> at $1 million? Jason Stoner would love to know himself. How did they come to know all of this? Someone was selling some information, but the web was very complex. Time to leave.

CHAPTER 43

Javier Henri LeCirac would have started his movie tomorrow had he known the intrigues, but instead he sat in his elegant and massive office overlooking Nice harbor. The setting sun turned the bright white yachts to a warm beautiful peach color. It was a quiet time for Javier after another busy day.

His office was massive, probably fifteen feet by sixty feet with fifteen-foot ceilings. All the furniture was very ornate, very refined, as were the massive walnut panels that lined the room.

Javier Henri had undone his Hermes tie, unbuttoned his Ascot Chang shirt and had propped his Ralph Lauren dress shoes on his massive walnut gold embossed desk. He leaned back in his chair. He loved this time of day, the rush of the corporate day was over, the staff returning to their homes, and Javier Henri was left to his thoughts.

And his thoughts turned to the lone crippled Mirage F-1B somewhere in a nondescript location on the border of Chad and Sudan. And then his thoughts turned to Kelly Grant, then back to the jet, then to Kelly. What a great combination, foreign intrigue, jetfighters, young beautiful girls. What made it more exciting is that in three to four days he would involve himself in both. He had purposely set up his schedule to clear it for these developments. At thirty-seven years old he did not need any more corporate life, at least for now. And he was uniquely qualified, as his father and his staff were highly professional, and Javier Henri could go off on what every thirty-seven-year-old male dreams of . . . adventure and young women. So very few men at thirty-seven had the chiseled looks, the money, the education, the discipline, and the style to truly due justice to this epic opportunity. But Javier Henri LeCirac did, he uniquely did, and the world should rejoice that such a man existed to seize the day, "carpe diem" it was.

As he continued to ponder the coming events, he needed at least two lead men to assist in the various details and research the coming events would require. He thought some more and then sat up at his desk to write down specifics.

The sun was just setting over Nice harbor and the combination of the rose-colored sky and the lights along the harbor and boulevard provided a perfect backdrop to Javier Henri's thoughts: a very glamorous backdrop, very intense adventure, very sexy, quiet femme fatal in Kelly. Javier Henri not only thought of the adventure ahead, but the beginning foundation of his latest passion, the Javier Henri movie version of a sort of French James Bond. But a more raw, real world version and this development in Chad and Sudan got his thoughts racing. And now he would have the time to act on this. It's good to be alive and be Javier Henri LeCirac at thirty-seven years old.

Well not quite . . . four billion people have been added to the world in fifty years. At that number no one is quite "special." And, of course, on any given day some twelve-year-old illiterate girl is giving birth in some slum in Bombay, Nairobi, or Jakarta. So much for modern life and the modern family; what keeps it all going is a massive dose of self-delusion, and the corporate mother/wife is leading the parade. Since her husband had acquired some skills and stature in "the company," she is afforded her relentless delusion by a pandering husband saying, "yes dear." No, the "action" men for Javier Henri must be single above all else.

It was dark out but Javier Henri's mind had just kicked in. The first guy would be Eric Olsen, a man thirty-one years-old from Oslo, Norway by way of Britain, and an MBA from LSE, London School of Economics. He was very smart, determined and in excellent shape for the coming events.

He had a taste for adventure that lay unknown, but that would change in three days when Javier Henri would call a meeting between him and the second guy.

The second guy on this "special project" team would be Pierre Patron, thirty-seven years old and born on Corsica to a French Foreign Legion sergeant from Spain and a local French woman. He had degrees from the University of Paris, but clearly had his father's genes for adventure. He had spent seven years in the French Air Force and had become a French jetfighter pilot flying the Dassault Mirage F-1B . . . the same crippled and orphaned plane sitting in Chad. Yes, Pierre would be invaluable. He did have a French girlfriend named Celine, and Javier Henri would have to make sure that was not serious. If they were serious, Pierre Patron was out, simple as that.

As Javier Henri's mind raced, he decided to add another name to the list, Brandon Craig. Brandon was twenty-nine years old, British from Birmingham and a budding writer/playwright, so he was generally starving. Javier Henri would offer a base salary to Brandon and bring him onboard to develop the narratives behind this budding adventure and to add imagination and creativity to the coming story. Javier Henri of course did not know the coming events would need no amplification. The events would be quite satisfactory on their own, maybe too much actually. Brandon had met Javier Henri at some movie conferences and writer's seminars as Javier did basic evaluation and recruiting for his movie development. He was a perfect fit as he was creative, but like most writers he was seriously underemployed. As Javier Henri's mind raced, he also decided to set up two to three small offices in his corporate compound to dedicate to the writing and creative staff for the movie project.

Javier was excited. Here on a nondescript evening at the office he decided to pull the trigger on his "side" projects. Just like that, he had started it all! It was a good time to be Javier Henri LeCirac.

CHAPTER 44

It was now 8 p.m. and Javier was still at his desk, and his mind continued to race on multiple levels. He called his house staff three blocks away to bring his dinner to his corporate office. He ordered a small steak, green beans, a small salad and, of course, wine. He quickly asked his head of house staff the status of Kelly Grant. She apparently had arrived two days ago with her allowed companion. Javier was happy, he asked his head of house staff to help her settle in. Javier Henri made a note to meet her next week.

While Javier Henri collected his swirling thoughts in Nice, France, Code 037 (Conrad of the postponed Rangoon negotiations) had skipped out of the ambushes in both Rangoon and Hong Kong. He then skipped to Nassau, Bahamas for a brief period to visit Erica and three days later was in Mayfair – London to say hello to Ashley Summerall. He discussed the upcoming weddings with both, then each went to bed with him. Another bachelorette party I guess. As Javier Henri dived into his steak dinner, a one Kent, or Conrad, or Code 037 was touching down on British Airways Flight 177, London to Cape Town, Seat 2A. It was 8:40 p.m. in Nice, 7:40 p.m. in Cape Town.

And in a narrow wretched back alley in the slums of Khartoum, Sudan a man dressed in poor clothing went into a dirty rundown mud hut off that wretched alley. He had his face and head covered with an old oily rag. The man sat down across from the sweating disgusting Said Alawid, the brother of the assassinated weapons dealer, Ali Alawid.

Once inside the poor man took his head cover off. It was the new three-star general, General Abdul. The general had come to welcome Said to his new home in Sudan.

As the night fell deeper into darkness, minds were racing all over the world. All minds were on adventure, intrigue and of course, the money. Well, except Kent. On this night Kent thought of one nineteen-year-old Lisa Aswanela and what lay under those hip huggers and halter top. She had arrived in Cape Town one day ago. The tires on the Aston Martin were still cooling from the trip.

Thanks to the Abbas brothers she and Sarah were staying in a five-star hotel in the harbor. Their first morning there finds Lisa bending over the balcony rail with a t-shirt on, a pair of raised walking shoes on . . . and nothing else . . . at all. As she bends over catching the fresh air, her very long firm legs are stretched out and for every male visualizing this picture; yes . . .but it is even better than that.

The view could send many men to the mental ward of the nearest hospital; slam dunk, industrial-strength sexual presence. Alex Kagamba must feel the vibe, and he doesn't even know Lisa is in town . . . yet.

Alex Kagamba is on the hunt through, the details have been attended to down to the chilled wine. Kent is on the hunt too, but just not so much attention to detail; actually, no attention to detail.

CHAPTER 45

The darkness fell on the dirty, grimy and narrow alley on the outskirts of Khartoum, Sudan. This particular alley was joined by hundreds more in an endless maze of low lying mud houses that encircled the more structured central city. The narrow alleys dominated these slum sections and what roads were there were also narrow and barely allowed beat up cars to pass. The people that roamed these alleys looked to be out of Hollywood central casting; wrapped in robes, brown skin, skinny and shifty eyes, fierce eyes, all seeing eyes.

The people of these vast ramshackle compounds lived simple, destitute lives. But also sprinkled among these populations were some of the hardest men on the face of the earth, and a level below these hard men were some of the shiftiest and slipperiest men on the face of the earth. And then the rarest of the species, a select few of the men were very hard <u>and</u> slippery. Please meet Said Alawid, the younger brother of Ali Alawid, the ruthless Sudan arms dealer. Mr. Ali Alawid used to be ruthless until his brain collected a .22 LR from a Walther pistol in Knightsbridge, London. With that event Said Alawid came to the front. And as disgusting and ruthless as Mr. Ali Alawid was, his brother Said was the true monster. With his brother living Said stayed barely under control, with his brother's execution the irrational rage of Said came front and center.

Said was in much better shape than his older brother, maybe only a 100 pounds overweight versus his brothers 170 pounds overweight. But aside from that he was just as greasy, smelly, rough and ruthless a predator. He just lived for money and the exercise of brutal power. If he had not been born Arabic in Syria, he would be heading a Mexican cartel in Tijuana, Mexico or a pirate clan in Somalia.

The men that worked for Said Alawid were of two types. The muscular killers and the skinny shifty "runners," and of the two the shifty "runners" were more cunning and dangerous by far. Nothing moved in these alleys without their knowing, and of course they were very religious. They loved money and yes they did pray five times a day, but that had little to do with the Muslim religion and a lot to do with . . . that almighty religion . . . money. They also worked for Said to get access to the women, whomever Said and his staff discarded. Sex, wealth and power, the triad of male existence, but these shifty men would never have power. They were the scavengers of the African plains. They collected scraps of money, information and women. They were essential to the "bosses" like Said but their loyalty was on a day-to-day basis, thus their danger.

For all the money Said and his brother made, they still stayed in their dirt slums to survive. They had nice villas and clothes but rarely stayed there, so the accumulation of money was apparently the sole justification for everything.

The room was small and dinghy with a single light bulb hanging down over a simple, beat up wooden table. Only General Abdul and Said Alawid sat down, the other seven men, four for Said and three for General Abdul, stood around the two men. And they sweated and swatted at insects as the setting sun marked another day ended in this collective dirt pile. The setting sun was a brilliant red from the dust and charcoal fires of destitute masses; welcome to Khartoum, Sudan.

The evening prayers would begin soon, but General Abdul and Said Alawid were not going anywhere. They talked, they sweated, but Said won that game; he sweated profusely and the smell permeated the room. General Abdul was unmoved, as he knew guys like Said used their disgusted presence to gain an edge in negotiations, and to get more money.

CHAPTER 46

The topic was "the new Sheriff in town," and that was General Abdul. He had been a faithful army officer posted to the dusty outposts of Sudan. But with his third star he became a player and was ready to cash in on his military career. So he was moving fast, as the sands shifted quickly in this world and someone else would want his payoff. He likely could dispose of some arms and ammunition, as well as a few military vehicles.

But General Abdul hoped to score big before his bosses could take inventory. Move fast enough and everything "lost" from the armory could be laid at the feet of the previous general.

And General Abdul knew of three select assets still off the books that would also be this big slam dunk payoff. But he needed to do this deal in the first four to five weeks of his tenure.

He had done his own casual research on this after getting his third star. He knew these assets had been locked away two years ago for special modification, and then the rush of the fighting in Western Sudan, the International Criminal Court coming after the President of Sudan over that fighting, and then the general corrupt chaos of the everyday situation in the Sudan military had left these three assets intact but forgotten. But General Abdul knew of these and in a perfect alignment of the stars, he was now in a position to make a deal with these three assets and he wanted to do it fast. And the market seemed perfect; after all, some shadowy fool in Rangoon was in the market to buy five MIG-29 nose landing gears for $1 million. Who pays that kind of money for parts to an old Soviet jetfighter? But you don't argue with money, and his new Indian buddy Raja Majani of Calcutta was on it. General Abdul would definitely strip six MIG-29's for that kind of money and Said Alawid would certainly shoot any moron arms dealer for running up the price. He wanted to buy at $50,000 per gear at most and then sell at $200,000 per gear, not buy at $200,000. Let me get this arms dealer and I will skin him alive, Said thought.

CHAPTER 47

It was now 8 p.m. and the negotiating parties were exhausted. The heat was terrible. The dust and charcoal smoke were terrible, and the smell was terrible. Not only from Said Alawid, but from the open sewer thirty yards away; the wind had shifted.

It was a miserable group in an even more miserable locale. With darkness came the incalculable threat of violence. The narrow alleys were wonderful killing fields in the day, at night they were just blind black horror. Said Alawid knew the alleys as well as his men, and he also knew the layers of traitors and thieves that populated these alleys looking for scraps . . . scraps of money, food, women . . . and scraps of information that would make the first three possible.

As darkness fell, Said Alawid became a little more relaxed, as he felt he owned the night in this wretched pile of dirt homes. The darkness turned the endless maze of alleys into a wretched horror show for the non-residents . . . and also for the residents. Anything that moved was a threat and the alleys were full of shadows, full of flicks of movement, some real and some imagined. Walk these alleys long enough and you end up in a mental hospital.

In Vietnam decades ago the Viet Cong had tunnels to live in, same deal. The Viet Cong who were not killed disappeared . . . into mental hospitals. Living in tunnels and narrow alleys wrecks the mind.

Said Alawid was curious how General Abdul thought he would navigate these strange alleys at night. They talked on. Said was upsetting the General, his offer for the three special systems was almost insulting. Said was offering $150,000 per item and General Abdul thought they were worth ten times that at the bare minimum. General Abdul thought he would shop this around; maybe the rogue buyer in Rangoon could help him. The Rangoon buyer seemed to have more money than good sense. Everybody likes those kinds of guys. He would talk to his Indian contact Mr. Raja Majani.

The only problem with opening the bidding was it took time. It's always a balance of time and greed. Take too little time and maybe you leave money on the table. Take too much time and the forces can close in and you end up <u>on</u> the table . . . dead, and then the next guy takes over. But General Abdul thought this Said guy is not going to be the one, just from his fat greasy smell alone. It was 9 p.m. and very dark in the dirt slums of Khartoum, Sudan.

Said was thinking maybe the next general after General Abdul would like his offer better. He hoped one day to be able to make a General Abdul "disappear," like his brother had mastered over the years. Until, of course, his brother "disappeared." At 9 p.m. the animals were stalking prey on the Serengeti, and the animals were stalking prey in the dirt slums of Khartoum, Sudan.

It was now 9:17 p.m.

In Cape Town Kent was gathering his energy to call Lisa tomorrow.

Javier Henri LeCirac had finished his meal and stepped out on his office balcony. His mind was racing on the excitement of a Mirage F-1B jetfighter, movies and beautiful young girls. It was good to be Javier Henri LeCirac.

Like Kent, Alex Kagamba was looking forward to seeing Lisa. His work was going very well and she was the perfect present. It was good to be Alex Kagamba.

Kelly and Abbey were settling into their plush quarters, they were like excited school girls. And besides actually being smart, they actually were young enough to be school girls. But their surroundings were the stuff of successful fifty-year-old's, not twenty-year-old's. They sat and talked to each other. Just panties and t-shirts, beautiful, firm, almost skinny legs were spread across beds and chairs as they talked. Victoria's Secret meets Nice, France. Meet Kelly and Abbey, reluctant sex goddesses.

CHAPTER 48

General Abdul thanked Said Alawid profusely for the meeting. If $170,000 per item was Said's best offer, he would surely consider it and get back to Said.

The guards started moving, at last their torture was over. My God, the smell, heat and close dirt quarters were beyond bearable.

Said offered General Abdul a place to stay in this mud hut. But you might as well lay in an open sewer with a gun in your mouth, to be more comfortable that is.

General Abdul declined. He led his guards out of the mud hut into the total dangerous darkness of the alleys. The General walked maybe thirty yards in the pitch black when an arm gently guided him into a small door. The General went in and then down two flights of stairs to an air-conditioned bunker with a King-sized bed, small kitchen and dining room.

The guards that had lost him were told by walkie-talkie to return to base. Plan B was in effect, and make no noise.

And the eyes that see and survive in these wretched alleys were not happy. Where had the General gone? Said would want to know. No information, no money and plenty of worries for Said.

But yards later another set of eyes were happy. They moved away after twenty minutes. By a satellite phone provided by their employer they whispered the news. Yes, Said Alawid was staying in a mud hut in the Khartoum maze and they knew where it was. This time the call did not go to South Africa but to Lebanon. Farsi Abbas thanked the man. It was 9:28 p.m. in the miserable dirt, dust and grime of Khartoum, Sudan. Said Alawid was happy, his offer was very low, but he thought the General had no choice. If the General thought he had a choice, maybe the next general after General Abdul "retired" would be more accommodating. The General could "disappear" the next time he was in these alleys. Poor Said Alawid, the General had already "disappeared" and Said didn't know it. The General was sleeping next door to Said, very safe, very comfortable. Said was left with a pile of greasy rags to sleep on in his crusty dirt palace.

And in Lebanon Farsi Abbas was happy with the business, but otherwise miserable. Money could not help this and he missed Lisa terribly. Lisa thought of him not at all.

CHAPTER 49

It was now 9:41 p.m. and Javier Henri LeCirac was not only still in his office, but in a feverish swirl of ideas and outlines for action. The crippled Dassault Mirage F-1B in the covert hanger in Eastern Chad was on the table. He would make calls to Dassault next week to get involved with the repair pieces, and he would assemble his staff. In parallel, Brandon Craig, the new-hire writer, would shadow the activities to begin the outline for the movie script. Eric Olsen and Pierre Patron would be activated as his special staff.

And the one and only Kelly Grant would be introduced to his staff exactly next Wednesday. Javier was too excited to sleep; God knows when he will go home. He called the head of his house staff to tell them to relax, he would not return until tomorrow night. He kept a large studio apartment off his massive corporate office just for nights like this.

CHAPTER 50

The next morning saw Kent wake up at 10 a.m. in a small elegant hotel in the Newlands sections of Cape Town. Lisa and Sarah woke up at 10:20 a.m., and Alex Kagamba had already worked three hours by that time.

The schedules were set. Alex Kagamba was to see Lisa Aswanela tonight at 7 p.m. He had detailed the schedule to the minute. He had never known such a startling sexy girl, much less been on a date with one. The dinner would be at the magnificent colonial hotel called the Mount Nelson.

Kent was to go to Cape Town harbor and board a military helicopter to go thirty minutes to the north of Cape Town. "They" had found him and wanted to talk. "They" could have done that at the cricket field across from his hotel, but now it's off on a helicopter to the dusty bush of the Western Cape. Maybe they had the shallow grave already dug. If he came back, he was to also see Lisa that night if possible.

CHAPTER 51

In a land far away the "dealers," the arms dealers that is, were in a frenzy. This great lucrative contract for five landing gears for a MIG-29 had come, then disappeared. Just like that, the man had disappeared from Rangoon.

Mr. Chaya Ptorn was not happy, nobody was happy. Chaya Ptorn had just finished another major drug deal with the guys from Burma's United WA Army and he was flush with cash, maybe $15 million. But a very easy $1 million from this Rangoon guy would have been better still. More, more, more, no matter how much you make there is always more and more. Money "1", Buddha "0", and it would be that way forever, Money "1" and Hindu "0", Money "1" and Protestants "0", and on and on. On the scale of the world's religions, "10" being the highest, it was money at "11.0" and any religion, just choose one, would come in at "0.7." That's human nature and that's just the way it is. God bless me but bless me with money.

Mr. Chaya Ptorn had risen to the top thanks to his contacts with the Thai military, who also worshipped money. His profile had become almost too big. He had elevated his "game" to fleets of Porsche SUV's. I mean, sometimes six or seven would convoy down the streets of Fang, Thailand, that had long been a major transit point for drugs from Burma and Laos. It was a modest non-descript town, so why does an arms dealer or drug dealer like a one Mr. Chaya Ptorn have to parade around in Porsche SUV's costing $115,000 and more? . . . because he can. But let's face it, Toyota SUV's would have done, those are the accepted symbols. Why elevate to Porsche? . . . because he can.

Over the last few years Mr. Ptorn's success had made him a bit more reckless; too much money, too much ego, too many women and as of late, too much meth . . . as in crystal.

Like the infamous Tony Montana of "Scarface" movie fame, Mr. Chaya Ptorn had committed the cardinal sin of dealing; he had started consuming his own product. It had only recently shown up in his behavior, not really bad yet, just a little erratic. More troubling was his head bodyguard known as Vanda Pntip. He was Chaya Ptorn's triggerman when he needed it, and now sometimes when he didn't need it.

Recently Mr. Pntip had stopped his Porsche convoy at 11 a.m. on the streets of Fang. He got out and executed a street level dealer at a street café, just like that, shot in the head. He stopped to light his cigarette, then casually got in the SUV and slowly departed. The police would get a bonus for their absence. The poor street dealer would be cremated at the pagoda tomorrow.

Arms dealers and drug dealers come and go, and it was not clear yet which way Mr. Ptorn was heading. But now he did want to see this guy from the Strand Hotel – Rangoon. The drugs were starting to take over, arrogance over modesty; nobody stands up Mr. Chaya Ptorn. Yes, getting a bit erratic, and drugs and loaded guns don't mix.

"Where is this guy?" Ptorn asked.

"I don't know boss, but we will find him," his head bodyguard replied. "But we can find him," he said again with a dangerous smile. The bodyguard Mr. Pntip now had a worthy target, not some scummy street dealer. The hunt was on. Mr. Chaya Ptorn now gets all his deals or somebody pays; the deadly threat of arrogance.

CHAPTER 52

That hunted man from the Strand Hotel – Rangoon was safe today. He had just landed in an old Huey military helicopter in the bush of the Western Cape Province, South Africa. Heat, sand and dust were everywhere. About fifty yards away sat a MD-500 military helicopter. It was a dark gray titanium color with blood red accents. Halfway between the two helicopters were two safari chairs. As Kent got out of the Huey, a tough lean man got out of the MD-500. He wore tan customized military clothing, wore the trademark Ray Ban military aviation glasses, and had a no nonsense walk. Kent had never seen this man.

The man sat down with Kent in the safari chairs. As the helicopters sat quietly, Kent and the man talked. This man is clearly a South African mercenary of some description, Kent thought. They talked for thirty minutes as the details were passed, and Kent had a few questions. More details were passed, and ten minutes later they got up and returned to their respective helicopters. As Kent strapped into the Huey helicopter, he thought there was something about this he liked; oh yes, the man was wearing a Bell & Ross BR01-93 GMT aviation watch. He had to be a good guy. But he also seemed familiar, had he been at the mercenary camp in the Eastern Congo? Hard to say, life is a blur at times.

If the Huey helicopter did not crash or it was not shot down, he would be calling a one long legged Lisa within an hour or so. He really looked forward to seeing her, as most men do. And a one Farsi Abbas of Beirut, Lebanon so wanted to see her. He was thinking of sending the jet to pick her up to meet him in London. This life was miserable without her presence. Men are so delusional. All the men chasing Lisa or fantasizing about her were delusional; well, except Kent. He was just a nature lover, in the form of an olive-skinned long-legged nineteen-year-old. Appreciate nature and then let it go and be free.

CHAPTER 53

Kent did call Lisa and she jumped with joy. Lisa's friend Sarah knew it wasn't Farsi Abbas. Farsi would give Lisa $50,000 and she would just yawn. Kent was coming to take her pants off for free, and she could not wait.

Lisa talked to Kent but told him tonight was not possible, but she would set aside the next two days after that if he was available. Kent said he was; who wouldn't be.

The schedule was set, Alex Kagamba tonight, then Kent for two days. If Kent left, she would likely turn her Aston Martin east toward Johannesburg. Farsi Abbas would try to change all of that, but he had not called yet.

CHAPTER 54

After Kent called, Lisa called Alex Kagamba. In her light sultry South African accent she told Alex she would meet him at the Mount Nelson Hotel, no need to do the silly date pick up routine. Alex offered to pick her up, but she insisted on driving. After all, Alex had not seen her in action, only on the Aston-Martin showroom floor in Sandton.

And arrive she did. The Aston-Martin looked spectacular and as one Lisa Aswanela unwrapped her legs to get out, she too looked spectacular. She was wearing her trademark low slung hip-hugging pants, the top blouse did go down to generally the beltline but was not tucked in. As such every movement showed the midriff skin, but only a glimpse, not over the top. She was in all black, including oversized black hoop earrings. Her wild hair was well . . . wild. She wore no makeup. It is likely a Lisa Aswanela type of understated but yet raw sexuality had never walked into the Mount Nelson, a sanctuary of old Victorian British South Africa, with magnificent British Colonial architecture. Alex Kagamba was standing at the door beaming, he would marry her tonight if he could. As usual the traffic stopped as Lisa walked through the lobby, the magnificent tight ass rolling with her stride. She flashed a smile to Alex, and he almost walked into a pillar. Just before she arrived at the Mount Nelson Farsi Abbas had called; Lisa had not answered and then turned her phone off.

"I see you got the Aston-Martin," Alex said to Lisa. "It's spectacular."

Lisa flashed a smile and said, "You can ride it if you let me ride yours, when you get it."

Alex was extremely well spoken but was a bit overmatched now, as Lisa had introduced the sexual flirting. Lisa was even a little excited, but would save that for Kent tomorrow. But Alex was quite a man himself, so maybe next time, yes, maybe next time.

Farsi Abbas kept calling Lisa furiously. With each dead-end call Farsi longed to see her more. If he could, he would have his pilot staff start the Dassault 7X right now and take him to Cape Town. He would if she was still in Cape Town. With each passing hour his home life in Beirut, Lebanon became more of a torture chamber. Four small babies, he had to be the good Muslim man, and a simple monochrome wife, she also must be a good Muslim woman. It would be fine if Farsi were a goat herder in the hills east of Beirut. But no, he chose to do arms deals, had become good at it, and was lucky enough to be born in the cradle of conflicts, so somebody always needed weapons. And Farsi Abbas always needed money . . . and there you go, the perfect dance partners.

He had become a very good trader of arms and with it came the ego. About a year ago he had become a bit more ruthless, maybe all deals should be his. Thus he had begun to quietly "eliminate" those competitors he could, he had the money now and he wanted still more.

Mr. Abbas of Beirut, Lebanon met Mr. Ptorn of Fang, Thailand; same profession, same greed, same violence. In the end Mr. Abbas and Mr. Ptorn had met the enemy, and it was them.

As Mr. Abbas ventured out into the world, the excitement, luxury and beautiful girls, those things available with his money, became intoxicating and relentless. The Lisa's of the world became available and by meeting Lisa early, he had been overwhelmed. Mr. Ptorn of Fang, Thailand was smoking crystal meth more and more and Mr. Abbas of Beirut was ingesting Lisa. Neither could stop, both were deadly habits.

Farsi Abbas called Lisa yet again, no answer. It was 10:38 p.m. Kent had strolled the tree lined streets of Newlands, Cape Town thinking about things, he had just gone to bed, it was 10:53 p.m. Lisa and Alex had ended a very fun, lovely, elegant, flirtatious evening and were standing in the dramatic entrance to the Mount Nelson. The valet brought Lisa's Aston-Martin around. It was the stuff of movies, the sleek Aston-Martin emerging from the black night slowly. It arrived in front of the dramatic columns of the Mount Nelson. Lisa thanked Alex and gave him a light kiss on his lips. She walked to the Aston-Martin, gave Alex one last flashing smile, and then the Aston-Martin slowly disappeared . . . until Lisa gunned it and sent a screaming exhaust sound through the Mount Nelson compound. Alex loved it; the Mount Nelson staff loved it. And there you have the perfect ending, a handsome young man, a scorching sexy young girl, an elegant backdrop, a more elegant meal, wine and evening, and then a screaming Aston-Martin exiting the plush Mount Nelson grounds. That's a wrap, send the film to Hollywood, the opening will be at the Beverly Hilton in Beverly Hills first week in May. It was 11:07 p.m.

CHAPTER 55

At 11:17 p.m. Cape Town time another call came from Farsi to Lisa. She picked up this time. The message was the same, I need to see you, I'm sending the plane in three days, where will you be?

"Cape Town," she said, knowing Kent would take up the next two days.

"Then stay there, I am coming with the plane, you need to shop in London for one week," Farsi said.

"I have little money," Lisa said.

"Okay, $200,000 should keep you busy," Farsi smiled, he felt better already.

"Okay, you are the man, I will see you," Lisa said.

She hung up, one week with Farsi, $200,000, not bad but that was one week of her life she would never get back, and she was only nineteen years old.

In a small compound west of London the conversation between Beirut and Cape Town was noted. Secure calls were made, people were notified. It was 11:31 p.m. Alex Kagamba was in bed but not asleep, he was busy undressing Lisa in his mind. Lisa sat on her balcony, letting the Cape Town harbor breeze go up her naked thighs. It was a sexual experience, Kent needs to be ready.

The next morning as Kent walked to breakfast outside the hotel a man approached, walked with him five minutes, and then disappeared. Kent went on to breakfast. He had two eggs scrambled soft, sourdough toast, hash browns, and a Diet Coke with ice please and, oh yes, a pineapple juice with ice please.

CHAPTER 56

On this morning in Nice, France the sun reflected beautifully on the harbor and also streamed through the fifteen-foot windows of Javier Henri LeCirac's opulent corporate office. Javier was up and assembling the immaculate Savile Row suit he would wear today. The walk from his elegant studio apartment to his elegant office would take five steps. He was happy, the last fifteen hours had been extremely productive. In the quiet, uninterrupted solitude of those hours he had assembled the plan to be played out on the hard-baked plains of Eastern Chad. Those plains held captive the wounded, covert, orphaned jetfighter, the Dassault Mirage F-1B, a sleek powerful fighter when it was healthy. Why had this lone jetfighter been treated so roughly and then left on the baked African plains? A plot Javier hoped was worthy of the Cannes Film Festival.

He assembled his special team. Eric Olsen would look at political and business issues and would have a small staff. Pierre Patron, the ex-French Air Force Mirage F-1B fighter pilot, would deal with aviation issues as well as doing research with buddies still in the Air Force as to maybe what this plane was about. He too would select a small staff of three or four to assist him.

And finally, Brandon Craig would be looking to develop the evolving story into a script. He was to do research on the conflicts in Africa, make contacts with authors, journalists, and movie people to get the raw background data to get the movie storyline moving. Javier was to assign his newly hired assistant Ms. Kelly Grant to this team, but as business or aviation issues came up, she too would gather those for Brandon Craig to blend into the fabric of the movie. She also was rather "safe" with Brandon, as he appeared to be gay at best, asexual at worse. Once Brandon saw Kelly Javier would know, not that he cared. Professional project execution was of paramount value, not someone's nightlife. Javier Henri was not immune to Kelly, but he had known so many beautiful girls he could stay focused, but she was different. She seemed immune to her own stunning presence. That was hard to find in this self-absorbed world.

Javier would first meet with Eric and Pierre today, and in two days meet with Brandon and Kelly. Two days separation should do it, Javier knew Eric and Pierre would be chasing Kelly from minute one, so separation was vital.

Javier Henri LeCirac was finally where he wanted to be, a project with mystique, adventure, Africa, jetfighters and a beautiful girl. The project had come and he was ready.

CHAPTER 57

Mr. Chaya Ptorn was having his own staff meeting in Fang, Thailand. He met with Vanda Pntip, his head killer. The only news Vanda Pntip had was how he had executed another street dealer, a 9 mm to the side of the head from three feet. Never saw it coming, Mr. Pntip smiled. Chaya Ptorn waved it off. "Where is the Rangoon man?" Ptorn snapped.

"Not sure boss," Pntip answered, "But I have my military intelligence contacts working on it, sir."

Chaya Ptorn had closed another deal and put $7 million in his bank account, but the mere $1.0 million deal he missed in Rangoon bothered him more than what he got. He wanted it all! The drugs and ego were starting to take over, but no one knew it yet, not yet.

The fact that a one Mr. Wei Kyi of Burma had tried to get the same deal also bothered Ptorn. Who was he to take a deal from the "master," the man was a third string dealer and confined to Burma. Who makes money that way! Mr. Ptorn was erratic, and he was sensing that himself. Maybe a few days gambling in Macau would loosen him up. He would like that.

He was to head to Mae Sai again soon to meet at the Burma border with Mr. Wei Kyi. He still did business with him, but now considered himself so superior. He was starting to feel superior to everyone.

CHAPTER 58

The two days in Cape Town that Lisa and Kent spent together passed like twenty-five minutes. Lisa spent most of the time in a t-shirt and nothing else, and Kent took advantage of that time again and again. Lisa just arched her neck, arched her back and let it happen. Whatever he wanted he could have. The world disappeared for those two days. And she loved every minute of it, as did Kent.

Kent came in from the balcony to find her bent over the couch reading a magazine. Her t-shirt was halfway up her beautiful, toned back. She looked at Kent but did not smile. He looked at her and did not smile.

As they lay sprawled on the couch afterward, they both laughed, sore and exhausted. Thirty minutes later it all ended, as Farsi called and Lisa took the call on the balcony.

"Be ready tomorrow, I will call," Farsi said.

"Okay," is all Lisa said and hung up. Back to work, she sighed.

Lisa had sent Sarah home by plane when Kent came into the picture. She would now park the car at the airport and return to Cape Town from London. Maybe see Alex Kagamba again, that would be nice.

CHAPTER 59

The next evening as the sun set over the horizon in Southeastern Angola, a beautiful Dassault 7X business jet was cruising at 37,000 feet toward Cape Town. It had refueled in Khartoum, would spend one day in Cape Town and then head to London.

It carried a pilot/co-pilot, crew and two stewards to assist with baggage, meals, whatever <u>she</u> wanted.

All was smooth sailing, except for the last ten miles it had been intercepted and trailed by a solid black jetfighter. The fighter had been launched out of a remote desert air strip in northeast Namibia. Code 017, Lisa knew him as Kent, had gone there this day to be at 37,000 feet this night. He did not know the crew's names or what they were to serve, and he certainly did not know the plane was for Lisa. He pushed the button, the missiles raced into the rear of the Dassault 7X, and a giant fireball fell to earth, vaporized flesh, melted metal. No one saw it, as this part of Angola is a giant black hole for radar coverage. Code 017 turned the airplane upside down and fell to 15,000 feet. He then dropped further until he was at 200 feet and screaming across the Namibian desert. As he taxied in, an expert crew came to the plane for maintenance. He had seen all of them before, but they were not friends. No one spoke, and Code 017 stayed the night in his usual suite.

It was only ninety minutes later that certain people learned the "target" was not onboard. No, one Farsi Abbas was actually calling Lisa from Beirut, he had business but would meet her in two days.

"Did the plane arrive yet?" Farsi asked.

"Not yet," Lisa replied.

"It will be soon darling," Farsi said. Then Lisa hung up.

No, it wasn't going to arrive. Mr. Farsi Abbas and you need to start saving for a new Dassault 7X tonight. Even the metal scavengers can't get much; the metal was basically crystallized from the intense heat. The listening post outside London informed "them" of the development, so plan B was started.

Lisa called Farsi after the plane was over one hour late, she would return to her hotel.

Farsi agreed and as he hung up, he turned pale. He hoped all was well. If not, he hoped the plane had had trouble and crashed, not targeted and blown up. Who could do this? He was used to being the hunter, not the hunted. Surely Said Alawid could not pull this off. Who could do this? And for the next two days seeing Lisa was not so important.

Farsi reported the incident to Dassault and as part of the Dassault engineering network, a report was passed to Javier Henri LeCirac and his staff. But Javier could not connect the dots, nobody could at this point.

Farsi wired $60,000 to Lisa and said there were aircraft problems and they must reschedule. He missed her so.

Lisa was so upset she took the $60,000, put it in her bank account, and used the down days to see Alex Kagamba again. On the third day she roared off to Sandton, South Africa, the Aston-Martin slipping through the air beautifully.

Kent called her as she sped across South Africa. They talked, laughed and hoped to see each other soon. Kent was calling from a special plane sent to pick him up. Ironically it was a Dassault 7X, deep titanium with blood red accents. When the plane finally touched down, Kent, as Code 017, would be exhausted yet again.

He needed down time bad, but "they" would know that, he would likely sleep for three days after packing three lifetimes in the last four days. That included the time spent with and on Ms. Lisa Aswanela.

Four hours into the flight, as Code 017 dosed, he saw a tough lean man walk by. They nodded to each other but did not speak. It was the same man that had met him in the bush of the Western Cape, the man who set up the mission. Code 017's Bell & Ross showed 11:17 a.m. in the skies above Zanzibar on the way to the British military base on Diego Garcia. The South African mercenary's Bell & Ross GMT showed the same time, they would be in Diego Garcia for supper. Code 017 would order pot roast, mashed potatoes, green peas and carrot cake. He would actually sleep for three days. The South African smiled faintly when he spotted Code 017's own Bell & Ross, a limited-edition red-faced version of the BR01-94. Only five hundred were made.

CHAPTER 60

Javier Henri LeCirac made the call to Dassault Aviation. He was inquiring about the damaged Mirage F-1B in Chad. Did Dassault need any onsite assistance? Were the parts made to specification by his company? Was any further technical assistance needed? He was speaking to the Senior Vice President for Mirage F-1B maintenance at Dassault.

They talked casually and Javier Henri found out the parts were still at Dassault, even though they had arrived two weeks ago. Javier had studied the invoices and he knew they had been paid for the parts. Why so late in getting the plane up to fly? It seemed another party was involved, and also Dassault had no one for such a hardship assignment.

And that said it all to Javier Henri. There was something special about this plane, but Javier didn't understand. The Vice President went on to say he had another problem and another hardship. A Dassault 7X had gone down in a remote area southeast of Angola, Africa and getting people there was going to be a bigger problem than the F-1B. Javier Henri took note and became even more curious. The movie storyline just got better, he was sure, even as he did not even know the storyline as yet. Again, Javier Henri said he and his staff would be happy to go anywhere to help their biggest customer. The Vice President did not need his help, but Javier had planted the seed and he was ready for the adventure more than ever.

CHAPTER 61

On the border of Angola and Namibia there was already a situation, and on the northern border of Thailand with Burma there was a situation coming. The Dassault 7X had melted down over Angola, thanks to an air-to-air missile from a British Hunter RF/F-07 jetfighter, and Mr. Chaya Ptorn was melting down thanks to repeated handfuls of his business product of choice, crystal meth; thanks to the notorious and brutal United WA Army. Yes, a real 20,000 plus army in the far northeast of Burma. They keep the product coming to dear Chaya. And Mr. Chaya Ptorn was cutting into his own profits by using more and more crystal meth.

Chaya had assembled a seven-vehicle convoy, seven Porsche SUV's. The sight of these expensive high-profile vehicles in the scrub-poor farming region of Mae Sai, Thailand seemed to be the height of arrogance. Chaya Ptorn had recently lost his concern for such issues. He wanted deals and money from deals, he wanted all the deals every time. That was the growing presence of crystal meth talking.

His convoy stream rolled up the main road to the border crossing. His SUV's did an orchestrated U-turn at the border and stopped. Out came a small army of bodyguards openly carrying Uzi machine guns. Somehow the Thai police and military were not around, funny how that happens every time Chaya Ptorn comes to town. He and his entourage streamed into the small house on the banks of the border river. Burma was fifty yards away.

Mr. Wei Kyi, the Burmese arms dealer, had been at the house for one hour with his two bodyguards. He dare not be late to a Chaya Ptorn meeting; the man had become ever more erratic.

The Chaya Ptorn entourage barged into the house and then into the room where Mr. Wei Kyi was. Ptorn had no less than eleven bodyguards with him. The Ptorn guards overwhelmed Wei's guards and stripped them of their pathetic K-57 Soviet pistols; each of the guards only had five bullets apiece. This had started very lopsided, and now Mr. Ptorn wasn't at a business meeting, it was an interrogation. He immediately started ranting to Mr. Kyi about the Rangoon deal for five MIG-29 nose landing gears. Because Mr. Kyi got involved he had disrupted Mr. Ptorn's "guaranteed" sale of five for $1 million. So now Mr. Kyi worked for him as payback. Mr. Kyi was in no position to speak as he was no longer a businessman, just Ptorn's prisoner. It had all happened in five minutes.

"So when this guy shows up again, your deal is my deal. Your commission is you get to live," Ptorn shouted in broken English.

"If you make the deal, I get paid. If I make the deal, I get paid," Ptorn shouted. "I get all the deals." Mr. Kyi's only hope now is that Mr. Ptorn would have a stroke and die right there. It didn't happen.

Ptorn ranted on and with each passing minute he became more rambling and more incoherent. His attitude became more violent. In three minutes it was all over, as Ptorn was losing his train of thought. This menace transferred to his bodyguards, particularly Vanda Pntip, the head bodyguard.

Out of nowhere Mr. Ptorn stopped, was silent for fifteen seconds, and then shouted, "Get my deal done, get it done now," he yelled to no one in particular. "They are all my deals, always," Ptorn thought, and got up abruptly and startled everyone. The tension went through the roof, along with Ptorn's blood pressure. Maybe the stroke was coming, Mr. Kyi could only hope, he was sweating. The stroke did not come.

Mr. Ptorn headed to the door as his guards shuffled rapidly. Mr. Kyi was close to shock, as were his unarmed guards. The shuffle continued as Ptorn headed for the door, chairs were being overturned in the scramble. Mr. Kyi was frozen with fear.

Mr. Ptorn left the room and then, in a fit of anger, again returned to the room door.

"Get it done, get it done," Ptorn raged. No one spoke.

Ptorn exited again. Vanda Pntip was the last one out of the room of the Ptorn entourage. He turned, smiled a demented smile, pushed his Uzi aside, pulled out a Glock 9 mm with special silencer, and put three 9 mm rounds into the chest of one of Wei Kyi's guards. Then walked over and put one in the fallen man's head.

As he walked to the door and smiled, he said, "Get it done." Pntip had gotten used to the random execution business. What a rush.

And across the river the same two covert spies as before saw everything go down. They saw everything except each other. Their reports back would detail the alarming turn of events.

Mr. Wei Kyi just stared ahead as the roar of the Porsche SUV's echoed down the narrow alleys of Mae Sai. The SUV's hit 70 mph within two hundred yards, all seven SUV's ripping out of town, not a policeman in sight. Funny how that happens sometimes.

Mr. Wei Kyi continued to stare, but the remaining bodyguard started moving the dead man. He dragged him down the narrow stairs and slowly got him to the top of the wall by the River. He then pushed him over the wall. The body splashed into the river and started floating slowly down. They were in luck, the man had landed right . . . he was mercifully floating face down. Karma was with them.

The slow destitute crowds crossing the border bridge would likely see the grisly scene and go on with their simple, subsistence lives. They were too tired trying to survive to be sad or shocked.

The SUV's continued ripping down the road. Mr. Pntip sat next to Mr. Ptorn, and with each passing mile their mood became lighter. They would bring the girls in tonight. They would bring the Johnnie Walker Blue Label and, of course, they would bring the crystal meth. Who knows, maybe this was Mr. Vanda Pntip's lucky day and he could bag another random execution tonight. The Porsche convoy came up on a Thai border checkpoint; they veered to the right of the slowing traffic and, throwing up dust and gravel, went through the checkpoint at sixty plus miles per hour. No one got in their way, so no one died. Mr. Ptorn was on the phone ordering up the girls and drugs. The border police almost seemed to salute as the convoy roared by.

CHAPTER 62

The sun was its usual blistering, tropical laser beam on this day in Diego Garcia. Conrad (Kent) had rested for two days and now expected the "visitor" at any time. It's best not to worry when "they" will come or what "they" will say, they are big boys, actually the "biggest boys," and Conrad could care less how they feel or how difficult their life might be.

In Nice, France things were merging with things in Beirut, Lebanon and both concerned the wreckage in southeast Angola. The man in Beirut, Lebanon thought of the sexy girl going from Cape Town to Johannesburg. The man in Nice, France thought of his meeting with the sensational twenty-year-old from London.

And in Fang, Thailand Mr. Ptorn and his "guys" were passing around the youngest and sexiest of the Thai and Burmese girls brought from the border. The poor girls never had a chance; sometimes two men at once assaulted them. The relief came only as the liquor and drugs made the men even more incoherent. The party abruptly ended when Mr. Vanda Pntip shot a young girl in the head, point blank. It was his second random execution of the day. The girl was thrown in the river and Mr. Pntip led to a bed for him to rest, it had been a long day for him. Mr. Ptorn had long since passed out, he had not moved when the gun was fired twenty feet away. Sweet dreams.

And in Khartoum, Sudan Said Alawid told the young Muslim girl to leave his quarters, he was through with her. Like Mr. Ptorn of Fang, Thailand his urge now was to do a "deal." Where is General Abdul? Said was in the mood to buy something for $170,000 and sell it for $700,000.

CHAPTER 63

Javier Henri LeCirac was in his opulent office in Nice, France. He was going full throttle on the mysterious French F-1B jetfighter situation, but also tracking the Angola situation.

He was a valued subcontractor to Dassault Aviation and had developed many contacts in the company from executive vice presidents down to line mechanics. Through his contacts he had learned that the replacement parts were about to be shipped. The repairs would take place next week, his sources thought. He wanted desperately to have his company "invited" along, and then he would show up. His father, as company chairman, would not be happy and God knows what would be the "Key Executive" insurance ramifications. Javier wanted to live his life, so who cares.

His sources said Angola was also on the schedule. Javier worked the politics in private; he planned to tip his hand at going only in the last minute. A few phone calls later and he had "wired" a potential "special technical assistance" from Dassault, but it turned out it was for the Angola Dassault 7X situation, not the F-1B. Javier Henri wanted both, he kept working the phones.

CHAPTER 64

The setting was opulent and elegant; it was in Javier Henri's office, complete with silverware and china. The girl had finally come. She had been hidden from Javier's business staff, so her arrival started a stir. It was Kelly Grant, at long last.

But that is only part of the story. The entrance was dramatic because Kelly had asked to introduce her assistant Abbey Bond at the meeting. Javier had agreed.

Actually, Javier Henri's staff was not invited, they just witnessed the arrival. Javier Henri would make the quick introductions as the girls departed. Now was the start of the multiple adventures, and he wanted to move forward. He could tell the girls were to be a distraction, but he didn't care. He would maintain order by controlling their exposure. They were so polite and modest; their discipline would help with controlling the men.

But there they were, and Javier Henri had forgotten how disarming and radiant Kelly Grant was, and the appearance of one Abbey Bond had left the suave dashing Javier a bit lost for words. How could two of the most elegant and sexy girls show up at the same place. Nature is not in balance when that happens.

Javier Henri had prepared himself for this arrival, but that was lost as the girls came into his office.

They were like school girls as they looked in wonder at the sheer size of this ornate and elegant office; the tapestries, the carpet, the marble, just overwhelming. It was more of a museum, just magnificent.

Javier let them settle in as he tried to settle down. The shock of it was, as fine and as stunning as Kelly was, it appeared to Javier that somehow Abbey Bond might be even more sexy and gorgeous. He tried not to stare and kept the conversation light. He wanted to talk to the girls for at least thirty minutes before business began.

They were modestly dressed; they looked to be Donna Karen brands, one a charcoal gray, one a deep blue. They each wore the pants version of the suit. The suit cuts were modest, but still could not conceal the likely shape and tone of two pairs of long, model quality legs. The dark blue suit on Kelly did highlight her pale thin, very white, skin. She wore little makeup, and she was ghost-like. And maybe it was the lights, but her eyes were a light crystal blue, a deadly combination. Her beauty and sex appeal seemed surreal even at 10 a.m. this morning in Nice, France.

Abbey was equally delicate and beautiful beyond all standards; a modest girl whose figure and thick blonde hair were not known to her. She had little concept of just how sexy she was, and thus she was the ultimate sexy.

Javier Henri tried to comprehend the unfolding situation but could not, it just was surreal.

Javier Henri asked the girls to summarize their activities and how the settling in was going. Kelly began speaking in a light feminine voice that was almost too delicate. Their British accent so charmed Javier Henri he was scarcely able to concentrate. Abbey watched Kelly and then glanced at Javier Henri, who in turn looked at her. She had the faintest hint of a smile, a very shy smile. Javier Henri could tell in ten minutes that neither of these girls had ever been around men much. They were innocent and precious. They were smart and articulate, but after that came the social and sexual wide-eyed innocence.

Incredible creatures they were. Javier Henri sat transfixed. These two girls were not to be hustled sexually, for some reason the reaction is for the men to just stand transfixed; a ghost-like siren beauty with an undertone of sexual presence.

CHAPTER 65

After one-hour Javier Henri sensed the girls were more relaxed. He explained to them that the projects he had were new projects with no history. He also said that Abbey should work with Kelly, since her resume and degrees qualified her. He had wanted just a companion for Kelly but since Kelly had found a very qualified girl, he would add her to the project and pay her a professional salary. The girls would be best friends and have a good and interesting job. The fact that two stunning girls would also be best friends simply defied the laws of nature.

A call came for Javier Henri that his assistant knew was important. He excused himself from the girls to go to his apartment off his office. Javier Henri listened intently for three minutes and then said, "Yes, I understand sir, and we would like to be part of it. You are so kind to invite us. I will send the names of our group by tomorrow," he finished. Dassault Aviation had invited LeCirac Industries Aviation on a fact-finding mission . . . to Angola. Be ready in one week.

After the call Javier Henri stood at his apartment window for almost five minutes. So it had begun. He didn't get the F-1B in Chad this time, but he was in. The F-1B would follow, he hoped. His thoughts then snapped back to the events at hand. He cleared his mind because he wanted to again experience the initial reaction to these two goddesses in his office. Were they really that startlingly sexy?

CHAPTER 66

And they were that sexy, no question. Javier Henri still found himself in a surreal world; the beautiful girls in his opulent office, and then the call including him on some adventure to Angola.

He told Kelly and Abbey that he wanted them to meet Brandon Craig. Brandon had been hired the same time as the girls, and he was to be the creative leader behind a movie. He was to lay the foundation as far as plot, storyline, locations, costumes, and well pretty much everything. Whatever might interest the girls was something that had to be done, the canvas was bare and there was no foundation or mold that had to be fit in. Javier Henri wanted them to work with Brandon for one month. If they found something they liked, great. If they didn't, LeCirac Industries was a $7 billion company, something would be found. But the movie project offered everything. There was the writing, there was costume design, there were budgets/accounting, there was management, and there was location scouting and travel management. This was a totally new endeavor to be run by twenty-somethings with only Javier Henri as the supervising adult. It doesn't get any better than this, since the money was being provided. They were to report directly to Javier Henri to cut out the bureaucratic shuffle that is built into these things. It also cut out the pack of sexually charged "dogs" that would come forth if these girls were to be put into everyday corporate life. He actually thought he might set up some small offices in the same building where the girls lived so they could explore the world at their choosing. Javier Henri may want to protect them, but he also had already taken their clothes off in his mind. Well, down to the panties. Mother Nature designed men to be sexual pursuers and women to be the receivers, and it worked to perfection every time, it seemed.

Brandon entered the office and the four met for one more hour to get acquainted and listen to Javier Henri outline the tasks. Javier Henri watched the interaction and felt comfortable. Brandon Craig was a creative, task-oriented guy and the girls' presence was exciting to him, but more as being in the presence of exquisite living art versus sexual interest. Javier Henri still wasn't sure what Brandon was, it seemed gay, then it seemed asexual. Either way he was the right guy as he had the movie on the front burner. What was clear was that the girls were comfortable with him; they had sensed what Javier Henri had sensed. Brandon was a creative guy and polite, and in the end there were two of them versus his one. They were comfortable.

Javier Henri said he would set up offices right on the girls' ground floor. As they sat excited, Javier Henri called his head architect to tell him he needed to develop five small offices on the ground floor of their building. There were a number of empty rooms there now, and the architect would draw up the plans in a week, there should be no problem. Until the offices were finished the girls would work in their apartments and meet with Brandon and his staff at Brandon's office. It was a done deal, they were off.

As Brandon left the office, Javier Henri talked to him quietly about an upcoming trip. Brandon would go as his "assistant," but also to start research and location evaluation as the "movie" guy. It was 11 a.m. in Nice, France. Javier Henri watched from his office as the girls walked away talking, two small tight asses swinging almost in unison, two exotically stunning girls who also had become friends. Nature could not be in balance for this to happen.

CHAPTER 67

The old Chevy truck from the 1950's rattled across the border from Syria into Lebanon. Two Arab men rode in the front and one man rode in the back . . . along with a goat tied to the side. There were two bales of hay for the goat to occupy his time. The man in the back had no diversion, just a very rough road and an old Chevy truck with shock absorbers that had worn out back around 1957. The trip went on for six hours.

Never try to guess the next mission, the man in the back had little idea exactly where he was but one thing was very clear, it was not Rangoon, Burma.

The journey through the city was slow and torturous, the route taken covered small narrow roads with lots of donkeys, goats, and street vendors on the road to keep the pace to about 10 mph. Maybe that was the objective, because by the time they reached the building it was 8 p.m. and this section of Beirut was very quiet.

It appeared to be a third string financial district. The men got out and went into the building through a back alley. They went up the stairs to the seventh story in an eight-story building. Two of the men left and the third one stayed, he was now alone and all was quiet. The man looked out the window as the old truck slowly rattled away down the dark deserted street. The goat was still munching away on the bale of hay. To the goat that bale of hay must have been like a Las Vegas five-star buffet.

CHAPTER 68

It was 10:17 a.m. in the third string financial district of Beirut. Two cars pulled up to the front of the bank across the street.

The man on the seventh floor took note. He went into position; the time and description were right. As he was making his adjustments, yet another two vehicles pulled up, again the time and description seemed right. In this situation things can get off schedule and out of line quickly, but the man on the seventh floor was calm. Someone was going to die, just not sure if it is going to be the right target.

Two men got out of the first vehicle convoy quickly. Having three seconds to decide, the seventh-floor assassin did . . . nothing. A single man got out of the second convoy and the assassin . . . did nothing. He did nothing for five seconds. Then he put a .22 LR bullet under the eye of the second man of the second convoy. It was like a pin prick, as the bullet is so small; the man stood still and then slumped to the ground. The bodyguard looked around quickly, to collect two .22 LR in his neck.

The assassin quickly laid the rifle down by a folder with a letter. He then executed his getaway. He walked across the seventh story to a window; the cable had been set up in the night. He slid down the cable to the sixth floor of the next building across a fifty-foot alley. He walked across the sixth floor to the other side, then repelled down on a preset cable. All the while the bustle of the daily street traffic went on, but likely someone was watching, maybe a lot of someone's.

When he landed in the street, he ducked in a doorway and took off his black outfit to show an orange and red outfit beneath, then down to the basement. He walked across the basement and emerged from the basement steps on a side street.

He got on the back of a motorcycle and left for the Beirut airport.

At 11:31 a.m. a lone man climbed the steps of a private Gulfstream 250, he was dressed in casual business attire. The steps were raised and the plane departed for Cyprus less than one hour away.

If all had gone well, the first man shot would be a Ramy Abdula, a notorious arms smuggler who had used Beirut as a safe haven for years, insulated from the ability of the powers to be to get to him. He had been immune to all the forces trying to get to him; well, right up to the second before his brain acted as a brake for a high velocity .22 LR.

As luck would have it, the two men to get out of the first convoy were Farsi and Yassar Abbas, come to count their money again. They had not heard anything and had not known anything was wrong until the bodies started dropping. The Abbas brothers went home pale and shaken. They would be dead if the assassin had not decided on the second convoy.

By 1:27 p.m. a man was swimming at a military base on British sovereign territory, the Island of Cyprus. He had flown in that day just after noon. His swim was punctuated by British Typhoon jetfighters roaring overhead.

In Nice, France Brandon Craig sat down with the two blonde girls from Britain. They would start the project for the movie, but they needed to get a theme first. They would meet briefly with Javier Henri tomorrow, if for no other reason than for Javier to see the girls again.

To the south in a place called Khartoum, Sudan Said Alawid had not taken a bath in six days, and yesterday was 110°F in Khartoum. He still had his deals, but he now missed his brother and Syria. All of his rants and deal makings meant more to him when his brother was alive. Now they were just deals, no one to show off for anymore. He was sure General Abdul would show up again, no one would dare outbid him for those two MIG-23's. Yes, two MIG-23's for $340,000 total, while some arms dealer in Rangoon was offering $200,000 for just the nose landing gear of the MIG-29. Crazy world.

The heat and smell overwhelmed all in the narrow back alleys in a place called Khartoum. Said wanted to talk to General Abdul again but then Farsi and Yassar Abbas also wanted to talk to the General. But they were shaken, as maybe Said Alawid knew they pulled the trigger on his brother in London and had tried to pull the trigger on them in Beirut today and had just missed, who knows. A dangerous business.

CHAPTER 69

The Abbas compound in Beirut was quiet, as in, "Who is being this quiet." First the Dassault 7X jet of Farsi Abbas disappears over Africa, and now two assassinations occur right in front of his eyes. Either it was just bad karma (Buddhism) or else someone was gunning for the Abbas brothers, and only Allah's (Muslim) "will" had saved them. In either case, Farsi and Yassar starting attending prayers just to cover their bases; Muslim prayers today, maybe Buddhist prayers tomorrow, just to cover their bases.

Farsi Abbas had talked to Dassault and Lloyd's of London about the disappearance of the Dassault 7X. Dassault had gotten satellite photos of southeastern Angola to look for possible crash sites. Dassault also had been talking to Total Oil, the large French oil company, about leasing their trucks/site equipment to go to the site in Angola and collect detailed evidence. Dassault also talked to French intelligence about events in the area that might have brought the plane down. The plane had disappeared from a high altitude, so it was unlikely some rebel militia had taken it down. If it had been shot down from 31,000 feet, then that would be a particularly chilling turn of events and none of this work addressed <u>why</u> the plane was chosen, or <u>who</u> exactly might be behind the Beirut assassination.

Farsi's thoughts of the long-legged Lisa had become secondary, and for the first time it seemed his survival was at stake, so thoughts of a sexy teenage girl took a backseat. The same went for Yassar.

CHAPTER 70

He had his Armani power suit on today as he talked to Dassault Aviation from his splendid corporate office. Javier Henri LeCirac was happy and full of life as these aviation adventures unfolded. He adjusted his $200 silk Hermes tie. The suit was a light gray, the shirt a dark blue, the tie a radiant light blue. The watch was a Cartier.

Using his father's and his own corporate influence he had managed to get into the door for both the Dassault crash site investigation in Angola <u>and</u> the onsite maintenance of the crippled Dassault Mirage F-1B fighter in the barren wastelands of Eastern Chad. This day, as most every day, it was good to be Mr. Javier Henri. Surrounded by opulent offices, a magnificent compound of townhouses just one mile away, the corporate jets and helicopters, and as the day unfolded, Javier Henri had already decided to take the Ferrari out for a spin along the coast this coming evening. The perfect climax to another perfect Javier Henri day.

Dassault was setting the logistics for the Angola trip. That was no small feat, as it would require the investigating party to leave Luanda, Angola and travel at least 700 miles into the wild raw terrain of outback Angola. There was also the danger of roving militias left over from the 2002 ending of the civil war. These militias were like roving packs of wild dogs. Still armed to the teeth and on the thin edge of survival, these gangs were not only wild dogs, but in many cases cornered wild dogs. The heat, the terrain, the dry countryside presented very dangerous obstacles themselves . . . and then there were these rolling militia gangs.

Javier Henri also continued to talk to Total Oil to get logistics support and also advice on security arrangements for his party. He would subsidize the Dassault effort and wanted to know these Total Oil guys.

As the details of these two upcoming trips began to sink in, Javier Henri started to understand that he was entering into a real and likely raw world of the real adventures. It had always been so exciting to think about and plan, but now the dreams were taking on the beginnings of reality. He was still excited, but that excitement was very much tempered by the reality that things were moving forward and that real adventures, particularly in Africa, had a very real and stark potential for life threatening adventure. Be careful what you wish for. It had all become more sobering rather than exciting. He would not tell his staff of this.

CHAPTER 71

Javier Henri's staff of Kelly Grant and Abbey Bond had grown accustomed to Nice, mainly because there were two of them and they both were quiet and conservative. But as they began to relax and did not have to fend off the young males alone, this comfort stirred a budding sexuality. They had not talked about it openly, but they had both watched the young males and were beginning to feel their sexual power, as well as their sexual energy. They had gone so far as to buy Victoria's Secret panties and had giggled their way through their own private fashion show. The girls were amazing sculptures of young, slim, firm girls and had any male seen them playing around in these briefest of panties, a stroke would surely follow. Neither had had a boyfriend, much less kissed a man. It was hard to see how that would play out right now. While Lisa of South Africa was one year younger, her exposure and involvement already with men would likely exceed Kelly and Abbey's entire life experience. Not that that is an advantage. Lisa's experience would likely age her rapidly emotionally, and the British girls could likely never have a wild, erotic sexual adventure with some guy.

After their private fashion show the girls simply sprawled onto chairs, one leg spread across the arm, and chatted innocently. They had no tops on, their blonde hair was everywhere except between the legs. They were slowly maturing everywhere.

They wondered aloud what this movie project was about. They had had only two brief meetings, but Brandon Craig was starting to add small foundations to it. Brandon had had several two-hour meetings with Javier Henri in the "big" office. The girls were still amazed at their own time there, it was so opulent and ornate that stepping back into the normal world just one hour later had left the girls a little let down.

Brandon had discussed costume design, location scouting, business management, lighting, scripts, actually everything with the girls. They would have their choice, but there was no rush as so much ground work had to be laid.

They were excited by it all. Who wouldn't be. Their quarters were new and redecorated, some interior designer from Paris. They had drivers and chefs at their call, but had not used either, they were too humble and conservative.

But the world was changing. As the night wore down, they wondered if the big office meant big "something" elsewhere, and they both giggled. But Javier Henri was on their minds, even as they did not talk about it, he was quite the male profile.

After a few more exchanges, they left for their own opulent king size beds and the 1000 thread count black Armani sheets. The carpet, tile and drapes were a rich gold, the bathroom fixtures were actually real gold. Life was good for Kelly Grant and Abbey Bond, aged twenty, stunning long-legged girls already living a very large life. Both went to bed in the same panties, no tops. Slowly they were getting used to being out of their clothes, and the males of the world would rejoice.

CHAPTER 72

He strolled down the exotic and extremely narrow alleys of Stone Town, Zanzibar. Stone Town was its own real-life movie set. Dark narrow alleys, shifty men in robes, street vendors passing by as if they were shadows. The alleys were narrow and bordered by four and five story buildings so that little of the tropical sun hit the street, and that is just as well as it was a piercing, laser-like tropical sun.

The smells drifting up and down these alleys added their own dimension. The smells were of cloves, basil, saffron, rosemary and a host of others. The smells swirled with the light smoke of the house fires cooking the daily meals. The people passed quietly, the women always veiled and in groups, the children following behind. But even the children seemed as quiet as ghosts. Rangoon, Burma and Phnom Penh, Cambodia were card-carrying Cities of Ghosts, add Stone Town, Zanzibar to their ranks.

The man continued to stroll. He had arrived via a commercial prop plane, Air Tanzania, two days before and had simply walked the alleyways and sat along the seawall and watched as Stone Town went about its business of survival.

On this third day he sat under a large sea grape tree on the beach wall. As he sat a very dark skinny man approached with two cloth bags. He leaned against the wall three feet away from the man. Five minutes later the dark skinny man left, he left with only one bag, he had said nothing. The man by the wall saw the bag and said nothing. In his world a bag left close to him was like a phone call to him. The man had left the bag, but he had not forgotten it. And the remaining man knew exactly that.

That remaining man was Kent Benson, because that's what his passport said. He was a businessman with a British passport, but he was not British and he was not on business . . . that he knew of. He had come from the British territory on Cyprus three days ago, and his butt was still sore from the long ride in a 1950 pickup truck from Syria to Lebanon.

He carefully picked up the bag and left. The bag went into a larger black backpack, he continued to stroll aimlessly. The bag was a bit heavy but it felt like the right weight to Kent Benson.

He strolled along the seawall on the western beachside of town and stopped under another large sea grape tree. He looked at the tree and remembered similar sized sea grape trees along a seawall in another dilapidated but exotic city . . . Havana, Cuba. His mind wandered to the young woman of the Floridita . . . let's see, her name was Eva, it seems. Yes, it was Eva, sleek svelte and quiet, all hiding a rampaging sexual energy. What a nice day to let the mind roam. And like Havana Stone Town, Zanzibar had virtually no traffic, so the mind could wander.

Kent Benson did not see the second man approach. He had come from directly behind Kent. He said nothing, again two bags. Five minutes of silence, and the man left with only one bag. The only difference was this man was large and fat and the tropical sun was killing him.

This bag was lighter, the man simply carried it. He returned to his elegant suite at the Serena Zanzibar, took a swim and then took a nap. A magnificent day in Stone Town, Zanzibar, the gentle sea breeze blowing the curtains in Suite 317, it was 2:15 p.m.

CHAPTER 73

He lay between her legs and kissed her deeply. She had very dark velvet skin, but not a Congo black. She was a nomadic tribe girl and her black was almost surreal, a velvet sheen black. As he held her she moved against him and her skin was scorching hot. That was natural, their skin does stay hot, thus the head to toe robes. As he finished and continued to hold her, the black skin was dramatic against the sheets.

Her face was of very fine high cheek bones, small lips, large elegant forehead, straight black hair, not so coarse. Pound for pound and inch for inch the girls of Somalia are likely the most exotic on the face of the earth. She was long legged, lean and firm. And he started with her again, and this time she wrapped the long thin arms and the long thin legs around him, lots of energy, and lots of movement. It was 10:27 p.m.

They woke at 4:31 a.m. and went to the balcony. She put his shirt on and nothing else. He had shorts on and nothing else. They stood quietly, his one hand held her hand, the other hand was gently put between her legs. They remained quiet and then she rested her head back against his shoulder, sighed a bit, and had a slow smile on her face.

She called herself Diane, and one year ago she was a normal girl in Southern Somalia, as innocent as Kelly and Abbey would ever be. But now she was quiet and not so innocent, but she was surviving better. She fell asleep on his shoulder, and he slowly took her to bed. They would sleep until 10:30 a.m. He would wake to the same sun and ocean breeze in Stone Town, Zanzibar with Diane as he did with Eva in Havana. That had been some short months ago and many long lifetimes ago.

The two bags had been opened and then put into one bag. One bag had a Walther P22 pistol with 100 rounds. The second bag had a full-on titanium silencer and it had been screwed on the pistol. The weapon was in the black backpack in the closet.

He walked Diane back to her room where he had found her on Suicide Alley and if that's not crazy enough, he had found her in the Happy Times Bar. And he was very happy he found her. He would stay in Zanzibar three more nights to get to know every inch of this Somali nomad girl.

CHAPTER 74

No, he won't spend three more nights in Stone Town, Zanzibar. He managed two nights with Diane, accented by strolls on the beach outside the hotel compound. She wore long robes, which occasionally blew open and the sun highlighted the long firm dark legs.

On the third day Diane stayed in the suite, as the man called Kent Benson, after all that's what his passport said, strolled again through the maze of alleys called Stone Town. He sat at a waterfront café called the Mercury Café when the man came.

They talked in quiet tones for five minutes. The man called Kent Benson listened, nodded, and said nothing. The man stopped briefing Kent Benson and sat at the table sipping his tea. Ten minutes later he got up and left. No one had spoken for ten minutes. As the man left, Kent continued to gaze at the sea from the ocean side restaurant.

CHAPTER 75

The Land Rover Defender came for Kent Benson at 1:00 a.m. As the Land Rover pulled up to the beat-up, dilapidated airport it went straight to the end of a very primitive airstrip. Kent got out and boarded the jet-black Learjet 45B, a jetfighter type business jet.

As the jet started its engines, the young Somali named Diane had been asleep for two hours. As the jet taxied, Kent thought of her, a magnificent four days with a quiet nomad girl. Her life would be hard and dangerous, most likely, but he hoped the last four days would give her good memories.

In Fang, Thailand Mr. Ptorn was ending another night of drugs and girls. He still had money and power in his arms and drug smuggling business, but he was edging to the cliff. But of course, they never see it coming. No one has as much time or money as they think they do. The perpetual self-absorbed arrogance that is the human condition.

Javier Henri LeCirac and members of his project team were fast asleep in Nice, France. His creative director Brandon Craig tossed and turned, the details of the movie project started to consume him. Kelly Grant and Abbey Bond slept soundly, the advantage of youth, stunning beauty and innocence. But sexual maturity was slowly gaining ground on them. They sprawled naked except for the briefest of panties.

General Abdul slept quietly in Khartoum, Sudan. He needed to move the MIG-23's soon before anyone noticed they were gone. He had his list of potential dealers; Said Alawid, Farsi Abbas, a new player named Alex Kagamba of Cape Town, and he hoped his guy Raja Majani could find that crazy buyer with more money than sense to buy the MIG-23's <u>and</u> the five MIG-29 landing gears for $1.0 million. Where was the crazy man from Rangoon, Burma?

General Abdul was always hoping for more money, more money. And with that drive he could connect with the other seven billion people of the world.

CHAPTER 76

It had come very quickly. The suddenness of the call shocked Javier Henri and left him excited and alarmed in equal doses.

A French Air Force C-130J would arrive in Marseilles in two days. It was an "embassy run" and would stop in Dakar, Senegal briefly, then Libreville, Gabon . . . Luanda, Angola. Javier Henri could bring four people, and Dassault needed their passport names and numbers today, actually within one hour. The Dassault team had been assembled, and the Total Oil group had leased three large military-type expedition trucks to Dassault for the expedition to the Dassault 7X wreckage in the wild southeast of Angola. Dassault was to bring eight people, and they would spend up to five days onsite collecting evidence.

Javier Henri thought quickly and decided on himself, Brandon Craig to develop the script, Pierre Patron the former French Air Force F-1B pilot, and a former Dassault engineer who had worked on the Dassault 7X. The reality of the African expedition hit Javier Henri in the stomach, and he felt a bit sick and weak. He had always dreamed of this since he was a boy, but always be careful what you dream for.

Javier met quickly with the chosen team and all were excited except Brandon Craig, who turned pale and became sick in his stomach, but did not throw up.

The rumors of the African expedition spread quickly within the company. The anticipation got everyone excited; everyone was excited except for the four people who actually had to go on this thing. And so all was set and the French C-130J was off into the night on the long, tortuous journey to Angola, its twelve passengers overwhelmed by the noise.

CHAPTER 77

The black Learjet roared off the broken runway into the steamy jet-black sky over Stone Town. Only the generators at the Zanzibar Serena kept the lights on, and there were few others on that night in Stone Town. Diane sprawled peacefully in a deep sleep, she also lay naked except for the briefest of panties; a fine-boned, velvet skinned, sleek sculpture of a young Somali nomad girl. Put this sculpture in stone and she is an instant masterpiece. Suicide Alley, Stone Town was dark and quiet. The Happy Times Bar on Suicide Alley, Stone Town was dark and quiet.

The jet headed to the southwest. The Learjet was chosen as it is a very fast business jet. The lone passenger did not know the destination or time line, but his "people" were in a hurry. The passenger did not know the location, but he would when he arrived . . . in that remote desolate desert . . . in Namibia, a barren airstrip with dirty beat up hangers and immaculate jetfighters.

As his jet gained altitude over Dar Es Salam, Tanzania, the French C-130J with Javier Henri and party was losing altitude over Libreville, Gabon, the hot steamy capital of the country.

That Libreville, Gabon was hosting a mysterious flight in the dead of night was not new, it was always a hub of intrigue. Never heard of it? Well, that is why it is always a hub of intrigue, because it is off the map.

The fact that some 3,000 French Foreign Legion soldiers were stationed in Franceville, Gabon, and Libreville was their transit point, kept it all interesting. Also, Libreville was home to the Bongo family, which had ruled Gabon for forty or more years. The young Bongo had taken over for his deceased father in yet another attempt to install a self-appointed "royal" family in Africa and the Middle East. The Africans hated the colonialists because they wanted their power! Given the power, they immediately set up their own "royal" mafia families. Thus the world was given Tunisia, Libya, Iraq, Egypt, Uganda, Yemen, Zimbabwe, etc., etc., and Gabon and Equatorial Guinea, and on and on.

Libreville, Gabon was also infamous as the hub of the mercenary cargo planes into the Republic of Biafra during that dirty, bloody, grinding civil war against Nigeria. The Biafra war is still known as one of the bleakest, nastiest, and extremely grueling wars of its time. It dropped humanity into the most desperate and bloodiest war, only matched by the Khmer Rouge of Cambodia a few years later.

As Javier Henri limped off the military plane for a rest stop, only Brandon Craig knew of the Libreville history, and he had only known of it for the last two weeks. In his research for the movie script he had stumbled across the Biafra war and then the role Libreville played in it.

He had immersed himself in it day and night because of its drama and because he never knew such a world existed. He had wanted to tell Javier Henri, as well as his associates Kelly Grant and Abbey Bond, but the schedule had become so compressed and hectic he hardly had time to eat, much less brief everyone on his research.

Now the shock, he was here! As they left the airplane he took note of everything, as it was all the stuff of legend, and he had just finished Frederick Forsyth's book, "Dogs of War." Even in the black night he saw an old DC-3 parked in the weeds off the runway and knew instantly it must have been one of the planes flying cargo missions into Biafra as it dodged MIG-21's flown by East Germans for the Nigerian federal government.

His mind raced as the development of the movie script became immensely easier now that he had actually set foot in Africa. He had been in Africa for fifteen minutes; it was 12:37 a.m. in the hot, steamy, wet blanket of a night . . . Libreville, Gabon, West Africa.

As they rode into town bone weary, every sidewalk and street corner was of interest to Brandon Craig. So this is where they walked, these were the cafes and bars they were in, these were the hotels where they stayed, these infamous mercenaries going to and from Biafra in that most bloody, dirty and infamous of African mercenary wars. He was totally exhausted and totally in awe. These were the same streets of the infamous Biafra mercenaries; he couldn't believe it, so excited and so innocent.

He now had the perfect job, to bring Javier Henri LeCirac his movie story and script. Javier Henri LeCirac was just tired; he slept in the seat in front of Brandon Craig.

CHAPTER 78

The next day changed Brandon Craig even more. In the blistering, scorching tropical sun of humid, moldy Libreville Brandon could see where these mercenaries gathered before or after their role in the Biafra war. By all accounts the mercenaries had done themselves proud in Biafra. A hopeless, bleak war in the tropical heat, little food, no medicine, yet they stayed and fought to the end when their Biafran black general told them it was over. He paid them on their contracts and told them to go home. But they had been brave, stoic and professional to the end.

And when they left they did so by way of an old cranky DC-3 that dodged the Nigerian jetfighters enough to reach Libreville, Gabon. As professional mercenaries are known to do, they just seemed to disappear, maybe to Cape Town, maybe Harare, maybe London, hell maybe Stone Town. No one is quite sure.

Thoughts were swirling through Brandon Craig's mind endlessly. Then he saw them on a downtown street as he headed to the airport. Two white males in a sea of black people, both thirty-five years old or so, lean, deep tan, deep lines in their faces; stern faces. Brandon had never seen a mercenary, and few would know if they had, but he assumed these men must look like them. The movie script was far richer already, and he had not been in Africa twenty-four hours. Brandon was exhausted and exhilarated, the rest of the Dassault/LeCirac team was just exhausted.

As they walked across the tarmac to the waiting French Air Force C-130J, it was as if they were in a steamy red-hot oven. This was the stuff of heat strokes. Brandon at twenty-nine years old felt it melt him, and he felt the true physical burden that must accompany fighters in these conditions. The mercenaries earned their pay just by showing up. As he walked up to the C-130J, he saw two other old planes parked in the weeds by the old DC-3 and he could only imagine the dark missions they may have been on in this darkest of continents. Heat and intrigue filled the air.

CHAPTER 79

The heat continued as the C-130J lumbered south. The plane was constantly rocking from the tropical, heated air columns. The Dassault/LeCirac crew was exhausted to the man.

As they crossed the border from the DRC Congo into Angolan airspace, the tropical terrain gave way to a grassland savannah and then to rather dusty red flat plains. And then they flew over Luanda, Angola, party central for yet another desperate brutal war and again featuring the infamous mercenary.

Brandon Craig had only been able to read one or two sources on the Angolan civil wars, but that was enough. He knew as soon as he touched the Angolan ground he would be able to sense the tragedy and violence of the place.

And he was able to do just that.

It was all a cultural shock. First Libreville, Gabon, now the dust and dry heat of Luanda, Angola. A whirlwind tour of the African mercenary wars brought to you by Thomas Cook tours. Please watch your step.

As in Biafra, Angola was a dirty difficult war. It had mercenaries on all sides, including the Cuban soldiers for one of the three parties.

The wars were terribly violent, but also terribly dysfunctional at times. The mercenaries here could be disorganized and erratic, and there were a number of psychopaths in charge. The wars dragged on and burned out most of the mercenaries. In 1976 those that had not burned out were captured and no longer subject to extreme mood swings . . . they were summarily executed in Luanda by their captors.

The wars kept going until 2002 when seventeen AK-47 bullets hit the longtime rebel leader Joseph Savimbi in an ambush. And those seventeen bullets allowed a twenty-eight year civil war to end in just six weeks. It's all in the numbers and if you can kill the No. 1 leader, often that is all that is necessary.

CHAPTER 80

The investigating crew was met by a French diplomat and by a Total Oil manager. Everything had been set up, the trucks, the supplies, the GPS, as well as two armed security men, ex-French Foreign Legion, provided by Total Oil.

Javier Henri asked when they should start, and the Total Oil manager said tomorrow. But both Javier Henri and the lead Dassault man asked for two days, and it was agreed. Not two days to hit the town, two days to go into a coma.

Brandon was also exhausted and also excited; an extra day to walk Luanda, the same sidewalks, the same street corners as the Cuban and contract mercenaries. He absorbed it all, and in two plus days on the African continent he had enough physical background data for two plus movies. Amazing, he didn't see the team members for two days; he didn't think they even opened their doors.

Brandon read the Angolan papers, he visited the cafes and he went to their parks. He was absorbing everything, and any eleven people he saw on the street could fill a movie. The movie backdrops were endless. "Blood Diamonds" meets LeCirac Cinema productions.

As he read the Luanda English newspaper, The Luanda Daily Standard, he ran across the ad for a Literary/Cinema festival in Cape Town. He tore the ad out, maybe Javier would spring for the trip, it was eight days away.

CHAPTER 81

The three expedition trucks slowly moved through the Luanda traffic. Maybe one hour to go seven miles on the potholed two lane highway out of town. The procession of people on foot was endless; carts, bikes, people. The trucks were loaded and heavy, and one truck had a fuel tank trailer. Once outside the city all prayed for just a small patch of paved road.

They made two hundred miles the first day, in a ten-hour day. The second day it took fourteen hours to go two hundred miles. It was only on the third day that their progress slowed.

A rogue group of ex-soldiers manned a desolate checkpoint to extort cash from mostly destitute local farmers.

And then their dream appeared.

The convoy emerged from the dust one mile from the roadblock. All six of the armed rebels cheered and shot their AK-47's in the air. The lottery had been won! Three French Total Oil trucks, the bandits would ask $1 million. Magnificent, wonderful, as soon as the trucks got here there would be some AK-47's put to some heads. If the money doesn't roll, heads will roll. Do not mess with young, drugged up, down and out players.

The bullet tore through the head of one of the rebels. The bullet came from the rebel's right. They in turn blazed away into the dust on the right side, and a bullet hit a rebel square in the chest . . . it came from the left side. The rebel guns blazed to the left side, and then another rebel fell, a shot to the throat. The three remaining started running, each got a bullet in the back. The hyenas would feast tonight.

The Dassault/LeCirac team dropped their jaws and went to a pale, pale complexion. The Angolan outback would like to welcome you to the area, cocktails at six. Javier Henri felt weak, they were 456 plus miles in, so to go on was a horror, to go back was a horror. And while Brandon had seen enough "location" shots in three days to fill three movies, all of that seemed totally irrelevant now. He just wanted to live.

The violence was extreme to Brandon, and now watching this violence shocked him to his very core.

The two security guys rejoined the trucks and never said a word. Brandon thought, "forget seeing a mercenary, here were two riding with them."

The trucks slowly passed the bloody bodies, no one from the investigation party looked.

At the end of this day they were only fifty miles away. The truck light shone brightly as they slowly ground down the miles. But exhaustion was their constant companion and they stopped twenty miles short, and most everyone fell asleep in their clothes right where they sat.

CHAPTER 82

They made it to the Dassault 7X wreckage at high noon the next day. They couldn't move before 10:00 a.m. Now they stood at the wreckage in the blazing sun.

But seeing the wreckage energized the group. The engineers started immediately looking at and photographing the wrecked plane; well, what was left of it. It was just melted metal, very black melted metal. Samples were taken and more photographs were taken.

Calls were made to France, advice was given and questions were asked. The satellite phones were burning through the minutes. Cell phones, electricity, even civilization did not exist here in the scorching barren area of the Angolan highlands.

There seemed little life here, and the sight of the crash made the scene that much more desperate and desolate. The sun was so hot that it soon drove the team back to the trucks. The team set up the camp about fifty yards from the crash site. Everyone rested until about 5 p.m., when they would spend another two hours analyzing the site.

During all of this Javier Henri was shocked to his core. He had been exhausted by the heat, the travel, the alien cultures and terrain. He could hardly keep his bearings, the change had been so extreme from his polished, posh life as a corporate manager and wealthy comfortable single man. He just could not believe this world existed. It had been all quite sobering.

As night fell the campfires were set up, the three trucks had been put together in a triangle for security. No one knew what was out here, roving bands of militia to roving bands of hyenas. No one would be sleeping outside.

CHAPTER 83

In just the three hours onsite it was clear that the Dassault 7X had incurred a massive heat event. All the technical team agreed on that point. Preliminary tests showed residue of explosives. But how could that be? And then Pierre Patron, the former F-1B fighter pilot, weighed in. From what he had seen and what the engineers had found he felt that an air-to-air missile could be involved. But how could that be, why would such an extreme event happen? This whole expedition had taken a bad turn. At the edge of civilization the members were already at the edge of their sanity, and they were losing it after just a few days.

At 9:47 p.m. it happened. Things were dead silent in the pitch black, each member in a personal coma of exhaustion and wild dreams in this barren land.

And then a roaring jet of some description came over the site at what must have been fifty feet. The team woke up in terror and disbelief. Now with this event so startling after the shock and punishment of the last five days, it was all becoming too much.

Five minutes later the jet came back from a different direction and if possible, an even lower altitude . . . maybe twenty feet or less! And again, five minutes later, a massive roar at an extremely low altitude. All were just sitting up, jaws dropped.

Then it came again, it seemed louder and lower than ever. Pierre Patron was pale white when he swallowed hard and told Javier Henri that it was a military jetfighter of some description, he was sure. He barely got the words out.

It came again and Javier Henri broke, he ordered his driver to take their truck out of the area. He wanted to get away from this site now! The other two trucks decided to stay. The driver suggested pulling into a dry riverbed one mile away with banks about fifty feet high for security. Javier Henri said yes, being alone in the truck in the small canyon seemed better, and he told the remaining two trucks they would return tomorrow.

It took them another two hours to move and set up, and now they were beyond exhaustion, just delirious, not psychotic yet. It all had become too much to bare, they were just hanging on. Be careful what you wish for.

The jet didn't return and everything was quiet, a dead quiet in the pitch black of the stark barren Angolan Highlands, Southwest Africa.

CHAPTER 84

The next day was bright and hot, waking to a new day of dead calm and quiet helped sooth the frayed nerves. Javier Henri's truck slowly returned to the site to find the Dassault engineers busy.

At this point Brandon Craig briefed Javier Henri on the literary/film festival in Cape Town in a few days. Could he go? Javier Henri said yes immediately, in fact they all would go. He was suddenly happy to think about the idea of a civilized world and an excuse to leave this most extreme existence. The heat, desperate poverty, the violence, and he had only been on a rather tame expedition, not the wretched warfare of Africa.

Javier Henri had his coffee and a reason to leave, so he had become ecstatic, maybe a little too much. Brandon and Pierre Patron hoped he could hold it together; they hoped they could hold it together.

Javier got on the satellite phone to Total Oil. He wanted to charter a helicopter tomorrow to take them out of this region and back to Luanda. He also called his staff to arrange their departure to Cape Town, and he wanted the best hotel. He desperately needed to be in civilization again. First class for everyone, just get him out of here alive.

CHAPTER 85

Only one man spotted it early and then he wasn't sure what he saw. It was a black spot very low on the horizon. All was dead quiet. He then pointed it out to the next two men who also spotted it. The black spot had become larger. All was dead quiet. By the time Pierre Patron saw it the black spot had become much larger, but still extremely low. He said to Javier Henri as they both stood near the wreckage, "That is a jetfighter of some make!"

Javier Henri stood transfixed by the unfolding event. They all did.

And then all was not quiet. The black jetfighter had come in hard and fast, maybe thirty feet above the wreck site. The roar was epic and shook the internal organs of the team. It was as if the world was ending and then it was over. The black jet never pulled up, it stayed down at thirty feet until out of sight in about ten seconds.

Maybe it was just coincidence and was a military training exercise. The team hoped so.

But Pierre Patron said no. The black jet knew the precise coordinates of the wreck and had flown directly over them each time, even in the absolute darkness of last night. Something else was up. The jet did not return, so no one was able to video or photograph it. Things became dead quiet again. The team continued to work but would always stop to check the horizon for the mystery jet. It did not return.

By 4 p.m. the team had settled down. But without telling anyone, Pierre Patron was still puzzled. He did not recognize the jet type of their visitor. It certainly was not a Mirage F-1B, the plane he flew, nor was it any other fighter he recognized from Europe or the United States. And where was it refueling to make this trip to the barren outback of Angola? Angola had no bases here and the flight from Luanda was too far without refueling, he thought. The Angolan Air Force had no aerial tankers either.

Maybe the extreme events of the last five days had ended. By 6 p.m. the team retreated to the trucks, but Javier Henri again moved his truck to the shallow river canyon. He was still shaken, maybe he would always be shaky now. Because of the quiet over the last six to seven hours, most of the team felt the worst was over. They settled in by the outdoor fire with steaks on the grill; the trucks had everything, including a small wine cellar. Oh, the French and their wine. Things had settled down enough that the Dassault team, plus the lone LeCirac engineer with them, had started to tell "war stories" about the previous five days. It had been maybe five times the adventure each had had their whole lives and some were over sixty years old. Now that it was over each knew that getting back to France would be like returning heroes with adventure stories that were true but hard to believe. It had been a very long intense five days. The short but dramatic stop in Libreville had seemed like six months ago, not six days.

Total darkness once again enveloped the small camp by the Dassault 7X wreckage. A bit relaxed, sipping a French wine, the steaks ready in ten minutes, the potatoes au gratin ready now. Total Oil Ltd. had engineered some great trucks, built in kitchens, nice sleeping quarters, showers, generators, even seventeen television channels, and all functioning in a place that best resembles the Africa of 1730.

Now the steaks were being served, the Total Oil chef had strawberry cheesecake set up for desert. It was 8:10 p.m. in this barren outpost in the Angola highlands.

CHAPTER 86

It was indeed a beautiful and calm night. The richness and blackness of the night seemed to have its own beauty. After the great meal the men would use the satellite phone to call home. At $15 per minute it was good to have old Dassault Aviation around.

They were right, the jet had not been back to blow exhaust up their noses at thirty feet and 500 mph. It would not come back at that altitude. From the north it was at least three hundred feet high. It was 8:17 p.m.

It was scorching the air at 500 mph and it held a 500 lb. centerline tank with white phosphorus that would soon scorch a small patch of ground next to the other patch of scorched earth.

The pilots looked at the computer screen and dropped the speed to 470 mph . . . exactly. The GPS coordinates were in . . . for a spot exactly fifty yards west of the crash site, basically targeted where the steaks had just finished grilling.

All was quiet in front of the roaring jet. The men chatted casually and relaxed . . . it would be all over soon . . . in seventeen seconds to be exact. The sound behind the jet was of the apocalypse, the sound in front an eerie quiet.

The 500 lb. white phosphorus bomb was released and all fates were sealed. The men actually heard the jet for three seconds as it passed them, their world vaporized. White phosphorus gives off a blinding white light when it explodes. The light is so intense it would blind a person from a mile away. It was like a massive welding torch.

The explosion generated a white orange mushroom pillar. Then the mushroom turned to a light gray, all visible if it had not been pitch black.

But it was pitch black and there were no spy satellites overhead, and the jetfighter flight crew knew that. It was 8:17:47 and it was very much over. The jetfighter of the apocalypse continued to roar south from the devastation, still at three hundred feet.

Javier Henri heard the explosion and was on the verge of a stroke, would this nightmare ever end. He went up to the edge of the rim but could not see anything except red glowing pieces of metal. In his best calm voice he called Total Oil and Dassault, he did not call LeCirac Industries . . . yet.

The swing shift command centers went into action.

Thank God Total Oil had a helicopter coming by at 7:30 a.m., they would bill $121,000 for the service but Javier Henri was happy to pay. And sadly, with the LeCirac engineer absent, they could carry more fuel. The helicopter would bring the drivers to bring the last remaining Total Oil truck home . . . not an easy feat itself. Now all Javier Henri had to worry about was being shot out of the sky by that black jet. It would be daylight on the trip back to Luanda and they would be sitting ducks. One week in Africa and Javier Henri was forever changed.

And at the bomb site all was hopelessly melted, and in less than ten seconds the whole world had changed violently and forever. It was 8:38 p.m. in the barren land they call the Angola highlands. French and Angolan intelligence would get the report as Javier Henri arrived back in Luanda.

CHAPTER 87

In a hanger in the vast wasteland of northeast Namibia a black British Hunter RF/F-07 taxied to a stop. A crew of twelve quickly surrounded the jet. The two pilots exited the cockpit, soaked with sweat and exhausted. Flying at 300 feet in pitch black is exhausting, as well as creating hallucinations.

They went to their plush quarters beneath the hangar, showered and went to sleep.

They would be in Cape Town in two days. The pilots did not know each other, but the pilot referred to as Code 037 had known this place before. He always flew low level missions at night and a few in the daylight.

CHAPTER 88

The helicopter did come to get Javier Henri, Brandon Craig, and Pierre Patron. The helicopter was not shot down on the way back to Luanda. Javier Henri's staff had set up the flights from Luanda to Cape Town by way of Johannesburg on Angola Air and then South African Airways.

Upon arriving in Cape Town Javier Henri sat in first class as the jet taxied to the terminal, only to be jolted by the sight of a dark titanium painted jet with blood red accents also taxing. He had a flashback but could not place it. That jet was noteworthy. He could not remember, so he used his cell phone to take a picture.

The three had come to Cape Town a couple of days early just to rest and relax and try to avoid a complete mental meltdown. They would stay at the Mt. Nelson hotel.

As they entered the hotel two men were on their way out. One was a tall handsome and lean man in his early 30's, the other a large man in his 50's, a much blacker man. The older man was General Alawambe Mosamba of the Ugandan Army, Western Forces. The younger man was Alex Kagamba, up and coming arms dealer and the man who couldn't forget Lisa Aswanela.

Had Brandon Craig known it he may have fainted. But as they passed each other in the front door, Brandon had actually walked by two players in the mercenary/arms/intrigue business. The film convention started in two days.

The titanium and blood red private jet had parked on a remote pad. Two, and only two men had gotten out. One was met by local people and driven away after handshakes. The second man just disappeared.

And the world turned. General Abdul was evermore desperately trying to move MIG-23's and MIG-23 landing gears out of Sudan. Farsi Abbas and Said Alawid were ever more desperate to do the deals before the other could do the deals. Both were also occupied as to whether someone was trying to assassinate them to get business or just to take them out of business. Life was a swirl, it always was in this niche of human activity.

And in Fang, Thailand Mr. Ptorn Chaya was at the top of his game, even as he slid closer to a full-on drug-fueled mental breakdown. He barely had time to complete the last $7 million deal before he dove back into a pile of Colombian cocaine and Burmese meth. His chief bodyguard had randomly killed someone today, so that part of his life was stable. Mr. Chaya's world had evermore become a mix of violence, girls, drugs, girls, weapons, girls, drugs, girls, dead bodies. And in his rants he, like General Abdul, wondered when the crazy man with lots of money would return to Rangoon. Mr. Ptorn Chaya wanted his money and his deals and this man was holding it up. His chief bodyguard would take care of that.

And Mr. Wei of Burma didn't want to cross Mr. Chaya, he just wanted a few arms smuggling scraps to fall off the table. He had a growing choice, do bigger deals or just live. He was leaning toward just live.

And that crazy man from the Strand Hotel, Rangoon, Burma, well he had just checked into a quiet hotel in the Newlands section of Cape Town. Maybe he would be in Rangoon soon or Bogota, or Havana, or even Bulawayo, Zimbabwe. He was just going to rest now, maybe go down to the harbor and remember Lisa standing on the balcony, or just sitting and watching the world go by; the Cape Town harbor was a great place for watching the world go by.

And a day later he did go to the harbor. He was lucky enough that day to see a couple of those rare sights stride by, the slim long-legged girls with thick blonde hair, the blonde girls of South Africa. In between them were the usual mix, three French guys talking fast, then a couple of tourist girls, then two mismatched black guys in which the big black man said, "And when will the arms be delivered," to the tall thin light black man. And the man just sitting there watching caught that information and watched intently as the two men continued to walk and talk. Of the three Frenchmen he noticed two were very thin and good looking, the third looked almost British, and he was. The third man was Brandon Craig.

Ten minutes later one of the three Frenchmen, Javier Henri, was hit by a random thought. The titanium and blood red jet at Cape Town was in fact the same plane he took note of at the Nice, France airport some time ago. It hit like a bolt, was there a connection? This new world of his was both exciting and threatening, but he was so happy to be back to hot showers, manicured gardens and the rich luxury of a suite at the Mt. Nelson Hotel. But was there a connection? The man that was on the titanium and blood red jet that day in Nice, France sat thirty yards away.

CHAPTER 89

In the bright sunlight of Dar Es Salaam, Tanzania General Abdul had landed on one of those endless rounds of "official visits" the world of parasitic politicians dream up to look busy, while doing absolutely nothing. General Abdul knew the useless dance, after all he had been in the real Sudanese Army and in a real hell hole in that fort in the western Sudan.

He shook hands and saluted the usual line of greeters. People in suits who could barely spell their name, but as a third cousin or the son of an aunt of the President of Tanzania they were now a deputy minister of something; layers upon layers of deputy ministers or special advisors taking up space and taking up money. And the money was never enough.

General Abdul knew the drill and had in fact joined the drill. He had two days of official visits, and then there was a three day stop in Zanzibar for a "cultural awareness" tour. Actually, there was only one day of official handshaking and meaningless chit chat; the last two days were set aside for real business, General Abdul's business, MIG-23 business.

It had to be done this way since Said Alawid of Khartoum, Sudan had "people" everywhere, and he lived twenty-four hours a day to make arms deals in Khartoum. Of course Said Alawid did make time to eat, and with extra time he would eat some more rather than bathe. The bath could wait until next week. After all, in 100° Khartoum with the dust, the dirt, the sweat, and the camels, what's the use.

General Abdul knew if Said Alawid knew he had also been talking to Farsi Abbas, then Said would go totally ballistic and shots would be fired. Like Mr. Chaya, Said Alawid wanted all the deals all the time. Now General Abdul was to talk to his own man, Raja Majani of Calcutta, in a place way off the Khartoum map.

General Abdul did check into the Zanzibar Serena before the shallow meetings began. He couldn't wait for it to be over, he was ready to do business for himself.

His convoy left the hotel and rolled slowly south. One hundred yards after they departed they passed Suicide Alley where a one Diane worked. But it was 10 a.m. and she would not be awake yet. She had not "worked" much, as the man named Kent Benson had given her enough to make her life easier for three months.

CHAPTER 90

The official part of General Abdul's day went well enough. But for each hand he shook, he also thought of his meeting with Raja Majani. It was time to get on with personal business, no more time for his country, Sudan.

And it happened the next day, but not in the day. General Abdul spent the day by the pool.

It was set at 7:30 p.m., not in General Abdul's elegant suite or in the hotel's elegant business meeting rooms. It was set in a narrow alley in a tiny room that had been set up by Raja Majani and a local contact. It looked like a perfect place for an assassination. General Abdul had just one bodyguard, he was clearly taking a risk, but he was only going to be there thirty minutes tops. Every minute after that it became more dangerous.

As they navigated the narrow alleys of Stone Town all seemed well, but you never know, each skinny little brown guy draped in robes could be armed to the hilt.

Lots of small people in robes dodging each other in the alleys, but only one was noteworthy, a beautiful exotic girl. Her head was covered, but you could not hide the refined beauty and sexuality in her face. She was long-legged and thin, maybe from Sudan. General Abdul would love to give her a ride home and then ride her, the smell of money always excited him.

The tiny dingy room had a single light bulb and a single fan; a little clay room that looked more like a tomb than a room. This wasn't going to last long. What is it with this business and the tens of millions washing around, that the guys in the business seem to live like scurrying starving rats. Well of course Said Alawid was not a starving rat, he was an obese rat. Tens of millions of dollars and they all seemed to live hand to mouth.

Mr. Raja Majani of Calcutta, India had little good news to report. The money man from the Strand Hotel Rangoon had left no tracks and had not been back. This man was clearly the man for the deal. He would save the time and tedious cheap dealing with the likes of Said Alawid or Farsi Abbas. He was offering three to five times the market price and didn't care. Maybe something else was up here, but General Abdul and Raja Majani didn't care, their plan was simple, take the money and run. An age old plan so true to the human condition. That is why eighty-year-old people line up at the lottery ticket stand every day in Florida, clutching and grasping for money even as they head to the grave, money twenty-four hours a day, seven days a week, and church two hours one day a week. And these people really believe they have religion. They do, it's just not the name of their religion. It's always money 1, religion 0.

CHAPTER 91

Two alleys over from the "arms conference" another drama was playing out. A large fat man had stopped the exotic nomad girl from Somalia. He had stopped her by putting his hand on her throat and pushing her to the alley wall. The robed small people continued to pass taking no notice, after all this happened every day.

The girl did not struggle and let the man put his hand between her legs. He smiled a smelly, greasy smile and kissed her neck. She looked at him and motioned to a yet smaller alley ten yards away, they could go there. The man smiled again.

He led her by her neck to the alley and again pressed his body to hers to keep her penned. As he kept his left hand on her throat, he fumbled with his right to undo his pants, he continued that wild greasy grin. He actually was going to get away with this, with this exotic beauty.

He even felt her hand rubbing his cock. This was going to be special before final evening prayers.

Except her hand was actually the barrel of an expensive Walter P22. She found his cock and pulled the trigger twice. The P22 is not a powerful gun, the bullets are small and relatively slow. But at zero inches into soft sensitive flesh, with lots of blood vessels, it is just as deadly. The gun firing into the flesh made virtually no identifiable sound. The pain was paralyzing. The man had frozen against the wall, so she fired again. Then she slipped to her right along the wall to escape the huge weight of this man, as his face slid down the clay dirt wall. Who knows if he is dead, but in twenty minutes he will be from loss of blood. She decided to leave her mark in her anger, she pressed the P22 between the cheeks of his massive ass and fired again. She floated away into the main alley.

She had done just as the man had said, the man who had given her the gun. Ironically, the man who had given Kent Benson the gun on beachside was an associate of the large fat man with four .22 LR bullets in places that cause extreme pain. His grunts could not be heard, as his face was buried in robes and the dirt. The girl put the gun back behind her right leg and continued to stroll toward Suicide Alley. She had done as he had told her to do, and she could now do it again, the first time is the most difficult they say. It was 7:47 p.m. in the dark and dirty, yet exotic alleys of Stone Town, Zanzibar.

The man who had given her the gun had only given her the gun, he had not given her the silencer. He could not, the silencer was hard to come by even for him. It was not just another silencer, it was a custom-made precision silencer made out of the finest aerospace titanium and it was all titanium, even the threads on bolts to the barrel. It was an exotic sculpture, an exotic deadly sculpture.

CHAPTER 92

The "arms conference" concluded with Mr. Raja Majani getting orders to double his efforts to find the "man from the Strand." Talk to everyone, get the word out General Abdul directed, time was not on his side. Soon the government would know of the MIG-23 inventory and he could not sell the planes for himself.

They left the dingy dirt room quickly and then went over two alleys. They would not go back to the hotel the same way. As they scurried to the hotel, they did pass the alley with a large hump under robes. They took no notice, it was likely garbage or such. They continued through the maze of alleys to the hotel. It had been a good meeting and General Abdul was hopeful. He had not seen the young exotic beauty on the way back; it was a pity, as he was ready for a young sexy girl. And that's the way it was this night at 8:03 p.m. in Stone Town, Island of Zanzibar, East Africa. The town was living up to its billing, it was dark, the alleys narrow and multiple layers of intrigue and mystery were alive and well. As flinty, narrow eyes peered out from dark dirty robes, they saw a lot and would report back. Not many secrets get past the narrow flinty eyes of the alleys in Stone Town. It was 8:07 p.m. as General Abdul re-entered the elegant hotel, only one hundred fifty yards away from the dirty grimy hole of a dirt room where the "arms conference" was held.

CHAPTER 93

Ward Kent and Winston Burton sat at an elegant white-linen cloth table at the Page and Bentley Restaurant. It was 12:57 p.m., 718 Madison Avenue, Manhattan, New York City. Ward Kent was comfortable in his gray Armani double-breasted suit, a black and blood-red power tie, cufflinks by Hermes, shoes by Ascot Livery Custom Boots, Mayfair – London. Winston Burton matched him with his all Savile Row London ensemble by Norton and Gieves and Hawkes. Both nursed their twenty dollar manhattans, where better to enjoy a Manhattan than at a power lunch in the capital of power lunches, midtown Manhattan, New York City. It was 1:07 p.m.

They both ordered the salmon, steamed rice, broccoli, a lobster bisque soup as a starter.

Winston Burton had flown into New York last night. He had two deals and as the pre-eminent international mercenary manager, Ward Kent always loved to see him. He brought great adventure stories, a great knowledge of all the dirty little wars ongoing and . . . it was always profitable for Ward Kent. What is not to like.

They caught up on details of their personal lives, the wives, the kids, the homes, the deals. Winston Burton outlined the general terms of two deals. One was somewhat above board for a government. Word was out that Sudan was looking to re-supply their army post, the one that had been leveled by the rogue black Mirage F-1B. Winston had some word that the strike had been orchestrated by some powerful brokers, but he actually didn't know who. Clearly it was a covert operation by some very capable players. At any rate the Sudanese politicians were looking to restock and were casting a wider net for reliable suppliers, besides the usual arms dealers. Farsi Abbas and Said Alawid would have been furious to know that their Muslim brothers in the struggle against the west, or the east, or each other, were going to some British imperialist Christian named Winston Burton.

But in this world there is little evidence that your "brothers" are your "brothers." It's all hype and marketing. Farsi Abbas is a card-carrying brother of the faith, but that had not stopped him from having Said Alawid's brother laid to rest with a small bullet in the brain that fateful day in Knightsbridge, London. Gaddafi of Libya, Assad of Syria, Saleh of Yemen, all have met their fate in the arms of their Arab brothers. We have met the enemy, and it is us.

Winston Burton felt that the Sudan deal would be north of $95 million. The second deal was a little more covert, it seemed a number of rogue nations were looking for MIG-23's. The MIG-23 was old but it had a low profile in the aviation world and was not seen as a proper threat, like getting MIG-29's or SU-34's. The buyers were below government level, but Winston told Ward Kent he was sure the deal was for some government who wanted them "off the books" and out of international sight. That deal was sized at $30 million plus, with specs and commissions and logistics more like $45 million. In total, Winston Burton and Ward Kent were looking at taking in $15 million each for arranging the financing, the acquisition of the weapons, the delivery, and the testing. Not bad for these guys, it should keep them in their mansions and private jets. Of course they were used to these deals and had other similar ones in the pipeline.

Ward Kent called for the sleek black company Town Car. The pair exited the restaurant on Madison Avenue, took the Town Car over to Park Avenue to let Winston pick up some premium Davidoff cigars at a specialty store, and then they departed for Ward Kent's suite of executive offices on Avenue of the Americas.

They would spend a further two hours discussing the deals and money Winston would eventually need to do the deals. Everything was doable and Winston felt confident the deals would come his way, as these levels of deals need a higher level of professionalism than is available by some of these "third team" players. Farsi Abbas, Said Alawid and Chaya Ptorn would cut Winston Burton's throat in a heartbeat if they knew his attitude.

Ward Kent ended the Winston Burton conference by calling his executive vice president into his meeting room.

"We need to start working on a $150 million credit facility for Mr. Burton," Ward said. "It is best if we could have the credit available within the next five to six weeks," Ward concluded.

"We will start immediately sir, and good to see you again General Burton," the vice president said.

Ward Kent and Winston Burton talked for fifteen more minutes, then Ward called for the special Rolls Royce. The car would take Winston Burton back to his suite at the Peninsula – New York. Tomorrow the helicopter at 34ᵗʰ Street would take him to his Gulf Stream 550, and Winston Burton would be back at his five-story townhouse on Berkeley Square – London in time for a late dinner. His house staff would prepare a Beef Wellington with all the trimmings, and that's how they roll at the top of this food chain, human style. Winston would light one of the $50 Davidoff cigars after supper and relax in his dark wood-paneled opulent smoking room, a cognac please James.

CHAPTER 94

The film festival started on time in Cape Town. The two days in civilized Cape Town had done wonders to settle the nerves of the Nice, France trio of Javier Henri, Pierre Patron and Brandon Craig. However, French intelligence had taken a special interest in the Angola air strike, it was a major shock to them as to what it was about. A small team had been assigned to start a trail to see how this series of events came to be. They had assigned a Didier Francois as their lead agent, and Didier Francois had already had three conversations with Javier Henri via the Paris to Cape Town link. Didier Francois' lead assistant was a Patrice Guiot, who had also talked to Javier Henri.

Javier Henri had started this project to add a little zip to his life and now, ten days later, he had gotten more than he bargained for. Talk about walking off the cliff. He felt he was in way over his head and he was thankful a French intelligence operative was onboard to lead him out of this.

Now Javier Henri and his two associates were wading into a swirl of cinema directors, producers and writers whose stories seemed to deal with African mercenaries and the military intrigue of Africa.

Javier Henri found it fascinating, and the events of the Angola outback seemed now to inspire him since he felt he was now part of the action. The rarified air of the African mercenary, he was sure the movie script was unfolding, as did Brandon Craig.

And let's face it, Cape Town had been ground zero for a number of African mercenary movies. In recent years there was Lord of War (2005), Blood Diamonds (2007), and Safe House (2012), all set in and around South Africa and Mozambique in general, and Cape Town in particular. There was even a recent real-life mercenary story of 2004-2005 when South African mercenaries were caught in Zimbabwe on the way to overthrow Equatorial Guinea, and all of this and more was on display at this small convention.

There were likely more than three thousand movers and shakers at the convention. Javier Henri was in his element, as there were a number of big players that were in the league of Javier Henri. They hit it off immediately, if for no other reason than Javier Henri was desperate for "business talk" after Angola and because the producers and directors in attendance had "profiled" Javier Henri and, most importantly, his money. His money brought the credibility. Javier Henri already had three major meetings set up for his Mt. Nelson suite tonight and tomorrow.

CHAPTER 95

For all of Javier Henri's swashbuckling convention ways, it was Brandon Craig who had stumbled on "the" story. In a corner of the Cape Town convention hall a British writer with experience in South Africa held forth at his own little circle. And as Brandon Craig approached the gathering, the audience had grown to more than thirty. Everyone listening intently to some story this guy was telling.

As Brandon leaned in he caught only bits of the story. What he did catch did have a compelling storyline to it. Something about a man code named "The 4th Mercenary" was the center of the trail that mostly seemed to center on an apocalyptic region called the Eastern Congo. The story seemed compelling indeed as Brandon Craig listened closer, he wasn't sure if it was based on truth or a story developed by this man. It was interesting, maybe an angle Brandon Craig could develop. The man was clearly looking for "investors" in his story.

The crowd cleared and a few left their cards with the man. Brandon Craig was the last to approach. Brandon Craig introduced himself. The man replied, "My name is Todd Blake of Johannesburg." And thus it began.

CHAPTER 96

Todd Blake, that Todd Blake who was the sole survivor of the group developing the novel about "The 4ᵗʰ Mercenary." Jeremy Keeler, Andy Morris, Frank Cramer and Bryan Norton were all dead in the wet, dark soil that is the Eastern Congo. They had left the world quickly and violently, and Todd Blake had been spared only because he had not set foot in the Congo. He had hoped to take advantage of the story with his friend Jeremy Keeler, but now he would carry on alone. He had the story all to himself. But he never knew why the four disappeared, and certainly not "how" they disappeared. If Todd Blake knew "how" they disappeared, he likely would let this story drop. However, he didn't and Brandon Craig asked Todd to come to a private meeting with Javier Henri tomorrow, Suite 327, Mt. Nelson Hotel, Cape Town, Western Cape, Republic of South Africa. Brandon said should he want to pursue it, there would be some money in it for him. That's all Todd needed to hear. Todd was all in at that point. You had Todd, as most people, at "money." The meeting was on.

That night as Javier Henri, Brandon Craig and Pierre Patron walked the harbor side they talked excitedly about the day's events. As they walked, a man was seated on a harbor bench, just sitting. As they walked by Brandon Craig used the term "The 4ᵗʰ Mercenary" and a bit of the story, but the man seated on the bench knew one thing, these three men he had seen earlier were not all French. One was clearly British with that accent. The man seated at the bench did not know that it was he, in fact, who was The "4ᵗʰ Mercenary." They had walked right by him.

If only Andy Morris and Frank Cramer could yell from the heavens. If only Jeremy Keeler or Bryan Norton could have yelled to them, "It's him, you have just walked by him, he is The 4ᵗʰ Mercenary!"

The man seated on the bench soon faded into the night. If anyone had been watching, they would have seen a single man emerge from the shadows, walk with this "4ᵗʰ Mercenary" for five minutes, and recede once again into the shadows. But no one was watching.

CHAPTER 97

He had two more days at leisure in Cape Town. Using a filtered phone he called the one and only Lisa Aswanela. They had a happy and spirited talk. He didn't say where he was, but she said she was going to Cape Town today for three days. The man she knew as Kent only had two days left in Cape Town, so he said nothing.

"I hope to see you soon Miss Lisa," as he said goodbye.

"I do want to see you too Mr. Kent," Lisa laughed, as she said goodbye.

The next evening as Kent sat on a restaurant balcony two levels above the harbor walk, he saw the same three men talking intently. He knew now two were French, tall and handsome, the third British with the look of an intellectual.

Then Kent saw it, at least one of the reasons Lisa had come to Cape Town. She walked arm-in-arm with a one Alex Kagamba, and a sight she did cause along the harbor walk. With her trademark hip huggers, bare midriff and her wonderful stride she did in Cape Town what she did at Mandela Square, Sandton, South Africa . . . she stopped traffic.

Kent smiled to himself, finally he had the chance to see her and the whole package. You don't get this view when you walk with her. She was beyond sexy, at nineteen years old she had become a sultry goddess, and Alex Kagamba beamed in her presence.

And Kent beamed too, as he had enjoyed her and her company for some time, but never got to just watch her from afar.

He also recognized the man, Alex Kagamba. He had been the tall thin light black man walking on harbor side with the large, very black man. The very black man being General Mosamba, Ugandan Army; they had been talking about arms shipments, he remembered well. And now she walked with this man, and then there was the Arab man from the Michelangelo Hotel in Sandton. Maybe a pattern here; not so much that Lisa gravitated toward arms dealers as arms dealers gravitated toward her. Although Kent remembered when she had come to his place on the Upper East Side, Manhattan that she said she did work for South African intelligence, as well as French intelligence occasionally, but not MI-6, British intelligence. That's a pity, she was the perfect Bond girl times three.

Kent was entertained because as Lisa walked within sight of the three men, their reactions were great, a mixture of nonchalance and then staring. The three men couldn't decide what to do. The two tall handsome French men obviously had known beautiful women, but Lisa at nineteen years old, her worldly air, those long firm legs and of course the rear view, well, it took Javier Henri and Pierre Patron to another level. Brandon Craig just watched and admired, it was just way out of his league, way out of his league. He would let the alpha males deal with that.

And so it was that evening at Cape Town Harbor the three men watching Lisa did not know that this stunning, spectacular girl had intimate knowledge of their "4ᵗʰ Mercenary," but she did not know him as "The 4ᵗʰ Mercenary." Now this "4ᵗʰ Mercenary" knew a bit about Alex Kagamba, but not his name. Alex Kagamba knew nothing about Kent, or Code 037, or The 4ᵗʰ Mercenary, or anything. All he knew was he had met an incredible girl that day at the Aston-Martin dealership in Sandton, that suburb of Johannesburg.

And at the end the three men at harbor side had spent two hours with Todd Blake today hearing about "The 4ᵗʰ Mercenary" plot. They knew he apparently existed out there somewhere, but they did not know where. They certainly did not know that as they sat harbor side watching Lisa, that this "4ᵗʰ mercenary" sat two levels above watching them. Of course the man watching two levels above did not know that he was "The 4ᵗʰ Mercenary" either. He worked in a shadowy world, so much so that at times he would not recognize his own shadow.

And so it was this perfect, crisp, light evening in Cape Town harbor. The sun was thirty minutes from setting and the evening crowd gathered for their strolls and restaurant appointments. No one would know all the levels of intrigue being played out right here . . . well, maybe "they" would know; yes definitely, "they" would know.

CHAPTER 98

The tropical sun was torching the riverfront, Rangoon, Burma. It was a still, steamy day and the subsistence population of Rangoon had taken their bicycles and trolleys to the shade of massive trees populating the city since the British colonial times. This was tropical Southeast Asia at its finest, a sultry relentless steam bath, no wonder people go crazy sometimes in this world.

Word on the street was "he" was back, or "he" was coming back. The prying eyes of the street level informants always told a story to get a little money for today and another story to get a little money for tomorrow.

The buzz was on and spread rapidly. It spread to the point that the "big boys" sent some staff into Rangoon. Mr. Ptorn Chaya and a one Mr. Raja Majani had done this. They had done this just as one of the most successful operators, a one Mr. Farsi Abbas, had heard from very discreet circles in Khartoum, Sudan of this possible covert deal. He wanted in but was behind the power curve, he didn't even know who to call, maybe Said Alawid, no, just kidding. Said would help only by putting a bullet in the head of Farsi Abbas; actually, exactly like Farsi Abbas had put a bullet in his brother's head.

CHAPTER 99

He had had no formal name for his short stay in the Strand Hotel, Rangoon, Burma a short time ago; he had left in a hurry. Now, as he strolled the chaotic streets of Calcutta, India "they" had named him Simon Greene and he had the passport to prove it. The passport was issued by the British Colony of the Cayman Islands. Yes, the British still had a colony, several it turns out, like the Falkland Islands of the South Atlantic and Bermuda Island of the North Atlantic. And though it didn't amount to much land, throw in the remote British South Pacific and lots of other outposts and the sun still doesn't set on the British territories.

Simon Greene landed in the dead of night via Air India, Bombay to Calcutta. Simon liked the old British names, not the Mumbai and Kolkata of today. It really didn't matter either way.

"They" had set up only one meeting for Simon Greene and it was two days away. So in the interim Simon Greene strolled the "streets" of Calcutta near his five-star suite at the Imperial Hotel, not far from the Queen Victoria monument. They were streets of swirling masses of humanity crammed ever so densely on the streets of the "formal" city. Outside the formal infrastructure set up by the British one hundred and seventy years ago was the informal city. The informal city was made up of a collection of cardboard, plastic tarp and chicken wire structures set up on bare dirt and extending as far as the eye could see. Calcutta may claim some thirteen million people, but actually no one even begins to know the population. Say it is actually twenty-one million and no one would bat an eye.

The settlements represent the basic subsistence of human life. There is no sewer, no water, only car battery electricity, if at all. The families of six to nine people per 130 square feet exist in a grim world of flies, open sewers, withering tropical heat, overwhelming smells and pollution from charcoal open fires and kerosene lamps, and yet more flies. And for what, no one surely knows, but from meager meals in old blackened bowls these people exist. Live is much too strong a word. They merely exist. And in their deepest misery with barely enough energy to walk down some soggy narrow sewer lane . . . they have ever more babies. With barely enough food to support the energy to breathe, they use that precious energy to have . . . ever more babies . . . to feed evermore the open sewer systems of an apocalypse called Calcutta.

In Simon Greene's neighborhood things were upscale. The families on a Calcutta block could open a seventy-year-old fire hydrant and bathe, and they did twenty-four hours a day, maybe 7,000 people per block. And at night in the formal city of Calcutta where they actually had sidewalks, some three million Calcutta residents would lie down as families to sleep, whole generations born, raised, married and died on the sidewalks.

One of the grimmest city services in the world are the Calcutta city workers who collect those who have died on the sidewalks the previous night. If a figure is still quiet on the sidewalk by 8 a.m., they are likely dead, collected by city workers in bags to be trucked to mass cremations. And with three million sleeping on the streets, thousands are left motionless each morning for collection.

So Simon Greene strolled through this surreal world of living souls, scraping desperately every day to live, but knowing in the end they will merely die someday on these very sidewalks. But in the meantime, they can dream and have their babies. What is a good disaster or famine without starving babies, India supplies them.

And stroll he did. He had started at 10 a.m. and in the blink of an eye it was 5 p.m. The endless people and bustle overwhelmed the senses but provided an endless, if stark stream of images.

Simon Greene strolled three blocks to his hotel. The hotel was situated on the swarming city streets but had developed a center courtyard for taxis and limos to enter, as well as for guests off the street.

And just like that Simon Greene went from the hectic helter skelter chaos of the Calcutta streets to the quiet manicured elegance of a British courtyard, all in a five-foot distance. It was surreal in its own right.

As he sat in these manicured gardens a limousine circled by with darkened windows, an Indian minister perhaps. But no, the man to emerge was Mr. Raja Majani. Interesting, Simon Greene thought, the Raja Majani he had met in Rangoon looked to be less connected than this Raja Majani. Raja may be an independent businessman, but it looks like official India knows and supports him. So he deals with a lot of players and is surrounded by intrigue . . . welcome to the world of the arms dealer it seems. Raja Majani obviously had other contacts today. Simon Greene just took note, he had one more day to rest and observe; maybe the other Raja Majani party would show itself, but likely not tonight, the meeting was on. Maybe Simon Greene would sit in the lobby and read the Financial Times just to enjoy the flow of guests passing by, a stark contrast to the grinding existence he had watched drift by today.

CHAPTER 100

The next morning Simon sat in the courtyard, such a nice place, and then he came. As Simon Greene sat in an obscure part of the center courtyard he spotted a tall slim good-looking young black man come out of the hotel entrance. And there he was, the same young man who had walked by him at the Cape Town harbor with the large black man seeking weapons, and most memorably he was the same man walking with Lisa Aswanela just five days ago in that same Cape Town harbor. Did Lisa know about all of this, it was hard to say. She was very clever and experienced at just nineteen years old. She seemed to be at the center of the vast arms intrigue network, whether she knew it or not.

And this new "player," the tall slim black man, was too young and polished to be connected to this "old money" arms business. But he must be somewhat successful as the Cape Town, Nairobi, New Delhi, Calcutta plane ticket was not being given away, nor was a room at the Imperial Hotel. A standard room went for north of $500, a suite started at $800, enough money for one night to keep two eight member "sidewalk families" living for one year.

The man being left out of these liaisons is the one man everyone needed to watch. That man, Mr. Chaya Ptorn, had continued to do great deals in Burma and Thailand, even as he descended ever more into a drug-fueled world of scotch, cocaine, meth and teenage girls. Over the last month his chief bodyguard had joined him in the drugs and alcohol stupor, and many nights the "partying" meant someone was going to die. Not by overdose, but by a random bullet into a random head, courtesy of the chief bodyguard. And things were getting worse, as the next senior bodyguard had become the "buddy" of the head man and he had taken to the approach from the old Johnnie Cash song, "I shot a man just to watch him die."

As is often the case, just as the drug and arms business is flowing in deals and cash, the head man is quickly and quietly walking off the cliff. Mr. Chaya Ptorn had just somehow stayed conscious long enough to put another $11 million in his account. Even with all the payoffs and overhead he had he still had the money to keep the party going at a high level.

Little did our Simon Greene of Imperial Hotel – Calcutta, Suite 317 know that he was on a path to intersect with Mr. Ptorn, nor did Mr. Simon Greene know how agitated and radical Mr. Ptorn had become because the "man from Rangoon" had not returned to see him and give him the deal immediately. Mr. Ptorn had become obsessed with it, it was the main thing he ranted about before he let loose with a few CAR-15 rounds and fell into a drug-fueled coma at 6 a.m. in the friendly town of Fang, Thailand.

Mr. Chaya Ptorn had become increasingly disruptive and "unreliable," and "they" knew about him and his disruptions. The man from the shadows at Cape Town was sending the Simon Greene of Calcutta right into it. But just not exactly now.

CHAPTER 101

And then it happened. No, not some low level air strike in the Congo or some assassination in Syria, what happened is Mr. Raja Majani met the Mr. Simon Greene, Imperial Hotel – Calcutta, Suite 317, 10 a.m., and Mr. Majani was right on time.

The meeting was cordial, professional and efficient. Mr. Simon Greene crisply outlined his list. First, two complete MIG-23 jetfighters with tandem cockpit (a two man cockpit), and he needed seven MIG-23 nose landing gears plus tires. End of story.

He was looking to acquire the full-up MIG-23 jets at $5 million apiece max and the seven landing gears at $300,000 apiece max. These prices would definitely get the deal done, as the max price was at least two times over the jet price and maybe five times the going landing gear price. Some arms dealers were going to be very happy. Easy money and quickly, maybe time left to shop for the private jet. "They" knew that but "they" also needed the systems, and they didn't need the money. That's probably the most powerful statement someone can make in today's world, "I don't need the money!" It just sounds so irrational in today's world.

They discussed general terms, as well as the need to actually see and fly the MIG-23's. So Mr. Majani must tell Mr. Greene where the jets will be located for testing. The locations could be anywhere: Russia, Ukraine, Angola, India, even old Libya and maybe even Sudan. General Abdul would like that, Sudan. India was out, Mr. Majani was Indian and was not about to deal with the arrogance and greed of his own people. "We have met the enemy and it is us." It never fails in human endeavors.

Of course it was understood the transaction would be "off the books," nobody goes to a private hotel suite to talk buying operational jetfighters. There would be staffs, committees, ministers, endless meetings, certainly not just two men doing the deal in a hotel suite.

Simon Greene said there was no strict timeline, but less than two months was the window. He only wanted to deal with guys who already knew the supply inventory and availability, he was not interested in bank rolling an upcoming arms dealer.

And by the way, Uganda could be a source. General Mosamba of the Ugandan Army, Western Force might get the MIG-23's. Better to fund his own little private army operating in the Eastern Congo. And who would get to General Mosamba first, an unknown Mr. Majani or General Mosamba's African brother, Alex Kagamba. And how would General Abdul of Sudan and General Mosamba of Uganda deal with each other if they found out the other was trying to "steal the deal."

In private arms deals there is little formal etiquette, but the madness does flow along certain organizational lines. Like the African wild dogs, they hunt in packs resembling violent chaos but they always alert their prey with their yelping barks. For the African wild dogs there is no need for stealth or ambush, when they pack up for the hunt they let the world know, and the world knows when they pack up "something is going to die." No need for stealth or ambush, let the world know "something is going to die."

As Simon Greene ordered lunch for them in his suite he had started the wild dogs of the arms dealers yelping, they would start to pack up from this day. Simon Greene and his easy money were the prey.

As lunch was served to Mr. Majani and Mr. Greene in Suite 317, Imperial Hotel – Calcutta, it had just turned 12:17 p.m. The masses outside scraped for bread crumbs in the dirt and inside, fifty feet away, the filet mignon was cooked to perfection. Mr. Majani had a light red wine with his filet.

The next day our Mr. Simon Greene was happy to do a "mission" so relaxed and simple. It was 6 p.m. as the Air India 747 taxied to takeoff, he sat in Seat 7A. He would be in touch with Mr. Majani . . . and others.

The day was winding down and the Indian horizon was turning its usual rosy glow. So beautiful, so tranquil, it's too bad that magnificent color was the product of some two hundred million charcoal fires lit up every day across the subcontinent. And you couldn't blame the peasants, for all of India's brilliance and engineering, there are six hundred million Indians who cannot read or write. So at the end of the day its very likely some of these people don't even know what causes the babies to be born. To them it is likely the wishes of one of the three thousand gods Hindu has, so good luck with all of that.

As the plane roared down the runway, Simon Greene was happy to live in a very small and rare world. It was a world of black and white; no one signed a contract with him until it was black and white, a focused mission, a necessary mission. This man did not belong to a sewing club, a knitting circle, a golf foursome, a booster club. He was always alone . . . but never lonely. He would arrive in London at 7:40 p.m., he settled back with a pineapple juice on the rocks, please.

CHAPTER 102

It had been two weeks they had been away, maybe six days longer than anyone thought. But they had survived it and Javier Henri LeCirac, Pierre Patron and Brandon Craig were ecstatic as they boarded an Air France 747, Cape Town to Paris. Javier Henri had lost his taste for private jet travel in Africa after the nightmare of Angola and that vaporized Dassault 7X. He had spent the most intense adrenaline-fueled two weeks of his life and, as he settled into his first-class upper level seat, he realized that for this 4ᵗʰ Mercenary character this would have been another day at the office . . . maybe even a slow day at the office. If he never set foot outside his office the rest of his life, the last two weeks of adventure would likely do him fine, even if he lived to be one hundred years old. Yes, definitely, that two weeks would hold him . . . for a lifetime.

But he also realized that the Angola adventure, followed by the four-day stop at the Cape Town Film/Writers Conference, had been epic. He and his team had gone a tremendous distance in setting up the script, locations, plots, and characters in his special project to produce a movie. He never expected to make so much progress so quickly and it was all due to this two-week adventure and, of course, due to the fact that everyone was still alive and intact.

Brandon Craig had been brilliant, what a good hire. He had absorbed all the events and put them in the context of a foundation for movie production. He also had kept Kelly Grant and Abbey Bond hopping back in Nice. Every day Brandon had a set list of new tasks for them to research from wardrobe to locations, to even script development. And the girls had been excellent, smart workers. Even as Brandon boarded the Air France 747 he had sent a three-page list of tasks and ideas for them to work on, and he set out a two-day work schedule for them to meet with him on all these issues upon his return. Javier Henri could not have been prouder of their efforts, they were already where he thought it might take eight months since everyone was so new to this industry.

But for all that euphoria, the issue of Angola balanced it out. French intelligence was getting more involved and Dassault had a top team of lawyers and advisors involved. Javier Henri had already had four or five conversations with Didier Francois and his associate, Patrice Guiot of French Intelligence – Paris.

The Angolan events seemed extreme even to French Intelligence. Where had the fighter come from? Exactly what type of fighter was it? Could the Angolan Air Force been involved? Why the devastating attack? Lots of questions, no answers . . . as yet. Since Nice was a beautiful city in the South of France, Javier Henri knew he would be seeing Didier and Patrice grace his palatial office in Nice, if for only the sun and sights. And these intelligence guys had not even seen Kelly and Abbey yet.

And this Todd Blake character, what was that about? Again, Brandon Craig had been brilliant finding that nugget in the swarm of "wannabees," writers, directors and producers, of which they were one. Of course the huge difference with Javier Henri was, and there's that word again . . . money. Javier Henri was one of the few guys there to make a difference because he had the money to do the movie. And after one day at the conference everybody knew that, so Javier Henri had access to as much talent as he needed, and Cape Town had a lot to offer being the Hollywood of Africa. Javier Henri had written a check from his personal account for $17 million to his new production company as a financial base. And that was just the base, money was not going to be an issue for this project. But already his team had been so very efficient, he couldn't believe it.

He and Brandon Craig had spent four hours at the Mt. Nelson suite talking to Todd Blake about the code name "4ᵗʰ Mercenary." Todd had outlined as much as he knew. The big difference in his story was that Andy Morris and Frank Cramer had been working for him, as well as Jeremy Keeler. Todd said the story as developed was true, and that the mercenary Bryan Norton had actually tracked down and seen the "4ᵗʰ Mercenary." Todd also felt Jeremy Keeler, Andy Morris and Frank Cramer had also seen and maybe talked to the "4ᵗʰ Mercenary." Todd had only a brief talk with Jeremy when the team was on the ground in the Congo, and that talk said all was well engaging with the "4ᵗʰ Mercenary." Then all was silent and no one ever returned, and no reports of anything, they just disappeared.

Javier Henri took notes, as French Intelligence would likely be his "buddies;" maybe he could get their take on it.

"And where was this "4ᵗʰ Mercenary" actually sighted?" Javier Henri had asked Todd.

Todd responded, "I have never seen him or heard him described, but our source Bryan Norton clearly saw him in two places and two places only. One was at several locations in Nassau, Bahamas, the other in the jungles of Eastern Congo."

Todd continued, "Bryan was a renowned African mercenary so he had the contacts in the Congo to pinpoint this 4ᵗʰ Mercenary, after that he just happened to spot him in Nassau by pure accident. Bryan had retired there. And as far as your script, you can add as fact that there was a young stunning Bahamian girl involved; light brown skin, light green eyes, long legs, a magnificent girl . . . and Bryan Norton saw her . . . and always talked about her, had talked about her, before Bryan disappeared in the Eastern Congo, as so many people do.

Javier Henri smiled to himself, there is truth to this, maybe, and the "4ᵗʰ Mercenary" is even providing the sexy girls to the story. He liked that, she could be added into the script along with the girl Brandon had seen at Cape Town harbor. The girl had been magnificent and Brandon was no threat at all, so he had talked to her about a movie and she had laughed. Brandon remembered her, who wouldn't. Her name was Lisa, Lisa something, she didn't say anymore.

So, after the meeting Javier Henri asked about the book, script, whatever existed. Todd said he had only forty pages of notes and comments collected at the point the whole project vanished into the Congo. They had been maybe ten percent into the project. Javier Henri decided to pay Todd Blake $10,000 for his notes, as well as to have Todd Blake on as a source of advice and insight. Todd was elated, god did he need the money!

"One final question," Javier Henri asked, "Where did you get your project team?"

"Jeremy Keeler knew Bryan Norton from their history of the African wars. I met Andy Morris and Frank Cramer quite by chance in a bar at the Polana Hotel, Maputo, Mozambique," Todd replied.

Javier thanked him for his time; he would have his staff organize the transfer of documents and the payment of the retainer fee. And that was that, Todd Blake was onboard for another African story. Javier Henri even liked the Mozambique touch, this script might write itself, he thought.

CHAPTER 103

Simon Greene of Calcutta had become the Jason Stoner of Upper East Side, Manhattan, New York City. He walked into his office on the Avenue of the Americas to find his "massive" staff of seven hard at work. It was their firm, he just had his name there but he was hardly there at all. The staff had their own projects.

But sometimes you are lucky, as just the day before Ward Kent had called to ask Jason Stoner to come by. While he was never there, Jason did maintain a nice plush office to look the part in case he had to.

Jason called Ward Kent to say hello and Ward invited him to lunch tomorrow for a two-hour consulting session on his views of the financial landscape, just some brainstorming, informal, no staff, just the two of them. Jason would be there and 1 p.m. was fine.

After the call Jason spent a wonderful two hours reading the financial papers on his desk; well, except for the wonderful orange paper of the Financial Times. Someone had swiped it, so he had the receptionist go down to the Avenue of the Americas, cross the street and actually go into the Financial Times Building to buy a copy of the Financial Times. And they actually had one.

He then started a side adventure. He called an Upper East Side – Manhattan real estate agent, the one and only Christine Alexander. She answered.

It had been some time, so the talk started rather formally. As it progressed Christy said she would like to see how the place turned out from her remodeling some months ago. Jason said fine, telling her he had only been home maybe five days total. She said she knew, as she had passed by many times and still had his key at her office. He laughed and thanked her for looking after everything; it felt good to have a friend in the city. They set the time to meet at 6 p.m., maybe he could buy her dinner. She said yes, she would like that, and the date was set.

Jason left the office at 2 p.m., jogged in Central Park at 3 p.m. and had showered and was sitting at his favorite bay window on East 67th by 4:30 p.m. He read some more and just took in the activity outside the window. So serene now, he just needed a slow mist to finish the day.

Christy dashed from the town car up the stairs to knock on the door at 6:10 p.m. She looked gorgeous, the blonde highlights, the Prada business suit and Jimmy Choo shoes. Jason answered and she stepped in.

He poured some wine as she walked around the place. Jason bragged on her remodeling and she laughed. It had been fun for her.

They sat on the living room couch and Christy's skirt managed to settle about nine inches above her knee, and she did nothing about it.

Fifteen minutes later it didn't matter, as Jason had gently pushed it to her hips. As they kissed and she walked to the bedroom ten minutes later, she was naked from the waist down and still fully dressed from the waist up.

The foreplay led to vigorous sex and with Christy providing much of the energy.

Afterward they lay quiet for thirty minutes and then Christy said, "I'm to be married in three weeks."

Jason said, "That's wonderful, but I don't think I will be invited."

"Not likely, you would stand out so bad, it's a small wedding, mostly family," she replied.

"Well, we have time before then I hope," he said.

"Yes, exactly two more days as he is on a business trip, the last one before the event," she replied.

"Is tomorrow good?" he asked.

"Yes, it is," Christy said, "But right now is good too," and she raised her leg up onto him.

And so it was at 117 East 67th Street, Upper East Side, Manhattan, New York City.

CHAPTER 104

The tension in the room was massive, particularly for the three Burmese men. They had simply gone to give Mr. Chaya Ptorn $300,000 as requested by their boss, Mr. Wei. In return they were to get a receipt and an invoice for the weapons. Mr. Ptorn was to deliver in two days. The $300,000 was so small that Mr. Ptorn went into a rampage on how rich and important he was and how useless they were. They submitted to his long rants that got progressively more violent. The bodyguards snapped the 9 mm rounds into the chambers as Mr. Ptorn became ever more dysfunctional. Mr. Ptorn was incensed Mr. Wei did not come, what disrespect! Mr. Ptorn raged on and on, sweating profusely by now as he had not slept in two days, crystal meth will do that.

Then in a bolt of lightning Mr. Ptorn shot two of the men in the head. He spared the third, but he just did, as the chief bodyguard had already had the gun to the man's head.

Mr. Ptorn told the bodyguard to throw the bodies out the window into the small river running between Tachileik, Burma and Mae Sai, Thailand.

He then told the last Burmese man that he should tell Mr. Wei he was on Mr. Ptorn's list. Mr. Ptorn was taking the $300,000 but Mr. Wei would not get his weapons, just a bullet in the mouth.

And so Mr. Ptorn continued his meltdown, and now there were certain Burmese generals and Shan State warlords who had Mr. Ptorn on their list. Mr. Ptorn had become so delusional and radical he actually thought he was running Burma and Thailand. And so far, he seemed to be right.

As they left the lone Burmese man in the room, Mr. Ptorn turned and fired another round above his head, the poor man just collapsed.

The Ptorn entourage swaggered through the narrow alleys toward their convoy. The chief bodyguard spotted a young drug-fueled thug on their way out and put three bullets in his chest. No reason, the thug had been in the wrong place at the wrong time, simple as that.

And that put Mr. Ptorn in a great mood. As the Ptorn entourage laughed and shouted their way to the waiting convoy of six Porsche Cayenne SUV's, all of the Mae Sai border market froze in quiet fear. They had seen this movie before.

As the convoy roared off, the Mae Sai police, border guards and military also stood in quiet fear. One mile away the convoy hit 70 mph, and they would likely kill some poor innocent street vendor on the way out of town.

On the phone in the lead car the orders were already being given for the liquor, the girls, and the crystal meth. A little more crystal meth and Mr. Ptorn would be awake for two more days. He was only forty-two years old but in full meltdown mode. He sweated profusely and laughed with his bodyguards about the just completed events. No regular laughs, no, laughs more like mental patients, a scary dysfunctional drug-fueled laugh. There would be no Burmese generals or Burmese warlords laughing with them. Theirs would be a cold hard stare. And so it was on the Burma/Thai border, it had been this way for fifty plus years. Another day at the office for the smugglers, killers and bandits of the Mekong golden triangle.

CHAPTER 105

Jason Stoner spent his two hours with Ward Kent in the most opulent of corporate surroundings. Ward Kent's office was massive and sleek. Black marble and titanium accents were everywhere, including what looked to be a titanium paneled desk. And in contrast there were bold blood red accents. And then it hit Jason, those were the same color combinations on the Dassault jet he so often traveled on. A connection? Jason didn't know, but he could ponder that in his subconscious.

His briefing to Ward Kent was just an informal discourse on the financial markets. In essence Jason said the wild, bloated and incompetent trail of clueless politicians and lawyers in charge of the country's budget would lead to a collapse of the health care system as the $700 billion Medicare system would become unsustainable. It could happen in less than five years. The Bush Administration funded two trillion dollar "wars to nowhere" with a trillion dollar tax cut. The shuffling bloated politicians of the Obama Administration have just continued the headlong race for the cliff. These financial actions could be prosecuted as treason in another age, as these actions clearly will destroy the nation, and the old people of the United States would not have it any other way. They are liquidating the society but don't care, they want their votes bought by Medicare and their children and grandchildren can go to hell.

The markets of course will ultimately rule, Jason continued. When the United States wants to borrow ever more money to fund the endless needs of the Peoples' Republic of America, the market will simply say no more to these bloated buffoons whose only skill is to compile a 2,000 page law, which means nothing. The law means nothing, as the government workers can barely read and write, much less manage a 2,000 page law. I mean, the IRS has a thirty percent error rate and yet the same dimwitted buffoons still shuffle off to work. Jason was trying his best not to sugar coat it.

It's hard to know where the cliff is that we are going off. It's certainly within five years, since the United States is "upping" the National debt by $1 plus trillion every six months. That could soon go to a three month cycle, meaning we could accumulate as much debt in an eighteen month period as the country borrowed in the first 225 years of its history. But not a word is spoken about this by either the Socialist Democrats or the Socialist Republicans. Welcome to the Peoples' Socialist Republic of America, it's been here since 1965.

They ended their session with some light banter. The weight of Jason Stoner's brief analysis weighed on Ward Kent, and it was an uncomfortable subject. Jason didn't really care; making the corporate world happy was not his job. These same buffoons dreamed up credit default swaps as a complex financial product when it was the same clueless piece of paper that meant little or nothing to a productive America. It was just self-absorbed MBA's dreaming up some words to chant over the phones, looking busy before they trot off to their $21 margaritas, loosen their ties and actually believe they are the financial warriors of Wall Street. America has been manufacturing self-delusion in epic amounts ever since the baby boomers began their shallow meaningless existence in the 1960's. Jason ended his discussion. They would stay in touch. Jason's financial team owed Ward Kent a detailed analysis in four months or so.

CHAPTER 106

Jason's two hours had actually worn him down. As he descended from Ward's 27th story suite of offices, he also tried to decompress. By the ground floor he actually remembered his "date" with Christy Alexander and that made the difference.

He walked home to East 67th Street from the Avenue of the Americas. The fresh air was wonderful. He would go for a run in Central Park, take a hot shower and wait for her to arrive at 6 p.m.

And arrive she did. It had started to drizzle, so she came in with tight jeans and a Burberry Raincoat. Underneath the raincoat was a Polo Ralph Lauren shirt . . . and nothing else.

They quickly settled down to a light white wine. After two of those she got out of her jeans and he played with her and she with him until she simply got up and put her knees on the chair in the bay window. It was dark out and with no lights on in his townhouse he thought it safe. She simply stayed poised, looking back at him with that magnificent blonde hair.

He only had this night so he made the best of it, meaning they started in the bay window, then to bed and then she slowly walked to the bay window again and mounted the chair, arched her back and waited for it.

She slept over, she really slept over, a dead sleep until 10 a.m., and then she told him in that wonderful sleepy and sultry voice that she had already taken the day off and then fell asleep on his chest.

She began to leave at 2 p.m. to go home and rest up for her fiancée. She kissed him deeply and asked if she could see him after she was married. That was very heavy and she knew it. As he looked at her in silence, he put his hand down her jeans and between her legs. Five minutes later he said yes. Then he pulled her jeans down and kissed her again, and she let him. Then she let him have it all again as if to seal their pack at a new level of lovers, a more dangerous level. She had a lot of sensual beauty to offer and it was all his whenever he wanted it. This day she had decided to cross a "life event" line. It had come to her quickly and spontaneously. She was calm in her decision, it was wrong by society's rules, no question, but she was at peace with her decision. She was calm and satisfied as he got on her yet again. She would sleep hard again tomorrow.

CHAPTER 107

Christy Alexander finally left at 4 p.m., and she was at peace with herself and looked forward to the days ahead . . . and not just her wedding. The black Sotheby's car picked her up on Fifth Avenue at 67th Street on this epic day, Manhattan, City of New York. It was not a bright sunny day, in fact it was gray and drizzling. It didn't matter, her life had changed dramatically. Given the heavy events and the dreary day, she was surprised how bright she felt.

The man in the overcoat standing on the Central Park side of Fifth Avenue saw everything. She was stunning and gorgeous, magnificent legs under her coat, looked to be Burberry or maybe Hermes. He had been waiting since yesterday and now he must wait some more to do his job. Her sighting had helped his long days. If he had been lucky, he could have asked the Burmese Consulate to the United Nations to give the message to the man from 117 East 67th Street when they saw him. After all, their offices were only a few doors down on East 67th Street and this man was headed to Burma. But of course the man from 117 E. 67th Street didn't know it, the Burmese Consulate certainly didn't know it, nor did the poor man sent to deliver the contract. His job was to be patient in the drizzle alongside Fifth Avenue, Upper East Side, City of New York. His best chance to speed his wait would be to spot some gorgeous, long-legged blonde walking down Fifth Avenue and he had just seen that, so he would wait some more.

CHAPTER 108

The harbor at Nice, France looked so peaceful. But behind the tall elegantly draped windows of LeCirac Industries things were at a fever pitch. They had been for almost three weeks now, since the return from the African "experience." Javier Henri LeCirac was amazed each day by how much energy had been unleashed from that winding adventure. It all seemed so surreal, who could possibly live that life. Todd Blake made the case that somehow "his" team had documented a real life guy termed "The 4ᵗʰ Mercenary" that appeared to have some strange existence. But now there appeared to be no one alive who had actually seen "The 4ᵗʰ Mercenary." Although unknown to anyone here, there was a certain young man who at the time was buried deep into the Congo jungle at a mercenary base who had helped Bryan Norton, and with Bryan Norton's help he had identified "The 4ᵗʰ Mercenary." And that young man was Trent Burton, the son of the one and only towering "Mercenary CEO" of Burton International, Winston Burton. He had left the Congo soon after the executions of the four people: Jeremy Keeler, Andy Morris, Frank Cramer and Bryan Norton. And when he left he had no clue that his idol Bryan Norton had been executed. He was clueless to this day, and his father would keep it that way. Trent Burton had returned to work in London and on this day had started his five-day vacation by stretching out on a lounge chair . . . overlooking Nice harbor . . . maybe one hundred yards from Javier Henri's magnificent office. If Javier Henri had known, he could have simply walked down to that lounge chair and said, "So tell me about this 4ᵗʰ Mercenary, what does he look like?"

But Javier Henri didn't know. And he would be even closer to the answer in yards two hours later when Trent Burton slowly walked back to the hotel and passed right under Javier Henri's window, just as Javier Henri was gazing out those very windows pondering the riddle that appeared to be this 4ᵗʰ Mercenary.

CHAPTER 109

Brandon Craig had proved to be brilliant. He had orchestrated his small team into a creative dynamo. He was so quiet and unassuming, but so brilliant and driven. He had kept everyone humming and not on humdrum small tasks. He had kept everyone thinking about all creative angles, major pieces to the formation of the movie. Javier Henri had seen this and had asked Brandon if he needed anymore staff. Brandon had said no, not at all. He had all he needed, as they were very smart and energetic, and to add staff now might slow them down. Javier Henri did insist Brandon get an administrative assistant to keep the calls and tasks under control. Brandon did agree to that.

The two weeks he had spent in Africa had been life altering. It had been like being on a very large movie set, but set in real life. The sights, the smells, he remembered it all. And burned in his memory were two instances he would surely capture in the movie. First there were the two tanned and hard men he had spotted in Libreville, Gabon, just classic mercenary type guys. The second was that incredibly sexy South African girl in Cape Town. The low-slung jeans just above her ass and the stride of her long legs, a great "female interest" profile. He actually planned to angle his way back to Cape Town just to try to find her. He would have to go again clearly for further "research." God, she was a goddess! But the movie was everything to him, and what a magnificent opportunity had come his way!

CHAPTER 110

Brandon's two assistants, Kelly Grant and Abbey Bond, had proven to be wonderfully creative, well-spoken and particularly focused on the job. They created on all levels, from costumes to locations to scripts, and he let them fire away with their ideas, most of which were useable.

As for Kelly and Abbey, they too realized this as too good to be true. They had a magnificent opulent lifestyle in the apartments, location, the maids and the chefs; all they had to do was just focus on their very interesting work. How does this happen to two stunning twenty-year-old's? They knew their luck and just made sure they did good work.

There were no boyfriends. Each had kept the other company, although they had gone to a new level of sexuality. They were aware of the men, but just not ready to get on that rollercoaster of hormones. They each had talked about when "it" might happen, and that innocence provided the excitement. Each had talked about how "it" might happen, and they even captured some of the thoughts for the movie, but they did not capture the most erotic thoughts. They just talked about those and those thoughts were the best when they had finished their day, taken a hot shower, and lounged around the apartment. Laying around mostly in just panties each girl only had the beginnings of a chest, just small tight breasts . . . no need for a bra. Basically two tomboy figures, very small hips and shoulders, long legs, small tight breasts, and very long blonde hair, each with the long "swan" neck of the nubile girl. They were clearly late blooming and now had the education to be more disciplined in the sexual arena. "It" would happen, it's not like its brain surgery. I mean, there are twelve-year-old illiterate girls in Bangladesh who have had sex. The act itself is right up there with drinking a glass of water, the richness comes with the complexities and the adventures of the interactions. And most people get those very wrong because that does take talent.

If somehow a camera could have captured it, it would be priceless. Two innocent young beauties lying on a couch, slouched in a chair, sitting cross-legged on the floor, or draped over a chair with legs casually flung over an armrest, the stuff of legends. And with it some talk of erotic adventures with men, followed by girlish laughs, innocent laughs. Make that DVD and most porn shops will go out of business. Most conversations ended with Kelly talking about her knees on an elegant chair and holding the back of the chair. That would be good, she thought.

And at the end of the day between their script scenes and Brandon's capturing the real life drama of Africa, they had managed to assemble 150 pages of script, scene description and character development. Not bad, and there were probably another 150 pages ready for production, as the outlines had become quite mature. Lots of work, but so much fun for the two young girls, and they were just starting to think about costumes and wardrobes.

This weekend Kelly would take Abbey in her black Porsche turbo to the Monaco harbor for the sidewalk cafes and some strolls along the harbor. Life is neither fair nor just, these girls proved it!

CHAPTER 111

And then there was the Sudan, Western Sudan, and then the subject of the Dassault Mirage F-1B jetfighter in Chad just over the border from Sudan. Javier Henri flinched and swallowed hard at the thought. Did he dare try another "expedition" to Africa after Angola.

He had learned that his aviation team had completed the repair parts for the jetfighter in Chad. He was hoping they hadn't finished so he could delay the agony of the "decision" to go or not to go. He let that go for yet another day. The parts had not been sent to Dassault as yet.

The plane itself still sat in that miserable hanger baking in the relentless sun of the Sahara. It had been closed up since that fateful day, except for French Air Force personnel checking on it every few days. Four French Foreign Legion troops were on station at all times. It was a curious situation that a beat-up F-1B jetfighter, in a miserable beat up hanger, by a miserable beat up dirt runway, in an endless expanse of miserable scorching land would be treasured this much. Why is that? The guards accepted this situation and had in fact joined the Legion just for this type of adventure and intrigue. Something was going on and they were "lucky" enough to be at "ground zero" for military intrigue. If Brandon saw these guys, they would go in the movie, textbook military adventurers, hard, lean, tanned and the stone-cold stare of killers, just legitimate killers for France on a formal military leash. Taken off the leash they become textbook African mercenaries.

To add to this intrigue Javier Henri had been visited by French Intelligence in the person of one Agent Didier Francois and one Agent Patrice Guiot. Javier Henri knew they would come, Nice was just too sexy and glamorous. He only hoped the two agents didn't spot Kelly or Abbey in the hallway. If they did, they surely would think they had been swallowed up by MI-6 British Intelligence and were in the middle of a real life James Bond movie, which maybe they were. With Kelly taking the Porsche turbo to Monaco harbor and Javier Henri planning to drive along the French Riviera this weekend in his Maserati, who knows, maybe they were. I mean, within thirty minutes Javier Henri would phone his personal chef for tonight's menu and wine order, and there was Pierre Patron, his French jetfighter pilot in residence, the private jets, the young girls strolling outside and, of course, back to Kelly and Abbey, stunning, sexy young girls walking the halls, I mean maybe all of this is too surreal and life has become the movie. After Angola, Javier Henri had a hard time grasping life.

The French agents did not disclose much, but it was clear that forces well outside normal were operating. They had established the plane belonged to the Abbas brothers and that they were known by French Intelligence as arms dealers. So the plane and an explosion could be explained, but this was likely an air intercept with a powerful air-to-air missile, and then the attack on the investigating team by yet another unknown jetfighter. That set of circumstances had quickly gotten them out of their "league." Who were these "big boys?" The Abbas brothers were still alive, and that part of the mission must have failed, but it just wasn't clear what was going on.

Javier Henri did not tell them about the Mirage F-1B in Chad. At least not yet, he would think about that.

CHAPTER 112

The patient man on Fifth Avenue had made his contact. It was at 7 p.m. the next evening, as one Jason Stoner strolled on Madison Avenue at 72nd Street. They had shaken hands, did their "good to see an old friend" routine, and then they passed, it had taken less than five minutes. The man disappeared west on 72nd Street, and at Fifth Avenue had gotten into a black Bentley limousine; it looked to have had the bulletproof treatment.

Jason Stoner had become Code 015.

Two days later a town car pulled up to the 34th Street heliport and a single man with one soft sided duffle bag got aboard.

The helicopter landed thirteen minutes later at a hanger at JFK International Airport. A black Range Rover picked the sole man up and drove him to a distant hanger. It was drizzling rain and foggy and as they approached the hanger, it emerged slowly from the fog. "It" was the dull gray B727-100 that had been transformed into a special war machine. It had hard points with weapons attached that were camouflaged to look like fuel tanks. The men were arming the weapons as Code 015 approached. He had missed the old war horse. Probes, antennas and weapons were all strapped to this monster. It was the end-all of airplanes and it was good to be "home," Code 015 thought.

He still remembered the dives and barrel rolls it had done to evade ground-to-air missiles in the Sahara a while back. What a ride, what an adventure! This was going to be exhausting, Code 015 knew that. This war machine did so many missions at once, all the while taking some poor operatives on yet more missions. The ultimate war machine and welcome aboard sir.

CHAPTER 113

One hour later Code 015 was strapped into his seat like he was in a jetfighter. And a good thing, it seems, as the large gray machine lined up on the runway taxied slowly and then came to an abrupt stop. Code 015 rocked forward in his seat.

Then nothing, just the high-pitched whine of three very powerful engines strapped to a plane built fifty years ago. Then the roar of three afterburner military jet engines, likely off the B1-B bomber, launched the B727-100 in short order. Even with the weapons it was likely at only thirty percent of gross weight. It lifted off at a 45-degree angle, and five minutes later it was escorted by three F-15 jetfighters who just wanted to see it up close and at work. It had to be a thing of raw beauty. After ten minutes the jetfighter escorts peeled off to return to base. And here we go again, Code 015 thought, as some flight crew member brought his pineapple juice on ice.

Six hours later over the Atlantic in the middle of the night a large air tanker came alongside the B727-100, and the plane dropped back to fill up. It likely just wanted to top off the tanks, as it had a range of ten hours. And the monster gray plane flew on and on . . . and on.

The sun rose to a blinding scorching torch, nothing like a twelve-hour flight and then to wake to a blistering sun. A five-star breakfast was available, but Code 015 wasn't eating. And just as well, because forty minutes later the B727-100 went into its patented 45-degree dive, then a 60-degree bank to the right for three minutes and a 40-degree bank to the left for one minute, then another plunge of 10,000 feet. What a brute of a plane and hats off to the flight crew handling this monster like it was a nimble little L-39 fighter.

They were lining up for something and then that roar of roars, the center tail stairs had lowered. Good luck to those operatives stepping out into this blistering void. They would be welcomed by mountains of sand and likely 120-degree temperature. The altitude now was likely 20,000 feet, once the roar stopped the plane buttoned up and roared back up to 41,000 feet or so. Code 015 would love to meet the flight crew some day and see the flight deck.

CHAPTER 114

They flew to the east for three more hours with no drama. Then suddenly, and it always seemed to be suddenly in this Apocalyptic Plane, they started descending. Not a smooth shallow descent, of course not, it was a spiraling bank of sixty degrees. Down and down it swirled. But from 41,000 feet it still took time at 10,000 feet per minute. This puts a lot of stress on the plane, but this plane was clearly built for it. He wondered if there were more of these; what a sight to see, four or five of these dark gray special military monsters lined up.

Down they spiraled until at maybe 1,500 feet they stopped the spiral and plunged to maybe 300 feet. Only at that point did things level out, but the massive roar of the engines would still cause great alarm to anyone in this plane. A standard issue American civilian would have already had a stroke for sure.

There seemed to be nothing around and certainly nothing to land such a plane on. And then suddenly the hard-caked ground met the plane with a tremendous thud, the rocks being thrown up under the plane. Then the brakes and the air spoilers, and then more brakes and more brakes, dust and rocks everywhere.

It suddenly hit Code 015, all he had to see was that dilapidated hanger . . . was it here?

As the plane slowly turned to go back down the runway, Code 015 sat up straight, alert for the first time in a sixteen hour mission flight from hell.

As they taxied for three minutes, Code 015 continued to search along the runway. He saw some nondescript small square buildings, but that was not the key.

Then it appeared, and it was the same hanger. If Code 015 wanted to show how smart he was he would have passed word to the crew to ask how the repair of the Dassault Mirage F-1B was coming along. However, in this business you never show how smart you are or what you know.

Was this his mission? He didn't think so, but maybe things had changed in sixteen hours. They likely had.

But the flight crew member came quickly to tell him to stay put. Code 015 did see three men exiting the plane, but not the hard military types, just men in their forties, more like technicians. They walked slowly to a small square building. And if Code 015's memory was right, there was a tunnel connecting that building to the old hanger thirty yards away. The hanger itself looked sealed and likely had not been opened since Code 015 had pounded the jet into this hard as brick runway upon that mission completion. That seemed like years ago but was probably only two to three months ago at best, he couldn't tell you. He took it a day at a time, a mission at a time, you really couldn't do it any other way.

Clearly Code 015 wasn't going anywhere this day, his small cabin compartment had been locked, he had checked it.

CHAPTER 115

It was 1 p.m. in Eastern Chad, no more than fifteen miles from the Sudanese border. It was likely 120 degrees outside, if Code 015 remembered those days. However, the plane apparently had some super auxiliary power onboard, as his cabin was only maybe 95 degrees.

One beat up truck had pulled alongside the plane, and Code 015 could hear freight of some description being offloaded. The men doing the unloading were French Foreign Legion. The cargo was not too large, toolboxes, small packages, and then one piece two feet by four feet plus. It was professionally packaged and based on the curvature of the package, it was clear to Code 015 . . . it was a replacement panel for one wounded Mirage F1 jetfighter. Code 015 would say he was sorry if he could.

And if he could see the small label still attached to the big piece, he could have made out the name LeCirac Industries, delivery to Dassault Aviation. But Code 015 could not see the packing label.

Then the cargo door was shut and Code 015 saw at least three crew members slowly inspecting the plane. A rock or a dent in the wrong place and this plane could be grounded. Taking a plane like this onto this runway in these conditions was very risky, but what else was new. This was not Southwest Airlines between Portland and San Francisco. If it was, this flight crew would not be there.

The sun beat relentlessly on the dark gray plane. If it could, it needed to leave within thirty-five minutes before the next spy satellite came over. This gray Apocalypse Plane would stand out like a white guy walking through the Lagos, Nigeria street markets.

And all movement had stopped outside the plane. Code 015's view was of a tortured, bright tan, scorching hot collection of sand piles with the occasional rough rock thrown in. The view itself was apocalyptic, like a hydrogen bomb had leveled the area. One great photo would have been this legendary plane parked in the stark ruins of the land of Eastern Chad. But no one was going to take any pictures, not even the spy satellites, the engines had started their whine.

It is likely the crew would try to launch in any case, as a stranded B727-100 on this airstrip in this location would have been the absolute nightmare, an absolute nightmare.

The key was to get this brute in the air as soon as possible, as one rock thrown up into the plane in the wrong place could be major trouble.

The plane taxied slowly so as not to throw up unnecessary sand. But taxing slowly when you knew the spy satellite was coming was its own torture.

As it hit the end of the runway it turned around, and with little warning it lit up the afterburners. They held the brakes until power built up, then released the brakes. The plane shot down the runway and lifted off the hard clay quickly, and everyone crossed their fingers. Was everything still functioning, were engines still at high power, or had they ingested sand that would grind them into malfunction and send this plane into a fiery death plunge?

Everything worked this time. And the gray warplane of the apocalypse had escaped one of its most dangerous missions, and that was simply landing and taking off on one wretched unforgiving runway in easily one of the most wretched and unforgiving places on the face of the earth. It had lived to fly another day. A lot of people would heave a sigh of relief to risk this plane in those conditions . . . well, something special was back there. And it wasn't Code 015's mission this time, he rode on with the Apocalypse Plane, just not sure where.

And far away from this nightmare of harsh hard land and relentless scorching heat, a man made a phone call. He made the phone call from a luxurious, elegant environment with a glamorous backdrop and a palm-lined harbor. The man was Javier Henri and his call was to Dassault Aviation. He was told politely by a Dassault Senior Vice President that Dassault had been informed that no onsite visit would be necessary, which meant no onsite visit would be allowed. The Vice President continued that all LeCirac parts were excellent and that payment in full would be next week. They could have lunch soon to talk business, Javier Henri agreed.

Javier Henri was relieved he actually would not be allowed to go to some bleak spot in Africa. He wasn't sure he would survive it.

As he gazed out his magnificent office at the flotilla of yachts, he thought of his movie project that was progressing so well, and in another world a man reclined in a large sophisticated warplane heading south further into violent Africa. Javier Henri wanted to make the movie, Code 015 was living the movie in real life.

CHAPTER 116

General Mosamba, Ugandan Commander – Western Forces was back in Cape Town. He liked Cape Town, who wouldn't? It was the most beautiful civilized city in all of Africa. Ironically, it had never been part of black Africa. When the Dutch came in the 1600's they found no one, and it was not until the 1800's when they had pushed far, far to the east did they meet the Zulu's and Xosha's. Cape Town had remained a very European city and General Mosamba enjoyed its treats, including the great restaurants and the young black girls who came here from all over Africa, just like American girls go to New York or Los Angeles to meet a guy who can improve their life. They don't go there to improve some guy's life, that's against the code and it's too much trouble.

On this day it was special for both General Mosamba and the upcoming arms dealer, a one Mr. Alex Kagamba. Today was much more special for Alex Kagamba, it was almost as if he was new to the world. He felt so alive, so magnificent. Sure his business was prospering, thanks to the orders for General Mosamba's "off the books" private army in northeast Congo, but that didn't begin to cover the glory he felt. No, this was different.

For as he left his condo this morning, he had left a one Lisa Aswanela smiling and quite naked in his bed. As he walked to his BMW to meet General Mosamba, he also got a sexual jolt as he walked by the Aston-Martin that Lisa had parked at his place. She was beyond sexy and charming. It was hard to imagine a girl so stunning, and she had ended up in his bed and was very energetic about it; all this at nineteen years old, quite surreal . . . and wonderful.

His latest deal with General Mosamba was well on its way. But the spectacular day did take a little bump in the road when General Mosamba told Alex Kagamba that the second of their two deals would be delayed. He was honest with Alex only because it was to the General's benefit and meant, that word again . . . money.

General Mosamba was going to sign the first deal today for $1.3 million. Relatively small, but at Alex Kagamba's level, very lucrative. Maybe he could get an Aston-Martin to match Lisa's. The thought of Lisa and last night got Alex upbeat again.

The second deal would have to wait a week or so, as he had to meet someone in Johannesburg. Read between the lines and there is another player here. Alex Kagamba knew this could be a tricky profession, but the excitement was there and now Lisa, so he maintained his cool with the General. Alex said maybe they could meet after next week to go over the second deal again. General Mosamba liked that idea very much, a return to Cape Town, but he would have to return to Uganda to keep suspicions down. He would make up a "ministers meeting" excuse to return to Cape Town. Then he would select his vendor for this round of arms. His private army in northeast Congo, Itreu District, was starting to pay off and he wanted to expand the number of boys in his units by at least seven hundred, no matter if he had to kidnap them, which was actually the only way to go with that number.

Alex and the General again retreated to the harbor side for their lunch and their usual stroll along the harbor. General Mosamba invited Alex to Uganda to see his little enterprise. Alex said yes, but was hoping not to go.

Alex couldn't wait to return to Lisa, who by now was likely stretching her long firm legs out on his terrace with his shirt on, just his shirt on.

And she was doing just that.

And one other thing, she was taking the call from Farsi Abbas, he would be in Sandton next week and wanted to know if she could she join him. Yes, Lisa said, knowing it would likely be just four days, and if he was happy, another $120,000 in her account. She would sleep in his bed, but there was likely to be no sex, just sleep. Unlike in Alex's bed last night when there was little sleep. She ended the call and dozed off on the terrace, quite an erotic sight.

CHAPTER 117

And so it was, Farsi Abbas had leased a private jet and was in the market to make a purchase. He was heading to Johannesburg for four to five days, then back to Mayfair – London to visit a little boutique shop that helped individuals procure $70 million toys. The insurance money had arrived quickly, it seemed the insurance company wanted to settle quickly and get this off their books. It seemed someone might have advised them on the nature of this murky world, and they would not be insuring Mr. Abbas' next private jet, so they settled quickly. Mr. Abbas was very happy about it until he thought about it, then he thought other forces were at work. He didn't know what was up, but his life had become stable and dull after the Syrian assassination, so he felt it wasn't about him.

Seeing Lisa again would solve a lot of his worries. He couldn't wait to get her in bed and have sex this time.

CHAPTER 118

So Lisa left the bed of Alex Kagamba in Cape Town to rip her Aston-Martin across South Africa to join Yassar Abbas in his bed. In the age old dance, the females just show up and the males lose their mind. Solid, smart, meticulous, successful men see her and her tight ass and long legs and become little boys, lost little boys.

Because she had spent almost two years with Farsi Abbas, she knew what he did and she knew where the money came from. And because she knew what he did, South African Intelligence knew and . . . French Intelligence knew, as one Didier Francois had called the Johannesburg French post and their "sources" provided the information on one Yassar Abbas <u>and</u> his vaporized plane over Angola. They knew he had sent the plane for Lisa Aswanela. That's what they paid her for. They had no idea who blew it up, no idea at all.

Lisa met Yassar Abbas at his regular two-bedroom suite at the Michelangelo Hotel. And she let him have some fun, posing for him in just a G-string and t-shirt. Middle Eastern men tend to be even more clueless than most, living in their manufactured world of sexual repression. Of course Lisa was something to behold, so it's understandable.

She led him to the bedroom naked where he "finished" before he could even start, but Lisa was still naked beside him, so he thought it was real; men and their relentless delusion. Alex Kagamba would be furious at this situation, Code 015 never flinched. It was not important for him.

CHAPTER 119

And on the third day they met the one Mr. Abbas and the general of the western forces, Ugandan Army General Mosamba.

It was their first meeting but General Mosamba liked the Farsi Abbas style very much, particularly after introductory cocktails at the Michelangelo lobby when Mr. Abbas ordered the Rolls Royce to come and take them to a secluded lunch. Alex Kagamba could not match that. General Mosamba was going to sit back and enjoy the ride.

And Mr. Abbas didn't disappoint. The restaurant, called Club 31, had a five-course meal set up with fine wine and premium Cuban cigars by way of Havana on hand. It was all so marvelous.

And General Mosamba was playing his cards, but in his head only. He was going to re-juggle his contract awards. Mr. Abbas was from the Middle East and Muslim and Alex Kagamba his African brother, so he was going to give his "brother" a little of the contract only to help him, the perks of Mr. Abbas were too good so far. He had $2.1 million in contract two, so he would give $400,000 to Alex Kagamba right away and a little slice to Mr. Abbas of $1.7 million, enough to pay for the gas on his Rolls Royce. General Mosamba had funds for an $8 million contract coming if his covert militia troops in the Congo, Itreu District, could rape and pillage the way he expected them to. He had copper and cobalt mines that should provide him with $10 million, and he needed to "invest" at least $8 million more to upgrade his firepower. He had set his sights on three more mining areas that he would have to "acquire," which means through the barrel of the gun, such were the ways of the Congo.

General Mosamba played his "humble" card, saying he was not in Mr. Abbas' league but would like to consider him as a supplier if Mr. Abbas had the time for him.

Mr. Abbas laughed, thanked the General, and said there was always room for the General. And there was because there was always room for money at the table. Mr. Abbas had never "done" Africa, particularly "black" Africa, but if there was money, he wanted to be in the room and he had heard there was money afloat, and he liked dealing with Generals rather than some rogue militia group.

For dessert Mr. Abbas recommended the ice cream with fresh strawberries. But the real dessert arrived as dessert was served. Lisa Aswanela had been asked to drop by at that time just to say hello and completely overwhelm the General. And she did in five-star spades.

But Mr. Abbas made it clear quickly that Lisa wasn't available, but maybe Lisa's friend Sarah would be. General Mosamba immediately accepted, sight unseen, but now he really had decided on Mr. Abbas, and being an arrogant African General he had also decided on Lisa. But that could wait until later when the money was bigger. Yes, Lisa was the ultimate goal. What a wonderful trip, great business and this absolutely stunning girl.

Lisa smiled at the General and excused herself. She turned to Farsi Abbas to say Sarah would call him to set up the details.

The throaty roar of the Aston-Martin of Lisa leaving was heard in the restaurant. The two men laughed, that was Lisa in her Audi R8 Mr. Abbas said. It wasn't though, Lisa had never told him about the Aston-Martin, he wasn't important to her.

She navigated the back streets of Sandton. She would stay at her townhouse tonight and pretend to let Mr. Abbas have more time for business.

About one mile from the restaurant her phone rang, it was one Mr. Alex Kagamba, he missed her. She laughed and said she had enjoyed the weekend also.

CHAPTER 120

As General Mosamba and Mr. Abbas were winding down the evening with a raspberry Mojito, Havana style, a raw and massive Apocalyptic gray plane was finally ending its relentless series of missions by slamming into a foggy rain-soaked runway in the Eastern Congo . . . the professional, very deadly, mercenary's camp buried in the valley of the rugged mountains.

Code 015 was beyond exhausted, and he could only imagine how tired the crew was. It was likely there were three separate flight crews and this mission had burned them all out, so the plane had to stop. And this was a good place to stop, deep cover in the heart of darkness.

Code 015 recognized the base as they taxied in the night. He was told he needed to stay in his compartment for ten minutes, then he could leave by the rear stairs in the tail. It seemed at least seven men got off before him, but who knows.

He was groggy and wasted. Two armed men met him and drove him to the same area and tent he had stayed in on the last mission. The tent had two subdued stars on the outside, a mercenary major general. Was this the place for the mission? He didn't know, they would tell him soon enough, hopefully after he had slept seventeen plus hours.

By the time Code 015 had collapsed into his tent bed in the wet primitive Congo, Mr. Abbas and General Mosamba were on their third Mojito and Lisa's friend Sarah had joined them. General Mosamba was disappointed Lisa did not return, it was no matter for now as he had Sarah, a fine young woman herself. He would wear her out.

By the time the General was immersed in his fourth raspberry Mojito, his best young guns in the Congo had overrun a militia camp outside their territory. The young meth-fueled teenagers laid waste to all thirty-five militia soldiers, executed forty-one villagers, and raped seventeen young girls. They had then raped the teenage girls all together and would march them back to their base as sex slaves and cooks. Doubtless many young drugged boys would be shot among them in their race to get to the girls again. Awe, the beauty of mother nature.

Getting wobbly and toasted in a fine five-star Sandton restaurant, General Mosamba received a call via his satellite phone. He listened to his trusted "Colonel," a twenty-three-year old veteran who had side stepped the drug feast to become a trusted officer. All was good news, they had expanded their territory and were within seven miles of the mining concession where the real money was. The General was delighted and said he would return shortly.

The General was drunk and happy. As his ride to the hotel pulled away, Mr. Abbas looked in the car and saw the General already had his hand up Sarah's dress. She relaxed and let him. She actually had one high heeled shoe on the front seat, maybe she liked the General, a very black and very large man.

Mr. Abbas called for his Rolls Royce and was very proud to have a new customer, his first in black Africa. Maybe he could sell weapons to General Abdul to fight General Mosamba, and weapons to General Mosamba to fight General Abdul. With the Dassault insurance money and a fresh $7 million from recent deals, he was ready to go private jet shopping. That meant a trip to London, he would take Lisa. His only disappointment this evening was that Lisa had messaged she would see him tomorrow.

CHAPTER 121

Mr. Abbas woke up and missed Lisa. Christy Alexander woke up in her small New York apartment and missed Jason Stoner, Code 015. She couldn't miss her fiancé, she saw him every day. Alex Kagamba woke up and also missed Lisa. General Mosamba woke up and thought of Lisa, even as Sarah lay next to him. Code 015 woke up and thought of nobody, he was still exhausted and did not know the next mission. He went outside to exercise for thirty minutes, came back into his tent, ate a sandwich from his kitchen, and fell into bed again with no thoughts of anyone.

The next day he had recovered some and walked around in his compound. And for the first time he recalled his previous trip to this covert camp. Only now did he recall the strangeness of the two young men (Andy Morris and Frank Cramer) coming to talk to him, and they had done it two days in a row. His life tended to be a little high octane, so these memories were only triggered by his return to this very camp. His flight missions had been so intense and his departure from base so abrupt he barely remembered the events. Still, it all seemed so unusual in a base so controlled and in such a covert location that their appearance was a mystery. And very clearly, they were not mercenaries in any manner. Very strange, Code 015 thought and then fell into bed again, thankful only that for two straight days no one had come to "visit" him. He fell asleep praying for a third day. It was 1 p.m. in the relentless wet and violent Eastern Congo.

It was noon at the elegant harbor of Nice, France and Javier Henri had just gotten off the phone with Todd Blake.

Ironically, as Code 015 was lying down, the telecom signals passing overhead between Johannesburg and Nice had their origin with the two young men Code 015 was puzzled over. Todd Blake had provided more detail to Javier Henri and Brandon Craig about The 4ᵗʰ Mercenary novel, but a lot of the story Todd had to invent because Andy and Frank never returned from their research trip. But based on Jeremy Keeler's input to him before all went silent, it was clear that Andy and Frank had not only seen but had spent some time talking to this 4ᵗʰ Mercenary. Then all went silent. It didn't take a genius to fill in the details. After all, this was the Eastern Congo. But the input was good, and Brandon could run with it. Brandon said he had the bulk of what he needed from Todd Blake but thought an additional $10,000 to keep Todd available for a bit longer wouldn't hurt. Javier Henri was happy to do that, Brandon had become a very trusted asset to his movie team. The script, descriptions, costume design, locations, etc. had reached 350 pages. Everyone was having the time of their lives, oh to be young again! Hard work, but fun work, particularly for two twenty-year-old's who were just experiencing the world.

CHAPTER 122

Six hours later at 7 p.m. Code 015 was up and sitting in his safari chair outside the tent, just sitting there trying to wake up from a long hard sleep. He was recovering, the energy was returning. The camp had become muted with the setting sun and the usual low lying clouds.

From his vantage point at the western end of the runway he noticed the landing lights of a small plane emerging from the clouds to the east. Nothing unusual, a few planes a day always came and went, and on intense days the jetfighters would emerge to do their business. The jetfighters were much more rare, as their presence meant some serious violence might soon disturb the low level of terror, and violence was so common among these poor people.

The plane touched down, a Caravan 208 seating nineteen people, but only eleven were onboard. It was coming out of Kigali, Rwanda on a special run for a one Trent Burton and assorted staff. Trent Burton had spent time at the mercenary camp, in fact thirteen straight months, much to the distress of his father, Winston Burton, the big cheese for this whole camp and the CEO of Burton International. Trent was returning for a staff visit to ensure the camp still ran to his high standards. Winston Burton used the camp plane for his son to avoid the random violence on the road from the Rwanda border. Every overland supply convoy seemed to have to fight its way through the random violence of the teenage killers.

As the plane slowly taxied to the end of the runway, Code 015 continued to casually watch it. And with the landing behind him, Trent Burton relaxed in his seat. It was good to be back for a few days, the adventures always started here.

Then he sat up very straight. Trent saw him and he was just sitting there looking at the plane. It was him, and Trent felt the man was looking right at him, just right at him. His pulse raced at the sudden surprise, and then he flashed back to the Bryan Norton task to spot this guy . . . and then Bryan Norton disappears and no one ever said anything. And then there he was. How long had he been here? Did Peter Hunt, a senior mercenary at the camp, know about this? Why was he here? Then Trent realized how extremely dangerous such questions might be in this covert deadly place. But Trent's night's rest had just been cancelled and if he wanted to know more, he must be very, very careful. In his mind this strange elusive guy had become the Pale Horse of the Apocalypse, the one that death rides on. It had been him, sitting there as if he were a shadow looking at the plane. None of this was comforting to Trent, but he also felt very, very alone. No one else really knew the drama associated with this 4ᵗʰ Mercenary. It was a special project for his idol Bryan Norton and the three guys he had brought to the camp. No one else knew or would come, just another shadow mercenary coming into the camp and then leaving the camp. Trent really didn't know the whole story. His task had been that of the spy lookout for The 4ᵗʰ Mercenary, but that job sounded a little ominous. It had been a simple job, an edgy job for Trent at the time. Now it seemed so dangerous, ominous and he felt so alone . . . so alone. And as he looked back through the plane, he could still see the man in the fading light just sitting there looking at the plane, The 4ᵗʰ Mercenary just looking at the plane.

As the plane taxied into the night toward the main base, Code 015 got up and went inside his tent. He knew nothing about what had just happened, he knew nothing about this "4ᵗʰ Mercenary" or who the "4ᵗʰ Mercenary" was. But he was in fact the "4ᵗʰ Mercenary" at the center of all of this. Ignorance is bliss.

CHAPTER 123

The day started dark and overcast at the mercenary camp, Eastern Congo. But they all seem to start that way.

Trent Burton woke with a jolt, remembering the evening episode with the "man" in the chair. He remembered him well from the time he came some months ago, the same tent, the same man. Now the "man" was back, how long was he gone? How long had he been back?

Trent Burton's tent was on the far end of the runway to the east, so he had the advantage of distance. Also, the men in that tent complex almost never went to the main part of the camp or interacted with the main camp.

After breakfast at the main camp mess Trent went up the small slope to the east with about a forty-foot overlook of the camp. It was 9 a.m. and Trent casually scanned the base. Then, with binoculars, he looked down the runway to the west and then to the tent compound where this man stayed. Nothing was going on.

He sat down and gazed at the camp, actually focusing on the operations to report back to the commander, as well as his dad, on the standards of the camp.

Ten minutes later he did spot movement in the far compound. Looking through the binoculars he saw a man emerge from the tent, a man he had not seen before. And then the man, The 4ᵗʰ Mercenary in the late Bryan Norton's world, came out. They talked for a further two minutes, and then the man walked towards a 4 x 4 Land Rover heading towards him with two armed escorts. The 4ᵗʰ Mercenary stood outside briefly and then . . . it appeared he looked right at Trent Burton. Trent could swear he was just staring at him. Was he? Trent swallowed hard and took the binoculars down. Then a British Hunter fighter passed over to land to the west and Trent, only twenty-five years old, almost had a massive stroke. One day back here and he was spooked, nervous and paranoid. Had that man been looking at him or the plane coming in?

He looked back at the tent and the man was gone. He was counting the hours before he left for London, and twenty-four hours had not passed, barely fourteen hours had passed.

CHAPTER 124

In a world where a leading politician can be named Sylvester Ntibantunganya, as was the case in neighboring Burundi, then you knew you may be in an extreme culture versus "western standards." Welcome to the surreal world, welcome to Eastern Congo.

This day also started as brooding, overcast, wet and foggy. The camp was quiet because getting to the runway was impossible and few trucks were leaving. Trent was happy to focus on his job and only occasionally looked up to see "the tent." Happily, each time he did look up the tent was quiet and even happier that he did not see this man. The weather was forbidding enough that if he did, the fog and shadows would have been the perfect backdrop to adding more to Trent Burton's sense of the danger and mystique he had already developed in his mind. The 4th Mercenary was happy to go about his business, as Trent was heading for the mental hospital all on his own. This 4th Mercenary had not a clue that Trent Burton was staging his own script for a mental breakdown. If the poor young guy did collapse, no one would be alarmed, this was the Eastern Congo, a long recognized time warp of violence, rotting bodies, drug-fueled teenagers with AK-47's dressed in blonde wigs, pink dresses, combat boots, and green sunglasses, with a string of AK-47 bullets as a necklace. Few left here mentally stable and functioning. None of the young boys left alive at all, reaching eighteen years old was middle age.

The day never got better; it was continually drizzling, then overcast, then another wave of low clouds and drizzle. By 6 p.m. things had already gotten dark, the camp had had a very good day, a quiet sleepy day. Trent Burton was able to stabilize and enjoy the peace.

But that changed. As Trent left his mess tent he looked directly at a monster Apocalypse Plane. It was dark gray and the fading light gave it just enough details for a massive menacing presence. The fact that the plane was being towed didn't help, as it appeared to be moving as a massive ghost. His shaky mental presence had just taken a step backwards.

The plane was intimidating no matter what the conditions, but poor Trent Burton had just witnessed the perfect storm of intimidation. The plane, the fog, the shadows, the Eastern Congo, Trent merely sat down, put his head in his hands and tried to breathe.

The crew was quickly preparing the plane. Ten minutes later the rear stairs came down. Trent looked up from his chair, he didn't want to but he couldn't help it. Five men came by a 4 x 4 Land Rover Defender, got out and quickly went up the stairs. "He" was not one of them, thank God, and no one looked his way. Trent settled down.

Three minutes later he was very unsettled. A lone 4 x 4 Land Rover Defender drove up and an armed escort helped a lone man out, and there he was. Another man quickly gave the man his duffle bag, and the man went up the stairs. He went up the stairs much too slowly for Trent's wellbeing, and Trent swears that about five steps from the top of the stairs the man looked directly at him.

Trent was losing it and was paralyzed by fear, he couldn't swallow, he couldn't breathe.

The man, the lone 4th Mercenary, entered the plane. And yes, he had looked in Trent's direction, but only to note what an absolutely terrible night to be trying to fly. He had no idea Trent Burton was sitting there, the fog and darkness blocked everything.

Trent had passed out, face into the mud. He was trapped in his own horror movie.

When the massive engines of the B727-100 started to whine, Trent came to. No one had even spotted him in the mud, the weather was just that miserable and dark too.

As Trent regained consciousness he was happy for the wet cool mud on his face, and he was happy no one had seen him faint. He didn't try to get up. He just sat there in the mud and watched this magnificent monster plane taxi to the runway.

It did taxi and then swung around aggressively to face west, the end of the runway lights barely visible. It didn't matter. With a light load and monster afterburners, it wasn't going to take long to get up.

And then it lit the afterburners and it all was a sight to behold, the stuff of legend. There were three massive torches in the gray wet fog. Many in the camp had come out for this display. A magnificent rogue military plane on steroids was roaring down the runway with menacing reckless abandon, it lifted off and for fifteen seconds the camp and the entire surrounding area was bathed in the most threatening apocalyptic but yet wonderful roar of these massive jet engines. For the mercenaries of the camp, it was a wonderful shot of adrenaline.

And then nothing, just the forbidding vacant presence of silence in the heart of darkness, and no one felt more alone and abandoned than one Trent Burton. And that was the way it was in another night of real or imagined terror . . . in the Eastern Congo.

CHAPTER 125

The imagined terror was in Trent's head. The real terror was only seventy miles away. But one massive plane with a raw menacing presence could bring its own terror, as it often did with just its sight. Its mission here was psychological, and it was just as good at that.

The world is small sometimes. General Mosamba's "hobby" in the Congo in the form of a growing savage militia was proving disruptive and a major concern to certain players. General Mosamba and particularly his proxy troops under his appointed Congolese Brigadier General Asamba had made the business relations in the area unreliable, so a recent contract was let at a very high covert level at selected cities. The wheels had turned and now action would be taken.

The raw gray plane from the mercenary base never got above 17,000 feet and then went into a shallow dive. The dive through the rain clouds was bumpy and sometimes violent. Not to worry, the crew loved this and the plane was such a structural monster that the weather was mild versus what it was built for.

It must have had exact GPS coordinates also; otherwise such a dive was useless. It did of course, and the crew system operators probably had all kinds of controls to do many mission things.

Then the plane dove aggressively but there was no way to tell the altitude, it was all pitch black. Code 015 would love to see the flight deck, it must be very impressive, as well as the mission control stations behind the pilots.

Then the plane dove a bit more aggressively, only to pop up into a forty-five degree climb with roaring afterburners. The plane continued to climb and climb, then at 20,000 feet it went into a shallow climb to 43,000 feet.

And in that dark wet jungle there were five hundred laminated leaflets scattered on the ground. The leaflet said simply, "We know you are here." The leaflets and the roar should give the killer boys pause, but probably not. First the boys could not read but they would remember the unseen roar, and that anyone would remember. It didn't matter; "they" were going to come anyway.

Some five hours later in the quiet of the tropical night a gray, raw Apocalyptic Plane slammed into the runway at Diego Garcia, British Indian Ocean Territories.

CHAPTER 126

And on this night as the monster plane taxied all was quiet on the narrow elegant streets of Nice. The hyperactive movie team had finally called it a night, and to a person they were quietly winding down their evenings. Even Javier Henri and Brandon Craig had decompressed for the evening. Kelly Grant and Abbey Bond slept quietly.

In New York Ward Kent was at a cocktail party on Fifth Avenue. He had received a call from Winston Burton that the credit line would be needed soon, as the contracts had been set and money spent. First there was a small amount for a special mission aircraft in Africa to start the first phase of the contract. That had just been completed.

Three blocks from where Winston Burton made his call to New York, Farsi Abbas was in a five-star boutique hotel. Tomorrow he would window shop for a new jet at a special Mayfair office. Lisa had just phoned Alex Kagamba in Cape Town to briefly tell him she would see him in two weeks or so. She needed to go to London on business in ten days and would stay for four days.

General Mosamba called Alex Kagamba to lie to him that he had only $500,000 left, but it would go to Alex. Alex was happy. Then General Mosamba called Farsi Abbas in London to tell him he had a $2 million-dollar follow-on order, and to say hello to Lisa. General Mosamba wanted Lisa, simple as that. Mr. Abbas would have to step aside.

And in Fang, Thailand Mr. Ptorn had returned home at 7 a.m. after one long night of loud music and drugs. And thanks to his bodyguards, two more dead bodies lay in the road. Not so much business anymore, just parties. Mr. Ptorn had become unreliable. He collected money with the barrel of a gun but did not deliver anything. He had mutated into a drug-fueled, third string thug but in the stone-cold efficiency of selected professionals, all those adjectives and all that venom and hate and fear were unnecessary. He simply had become unreliable.

CHAPTER 127

But what Mr. Ptorn wanted he got, at least according to Mr. Ptorn. And word on the street is the man from Rangoon was in fact returning to Rangoon. That was the word on the street, and no one ever really contested the "word on the street" or where the word came from. No one ever contested the word on the street, it seemed. They should have.

But Mr. Ptorn had let it be known he wanted the man to return and he apparently was coming. Why wouldn't he, Mr. Ptorn had spoken.

And the man did return as Code 015 to the professionals that matter. He had his suite at the Strand Hotel but he would not sleep there, not with a Mr. Ptorn and his pack of armed psychopaths.

He set up shop at the Strand and waited. There would be no name for him, just business. No cell phones, no internet, no Facebook, this area had been deemed for business only, hard business; no plastic play toys, no Googling or other childish mannerisms like Yahoo. Where do these people come from anyway?

The word passed quickly. Mr. Majani called from Calcutta wanting an appointment, not realizing this was the same Simon Green he had met for the MIG-23. Mr. Wei called also but just to apologize, he couldn't come primarily because, thanks to Mr. Ptorn, he could not go anywhere. He was a marked man by the lunatic Mr. Ptorn.

Through the swiftness of the underworld Mr. Ptorn called. He mostly shouted and said that he would send his team to pick up his money. He said he was fining Code 015 $3.3 million for something like being late, or making Mr. Ptorn wait, or because it was Wednesday, or because it was a full moon. No money to him, then his men would handle the rest.

Code 015 acted his part and begged Mr. Ptorn to let him bring him the money. He understood about Mr. Ptorn's fine and would pay it . . . and he still wanted to work with Mr. Ptorn on future weapons' deals.

Mr. Ptorn, being a volatile bipolar train wreck, started laughing and saying yes, yes, yes. He became giddy and chilling. He said he had changed his mind and wanted $3.7 million, then laughed again.

Code 015 spoke softly saying $3.7 million was fine, but that would be the limit of this "fine" this time. If he was late again, he could be fined again. Code 015 then navigated the terrain. Did Mr. Ptorn want the money delivered to Fang, Thailand or somewhere else? Mr. Ptorn quickly became the other pole. How did he know about Fang! You come to Fang and you will be roasted like a cow.

Code 015 softly said he wasn't coming to Fang but if Mr. Ptorn wanted his money, it would be delivered on a mountain road outside of Pai, Thailand. Code 015 said quietly that if Mr. Ptorn did not show up at 7:45 p.m. at a certain mile marker, there would be no $3.7 million now or in the future. The meeting would be in two days.

Mr. Ptorn went ballistic. No one gives him orders! Code 015 quietly said he had just given him an order, but he surely did not have to take it nor take the $3.7 million in untraceable U.S. dollars.

Mr. Ptorn went more than ballistic, the nerve of this guy. Who is he, where is he now? Code 015 said it didn't matter, check your email Mr. Ptorn, the directions are there, make yourself happy. Code 015 then hung up. A note at the bottom of the email clinched the deal, "You can bring whomever you want!"

CHAPTER 128

In two days Mr. Ptorn would show up with his army. This guy's dead, dead, even $3.7 million will not save him. Mr. Ptorn let his two senior bodyguards know of the plan. They also became enraged. They would clean their weapons and bring extra ammo, and notify the police and border police not to bother patrolling that stretch of highway between 7 p.m. and 9 p.m. They would own that road.

All of this was to go down in two days, so now is the time to party, tomorrow is business. And so it went on yet again, the drugs, the liquor, the girls, although the girls were not necessary so much anymore as the drugs and alcohol left the main players useless. But the lower level bodyguards had their appetite satisfied. So off Mr. Ptorn went into his delusional toxic waste dump. At 3 a.m. most were passed out, except a one Mr. Vanda Pntip. The head bodyguard had enough strength to walk into the street, stand in the middle and put three bullets into the chest of the first two motor bikers coming by, wrong place, wrong time. Mr. Pntip then wobbled back to Mr. Ptorn's compound and passed out on the patio. It had been a very good evening. Tomorrow would be better.

CHAPTER 129

The convoy of five Porsche Cayenne's was following the weaving mountain road out of Pai, Thailand. It looked like a trail of sparkling diamonds.

It was a relentless frenzied march accented by the brilliant white of the Porsche Xenon headlights. It was 7:50 p.m. and Mr. Ptorn was five minutes late, but then Mr. Ptorn is never really late, when he shows up is exactly the right time.

The convoy could be seen from a mile away but just momentarily, as the road dove in and out of the mountain terrain.

The mile marker for the meeting and negotiations was at marker eighteen outside of Pai and was clearly marked. The roadside bamboo hut was just after that. The mountain fell off quickly from the road, so the bamboo hut was some ten feet above the ground in front and some eighteen feet high in the back. The hut was supported by stilts and although the hut was only fifteen yards from the road, all fifteen yards had to be covered over a narrow ramp from the road to the hut.

Code 015 stood inside with the cases of money on full display. He was all alone and there was a single fluorescent light on in the hut. It was very Spartan in the hut and you could hear the convoy coming. There was no tentativeness in the convoy, it was rolling. It only slowed down when it was just short of the hut. The SUV's moved in formation with the first SUV stopping past the bamboo ramp to the hut, the second SUV stopped right at the ramp, and the last three stopped in a tight formation behind the second SUV.

The third SUV actually put on the blinking hazard lights. The fourth and fifth Porsche SUV might have also, if any of the six bodyguards were still alive.

As the SUV's were rolling to a halt, two men in all black came from the left and two men in black came from the right. Proceeding quickly on each side of the cars they put 9 mm rounds into the rear seat and the two front seats. There was no sound, just your basic Sig Sauer P250, 9 mm, full titanium, silencers attached. There was no hesitation, just execution, piff, piff, piff into the head, neck, chest, wherever, just do it; piff, piff, piff, piff, piff into the next two Porsches. They were coming from the back and they were essentially invisible in their all black outfits and the black night outside of Pai, Thailand. Piff, piff, piff, it continued. By this time, meaning like only one minute plus later, the second Porsche had emptied and was heading for the bamboo ramp, completely innocent of what had happened behind them.

The charge was led by Mr. Ptorn himself, he had worked himself up into a stroke-inducing rage. Crystal meth can do that. He was followed closely by Mr. Vanda Pntip, his head bodyguard and head executioner. The final man out of the second Porsche was also a senior bodyguard. Both bodyguards would be late for their next party, as five feet onto the ramp both were hit by three 9 mm bullets each. Five of the bullets hit the two torsos, and then a single bullet had hit Mr. Vanda Pntip at the base of his skull. Part of that mess ended up on Mr. Chaya Ptorn's back. Mr. Ptorn would be enraged by the disrespect to him! But Mr. Ptorn was laser focused on Code 015 until the bodies hit the ramp and caused Mr. Ptorn to lose his balance on the rickety ramp. He turned quickly in irritation, only to see two large bodies crumbled on the ramp. He stared for maybe five seconds in total shock, who wouldn't be, then Mr. Ptorn turned back to face Code 015. Mr. Ptorn collected three shots to the chest from Code 015 and three from the back by a backside party.

Maybe three minutes had passed.

There were eleven bodies from the Mr. Ptorn party. And the lead Porsche in the convoy, having seen the death on the ramp, just sped away. They were bodyguards, and now they were guarding their own bodies.

It was of no importance now. Three of the all-black men had gone to the other side of the road some time ago and were picked up by a nondescript farm truck. They were three Burmese mercenaries from Shan State, Burma. The 4th Mercenary had already gone down the steep slope into the bush. The slope would stay quite steep for almost half a mile, steep and infested with vines and brush; clearly a nightmare in pitch dark. About one hundred yards down the man put on his headlamp.

Code 015 was to follow just as quickly. However, as he also went to jump from the ramp and head down the steep slope, he wasn't as lucky.

It was only a three-foot jump from the ramp to the slope but as Code 015 jumped, he caught his foot on Mr. Vanda Pntip's lifeless body. That put him into an awkward position and he fell and hit his right shoulder and right knee on the ground with a thud, and then he proceeded down the slope with his face raking up the vines and brush. He got up and continued down the slope, but with very significant pain in his shoulder and knee. He went down one hundred yards and he had to switch on his headlamp. He met up with the other man at two hundred yards down the slope.

The man looked at Code 015 and said, "You didn't come out of that so well," it was the accent of a white South African.

The man checked Code 015's face, which was bloody from numerous scratches but nothing serious. The shoulder was bruised, the knee jammed, but it didn't matter, they had to move. The South African moved much quicker than Code 015. It didn't matter much, as they were to stay in the mountains tonight. And they did.

CHAPTER 130

As light hit the mountains, Code 015 found a stream to clean off the caked mud and blood. Both men looked a bit worn but that would be okay, they just couldn't be too worn.

The truck was fifteen minutes late, but it was of no consequence. The fact it had come and was a Thai Lanna Adventure Tour truck was everything. Two beat up white guys in an adventure tour truck was common in this area and would pass border checkpoints with little notice. Just crazy tourists. And Mr. Ptorn had called off the checkpoints in the neighborhood, as he didn't want to be bothered by them looking at the cases of money. But there was little money, just stacks of paper with a $100 bill on top. The bullets were real. Code 015 had left the fake money cases, let someone else figure all that out.

The contract completed, the two men were heading to Chiang Mai. The South African mercenary would be in Bangkok tomorrow and at 1:30 a.m. the next morning on a Thai Airways jet, Bangkok to Johannesburg.

Code 015 might have moved fast too but the shoulder and knee hurt, thus a pronounced limp. And his face was scratched up, no need to tip off the authorities, so he would stay in Chiang Mai for five days to recover in the arms of Rin.

But Rin was not around, they always are disappearing. So Code 015 slept by himself for two nights. On the third night he limped to one of his favorite clubs. Not a rowdy bar scene with forty-year-old Thai hookers who looked like truck drivers and who were more beat up than he was. They were way past the warranty. No, he went down a little alley where the lady manager filtered out all except the young, tender and innocent. And after one hour of watching and sipping a beer . . . well, her name was Kat, nineteen years old and beyond petite and sexy. Not very experienced, but petite and sexy. He spent the next three nights with her. It was memorable because inexperience can be so sexy.

CHAPTER 131

The Thai tuk-tuk wove through the narrow back alleys of Chiang Mai. You have to love the tuk-tuk sound, it's a nice deep raspy roar and all on natural gas. Kat had put on her short shorts, flip flops and little halter top, and kissed Code 015 deeply. He would see her soon if he could, you don't see a twenty-one-inch waist very much, if at all. And Kat would likely hit a twenty-three-inch waist by twenty years old. It was the perfect cure for a bloody beat up body.

Code 015 actually wasn't sure where he was going. As the tuk-tuk ripped through the lanes to the Chiang Mai airport, Code 015 flipped a coin. Heads to Nassau, Bahamas, tails to London. If the coin is lost, back to Chiang Mai and Kat.

Code 015 did catch the flip and it came up tails, to London it is. Maybe just sit in Hyde Park and read the Financial Times. God that sounded good, no air strikes, no headshots, no psychopaths, no sociopaths . . . for at least a week, maybe ten days.

As British Airways 71 Bangkok to London soared over Nice, France, Code 015 was in 2A watching the French Riviera go by. How long ago was it when he was in Nice, France and Monaco? His best answer was likely it was two lifetimes ago or three months, both good guesses.

As the plane cruised by Nice, on the ground the Javier Henri LeCirac film project had been operating at a frantic seven days-a-week pace.

The pace was frantic but productive. The document describing everything, from the costumes to locations to the cast and the script, had grown to over five hundred pages. Javier Henri thought it was incredible progress. And after seven to eight weeks of relentless creative work, Javier Henri demanded everyone take a ten-day break. He demanded it even as Brandon Craig resisted it. Javier Henri told them not to show up for work.

Brandon Craig decided just to work at his apartment, maybe go home for three or four days. Kelly Grant and Abbey Bond decided on going back to London for the whole ten days. Kelly would head to the Northolt area to visit her parents for a couple of days, then spend some time with Abbey in London.

They had been away on a real job for twelve weeks and coming back things felt different. It had been a whirl, but the work was excellent and their support system five star. I mean, where can two twenty-year-old's get this job plus elegant apartments in a massive elegant compound two blocks from work and the magnificent Nice harbor. And then Javier Henri throws in the Porsche 911 Turbo for Kelly, it all was surreal. So London it was for the girls.

CHAPTER 132

On the third day a man called Kent, the old Code 015 name was put to rest, strolled to the west side of Hyde Park around Lancaster Gate and sat down. He had his Financial Times, Wall Street Journal and New York Times, so he was set for three hours. The weather was cool and overcast and since this was London, what else was new.

As he buried his head in the paper, he had no idea when she came. But he finally looked up to catch her out of the side of his vision. He immediately remembered her, her stunning delicate beauty was there even as she covered it up with a scarf. She had been the one who had started the friendship with another young beauty in this very section of Hyde Park.

Oh well, he just kept reading; God knows the looks she gets every single day, every single day.

Thirty minutes later he looked up from his intense reading to see she was still there, she even gave him a glance and the shyest and most introverted of smiles. He gave a small smile back and continued reading, as did she.

Thirty minutes later he emerged from his reading again to find her still there quietly reading a thick bound document. He read only fifteen more minutes, then he got up to leave and they again exchanged small smiles. As he left the Hyde Park gate to walk up Bayswater Road, he looked to his right to see she was still there, a very quiet, very blonde beauty sitting and reading a large document. It all was very charming considering she was so young. No iPad, iPhone, etc., etc., just a quiet girl in a quiet park, very charming, very endearing.

It was 3 p.m. and Kent limped back to his condo . . . right across Bayswater Road from the park. He would sleep for twelve hours.

CHAPTER 133

The next day started quietly for Kent. He sat at his grand circular window overlooking Hyde Park. He could see the bench where he would again read the Financial Times. He wasn't sure when he would start.

His small place on Bayswater Road was at the penthouse level but the residence was small, just one large bedroom, a library/reading room, a small dining room, kitchen and one large bathroom. He only had the one large circular window. A small quiet retreat from the erratic, radical, violent profession he had. He had several of these places around the world to recover from the traumas and, yes, his knee was better, as well as his shoulder. He still had a slight limp.

This was going to be a leisurely day, he had no idea when he would leave his place to buy his Financial Times and New York Times. It was 10:31 a.m. at Lancaster Gate on Bayswater Road, City of London. A private jet from Johannesburg landed at City Airport at 12:07 p.m.

CHAPTER 134

It was 1:27 p.m. when Kent took the elevator to the ground floor. He walked up Bayswater Road past the Black Swan on a stroll toward Oxford Street where his papers waited for him. Thirty meters past the Black Swan, a black Bentley limousine came from his back. It would have been fate and ironic had she been looking his way. But she was gazing at Hyde Park as the limo glided past. Lisa Aswanela did not see Kent. Kent took note of the Bentley but did not see Lisa.

At 2:17 p.m. Kent had settled into his bench at Hyde Park, and for the next two hours plus he would be in his own world, a silent world where he was very alone, but in no way lonely. In its own way it was another day at the office in his world, just without air strikes, assassinations, hot deserts, arctic cold, jetfighters and fast cars. A world of immersed concentration on the papers intruded by short periods of just gazing at nature in Hyde Park, quiet, magnificent quiet.

After one hour he looked up from his paper . . . and had no idea when she had come. As soon as he dropped the paper, she looked over and gave a shy smile. Kent smiled back and said hello.

And today she wanted to talk. So he read a little and talked a little, and she did likewise. Kent finally asked what she was reading and she said it was extensive notes for a movie. Kent asked if she was an actress. She smiled and said no, just an assistant. Kent was intrigued nonetheless.

An hour passed. At their next chat she asked if he lived in London. He said yes, actually right across the street.

And then Kelly had decided. She said, "Should we go there, I can tell you about the movie?" She was blushing deeply, and her thin pale skin had become a light rose color, her voice so light. Kent knew what this was about and said yes.

Some girls plan to lose their virginity to first sweethearts, some to first husbands. Kelly had decided she didn't want to know the guy, and he should be older. She had only decided yesterday.

"By the way, my name is Kent, Kent Weston," he said.

"And I'm Kelly, Kelly Grant," she responded.

CHAPTER 135

As Kelly was taking off her jacket and scarf, a one Lisa Aswanela was sitting with Farsi Abbas in Mayfair – London for yet another private jet presentation. She wasn't bored, the sums involved kept her interest and the planes were magnificent.

As Lisa listened to another presentation, Kent had gently removed Kelly's shirt. She was not wearing a bra as she was not developed, just little perky breasts, and she had never felt her nipples so hard. Kent spent a long time feeling her and kissing her. By the time he finally led her to the bedroom she only had her panties on and was light headed from the drama of it all. The first time can be like that.

If Lisa had known, she could have coached Kelly. But Lisa was looking at a slick brochure of a jet when Kent finally had Kelly. But Kent, knowing the situation, was very gentle and somewhat brief. If Kelly was comfortable, there would be plenty of time later.

And she was comfortable. There was only an hour between her first time and second time, then she fell asleep on Kent's chest. It was 5:10 p.m. Lancaster Gate, London.

And so it was, the young, delicate, quiet and hauntingly beautiful girl named Kelly had decided to eliminate all the fraudulent and hyped drama of the female virgin by ending it with an anonymous stranger whom she knew nothing about. She had sexually exploited him, but the world never thinks of it like that for men. They tend to be sexually disposable to the females. Nobody cares about male virginity, so why worry about female virginity. Well, there is one reason that comes to mind . . . money. Nature had made men very sexually active, and thus females are natural drug dealers. Pay me and get sex. And it is not just prostitutes, the whole world's culture is set up to trade a daughter to marriage to get a cow, or some corn, and then you can take her for sex. And now with a money based society, $300 will get you a young girl, and the mother of the young girl will be happy to get the money and have one less mouth to feed. Even in western societies the suburbs are full of prostitutes who just have one customer, the customers are called husbands.

Men have sex because they were built that way; women have sex for babies because they were built that way. The women just like to be paid for their efforts. It is about the money.

CHAPTER 136

Kelly woke at 6:30 p.m. and whispered to Kent that she should go. Kent whispered back, where are you going? She said nowhere. Then stay here tonight. And she did.

But in the morning the reality of a new day struck and she left from the Lancaster Gate subway station, heading to Northolt to visit her parents, and to pretend she had just come to town for two days. On the third day she would return to Kent's place on Bayswater Road, and by the time she returned to Nice she would be well past a virgin.

And on the third day she did return and Kent met her on the street above the station. It was 9:30 a.m. and as they kissed and talked, a black Bentley limousine was approaching. The occupants were on the way to continue to shop for a private jet . . . and to shop in general. When you are looking for a $40 million jet, it's not an afternoon thing.

This time the sexy girl in the Bentley was looking ahead and did not miss Kent, and especially she did not miss Kelly Grant. Another day, another fate was working. The Bentley was a hundred and fifty yards away when she spotted the two. And she knew Kent right away, and she knew Kelly not at all. But Lisa did focus on Kelly, and her sense was she had never seen a girl with more magnificent hair.

As the Bentley cruised closer, the face Lisa saw was beyond sexy or beautiful. This young girl had the serene quiet ghostly beauty that many would believe should, or could not, be touched by mere mortals.

At seventy yards away Lisa asked the driver to slow to 20 mph. The driver did and Lisa gazed intently at the couple, looking briefly at Kent again, but returning to laser focus on Kelly. Being a professional, Lisa did not put the window down to yell hello. The Bentley merely glided past the couple at 20 mph. Lisa gave a quick glance back and then said the driver could resume.

Farsi Abbas had taken note of Lisa and asked if she knew that couple. Lisa said no, she was just looking at the neighborhood. Farsi Abbas had seen the couple too, he looked at the man and would remember, who wouldn't remember. Farsi Abbas had never seen a girl like that, and you remember a man with a girl like that. But Lisa was his, and he asked her if she wanted a place in London. Lisa said "maybe," if only to make this exotic blonde have to share Kent with her. And Farsi Abbas would have to shell out $3 million plus so "his" Lisa could have access to another man that she actually wanted to be with. But Farsi would do it.

While women tend to be self-absorbed, men truly are self-delusional.

And the world keeps turning.

The Bentley continued to Mayfair – London for another elegant five-star meeting with the private plane brokers. Actually, today the brokers would go up a notch to the Gulfstream 650. At $70 million the plane was clearly out of Farsi Abbas' range, unless he started to sell arms to all of Africa . . . and southeast Asia as well. But the brokers knew male vanity more than they knew the planes they were selling. And after seeing Lisa the brokers "knew" their customer, time for some fun.

As the Bentley was parked and as Farsi Abbas and Lisa Aswanela were being walked to the plush offices, the young Kelly had her knees on a chair leaning on its back facing the large circular window. As she arched her back and let Kent gently remove her panties, she saw the bench where she had first met Kent. This seemed like a movie, maybe she would add it to the script. Yes, definitely she would. But by now Kent had gently come up from behind her, one arm around her tiny waist, his other hand on her tiny breast. And this time he stayed on her, but slowly and for a while. Just before she closed her eyes to fully enjoy the raw sex, she glanced once more at the bench where it all began. Then she closed her eyes, arched her back for him, put her head on the back of the chair and closed her eyes. She was comfortable and aroused, he could take as long as he liked. And he did. Kelly had five more days in London.

CHAPTER 137

As Farsi Abbas listened to the Gulfstream 650 presentation, in his mind he was trying to decide how he would ever come up with $70 million. I mean, who buys such planes. And in his self-delusion the thought of jetfighters came to his mind. Then he had heard on the street that the MIG-23 was in play somewhere. Cuba? Angola? Sudan? Libya? He made a note to research that. Selling jetfighters could get some serious cash flow going.

And he was right. As he made his note in London, a one General Abdul was in Khartoum, Sudan telling Mr. Majani he needed closure within fifteen days on two MIG-23's. It had gone to two MIG-23's because he had found another one no one knew about. General Abdul wanted $5 million, a set price.

The jackals were circling. Of course Said Alawid wanted in on the action, and it was only right the contract go to a fellow Sudanese. As General Abdul talked to Mr. Majani in Calcutta, Said Alawid was resting his fat, sweaty, smelly, dirty body in his favorite place, a barren dirt place of slums outside of Khartoum. All Said Alawid wanted to do was count his money and make more . . . praise Allah. His only use for money was to buy lots of food, eat it, sleep and wake to count the money again. And to count more money he wanted General Abdul to sell him the MIG-23's for $1 million. He could resell them for $15 million, and thus have more money to count. Greed is good. If he didn't get the deal, well, how good could a fellow brother be to betray his own kind and Sudan.

So Said Alawid sat in his dirt hovel and called General Abdul. Said wanted another audience with the General, like last time at his place. The call went through but General Abdul told his assistant colonel to kill it. The general was busy, but not that busy. The General was talking to Mr. Majani and whoever else . . . just not Said Alawid. If Said knew this, it is clear he would have been a bit more aggressive. It was "do not cross Said Alawid," the sordid, obese lord of greed who spends most of his time sitting on a pile of greasy blankets buried in a maze of narrow filthy alleys on the outskirts of Khartoum, Sudan. Not such a sweet deal, even if it was a sweet deal. And it wasn't, it was a delusional grab for money, as if General Abdul was some dimwitted ten-year-old. The general thought Said Alawid probably couldn't even spell MIG. But he had to be careful, Said Alawid was a dangerous egomaniac. How that happens when you sit on a pile of dirt in an area of Khartoum that itself is a pile of dirt, all the while weighing in at 370 pounds and the smell of a bad herd of camels, is hard to explain. General Abdul just knew as lost as Said Alawid was, he was dangerous just because he was so lost . . . and as usual Said was the last one to know how lost he was. But Said Alawid had four scruffy equally lost bodyguards, which made him dangerous. They hung with him because he was their hero, as bizarre as that is. Africa is filled with these guys. Every rebel militia starts this way.

But a call did come in that General Abdul would take, a new player. And how it got out on the MIG-23's he did not know. With this call General Abdul knew he had to sell very quickly, the "market" knew.

CHAPTER 138

A fellow general was calling, a General Mosamba of the Ugandan Army, Western Forces. The two generals had never met, but they knew each other. Selling a country's military hardware was the reason people make "General" in Africa. They greeted each other with warm hellos, they were in the same business.

General Mosamba was calling to inquire about MIG-23's, not to buy, just to sell. If General Abdul needed more to sell, General Mosamba had them. It seems the international arms community had heard of the MIG-23 demand, maybe by way of the Cuban deal, or Sudan, or maybe some arms dealers "chit chat." But there seemed to be more sellers than buyers out there before, and now General Mosamba jumps in to put more on the market.

They talked politely for ten minutes and concluded with General Mosamba telling General Abdul that he had two new sources of arms if he ever needed help; one was a Farsi Abbas, and one Alex Kagamba out of Cape Town. General Abdul thanked him and hung up, not being sure what that was all about . . . well, except it was about money and how to get more of it. The World Health Organization (WHO) had never looked into that disease. Of course the WHO had the disease as bad as anybody.

CHAPTER 139

Kelly sat curled up on Kent's couch, content to read her movie document. Kent had become curious about the thick document, it seemed a bit much for such a young girl to be trusted with.

As he came in with groceries, he saw her with it again. He told her it looked like an interesting document, what was it? Then they both realized they had spent a lot of time in bed without having the slightest idea of each other. In other words, it had been perfect.

Kelly in her youthful innocence was open about it, she was working on a movie production. Kent slid in behind her on the couch and let her lean back against his chest. They thumbed through the pages together, as Kelly described the project.

The movie's working title was "The 4th Mercenary," Kelly explained, based on an unwritten novel by two guys who went to the Congo and never returned. Kelly told Kent that her boss, Brandon Craig, had set up the foundation drawing on the old mercenary havens of Biafra, Gabon, Angola, South Africa, Rhodesia, etc.

What Kent didn't know is that the story being told was generally about him. What Kelly didn't know is that the man she was leaning on and embracing was in fact the very man her movie work was to be based on. And both were beyond any comprehension that this was the situation. The real "4th Mercenary" had casually put his arm around the girl making the movie about The 4th Mercenary.

As Kelly explained the broad base of the movie's foundation, Kent asked questions and never felt any connection. There were lots of novels on African mercenaries. Everyone's favorite was "Dogs of War" by Frederick Forsyth; his own favorite was "A Coffin Full of Dreams" by Frisco Hitt. So they talked on for two hours or so, then they fell silent and then they fell asleep.

They were still napping at 4:37 p.m. when the Black Bentley cruised below them on Bayswater Road. Lisa requested the Bayswater Road route, Kent's situation and this exotic mystery blonde "Lolita" was so intriguing. Lisa had her own movie going on in her head. Farsi Abbas sat quietly in the Bentley; how do people come up with $70 million for an airplane!

CHAPTER 140

At a sidewalk café in the Nice harbor another scene was developing for the movie, maybe fifty yards from where Javier Henri and Brandon Craig were developing the scenes and concepts.

Under the colorful orange umbrella, with the yachts in the background and the numbers of the beautiful people sitting at the tables, two men in their thirties were sitting and talking. To complete the scene, the two men were agents from French Intelligence in the person of Didier Francois and Patrice Guiot. To complete the picture, both were wearing their best fine cut suits and aviator sunglasses by Hermes. After all they were to meet Javier Henri LeCirac who looked like he came off the front page of GQ every day.

They had told Javier Henri they were in town and wanted to speak with him again. They were here now doing some "covert research" and generally enjoying themselves. After all, why be an intelligence agent if you can't sit at an exotic harbor side café and be mysterious . . . and please remember to bring the aviator sunglasses.

But at the end of the day, French Intelligence still could not get a handle on the Angola airstrike. They could not piece together where the jetfighter came from or even what kind of fighter it was.

In the next month if they did not get some concrete evidence, they likely would put the data in the computer and move on to the next mystery. However, one mystery they would not likely be exposed to is the mystery of the lonely Mirage F-1B secluded in the miserable overpowering heat of Eastern Chad. That mystery was not even fully known by French Intelligence, and it was clear they were not allowed to know or solve this one. In a world of shadows some shadows will remain shadows to even major power organizations.

The intelligence operatives continued their meal and also continued to drink in the glamorous backdrop of the Nice harbor. They were to meet Javier Henri in the next hour. The elegant offices were across the street, so they could relax and consume the sexy atmosphere.

And sexy it was. As they chatted about the yachts, a young slim girl strolled along the harbor walk, short shorts, long brown hair, but a very wide brimmed hat was disguising her face, all the more intrigue. They gazed at her, with a few glances at her friend, an average girl stuck with a spectacular friend.

As the operatives were being entertained by that scene, they heard a high-pitched whine on the street by their café. They quickly turned to see a bright yellow Ferrari being driven by a young blonde in a bright yellow outfit. Their luck held as the young woman gunned the Ferrari and then swung into the valet lane of the operative's café. She quickly got out and pulled her yellow skirt down, but that didn't take much as it stopped at least seven inches above her knee. She was likely twenty-five years old and had oversized sunglasses on. She went into the building of Javier Henri's office. It was good the guys had their aviator glasses on because between the yellow Ferrari and the blonde girl in yellow, the glare was considerable. But they did have the glasses on, so they were able to see every inch of her; after all, it was their job to notice the details.

As she disappeared into the building, an Aston-Martin and an orange Lamborghini cruised by driven by young Middle Eastern guys trying to make an impact on the young girls of the French Riviera set.

Before the operatives had to meet Javier Henri, they were treated to a stunning girl who actually looked Arabic. If she was, the Muslim moral police would have had a stroke both because she was wearing very little, but wearing it very well. Her hair was jet black and her shorts and halter top were also black. The oversized sunglasses were Channel, and she was striking and sultry looking and maybe all the more so because she did look Arabic. Seeing that in Nice was like seeing a lion with a white mane in the Serengeti.

Then it was time for their meeting with Javier Henri, but the spell was hardly over. As they walked into the ornate suite of Javier Henri, they spotted the blonde in yellow walking out.

She was not dressed for business and she had only been there about fifteen minutes, so it was obvious she was a girlfriend and the Ferrari belonged to Javier Henri. That certainly fit the analysis of the two French operatives. And their attention to detail paid off, for as they entered Javier Henri's suite, they both stood for ten seconds outside the door to watch the small firm ass navigate the hallway. It's too bad they could not be at the café to see her rip out of the valet space in the yellow Ferrari, while Javier Henri works relentlessly on the main industrial business, the aviation business and the movie. The girl in yellow disappeared and the operatives returned to the real world.

CHAPTER 141

General Abdul's office in Khartoum, Sudan was neither elegant nor ornate. And the thought of a luxury harbor in Sudan was beyond ludicrous. The weather was hot, brutally hot, and General Abdul's window air conditioner was laboring gallantly but losing the battle. The General was in a light sweat.

Said Alawid was mired in his mud hovel amid the blinding heat. He was enduring two additional handicaps, the insects and the fact that he had not bathed in five days.

The General was on the phone to Mr. Majani in Calcutta. The General was out of time. He had selected Mr. Majani to move his two MIG-23's. He had heard about the "big man" in Sudan, the one Farsi Abbas, but he didn't show up for this deal. Farsi Abbas knew all the "big boys" in the Sudan government and General Abdul didn't need that. Farsi Abbas could get the official Sudan arms' deals but not this one, an under the table deal with under the table money. If Mr. Abbas found out about the deal, he could take General Abdul out. Farsi Abbas was that powerful in Sudan, but right now Farsi Abbas was still shopping and playing. He wasn't playing with Lisa as yet, so he kept trying and he was losing track of business.

Said Alawid was becoming furious, as the General was not allowing him to steal this deal. Like Farsi Abbas, Said Alawid felt he had a license to kill also if things don't go his way. But unlike the late Mr. Ptorn, Said Alawid was not losing touch because of crystal meth or some other toxic drug, he was losing touch because he rarely went anywhere anymore.

Said Alawid stayed confined to his dirty and dusty little mud compound in the narrow wretched back alleys of his slums. At this time he had not left his "business center," his eight foot by ten foot room in the mud hut, in some seven days. Said Alawid himself realized that someone must come clean this hovel and him soon, as he had developed several open sores that were just getting worse.

So after trying to get General Abdul on the phone again, Said Alawid asked his bodyguards to hire some cleaners to come to his room. After his room they could clean the rest of the mud hut, and that should do for the next year. Living in the incredible squalor as you try to make millions takes a certain type, and Said was there. He was the opposite of his brother Ali Alawid. Not opposite in size, both were north of three hundred and fifty pounds, but opposite in their lives. Ali Alawid moved around, saw the "players," ambassadors, secretaries, etc., liked living large and doing his arms deals. Ali Alawid also liked his ladies and was a good dresser, even if it did have to be specially made at XXXXL. Of course for his troubles Ali Alawid collected a well-placed bullet to the head in Knightsbridge, London that fateful day, courtesy of the equally vain and high-living, a one Mr. Farsi Abbas. It didn't matter to Said Alawid who actually killed his brother, he was going to kill Farsi Abbas for it as well as Farsi's infidel ways. It was rumored Farsi had sex with non-Muslim women, so that's a death sentence right there. Although had Said Alawid ever seen Lisa, he would understand and kill Farsi Alawid just to get to her.

Since the day his brother was gunned down, Said Alawid was happy to be a filthy recluse because his whole life he had been looking for a reason to be a recluse, and being a recluse in a maze of fly infested alleys in one hundred degree plus heat seemed to be his calling. But he still liked his deals, and he still liked his money. He just could not pursue the deals like Farsi Abbas, two arms dealers who could not be more apart; Farsi Abbas with the private jets, Rolls Royce's, 3,000 square foot suites and one very, very sexy escort girlfriend in Lisa. Said Alawid was just dirt, filth and squalor, no car, much less a plane, just sitting and eating among the smells and heat; two Arab brothers living on the same planet, but two extremely different worlds.

So there these two were. Farsi Abbas was going to lose the deal with General Abdul, as he was too busy trying to spend money to keep Lisa. He was still in London trying to decide on a new private jet. And now Lisa wanted to look at apartments in the Bayswater area of London so she could "see Farsi more," she said, but to really keep Kent company she hoped. Farsi would owe her $200,000 plus for her time in London this time, and he may have to add $3 million to that if she seduced him into a condo in the Lancaster Gate neighborhood.

CHAPTER 142

As events winded through the maze of life, General Abdul made one last fateful call to Mr. Majani, Calcutta, India. Mr. Majani was waiting for the call. In his office overlooking the Queen Victoria Memorial, Mr. Raja Majani had a splendid view and an elaborate office, even if less than two miles away was relentless squalor and likely two hundred thousand people sleeping on the streets every night.

General Abdul said to make the deal $5 million, fixed price, US dollars, delivered to Khartoum at night on a date to be specified by General Abdul. That was what he needed, quick quiet execution, he only had a few days. After that Farsi Abbas will know of the deal somehow and either take the deal himself for $1 million or tell the powerful Sudanese authorities of the whole scheme. And Farsi Abbas could do that, under all his clean cut polite charm was a ruthless dealer of arms and he had "taken out" so many already, even Sudanese generals.

And Farsi Abbas could turn a $4 million or $5 million-dollar profit from this in four weeks. With his escalating lifestyle, it actually would not help that much. With Lisa his lifestyle had become very intoxicating, and he was addicted to it as much as the bullet riddled Mr. Ptorn had been to crystal meth. If General Abdul could get this deal done before Farsi Abbas got on the trail, he would profess innocence and ply Farsi Abbas with official Sudan arms business, as the Sudanese generals had done for many, many years. You don't shop for private jets like Farsi does by not getting your deals.

Mr. Majani called a contact named Simon Green to pull the trigger on this. Mr. Green "was out" at the moment, according to his "staff," but they would set everything up. Mr. Green would call him back soon.

In the space of those two phone calls, General Abdul had at least three assassins with his name on their list. Mr. Said Alawid, of course, Mr. Farsi Abbas when he found out, and at least one from someone in the Sudan military who would be slighted because General Abdul had not included them and who would believe being a three-star general could bring so many headaches and so little power. The graves are full of three-star generals, none of whom died "in the line of duty," unless corruption is in the line of duty . . . and it turns out . . . it is in the line of duty, welcome to Sudan.

CHAPTER 143

Kent, Kent Weston as Kelly Grant knew him, was sitting on his favorite bench in Hyde Park reading the Financial Times. Kelly Grant was back at his condo, she would join him in thirty minutes to soak up the solitude and fresh air of their little corner of paradise.

Kelly stood at the large circular window looking down over Hyde Park. She was not watching anything in particular, just a quiet gaze reflecting on the huge swirling events of the last four days. If ever there was a defining moment in her young life, it had been these four days, just four days and all had changed dramatically. She looked forward to going back to work on the movie project in Nice, but right now she was just soaking up this new world.

She glanced down to the bench where Kent sat reading, and there he was just like the day they had met and then boom, it all started . . . and she had started it without real rationale or reflection and it had turned out well. It had been free, easy, natural, and she had been lucky, as the first time can be so traumatic. It had been quite erotic for Kelly. She would never forget the time she spent bent over the chair gazing at Hyde Park, her perky ass in the air for Kent.

As she reflected she saw movement out of the corner of her eye. Jolted to reality, she saw a man in a stylish overcoat approach Kent, say hello, and sit down next to him. They did not seem to be friends, so Kelly watched intently. It seemed a bit mysterious to her, like out of a spy novel. A well-dressed man approaches another man on the park bench, they talk, then the man disappears after five minutes. Maybe a scene for the movie, Kelly thought.

And just like that the man did leave, he had not stayed five minutes. Kelly felt a lump in her throat from the tension she felt. Kent resumed his reading as if nothing had happened. Wow, for some reason that little event had sent chills through Kelly, maybe this movie project had spooked her, the movies meet reality. Her imagination had certainly taken off and she had added some thirty pages of notes on Kent, their encounter, the scenes, the location backdrop, all to go into ideas for the movie. In her ten-day "vacation" she had never been more productive or creative. She could add ten more pages right now. She scribbled notes for twenty minutes and then headed down to see Kent. She would pretend to just meet him, flirt with him, they would laugh, and later if she had her way, she would end up on her chair ready for Kent.

As she left the window, a sleek black Bentley again traveled up Bayswater Road. It passed under the large circular window just as Kelly turned to go. The two occupants were the same. Lisa gazed at the sidewalk but saw no one that looked like Kent. But he was only thirty yards away sitting in the park, the vegetation hiding his location from the street. She would leave London in a day and she was ready. She tired of Farsi Abbas quickly, and a week was too much. Even the $300,000 he would lavish on her made no difference, he had taken a week of her life. She was ready to be young again, ready to be nineteen again. The money she had earned had been spectacular but it was slowly taking her soul. She wanted to see Alex Kagamba, she wanted to see Kent . . . if she could find him.

CHAPTER 144

Only five minutes after the Bentley glided by, Kelly Grant crossed Bayswater Road. She did flirt with Kent but decided to sit close to him in the end. They had one more day together and then Kelly would return to Nice and the movie project.

She talked to Kent about his plans, and he said he had to leave as well. To return to London when? He didn't know, but he would call her . . . if she gave him her number. After an intense four days he had never gotten her number. And his number? Well, he only had the line number in his condo . . . but he could always call her. And he got her number.

They sat and read like "old times." She actually continued her movie notes on the recent developments. So she was writing notes on a possible profile of this "4ᵗʰ Mercenary" movie, as she sat right next to the actual "4ᵗʰ Mercenary" of the Andy Morris and Frank Cramer work, and less than a mile from where Andy and Frank had stayed . . . when they were still living.

Only a mile away in a five-story townhouse on Berkley Square, Mayfair – London a one Trent Burton sat in his father's library. He had returned to London from the Congo and had resumed his duties with the company in London. But he had not forgotten, and maybe never would forget the haunting trauma of seeing this elusive mercenary from the Congo camp. It all would have meant nothing except Bryan Norton, his hero, had asked him to specifically watch for this man. And when Trent did see The 4ᵗʰ Mercenary, the tension was amplified.

What Trent did not know is the man he spotted for Bryan Norton in the Congo was known as the "4ᵗʰ Mercenary," he was just an elusive guy to Trent. But in the end and at this time, Trent was the only person to actually see The 4ᵗʰ Mercenary in the Congo. Were Trent to now see this man sitting in Hyde Park, it likely would put him over the edge. Even the stunning presence of a one Kelly Grant could not save him.

As Trent sat in the library, his father fielded a call. It was a wealthy prominent businessman seeking some background on past situations in Africa, military as well as mercenary, just general stuff. The wealthy man had a project and needed a "technical" man to tell him how it really was. Winston Burton could help, he thought it would be interesting, so they agreed and Winston Burton would help. And Javier Henri LeCirac thanked him from his office overlooking the Nice harbor. And how is your father, Winston asked?

"He is doing fine sir, I will say hello for you," Javier said. "Wonderful, do take care Javier," and Winston said goodbye.

CHAPTER 145

Kent and Kelly strolled to the Bayswater condo, as it was getting dark. They had spent the entire day soaking up the fresh air of Hyde Park.

When they hit the apartment they had a snack and then went to bed. It was 7 p.m. At 2 a.m. Kent woke Kelly for a final time to make sure she would remember their times together. She would have anyway, but she was glad he was thoughtful.

The next morning Kelly and Kent stood on the sidewalk, as Kelly prepared to leave and return to Northolt to catch the LeCirac corporate jet back to Nice. She would meet Abbey Bond there and they would slowly catch up on things. Kelly thought it best to let her story mature a bit before telling it. It all had been so surreal, now it seemed overwhelming. She would tell Abbey in due course.

It wasn't a quick goodbye, it was a gentle lingering, a soft chat if you will. And they delayed their goodbye long enough for one last pass of the Black Bentley.

Farsi Abbas and Lisa had one final visit to the private jet market office and then they were gone too. Farsi Abbas had not decided on anything because for the first time he was short of money.

But Lisa had watched every day and did not miss today. As the Bentley slowly cruised by, there she was again, the haunting blonde beauty. Lisa focused intently on her and her delicate white skin. Her light blue eyes seemed even more surreal than before. Kelly had both arms gently around Kent talking to him. Lisa focused next on the long thick blonde hair and her swan neck. Talk about nubile, Lisa felt old. Kelly seemed from another world, she was so pale, particularly to Lisa whose world was so dominated by olive skin and black skin and black hair.

Lisa was a bit jealous. Then she realized that she had not actually looked at the male Kelly was with. She assumed it was her Kent, but in truth she had not looked in the short time she had.

It's not unusual. A female rarely notices a male unless he is with a woman she finds to be competition, and then she will notice. Lisa had done that the first time but not the second, she was sure it was Kent . . . but she didn't look at him. She didn't have time, so the stunning female took priority.

Kelly gave Kent a long kiss and then walked to the Lancaster Gate subway station. But Lisa had not looked back.

Kent watched her walk away. After fifty yards Kelly turned, looked and waved, Kent was still standing there. At one hundred yards she turned again and he was still there, and he waved a last time.

As Kelly went into the station to wait for the train she realized he had her number but she knew nothing of him, where he was going, when he would come back. She just kind of knew nothing. Maybe it was best because losing her virginity this way was her plan, and it had turned out perfectly. She would remember this for a long time, certainly past her marriage and the birth of her children. It had been a defining moment in her young life and for all the extreme risk in her plan, it had turned out perfectly. Thirty minutes after Kelly took the train, Kent arrived at Northolt by helicopter.

Maybe one day through a maze of twists and turns she would eventually find the irony of ironies, that the first man she had spent time and slept with was actually the basis of her movie project. If only Andy Morris and Frank Cramer could scream from the heavens, "That's him, he is our 4th Mercenary!" Andy and Frank had walked by his place all the time when they were alive, never knowing. And now Kelly did not know . . . and you know . . . maybe she is better off for it. Trent Burton only knew the man on sight and he was ready for a mental hospital. But Trent also would not match the "4ᵗʰ Mercenary" to this man. Only four people ever could match this man's face with the concept of the "4ᵗʰ Mercenary," and each of those four people had been eliminated at the same time in the wet forbidden hills of the Eastern Congo.

CHAPTER 146

As the dark titanium plane with the blood red accents taxied at the Northolt Airport, it passed the LeCirac corporate jet just as Kelly Grant and Abbey Bond were walking up the stairs. They turned to see the plane; it was quite beautiful . . . and quite loud. They took note of the dramatic striking color and continued up the stairs.

Kent Weston, as the young Kelly knew him, was sitting on the other side of the titanium jet, so he did not see Kelly. It didn't matter now as he had his mission assignment, the real world always faded to the background with that condition. He would be Code 087 to some, and Simon Greene to a one Mr. Raja Majani. He was the Simon Greene in Calcutta looking to buy a MIG-23, and now Mr. Majani was to meet him in Muscat, Oman to hopefully finalize the details before General Abdul ran out of time.

The titanium Dassault 7X Tri Jet touched down at Muscat International seven plus hours after leaving London. Kelly and Abbey had long since arrived at their apartments. They would spend the next week trading stories of their ten days off. But Kelly would wait to tell the Kent story; it all seemed so surreal now, those five days with the guy named Kent Weston. But she did have fifty pages of notes from those days, all ideas for the movie, from the sex to the man visiting Kent that day in Hyde Park. The movie would need sex scenes, and until four days ago she would have no idea what to write; now it was all clear to her. Brandon Craig would be interested.

And a day after he was Kent Weston he was Simon Greene and in his suite at the Grand Hyatt – Muscat. Raja Majani had also checked in, so Simon Greene invited him up to his suite.

After ten minutes the man called, Simon quickly went to the bottom line. He would buy the two MIG-23's, plus two spare engines, plus a full load of fuel for both jets for $5.7 million. The planes must be flyable and ready for inspection in four days. And if all was in order, the money would be transferred as the jetfighters took off into the night at 8 p.m. Khartoum time on that fourth day. Tomorrow would be day one, Simon Greene said. The engines would come later.

Mr. Majani took notes furiously, all was to his liking and he hoped General Abdul was ready to move. Mr. Majani was also doing some simple math as to what his commission would be on $5.7 million. In the margins of his paper he wrote $700,000, and that got his blood flowing more than two nineteen-year-old starlets from Hollywood.

Simon Greene asked Mr. Majani to make the call now in his suite, out in the hall, or in Mr. Majani's own suite. It didn't matter, but Simon Greene wanted the answer and the details within two hours. Mr. Majani could find Simon at the pool or walking the beach, but Mr. Majani needed to close and now.

Mr. Majani nodded again and again. He said he would do it. It is the thrill of the close that keeps the sellers waking up every morning. Mr. Majani had navigated meetings in Rangoon, Calcutta, Stone Town, and now Muscat, Oman to do this deal. Between the intrigue of those cities and the sale of jetfighters . . . well, it doesn't get any better. He would like to be on hand for the final transaction but he was not sure he would be invited, and he wasn't sure he wanted to see so many of the faces of the people in this deal. That would likely be dangerous.

Mr. Majani excused himself to make the contacts. It should work, as General Abdul had little time to be picky and had no other dealers he wanted to sell to. Said Alawid had become quite the delusional sociopath sitting in the hot stifling dirt of his wretched mud "business headquarters." And at the other end of the lifestyle spectrum was Farsi Abbas, a slick charming ego-driven man whose opulent life style and major male "toys" masked his cold drive to win everything. General Abdul knew through Sudanese intelligence what happened that day in London when Said Alawid's brother, Ali Alawid, was assassinated outside the Sudan Embassy. Dear old Farsi Abbas had him taken out. One day General Abdul would get around to telling Said Alawid that story, if for no other reason than to watch to see who takes who out. General Abdul would not miss either one.

CHAPTER 147

General Abdul listened intently to Mr. Majani. Mr. Majani spoke continuously for ten minutes. Then General Abdul said he would call him back within fifteen minutes. When the General hung up, he said to himself, "finally." The General then made three phone calls in a row, each only taking about three to four minutes. He had lined this up some time ago.

One of the MIG-23 jets would need to be flown into the airbase thirty miles north of Khartoum. That was to be done tonight. The other jet was already there and had been inspected and flown yesterday, it would be polished up and ready. The jet coming tonight would go through the same process and be set by tomorrow night. So the four days was just right.

Mr. Majani said that a small party would come to Khartoum on the morning of the fourth day. At least two of the men would be the technical inspectors and they would need to be taken to the planes immediately. The other three men were to stay at the Conrad Khartoum Hotel until 6 p.m.

They would then leave the hotel on their own but would need to be "smuggled" into the base for their own inspections. Two would be pilots and would do their own assessments. The third man was Simon Greene and he would also judge the deal. And in the end, he was the "man," meaning he was the man with the money. The man with the money is always the "man."

General Abdul pulled the trigger. Let's do this for $5.7 million, the four-day schedule is a go. Mr. Majani hung up and started counting his money. General Abdul hung up and started counting his money.

CHAPTER 148

The other private jet leaving Northolt that day was the chartered jet of Farsi Abbas with his obsession, the one Lisa Aswanela. The chartered jet was a Gulfstream 250 with an opulent interior. There were only three onboard, Farsi, Lisa and a steward to take care of them.

Their first stop was Rome where Lisa would depart via commercial jet to Johannesburg. She preferred to just leave from London, but Farsi had become very possessive and insisted she spend the last day and a half with him.

From Rome Farsi would take the chartered jet back to Beirut and his waiting family of five. While Farsi circled the globe in five-star style, his family had not left their block in Beirut.

As soon as Lisa got off the jet and finally saw Farsi taxi away, she called Alex Kagamba in Cape Town. Between having to "exist" through ten days with Farsi Abbas and seeing her Kent of Johannesburg with some young nubile blonde siren on the streets of London, she needed some proper male company, she was feeling lonely and neglected. She talked to Alex only a few minutes to tell him she would be in Cape Town within ten days. Alex was ecstatic and then some. Lisa would be in Seat 2A, Alitalia Air, Rome to Johannesburg.

As Farsi Abbas settled into the flight to Beirut, he got a call. A deal appeared to be going down in his very own personal arms dealing backyard while he had been dancing around London playing and shopping. Farsi was first shocked and then angered. How did a deal in the Sudan go down without him getting first shot? He felt a little embarrassed, since instead of taking care of business he had been playing in his sandbox with Lisa. Still this would not stand.

You don't get to Farsi Abbas' level in Sudan without a complete system of spies. He had heard from his key guys and one of them was even reporting from the very hangar where the first MIG-23 sat waiting to be sold in the next three days or so. And that operative already knew that yet another MIG-23 might be coming to be sold as well. The man said he was not clear who the big VIP was for this, but he would stay in touch.

Farsi Abbas immediately called his "big guns" in the Sudanese government telling them of his information. They each professed shock and anger. Who is doing this and more important, where is their cut of the commissions? Farsi hung up knowing full well these parasites were lying. They always lie and Farsi wrote their names on a list, his "list." But in the shady, back-stabbing, greedy, turbulent world of international arms dealing, there is no clear path to who is lying and who is telling the truth. Mr. Ptorn of Thailand was Farsi Abbas' equal in southeast Asia arms dealing, but he died with a body riddled with 9 mm bullets because he believed a man who was clearly lying. Mr. Ptorn's body and the other ten bodies slumped on the road outside Pai, Thailand proved that. Now Farsi Abbas clearly believed he had a whole host of his VIP "friends" in Sudan lying to him . . . when, in fact, they were telling the truth!

Farsi next called his brother Yassar to debate the next step. Clearly Farsi must do something to protect his lucrative turf in Sudan. And just like that all the fun times in London with Lisa and the private jet shopping had vaporized. He now only remembered those days with some pain, as each day he played in London some new deal had come up and passed him by as he played and played. He also had spent and spent. Of course the biggest was for Lisa, he had given her $300,000, and for the first time Farsi was upset with her. She seemed to be a burden just playing to his ego. He had never thought that before. But in the end Lisa was not playing him . . . as always, the male only plays himself . . . women rarely waste energy playing a man.

Why bother when he will do it to himself . . . every time, without fail.

On the subject of money Farsi also snapped to attention. Lisa was so intoxicating that since he met her he had taken it up two or three notches. The deals kept coming, so the money kept flowing. But having to buy a new private jet to replace the one that had been "assassinated" over Angola had woken him to the massive cash flow it took to keep one in the air. He needed to sit down with his accountant in the next day or two in Beirut to go over the "numbers." He had lost track of the money numbers, something a Lebanese Arab would never do . . . well, except when there is a young sultry long-legged woman involved. And Lisa fit that description perfectly.

CHAPTER 149

It was show time, no nonsense show time in Khartoum, Sudan. All was in place. The second MIG-23 had landed under cover of darkness last night. The special contract technicians were on hand to inspect the second MIG-23. At 11 p.m. they had confirmed a go.

The two Ukrainian contract pilots had also come into Khartoum under cover of darkness. Simon Greene was the point man and he would execute this deal with aggressive precision. The crew relaxed during the day, a good idea as it topped 107° in the relentless desert heat of Khartoum.

The city seemed subdued and smothered in the sweltering heat. Mr. Said Alawid was truly suffering in the dirt and grime of his mud hovel. The open sewer was beyond wretched on these days.

Mr. Farsi Abbas was burning up the airwaves to Khartoum trying to catch up and find the status of this rumored MIG-23 deal. He was planning to head there in two days to come face-to-face with his Sudanese contacts. He wanted to know why they had not set him up to do this deal. How did this deal get away, was there some guy "cheating" the system?

General Abdul was already at the base. He had arrived at 10 a.m. and he would wait there. He did not want to show up at the base just in time for two MIG-23 jets to depart. He would plan to leave very visibly at say 2 p.m. to let everyone see him leave. After that he would sneak back in, do the deal, and then sneak back out. He would have to slide under a military truck carrying food to the base to do that. He had set up the truck to come in at 6 p.m., offload and leave the base at 8 p.m. By his plan one of Farsi Abbas' operatives, a Sudanese Brigadier General, would be on the base when the jetfighters departed. General Abdul knew Farsi Abbas was too powerful in Sudan to assume he would not know about this.

Mr. Raja Majani had called to Khartoum to see if all was well. He was so stressed, he wanted to be there but had not been invited.

So for a short time, Khartoum was arms central. The dealers in Calcutta, Khartoum and Beirut were dialed in, even as they might not know it. Even Winston Burton in London knew this was a special day for some of his clients, and he hoped all would go well.

CHAPTER 150

At 7 p.m. the two Ukrainian pilots left the hotel through a back door. Mr. Simon Greene walked right out the front lobby, a casual stride but focused, focused because he missed seeing a stunning young Sudanese girl at the front desk. She had the fine-boned, velvet black skin and chiseled looks that only Sudan can produce. That would have to wait.

The men met in the parking lot and left immediately with a Sudanese driver. At 7:30 p.m. the men hid in the back as the car entered the base. They immediately went to the darkened hangar where the MIG-23's were. With light's out, the planes were towed out to the end of the runway.

Simon Greene met General Abdul. And if they had time, they would be able to establish that this Simon Greene was the same Mirage F-1B pilot who had leveled his base in Western Sudan. He was also the pitiful man who had come to General Abdul's base to plan the attack. General Abdul was only alive to make this deal through good luck, he had missed the devastation by only ten minutes but certainly witnessed the firestorm. Now this same man was back to shake his hand, but no one knew this story.

Simon Greene had made a command decision in the last five minutes. The pilots were going to go to the planes and fly them away. No tests, no touch and goes, just start the engines and blaze away. There was a risk in this, but Simon Greene decided to just go for it.

He wired General Abdul the first $3 million immediately, as they stood in the darkness. The remaining $2.7 million would be wired five minutes after takeoff. What General Abdul didn't know is that Simon Greene was going to be in the cockpit of the second MIG-23 when he wired the money. And he was.

He excused himself from the General and disappeared into the darkness. The Ukrainian pilots were already in. As Simon Greene strapped in, the pilots started the engines.

And fifty seconds later a startled and shocked General Abdul watched as the MIG-23 lit the afterburners and roared down the runway. Simon Greene had faded into the darkness and did not return. Within thirty seconds the vibrating roar of the MIG-23's had left an eerie silence. General Abdul stood in the dark silence, his jaw dropped as he felt he had been screwed, really screwed, but he had little time for pity as he needed to get off the base quickly without anyone seeing. Just as he was sure this sleazy "arms dealer" had done him in, a message came on his phone. "Here is $3 million, keep the change, Simon Greene." The General then smiled and pumped his fist, nice doing business with you Mr. Greene. It was 7:47 p.m.

CHAPTER 151

The two MIG-23's never got above two hundred feet as they roared to the west. Seven minutes after takeoff Simon Greene gave them the coordinates for a lonely beat up airfield. It was twenty-seven minutes away. The sound of two MIG-23's roaring two hundred feet off the deck would likely kill some camels of heart failure.

Flying at two hundred feet in pitch black is a difficult job, as there is no sense of space or time. Even the twenty-seven minutes it took to get to the airstrip required a lot of focus; everything was so surreal in the total darkness . . . and at 500 mph.

At three minutes out from the base Simon Greene spoke briefly and some makeshift runway lights came on. The jets climbed to one thousand feet and then dropped onto the runway. It wasn't pretty. The jets slammed into the baked clay and sand, the MIG-23's massive shock absorbers being stretched to the limit. Rocks and sand were flying everywhere. The jets were swerving and throwing up a storm of sand and debris. It was as surreal as the short flight. But in the end they managed to stop the jets just fifty yards before the hardcore desert began and a sure wreck and fireball.

They shut down the engines and all the landing lights were killed. The violent landing with the shadows and the bright landing lights gave way to pitch black and eerie quiet.

Simon Greene told everyone to stay put, and five minutes later two tow vehicles came. And after all the roar and rough dust on landing, the three pilots sat quietly with open canopies and enjoyed the quiet of another desert night in Chad as they were towed in.

Slam, bam and just like that this mission was over, but the swirling levels of intrigue it had stirred up had only begun.

The Ukrainian MIG-23 pilots were hustled into a nondescript truck and carried one hundred miles to another dirt airstrip. There they were hustled onboard as the only passengers on a small military transport and flew three hours to a field outside Ndjamena, Chad. Two hours later they were on an Air France flight to Paris. By the time they spent the night in Paris, the next morning would be surreal . . . did all of that just happen. One thing for the pilots, since they could fly the MIG-23's and stay straight without diving into a bottle of vodka, they were sure to get some additional "contracts" now that the MIG-23 was part of the fleet.

Simon Greene stayed at the beaten, tortured heat-soaked "base" in Eastern Chad. The next day he left his underground bunker and walked to the hanger, and there it was, the infamous Mirage F-1B jetfighter. He noticed some new panels. The security was very tight but Simon Greene had access, he was a three-star level mercenary pilot on this base, maybe the only one with access . . . this location was very special in a very special world. He wasn't sure what the schedule was but it didn't really matter, he would relax at his desert "resort," a desert resort that may be the most pitiful desolate and heat-racked piece of land on the face of the earth. It didn't matter, this Simon Greene was used to oscillating between the posh luxury of a suite in Beverly Hills, Honolulu or Monaco, and then heading to this pitiful place or one of equal misery in the Congo, Burma or Somalia, or maybe some miserable jungle in Colombia. It was all good, although he did need to head to Nassau, Bahamas to check his accounts. Sure there was the internet, but he was going into the actual bank lobby and talk directly to a human being. And that's the way he rolled.

CHAPTER 152

As Simon Greene strolled and looked at the magnificent lines of the Dassault F-1B, another set of lines were boarding Alitalia 802, Rome to Johannesburg by way of Nairobi. Lisa had spent the night in Rome, it was wonderful, just a quiet night, and particularly great because . . . no Farsi Abbas. She was being paid an absurd amount of money for being a pet and companion, yet it was an ever more tiring job for which the pay did not seem enough, as bizarre as that sounds. Now she was upbeat as she was heading home, and then in a week or so she would see Alex Kagamba. She was ready for a man between her legs, and she still had thoughts of Kent and the haunting beauty of the blonde at Hyde Park. Lisa could just see her undressed and Kent having her, maybe even the knees on the chair with that little butt raised. It was one of her favorite positions, and she would love to meet the nubile blond to ask her, her favorite position.

As Lisa was nurturing her apple juice, she noticed the tall elegant Italian copilot and he noticed her. They nodded to each other acknowledging that they both were the beautiful people of this earth. Lisa was sure the Italian would find time to say hello, after all it was five hours to Nairobi.

As Lisa thought about the coming weeks, she was so absorbed she did not notice that a male passenger had settled in next to her, a young pleasant looking man who was never a threat to sexy women, so the women were almost always friendly.

They said their simple hellos and then the young man became involved in his work. And he stayed involved with his work until about one hour out of Nairobi.

Lisa got into a light chat with him, which developed into his work. He was doing development work on a project that had to do with story themes and locations. He asked her about herself and she said she had done some modeling and acting, and she wasn't lying. Her whole time with Farsi Abbas had been a year long acting job, off Broadway of course.

Their light conversation was interrupted by the Italian pilot who did the usual "fly-by" with his card, his Italian Riviera smile and invitation to dinner. Lisa didn't say no as she was feeling the need to take on a number of males now, the freedom from Farsi Abbas was intoxicating and she would take more and more.

As Lisa was diverted by the pilot's conversation, the man next to her had time to assemble his thoughts and piece together his memory.

As Lisa returned to their conversation, the man had put it together. He told Lisa that maybe she had been in Cape Town, say six to seven weeks ago. She said yes, that's right. The man said he had teased her about being in a movie. Lisa thought about it, and then laughed. It was true, and now she placed this chubby young man. Yes, it was him. They laughed, truly a small world.

The man in Seat 3B was Brandon Craig, he was doing location research and on the way to see Todd Blake in Johannesburg, the same Brandon Craig who had survived the violent air attack in Angola to end up living the good life in Cape Town at the film festival, and in the process discovering Lisa Aswanela on the harbor sidewalk. The ironies were everywhere.

Their world connected in more than that way, the very aircraft wreck in Angola that had put Brandon Craig in ultimate danger, that very plane was on its way to Cape Town to pick up this very Lisa to bring her to London. And few would ever know that the jetfighter that had downed that plane was piloted by the same man known as The 4th Mercenary. And that same man had by chance met and been seduced by Brandon Craig's top assistant, Kelly Grant. The 4ᵗʰ Mercenary was everywhere . . . and he was nowhere.

As the plane touched down in Nairobi, Brandon Craig insisted on getting Lisa in the movie. Lisa didn't say no. Brandon was leaving the plane in Nairobi to scout locations but would be in Johannesburg in three days, could he talk to Lisa then? Lisa didn't say no. Maybe she would even come to Nice sometime, and he would lay the whole project out. The project would definitely feature young sexy exotic girls, and they don't come anymore sultry and exotic than Lisa Aswanela. Maybe if Lisa came to Nice she would meet the Kelly Grant of Kent and Hyde Park fame. And there you go; the ironies keep piling up. Throw in Trent Burton, who was the only man to place The 4ᵗʰ Mercenary face with the infamous Congo mercenary camp, and eventually someone would map the relationships and all their lives and survival would be infinitely more perilous.

But ignorance is bliss, and Brandon Craig got off the plane recharged about the project. Lisa would clearly light up the screen, exotic sultry and long-legged, and Brandon Craig did not even know about the Aston Martin parked at her townhouse in Sandton. Nor did he know about the French or South African intelligence connections. Ignorance was in fact bliss, and Brandon Craig was sure he had found the first live body for the movie. And what a body she did have, she could easily take this to the next level. Brandon Craig was sure of it.

CHAPTER 153

Far to the northwest of Nairobi the man in these conversations was still at the blast furnace of hard clay and blasting sand. He had "cooled his heels" at this wretched hole for three days now. And it was a hole. Simon Greene's quarters were thirty feet below the desert. In his complex things were very cool and comfortable with all the right amenities; it's just as he went to the surface that the apocalypse appeared. There was actually no sign of life here, just endless scorching desert. Simon Greene would be patient, "they" would call, he was sure of that.

In Cape Town Alex Kagamba was excited about Lisa's arrival next week. He was also happy about his latest deal with General Mosamba. A small one, but it seemed General Mosamba was ramping up for something and it didn't involve his Ugandan Western Force. Alex Kagamba was not in this business to judge ethics, he would judge cash flow.

General Mosamba was up to something and he needed to arm his new army, the new army in Northeast Congo that he had formed to take over a five hundred square mile stretch to get to the "mine." The mine had something to do with rare minerals that the West used to make electronics and cell phones or something. All he knew was the stuff was moved in one hundred-pound bags and could bring real money. General Mosamba knew he could get some airlifted to Kampala, Uganda, then truck it to a warehouse in Mombasa, Kenya, then sell it to the Chinese, Europeans or Americans. To do that, job one was to slaughter probably three hundred soldiers of the latest warlord to hold this territory. There had been so much fighting lately that only a small part of the ore had been moved, but it did seem the latest warlord had a privileged position and was business-like. General Mosamba didn't care, he was going in.

General Mosamba's target warlord, a self-styled General Simbas, had just taken a call from a Winston Burton. General Simbas was standing in the black mud of Northeast Congo as the rain came down. Winston Burton was standing on a polished black marble floor in his office complex, Mayfair, London. When the phone call ended, General Simbas waded through mud to his wrecked Soviet Jeep, Winston Burton skipped down the marble steps to his waiting Rolls Royce. But General Simbas was a very happy man, he had received the blessing of Winston Burton, it was better than the Pope, and his recent trouble with the "new" General Mosamba might be over, at least the right guy was on his side . . . at least for now.

CHAPTER 154

It is Ta205. That is the element designation for tantalum ore, that earthen ore that is a must have for the one billion plus cell phones made every year around the world. That it is produced in the most primitive violent and subsistence cultures on earth to be used by a vast majority of the slick well-spoken and educated set, is just one of the endless ironies that is human existence.

The miners themselves often had shovels as their only "capital equipment." It was grueling work in the extreme, not only because of relentless rain, but when the sun was out it was brutal and laser-like. The ore was loaded in one hundred-pound sacks and muscled out of the open pits by another segment of young illiterate workers. No one in this group would see forty years old. The labor, the food, the fevers would see to that. And if not, then likely the boy soldiers who policed the pits and played God whenever they got enough drugs in them. It was a grueling thankless existence, all for the Ta205, an abstract concept lost on most people but certainly on the simple men just trying to live just one more day.

Most of the tantalum ore is dug by hand in the DRC Congo. But as you would expect in one of the most tortured landscapes on earth, the Eastern Congo, they had found a small area producing tantalum. And once that area was found the warlords soon found the pitiful miners to dig the ore out in pits up to fifty feet deep. And the whole "Blood Diamonds" story starts again, except this time the miners risking their lives don't comprehend why this "dirt" is worth anything. At least with diamonds there is a human connection to the sparkle and colors. Here it is just dirt, but they dig the dirt for, there is that word again, money. And not just any money, but the worn dirty tattered money that is the Banque Centrale du Congo Franc. To see an American money bill is to drop to your knees and thank God, as an American dollar bill is more mesmerizing than a diamond stone. And it should be, as it is rarer than diamonds in the Congo.

And into this rotten abyss steps large, confident General Mosamba, the Commander of the Western Force-Uganda and the self-appointed Supreme Commander of his growing DRC-Congo militia. His eyes are set on the tantalum ore fields of the North Kivu Province. These fields were an unexpected find, as most of the real tantalum is in Katanga Province to the far south in DRC-Congo. But a small field is fine for now as General Mosamba, just like General Abdul of Sudan, was recently promoted so he is eager to turn his position into real money.

The only downside General Mosamba can see is that this local Congo warlord, General Simbas, has started to stake his claim also. Another downside unknown to General Mosamba is that a man in the person of Winston Burton has decided that General Simbas will be his "man" to protect and stabilize the region around the mine fields. And the credit line Winston Burton set up with Ward Kent during that power lunch on the Upper East Side of New York City is where Mr. Burton has the advantage. Mr. Burton provides order and stability so that a critical global commodity gets to market. Lots of companies pay very well for that service, and that elaborate professional mercenary camp in South Kivu does not run on charitable donations.

Recently General Mosamba sent a small force of Congolese hired guns to take out twenty or so of General Simbas growing militia. General Simbas took note and reported back to Mr. Winston Burton, so now it was game on.

To field an adequate team General Mosamba would need the services of Farsi and Yassar Abbas, and he would have Alex Kagamba in reserve with contracts and help the young man grow his arms business.

Farsi Abbas was the key man. He was powerful and now rich and his contacts went high in places like Sudan, Syria and South Africa. Farsi Abbas also had Lisa Aswanela and the General thought her to be as big a prize as "his" now tantalum mine. He couldn't wait to get her wrapped around his large black body. She won't be able to walk for a week, and he smiled broadly at the thought.

Alex Kagamba was thinking the same thoughts about Lisa, except he was in the place of General Mosamba. Alex did not have a clue how complicated Lisa could make his life or all of these lives. First there was Farsi Abbas, a ruthless arms dealer who obsessed about Lisa. Then we have General Mosamba who expects to be a big customer of Farsi and who also lusts after Lisa. And then General Mosamba, who Alex expects to become his big client, may want Lisa as Alex Kagamba's "kick back" payment for arms deals. Lisa is a valuable property no matter who the player is. Valuable except for a guy named Kent Benson. He treasures Lisa as much as the next guy . . . but he is not bidding. It is only worth something if someone will pay for it, whether its sultry long-legged girls or what looks to be common dirt . . . but isn't . . . it's tantalum.

CHAPTER 155

The road out of Eastern Chad was not much of a road at all. The Simon Greene of the Sudan MIG-23 deal was being moved overland. He was wrapped in robes like a Tuareg or Bedouin nomadic tribesman, not only to disguise himself but also because the 20-mph wind from the west was like a blow torch in his face.

For him to be on the move this way meant contracts were delayed or the runway had become so rough as to be unusable. No one told him which one it was, so he was stuck in this beat up two-ton military truck with two escorts, guys that looked like they had come right out of the French Foreign Legion recruiting poster. The truck was much more powerful than it looked and carried a big cargo under a tarp in the rear bed.

Simon Greene was known as Mr. Stanley to the two soldiers or mercenaries. Mr. Stanley was not quite sure of their status, no one spoke much, but he thought they were mercenaries.

The terrain was from a devastated planet unlike earth. The three men carried as much water as gasoline, but the truck was loaded with both. Mr. Stanley assumed a long journey and the two men agreed, it could be as far as into Niger, which would be at least eight hundred miles. It wasn't clear why this journey was necessary for Mr. Stanley, but often that was not discussed with him.

The first day passed as you would expect, endless sand dunes and endless heat. Mr. Stanley had the back seats of the truck to himself, so he tried to relax while basking in the 125° resort weather of Chad. The two men switched out driving every six hours or so, and after thirteen hours they stopped and pitched camp.

The "camp" was merely a set of tents that attached to the rear of the truck. It was well designed with compartments for each man, and the prepackaged meals were quite good. There was plenty of cool water, so it was restful and everyone was asleep by 7 p.m.

Mr. Stanley woke at midnight and took a brief stroll. The stars overhead were miraculous, so bright in the complete absence of light in this desert. The temperature had dropped to 90°.

As Mr. Stanley strolled to the front of the truck, he found one of the men sitting on the massive front bumper with an AK-47. While the desert looked vacant and barren, it was still dangerous. Over any dune could be the random roving gang of Arab men, and the truck and supplies would be an inviting target.

In fact, as the two men relaxed at the front of the truck, Mr. Stanley thought he saw a glimpse of light a mile or so away. The soldier saw it too. So now both were awake, but the next hour did not produce a repeat sighting and Mr. Stanley returned to his cot as the second soldier took his watch until dawn.

At dawn the men had breakfast and a short stroll. One hundred yards from their camp Mr. Stanley found a whole series of camel prints. Either a caravan had passed without anyone knowing it, soldiers or camels, or the camel group had come to spy on the truck and then had moved on . . . for now.

The bright desert sun made all of those ghosts disappear for now. The truck was refueled, and this lovely rugged truck started again on its tortured journey in a tortured land.

CHAPTER 156

As Mr. Stanley subsisted in his world in the furnace heat of Chad, his new acquaintance Kelly Grant of London and Nice had continued her luxurious existence in Nice; wonderful food, great projects, posh furnishings everywhere, and her friend Abbey Bond to laugh and play with. She did remember Kent, maybe he would call, but her life was grand and she was so balanced to be so beautiful that she did not dwell on imagined soap operas in her life. Women love soap operas so they create them out of thin air, they have to, as the deadly boredom of suburbia is a creative wasteland. There are no soap operas, but they create them out of the flimsiest material.

Kelly continued to work the movie and she had narrated the London scenes into a plot. She included a rather racy description of the sex scenes and thus created a massive buzz in the offices. Did she just imagine those scenes or live them? She looked too innocent to live them, but that was what the buzz was about. Did she or didn't she? Fantasies took off and Brandon Craig loved her work.

And in Johannesburg Brandon Craig did meet Lisa Aswanela at Mandela Square for lunch. And as usual there was a willing troop of male onlookers. Lisa did agree to work with Brandon Craig, the project sounded interesting and it seemed real. Part of the projects credibility was just the appearance of Brandon Craig. He just was not a physical or social threat to Lisa, and she found that endearing. He was studious and disciplined and even if she said "let's go to bed," it's likely it would have gone over his head. Brandon felt Lisa didn't need the money, but he offered her a "retainer" of $3,000 on the spot. Lisa declined, and said once she had done something for the project they could talk money. Lisa needed the project and mental stimulation far more than she needed the money . . . and she was only nineteen.

The British writer Todd Blake was 47-years-old and desperately needed the money. He met Brandon Craig the next day after the Lisa meeting and again in Mandela Square. Todd had memories of how he and Jeremy Keeler would meet here to dream about the "big score" they would make with the "4th Mercenary" book and movie. It had only been a short six or seven months, but it seemed like a lifetime ago. All the promise of those times vanished in a black sinister haze of violence that Todd Blake could only imagine, as no one had ever heard anything of what had happened.

At least with the Brandon Craig project he had a lifeline to make a little money and also talk about his friend Jeremy Keeler to someone.

Brandon Craig was trying to get some picture or framework for this 4th Mercenary in talking to Todd. Todd was honest, he said he could provide a clear picture of Andy Morris and Frank Kramer but that was it. Their research subject seemed too elusive and if they actually saw or talked to the man, it was not clear. Todd Blake could recount the intrigue leading up to the supposed meeting with the "4th Mercenary" in the Congo, the random luck of Bryan Norton in Nassau, Bahamas, the random luck of Trent Burton spotting the same man in the Eastern Congo, and then nothing. Bryan Norton actually had photos of the man from Nassau, but they were likely disintegrated along with Bryan Norton's body on that lonely slope overlooking the mercenary base in the Congo. So Brandon had a blank slate to develop the "4th Mercenary" as he wanted, but Todd Blake had been useful because the events that Todd Blake did know about leading up to the disappearances would be quite useful. Todd did recount how Bryan Norton had gone on and on about some fabulous young Bahamian girl with light green eyes who The 4th Mercenary had been with. That was stuff Brandon could use for his project. What Brandon could have used also, had he known, was that the light green eyes of Erica the

Bahamian girl would have contrasted perfectly with the light blue eyes of his British assistant Kelly, and both had slept with The 4th Mercenary. Now there is a movie. But nobody, the girls, Brandon Craig, Todd Blake or Javier Henri knew anything. Throw in the magnificent Lisa and no one could put the pieces together. Not everything in this world needs to be known.

CHAPTER 157

The subject of all these discussions was just trying to survive the second grueling day in the endless tan landscape of massive dunes that is the Sahara Desert.

Mr. Stanley was pulling a four-hour drive shift as the other two men had hit the wall of exhaustion. They had not seen anything at all, all day.

It was 4 p.m. and the two men were still in a coma of sleep. Mr. Stanley decided to end the torture for today. About two miles ahead was the sight of three lonely palm trees and that was mission objective, just make it to the three palm trees. There was likely water there, but maybe twenty feet below the sand. That is the only way those palms could be living. However, they didn't need water or anything, they needed only rest. Mr. Stanley would position the truck away from the palm trees by two hundred yards so that there would be no reason to come close to the truck.

The truck itself had become quite impressive to Mr. Stanley. He had not seen in the back and was surprised by the size of the water/fuel tanks and was also surprised to discover a massive Russian machine gun that fired explosive rounds the size of a large cigar.

He now paid attention to this truck. With the load of fuel, water and now this massive gun with some two hundred rounds of very heavy bullets, this truck must be a turbo diesel with 700 plus horsepower. It was a six-wheeler and had navigated through the treacherous sand without too much struggle. The bed was very large, and the last space was used by three coffin-like structures. And the final touch to this beast was three air-conditioned compartments, one for each guy. They were to be used to recharge the men as the trip became unbearable. It had hit 45°C today and had become life threatening. In fact, he needed to get the men up and drinking water, a five-hour sleep without water is life-threatening here. The wind blasts from the east hit 30 mph and scorched everything it touched, a massive blowtorch under a laser piercing sun. It was clear after only two days that they were all on the thin edge of survival.

As the blistering sand hit Mr. Stanley he opened the truck door to wake the men, only to suffer a burn from the door handle.

The men were in decent shape, but Mr. Stanley hustled them into the shower alongside the truck and each got one-half gallon of cold water. One thing this truck had was the fuel, water and power systems to give them a chance. Then he put them in the air-conditioned compartments for a three-hour rest. At that time one would come on to watch and Mr. Stanley would shower and rest, he had hit the wall as well.

And what was all of this about anyway, some kind of desert boot camp. Mr. Stanley had not a clue at this time.

CHAPTER 158

As the blow torch sun began to set in a territory Mr. Stanley guessed was between Chad and Niger, Kelly Grant, Abbey Bond and Javier Henri LeCirac settled down at a harbor side cafe to enjoy a light supper, as a cooling breeze came off the Mediterranean. Life was smooth and good. The Porsches cruised by, the Ferraris cruised by, the light chatter, the laughs, it was a world away from most peoples' lives and it was a universe away from Mr. Stanley's existence. Kelly would not be able to comprehend the difficulty he was currently in, and she would likely not recognize him as the Kent she knew from Bayswater Road and Hyde Park. His skin was deep brown.

Brandon Craig was enjoying another sit down with Todd Blake in Sandton, South Africa. He had some wonderful notes and themes for the movie from their discussions. The crisp air of Sandton was very pleasant tonight and the wine chilled to perfection.

Little did Brandon know that Lisa was only five minutes away by her Aston Martin, but he would call her tomorrow. That meeting also held a lot of promise for the movie, his first casting decision.

Alex Kagamba was set for Lisa Aswanela in Cape Town. He too was relaxing at harbor side Cape Town with a light supper, as the sun set over the cool Atlantic Ocean. Only poor Farsi Abbas was not doing well. He was in his standard bland apartment in Beirut with his family. He was screaming into the phone at some poor deputy minister in Sudan about his missed MIG-23 deal. He knew the fighters were gone, as his source at the base told him they roared away and never came back.

Then Farsi's phone rang, he just hung up on Sudan and turned into the slick soothing smooth operator he could be in an instant, it was the new client, General Mosamba.

General Mosamba was ready to do some business. Farsi turned into a charmer and a meeting was set for next week. Where? General Mosamba was not too subtle and he was quite used to the arms dealers providing the girls. With that, General Mosamba said he wanted to meet wherever that Lisa girl would be. Farsi Abbas was afraid of that and now he had a problem on his hands, a big problem. He felt like putting a bullet in the black man's head, he would never touch Lisa! But you would never know it. Farsi laughed and said he would certainly do his best, if not Lisa maybe Sarah, Farsi suggested. General Mosamba laughed and smoothly said Lisa would be preferred now, maybe both later. The two smooth brutal males exchanged their warmest regards, as they both clenched their fists and reached for their guns. The call ended on the politest of terms with Farsi saying that General Mosamba had excellent taste and Lisa it would be. He would have to arrange it, but they could meet in Sandton next week, say in eight days. The General said yes. Farsi would catch a break, as Lisa would disappear to Cape Town in six days. As Farsi hung up he was livid with anger, but what did he expect, it was only business. But even the slyest male crosses over into irrational rage when a certain woman is involved. The slick Farsi Abbas had become a danger to himself with Lisa. It happens every day. The men do it to themselves every day, and the world keeps turning.

CHAPTER 159

Mr. Stanley was at least lucky to have two professionals onboard. Right at three hours one of the men came out to relieve him. All had been quiet except for these small instances of what looked like a flashlight to the west. It looked like the same light from the first night. Mr. Stanley said he heard nothing, but the total blackness was so overwhelming he was not sure of anything. He suggested they all go to the night goggles; the darkness was so complete that any danger would go undetected until too late.

The man agreed. In another four hours the next man would come. Mr. Stanley was going to shower, drink a gallon of cold water, and hit his air-conditioned coffin.

As he was leaving, the man gave him a large rugged cell phone. He said his orders were to wait two days and then give the phone to him. It had fingerprint recognition and would detail the mission, as well as what the three very rugged protected switches were for.

Mr. Stanley took it, then took his shower and went to his coffin to be cool, look at this device and sleep, sleep, sleep.

CHAPTER 160

And so, it was to be. Mr. Stanley's reward for the intricate maze followed to get the MIG-23's was to be awarded a life-threatening march across endless desert in 125°+ weather. Mr. Stanley didn't take it personally, it was just business. There were no Employee of the Month awards in this business, there were no promotions to regional vice president, and there were no award banquets. There were simply some special contracts to be completed and the reward was a lot of adventure, a few young long-legged girls and then, well, there was the contract I suppose. In the end it just beat being shipwrecked in suburbia. Compared to the wife, the kids and the mortgage, well, this wasn't that bad.

The device outlined the mission, and it appeared there were at least three more days of this desert death march before it was "go time." Apparently the client wanted a long march so the surprise would not be believed afterward. It was one of those, "there is no way they would have crossed that territory," and then they . . . crossed that territory. Sounded interesting to him, our exhausted Mr. Stanley, and then he fell into a deep sleep, a sleep just barely above a coma.

CHAPTER 161

At the weekend Kelly Grant and Abbey Bond ventured to Monaco just to stroll, look at the shops and do lunch on the harbor. They were dressed conservatively but still projected a quiet and stunning beauty. Kelly still had not told Abbey of the exploits with Kent in London, maybe there was no need to, time had passed. But Abbey did notice Kelly carried herself a little differently, a little more knowing, a little less innocence.

Brandon Craig met Lisa at Mandela Square. It was a good meeting and Lisa said she was interested. Brandon said he would formalize this in the next week or so when he returned to Nice. As the project developed over the next two months, he would lay the whole concept out. At some point as things matured Lisa could come to Nice and Monaco for two weeks, one week of working and reviewing the project, and one week to play on the French Riviera. Lisa laughed, she would like that and the Porsches and Ferraris of Nice would fit nicely with the Aston Martins of Sandton, South Africa, and Lisa strolling the beaches in some kind of thong would be epic. Javier Henri LeCirac and his buddies would have an exotic animal to pursue. The beautiful people were alive and well.

The wretched and oppressed were not doing well, in the best of times they don't do well. But these had not been the best of times, not since the colonial times when North Kivu Province was part of the Belgian Congo. Now another of the countless warlords of the Congo was muscling in on other countless warlords trying to get a few bags of ore out for a little money. And General Mosamba's group had just surrounded thirty-five of General Simbas' group and had executed thirty of them, keeping five to work as slave porters or workers in his camp. It was the same old story. The thirty were marched only a hundred yards into the jungle and then simply shot. The boy soldiers as usual used way too much ammunition, to the point that threads of clouds from the firing drifted out of the jungle into the pitiful dirt village. The stench of gun smoke, the stench of death, in a way it wasn't slaughter, it wasn't brutal . . . it was the Congo being the Congo.

General Mosamba got the call from his lead commander. General Mosamba was ecstatic; this was going to be a celebration given some more boys and weapons. He was going to get the funds and then call up Farsi Abbas to get his weapons, maybe give some business to the young Alex Kagamba. He would celebrate with a week on Lisa, Lisa was definitely in the mix and Farsi needed to deliver on that as much as the weapons the General would order.

Meanwhile the other warlord, General Simbas, had heard of the execution of his troops near the village of Nia-Nia in the far northeast of the Congo. He needed to meet his enemies soon to at least stop their successful attacks. This was the third in a row, and his teenage soldiers would switch to the side that had the best drugs and killed the most if he did not make a change soon.

General Simbas placed a call by the satellite phone to Winston Burton. The retired general answered and listened for five minutes and then said he would begin the move soon.

As Winston Burton hung up he returned to his Beef Wellington dish at the LaSalle-Mayfair, London restaurant. He continued his conversation with Ward Kent of New York City, then Winston Burton added as an afterthought that he would need to tap about $30 million of his new credit line. Ward Kent said it would be arranged.

As the men continued their lunch a magnificent dark green Rolls Royce waited at the curb outside. There was room for only two such vehicles in front of the restaurant, the other spot was empty now as Farsi Abbas was still stuck in the dreary Beirut suburb with his extremely boring family existence.

CHAPTER 162

The next two days in the Sahara Desert were the same as the first two. Grim, endless, bleak, barren, scorched, gritty, apocalyptic, seared . . . and, oh yes, grim, endless and bleak. You get the idea. At this point Mr. Stanley was dedicated to minute by minute survival. The world of Hyde Park, London, Kelly Grant, Lisa Aswanela, Eva of Havana, sidewalk cafes in Nice or Chiang Mai or South Beach . . . everything went so far back in the recesses of his mind that they seemed no more than surreal fantasies from several lifetimes ago.

The only reason, the very only reason this mission was going forward was simply the truck. Each day it became more of a marvel. The engine was relentlessly powerful, the cool water seemed endless, and the air conditioning in the cab and sleeping quarters was clearly the only reason the three were alive. The fuel supplies stored onboard also seemed endless. There was little stress each day as this massive machine seemed to take the extreme heat and endless sand in stride.

It was clear that only three men were selected, because with each man added the stress on the capacity of the systems needed would escalate. With three men everything was fine, but add a fourth and all systems would be stressed. The truck had an array of auxiliary tanks and auxiliary motors to meet the mission. Running low on fuel, then another tank was selected and turned on and the valued fuel flowed. They likely consumed 50+ gallons a day, so on this fourth day they were into the fourth tank with plenty of fuel left. One thing in their favor in this fourth day with the burning of the fuel and consuming water the truck was likely 1,000 pounds lighter already, that helped on its power requirements. But in the end it was the truck and its intricate design and special systems, which was the only reason these three guys were still alive and actually quite strong. They had switched to the air-conditioned cab on the third day, and they sat in 70° comfort with cold water as the landscape outside the dark tinted windows hit 130° during the mid-day. Their sleeping coffins also kept them at 70°, even as the oven-like evening still stayed at 105°+.

They saw nothing, absolutely nothing. The three palm trees from the second day seemed a distant memory. On they went. Mr. Stanley took his four-hour shift driving to make sure everyone was strong, as each day they got closer to the mission objective. Mr. Stanley was the only one with the mission details, but he would brief the other two men tonight. They had been great professionals, hard, lean and steely-eyed men, clearly from years with the French Foreign Legion . . . but no one talked about that . . . they actually talked very little. It seemed each man was saving energy, focusing on the blistering barren landscape, but with thoughts of the unknown mission ahead.

And on this fourth day Mr. Stanley viewed the inventory of the weapons onboard. He would brief the two guys tonight. In addition to everything else, the truck was loaded with a tremendous amount of firepower for three guys. If they had in fact developed a complete surprise package for their mission, they would be able to choose what they wanted to use and when they wanted to use it. But of course the special cell phone had the whole order of battle laid out, and it certainly seemed more than enough to do the job. Time would tell.

CHAPTER 163

Farsi Abbas had his chartered Gulfstream IV touch down in Khartoum, Sudan. It had taken him two days to line up this charter, then he had to pay an extra $100,000 to get it to land in Beirut. Beirut wasn't that volatile but it was next to Syria and the fighting, and therefore the charter companies could put an extra $100,000 in their pocket. Next time it might be more. Farsi Abbas made a note to himself that he needed to buy a private jet, he had shopped long enough. He and Lisa would hit London again, buy the jet and then spend ten days just relaxing in London, maybe fly to Paris or Milan for a day or two, then back to London. The thought of that lifted his spirits and he would use the thought of the London trip to get him through the next two weeks or so.

First up Khartoum, then Sandton to meet General Mosamba, and then there was the Lisa issue with General Mosamba. Things were rocky enough without that.

Khartoum was brutally hot, even in Farsi Abbas' five-star hotel. Given his special status in Sudan, he called the government contacts to his hotel and then turned up the air conditioner.

The first two officials came and after enduring Farsi's rant, calmly and meekly told him what little they knew. The whole weapons deal was done quickly and quietly, they said. With the recent promotions in the military it was hard to know if the "old" generals or the "new" generals were behind it. It wasn't the "old" generals, Farsi Abbas exploded, they know this game and the power. So who are the "new" generals?

The men had done their homework knowing this was coming. Their story had two major points to soothe Farsi Abbas. He picked up on the fact that a new Brigadier General had actually been on the base when the MIG-23's took off. No other generals were seen. Secondly, their reliable sources in the Khartoum mud slums had seen a military party pay a visit to a one Said Alawid. That had been some weeks ago. They didn't know the details of it or the actual identities of the military party, but the shifty eyes of the alleyways in those miserable slums clearly saw military uniforms go into the Said Alawid mud compound area.

Farsi Abbas instantly became the smooth charming salesman that kept him at the top of his game. He became gracious and the men relaxed. To keep the good vibes going the men also said that a new three-star general, a General Abdul, was planning to meet with Mr. Abbas to discuss future requirements. And just like that General Abdul had cleared the deal. Farsi Abbas just wanted heads to roll, the parties didn't actually have to be guilty. Farsi had a new young Brigadier General on his radar and that miserable smelly rat, Said Alawid. Farsi saw it this way, Said Alawid was trying to cut him out and Said Alawid was getting into the new generation to do it. And Farsi knew Said Alawid was playing the "help a poor Muslim brother" routine so he could completely rape and pillage that same Muslim brother. Said was offering $300,000 per MIG-23 tops so he could move those same planes a week later at $2.5 million. Nice work if you can get it, but more than his greedy business way. Farsi despised the massive heap of dirty rotting flesh Said Alawid was. His older brother was obese and disgusting, but he did take a bath every two days. He also was a "respectable arms dealer," if there is such a category and that was worth something. What it was "worth" was when Farsi Abbas put a contract out to kill Ali Alawid, he did it professionally. Ali Alawid was killed quickly and humanely in the affluent streets of Knightsbridge, London. It also was done in the quiet opulence of Ali Alawid's Bentley limousine, that's as respectful and as quiet as it gets. Farsi Abbas would not go to that expense for Said Alawid.

Of course Said Alawid also had plans for Farsi Abbas. Farsi was his own version of sleaze to Said Alawid, as bizarre as it is on the surface. Farsi with his polish, private jets, Rolls Royce's, Bentleys, penthouse suites, etc., etc., was not right to Said Alawid. Money to Said was a religion stronger than Islam, and you don't disrespect money by spending it. And on the Muslim level Said Alawid was sure Farsi Abbas went to bed with every non-Muslim woman he could find or buy, and that was not right.

As the two government men left Farsi Abbas' suite, Farsi was talking quietly to another party. The party was located in Khartoum, but not the nice part, in fact the man on the other end just happened to be navigating his way over an open sewer in a mud back alley that measured maybe ten feet across. The open sewer had a nice flow to it . . . and it was 107° in that cramped alley with twenty-five-foot high mud walls on each side. You get the picture.

CHAPTER 164

Brandon Craig returned from his African trip ecstatic. Meeting and "signing" Lisa had been epic. Brandon Craig thought the chance of his seeing this nineteen-year-old goddess again after Cape Town was zero, and then she shows up in the seat next to him! All of that went well, as she was onboard for a part in the movie and he couldn't wait for her to come to Nice.

The project was progressing rapidly and Javier Henri continued to be amazed at the progress and pace, and especially the creativity of his small team. He gave Brandon Craig full rein now, as he was so efficient and creative. He had read Brandon's project notes and developing storyline and thought it to be very clever. This would be an excellent movie and Javier Henri thought that before he had even gotten to Kelly Grant's script development, which had some very definite sex scenes and drama. The development team was still in a buzz about Kelly's input and where she might have gotten it. She was far too shy and private to actually have lived that, it seemed. It was a mystery, a good mystery, and Kelly had only used the first two days of her five days with Kent. There was more to come.

As another crisp day was winding down in Nice, a nice sea breeze came off the harbor. Kelly and Abbey Bond decided to dine at harbor side and again soak up their fantasy life. As they chatted Javier Henri cruised by in the yellow Ferrari, he honked and waved, then hit the accelerator to let the Ferrari whine loudly. Everyone smiled, the beautiful people were alive and well. A bright orange Lamborghini trailed the yellow Ferrari with its own whine, some thin Italian guy with long hair. Oh, to be young . . . and rich . . . and in Nice.

CHAPTER 165

As the fourth day wound down in the baking oven that was the Sahara Desert, Mr. Stanley was back at the wheel of this wonderful rugged mammoth truck. It had topped 140° today with an east wind at 25 mph. As the blistering and violent orange sun began to set, the light fun atmosphere of the Nice harbor was completely lost on these three warriors. The truck had saved them, no doubt, but they were still bone tired and sand was everywhere, including their mouths.

Mr. Stanley now stopped and referred to his rugged cell phone-like device with the three toggle switches and switch protectors. He had briefed his two associates last night, so now they were entering the operational zone. By Mr. Stanley's references they were maybe twenty miles from the spot they would need to be. With this device they could hit their required spot within ten to twenty feet and that was good enough. But they needed to be there at 9 p.m. or after, not 7 p.m., so they would stop right here and begin the system checks on all the weapons and devices. The main mechanical weapon was a 12.2 mm Soviet machinegun. It looked prehistoric, but it also looked very, very deadly, a raw kind of deadly with a massive steel barrel. Everything looked raw and thick and heavy, and it was. They had exercised the gun yesterday and it operated with a heavy thud rather than a crack, and the explosive tip bullets threw up thirty-foot mushroom clouds wherever they hit in the scorching sand. The sound was pure adrenaline to the males, and the resulting thud of the explosion and mushroom cloud put it over the top.

The order of battle indicated that precision was not needed, the explosive-tipped bullets from the prehistoric slab of heavy steel would take care of the inaccuracies. Also key to the brief was the location of a 3000-gallon storage tank of gasoline. The tank was buried in the sand and was made of fiberglass to mitigate the fearsome sun and temperatures of this section of the Sahara. But its general location was guaranteed and should be the first priority target. Hit a 3000-gallon gasoline tank with a massive explosive-tipped round and a lot of the follow up work takes care of itself.

There were likely thirty-five or so heavily armed and radical fighters in the camp, most would be in the camp at 9 p.m., and in this deep remote hostile location few sentries were expected . . . who the hell is going to drive four days in 130°+ temperature to get to thirty-five radicals.

But given the conditions it was estimated the fighters were in poor condition, they had lots of water and food but little cooling capacity. And what they did have was unlikely to cool to less than 100°, so the soldiers were heat-stressed in the best of conditions.

The soldiers of course were not active, any activity would literally kill them. These guys needed a safe place and a safe place to plan the future. The cell phones and internet had now worked against them, so they just went silent with their best fighters and suicide bombers. And here they sat staying low until the right time. And here they were safe, a remote pure type of safe.

CHAPTER 166

In Nice, France, Sandton, South Africa, and Cape Town, South Africa things were winding down, a little television and a little wine, then to bed. In London, Khartoum and New Delhi things were quiet, people putting the cap on the day. And in the Muslim fighter camp things were quiet, a dead quiet, as the vast scorched earth around them had nothing to say; the wind continued to whisper over the dunes and suck the moisture out of every living being.

The truck had been crawling along for one hour and the twenty miles had been covered . . . well almost. Night goggles were on and the game faces were on. Personal machineguns and pistols had heavy silencers, and each man was loaded with magazines.

Mr. Stanley had each man stay in the cab until the last moment. The movements had been practiced to ensure a minimum of effort, because even at 9 p.m. the heat was still 115° and the dryness could put someone in a coma in a very short time. Each man had basically a three-gallon slab of ice on their back with the camel drinking system set up. Every man would basically have a continuous source of water. The slab of ice was necessary, as cold water turned to hot water in probably fifteen minutes in these conditions. The ice probably bought them an extra twenty minutes of cool water, plus the advantage of a massive ice pack on their back to act as a heat sink. Without these advantages the mission would likely be undoable. That is how brutal the elements were. For these thirty-five or so fighters to subsist here they had to be very hard, very hard. But the advantage was clearly with the three guys, because even a fifteen to twenty-minute firefight means these thirty-five guys are likely in a coma. They just could not keep cool or hydrated enough to actually fight in this place, and critically as back up each man had another two packs of three gallons frozen to ice. Should they need it they could change two more times to ice and cold water. A special freezer in this truck was designed just for that. This truck was incredible and a joy to look at, right out of the "Road Warrior" movie. Say hello to Mel Gibson.

CHAPTER 167

Mr. Stanley was driving at 10 mph and looking at his device. There were no sentries. There may have been earlier and they may come later, but anything past fifteen minutes becomes dangerous and they needed to climb a one hundred yard long dune to start those sentry duties, just brutal. So the coast was clear for now. Whoever wanted to stop this or sound an alert had just lost, the thirty second window they had to do that . . . had just passed.

The two mercenaries were out of the cab and onto the gun in fifteen seconds. The gun was raised on pneumatic stilts behind the cab in fifteen seconds. One man sat in a chair behind the gun, the other fed the bullet belt into the raw monster. The truck was at a pre-position, so the gun was at an angle of 10° off center and a 2° depression and would put the rounds into the gasoline tank. Then the gunner could spray the general camp at will. And he did.

The first three thuds of the gun rocked the big truck, and only three seconds later the heavy rounds began raining down. Two bullets exploded and the men had to switch to filtered goggles, as the flashes became so bright. Somewhere in the mini explosions came the big one. A vast massive flame flew up from the ground, easily three hundred feet in the air . . . that was 3000 gallons of gasoline. The heat virtually melted the camp, the ten trucks in the camp all were in flames, and each in their own time blew up with their gasoline tanks.

Mr. Stanley could see a number, likely five to seven men, running with flames on them. The other thirty men never had a chance, just melted down where they were.

The gunners in the back stopped with the large explosive bullets. They next raised up a mounted small "Stalin Organ," another raw device. This was a serial rocket launcher but only had six tubes versus twenty-four tubes for the real thing. The men got off the truck and gave Mr. Stanley the signal. He flipped the switch to rain all six rockets down onto the camp. It was clearly overkill, nothing much remained by the time the rockets went off. Seven minutes had passed, it was 9:27 p.m. Kelly Grant slept softly in her bed.

Next came the hard part.

Mr. Stanley, by the order of battle, was to sacrifice the truck. Each man got their ice packs out and stood clear. Mr. Stanley went through the checklist, and as the truck moved slowly forward he jumped off. The truck edged over the top of the sand dune and headed into the depression where the camp had been vaporized. Using this special device he was able to speed the truck up to 30 mph, that was enough.

Mr. Stanley checked to see if each man had his flash goggles on, they did. Next Mr. Stanley flipped up the three protective switch covers and then flipped up two of the switches. As the truck approached the melted mess, he flipped the last switch. And then came a brilliant white light, an intense vaporizing white light, it was two hundred pounds of white phosphorous and it just melted the whole beautiful sculpture of a magnificent truck. And that heat set off the remaining seventy gallons of fuel in the truck, the encore to a spectacular but sad sight for the three guys. Four days on that truck had seemed like four years, and the engineering had been flawless. They knew they were literally toast without the truck. It was a sad and sober moment for the guys, they watched as the last pieces of their friend melted down. It was a highly successful mission, but there were no celebrations.

The men simply turned and began walking into the endless darkness to the east. If all went right, by two hundred yards they would hear the chopper. Mr. Stanley's device showed it may be three miles away. That was good because at this point even with three ice packs and eight gallons of water apiece they would have one day to live. Should their employers wish to clear up all signs of this contract, just don't send the chopper. It had happened before.

But the chopper did come and they got winched up onboard, and no one shot them. It had been a good day, a good mission. But as they looked back at the dying flames and debris, each man was quiet . . . they did miss the truck.

It was now 9:57 in the middle of nowhere. The chopper slowly left the vast empty brutal landscape. The leveled camp would collect tomorrow's sand, and the desert would have nothing to say about these events. The blowtorch wind would whisper again over the desolation and bleakness that is the Sahara Desert.

The waitresses along the French Riviera were clearing the elegant tables from another night of dining and refined relaxation. The harbor lights danced in the waters, the sea breeze was crisp and the Ferrari's left for the elegant townhouses.

In the end all men die, few ever live, and those few who had lived today were not the ones driving the Ferrari's to the elegant townhouses.

CHAPTER 168

Farsi Abbas' rented jet left Khartoum at 10:31 a.m. heading to Johannesburg, South Africa to get to Lisa before his new client, General Mosamba, came in tomorrow. Farsi had spent a lot of energy to ensure the Sudanese officials knew he expected to stay on top in the arms business.

There was nothing unusual about the events at the Khartoum airport for his departure . . . well maybe one.

Farsi Abbas was five steps up the stairs to his Gulfstream 250 when he turned and came back down the stairs. A well-dressed Sudanese man spoke to Farsi Abbas for five minutes, then shook the man's hand, smiled briefly and returned to the aircraft stairs. The man had brought a little good news from the government, and in two weeks Farsi would meet General Abdul who hoped he would bring Farsi more good news, and Farsi relaxed a bit as he headed for Johannesburg.

But the relaxed environment did not last very long. As soon as Farsi Abbas walked down the steps of the Gulfstream in Johannesburg, another man met him and briefed him for five minutes.

It seemed the good General Mosamba had already arrived and wanted to meet Farsi Abbas and Lisa Aswanela this afternoon. Apparently the General had detected Farsi's reluctance to give him Lisa, so the General wanted her all the more. He also had $20 million to spend on arms, so we will see where Farsi stands, the money or the girl. If no girl, General Mosamba was ready to go to Alex Kagamba in Cape Town. Ironically, if the General did that he would eventually force Alex Kagamba into the same decision . . . once General Mosamba found out Lisa also spent time with Alex. It was all getting a bit complex, but not one of the parties knew the exact complexity.

Farsi Abbas called General Mosamba only as his Rolls Royce pulled into the Michelangelo Hotel entrance. He asked to meet General Mosamba at 7 p.m. for supper, as he had just arrived and had not spoken to Lisa as yet. For his part the General smiled to himself, he enjoyed turning the screws on this Arab, an Arab who had accumulated one of "his own" people. Of course that was pure arrogance, as Lisa and the General had nothing in common. Being "African" was just another scam in a long list of political scams on the continent.

When 7 p.m. came, the two men met at the Michelangelo five-star restaurant. Farsi did not try to contact Lisa, as the whole General Mosamba – Lisa situation left him sick. He could not bear the thought.

As they sat down General Mosamba did not ask about Lisa, he would let Farsi squirm. Then the General got a call, it was Alex Kagamba. He excused himself to take the call out in the hotel lobby. As he did, Farsi frantically called Lisa to at least say he had talked to her. She answered. She could, as Alex had left to make a call at that moment to . . . General Mosamba in Sandton.

Farsi quickly asked where she was. She said Cape Town. Farsi was agitated and also relieved. He calculated his time in South Africa and asked if she wanted him to come to Cape Town in two days. She said no, she would return to Sandton soon, she would let him know in two days. But she knew she wasn't going to return then. Everybody was bobbing and weaving trying to cover their tracks or find the tracks of someone else.

General Mosamba returned to the table with Farsi. Alex Kagamba returned to the table with Lisa, there were smiles all around as deceit, deception and deals were floating around.

General Mosamba asked about Lisa and Farsi did something he rarely needed to do . . . he told the truth . . . because it was to his advantage to tell the truth now. He told the General she was in Cape

Town, true, on a modeling assignment. Although Farsi meant that as a lie, it was close to the truth. The General was disappointed but also excited, he had never been with a model and in Farsi's mind he never would.

CHAPTER 169

General Mosamba left the meeting with Farsi Abbas with his $20 million arms purchase on hold. He would have signed it gladly if Lisa was available and there you go, some very expensive sex. But in the grand scheme of things maybe not so bad if you believe that there is "sex for money and there is sex for free . . . sex for money is cheaper." Just ask the King of Swaziland, he has thirteen wives. He is the absolute ruler, but I doubt he feels very rich or very powerful.

So General Mosamba shifted to Alex Kagamba to keep an alternate supply available. Farsi Abbas wasn't much on competition, so if he found out about Alex Kagamba, both Alex and General Mosamba were expendable. Farsi had reached the peak of international underworld influence. Now several governments were answerable to him, and he didn't hesitate to take out any bumps in the road he traveled. When Ali Alawid was eliminated in Knightsbridge, London it was just another in a long line of "adjustments to the competition," as Farsi Abbas termed them. Ali Alawid had been a private arms dealer but it didn't matter, government or private, stay out of his way. Farsi had actually eliminated the three-star general in Sudan whose position General Abdul presently had. So Farsi was glad General Abdul was ready to place an order, it makes Farsi's job smoother and the money easier.

When General Mosamba did meet Alex Kagamba, he had decided on Cape Town. He felt it better not to talk to the competition under the nose of the other guy. The General was wise, even though he did not really know how ruthless Farsi Abbas could be.

Alex and General Mosamba met after two days, and General Mosamba spent the first hour complaining about this Farsi guy not turning over a girl named Lisa to him. The General did not mention the name Lisa until forty-five minutes into his rant, at which point Alex Kagamba almost had a stroke. It couldn't be the same Lisa, could it?

Alex subtly asked about this girl and then General Mosamba launched into this graphic description. Long firm legs, low slung jeans where you only need an inch or less in front to get your hand down them. The wild hair, the tight midriff, the sexy chiseled face, smooth light olive skin. Alex Kagamba was getting sick and he was not able to wrap his mind around this from about five different angles.

Alex Kagamba had always had supreme confidence around the ladies, and here comes this African goddess who is also smooth and confident and apparently keeping a stable of arms dealers on her arm. The only saving grace was Lisa did not know that Alex was in the business. And now Alex only knew about two parties, but the connection told a lot. Alex was in pain listening to General Mosamba describe how he would undress her and get between those wonderful legs. General Mosamba concluded his porn brief by saying whoever can deliver Lisa or the equivalent was going to win some big business. Alex responded a subdued "yes," but he was sick, confused, shattered and puzzled. To end this torture he asked to meet General Mosamba tomorrow. Alex only wanted to talk to Lisa to get some facts. If Farsi were to learn Alex's name from Lisa and know she had gone to Cape Town to see him, the danger level for everyone would go off the charts. Once Farsi Abbas gets started, no one's immune to his personal justice system. Alex Kagamba did not know anything about Farsi Abbas, but he could fill in the blanks. After all this was the international arms business. Alex hoped to make his money quickly and then depart the business, but it was never that easy.

CHAPTER 170

Alex Kagamba said his goodnight to General Mosamba, he would let the General find his own woman tonight. He was just weak from the whole wicked irony and turn of events. He was weak from it all.

As soon as he left the General at the extremely elegant Mt. Nelson Hotel, Cape Town he was on his cell phone.

Lisa answered and said a sweet hello. Alex was subdued and simply asked where she was. She said she had to return to Sandton tonight and was at the airport. Alex Kagamba was relieved but also agitated. He didn't have the stamina to see her and confront her, so her leaving was a relief. He simply talked to her a few minutes and said he hoped to see her again soon. Lisa said she hoped so, she liked being with him. That perked Alex up some, but not enough to counter the blows to his ego that had been dealt in such a short time. He needed at least a week to sort the tangled web of emotions and events that were before him. He drove to his apartment in a complete numb trance. He had not one idea about how to analyze or comprehend this.

CHAPTER 171

It now had been three days since Farsi Abbas had left Khartoum, Sudan. And on this night three lean, hard men navigated through the treacherous filthy back alleys of the Khartoum mud slums. It would have been impossible to ever locate a door of a non-descript mud hut in this endless sea of mud huts, alleys and pitch darkness. These men were not that versed in slums in general, and certainly not this one. It was unknowable, except to the thousands of wretched, wasted souls who had to subsist in one alley or another each day.

It was unknowable to these men but they didn't care . . . they had a device, and thanks to a rail thin shifty little man in mangled robes they had a beacon to home in on. It was 8:42 p.m. on a moonless night. Moon or no moon it didn't matter, these alleys were so narrow that little light ever showed up at night.

On the men went in the stench and slop of the alleyways and open sewers. They made several wrong turns, even with the beacon. It was a full forty-minute hike through the night heat and the very smelly oven-like alleys. If anyone expected them, they would have had no trouble finding these guys.

But no one expected that just for $300 this little shifty, beady-eyed rat would actually lead these guys in. He had planted the beacon in the side of the mud hut last night, and he waited in the shadows at the target location. He wasn't supposed to be there, but he couldn't pass it up and if the men found it, maybe they would give an extra $100.

He saw the three shadows approach and he knew it was them. They were too fit, muscular and healthy to belong in these slums. They got more to eat in one meal than anyone in this slum would get in a week. But it didn't matter how weak these slum people were, against all odds they had kids and then more kids. Where does that energy come from? Someone needs to do that study.

The men also had a device to simply open the door. Mud hut doors are basically un-lockable, so the men pried the door open in twenty seconds.

The four bodyguards were subdued and groggy because even one beer in this putrid hot hellhole leaves you weak, and they had also suffered through another endless day of heat in the hut or the alleyways. They were bodyguards here because they revered "their man." Why? You would have to ask them.

But actually it would be too late to ask them, as they were all executed with three bullets each. Then the three entered Said Alawid's room together and there he was, a massive man in filthy oily robes. He looked up quite simply, and there was little drama now. The three men simply stepped in the room and rained head shots on poor Said Alawid. The three men were told specifically to take head shots, as it was likely that torso shots would never reach vital organs given the three hundred pounds of massive rolls of fat encasing his body. And it is true, even a 9 mm fired at close range would likely not penetrate to vital organs. It would hurt like hell, but it won't be fatal. The head shots were very fatal, in total there were nine of them.

The men exited the pile of smelly mud and the air outside was a relief, even as foul as it was. But this was only the beginning, tomorrow at sunrise the overwhelming stench would be joined by five already rotting bodies. The three men thought about this as they left. Nope, tomorrow would be a very special hell for these people.

The little man followed the three men pestering them for a $100 tip. He kept pestering and following the men for some fifty yards until one of the men turned and dropped the poor wretched man with two head shots . . . at close range. All the shots tonight had very successfully gone through three all-titanium silencers, so the sounds were just background noise, little "piffs" in the night. And like that there were six dead rotting bodies in a place saturated with dead rotting bodies, most of which were technically still alive, but just technically. The three men stripped off their clothes and shoes, threw them into a barrel and burned everything with gasoline.

Driving away the leader made a three-minute call. And in Sandton, South Africa Mr. Farsi Abbas smiled . . . he wished he had Lisa there to celebrate. She was coming to Sandton, but she had never told him. That might put her in danger, Farsi Abbas was on a roll.

It had turned 9:37 p.m. in Farsi's elegant opulent suite. It was the same time in the stench-filled mud hut of the executed Said Alawid.

Farsi Abbas knew there was one remaining Alawid brother named Saif Alawid. But he knew nothing of him and thus it was likely he was not in the arms business, which would allow him to live, otherwise he was next.

Farsi had known about Said Alawid for some time and how personally disgusting and greedy he was. Farsi knew as soon as the contract on Ali Alawid was completed, it was only a matter of time before Said Alawid followed. The wretched mud slums had not saved Said and Farsi was not sure why Said ever thought they would. He guessed it was Said's only hope, but a hope in vain. And the world kept turning.

CHAPTER 172

The three men of the Sahara contract reached Dakar, Senegal at 3 a.m. on the same night they vaporized the thirty-five armed militants. The two men with Mr. Stanley left on separate planes in the same still darkness; their planes were parked at the end of the runway under armed guard. They briefly shook hands, said "well done" and that was it, another day at the office. Their plane, a Gulfstream V, roared in the still black air and headed south, likely South Africa, maybe Angola.

Mr. Stanley was left by himself in the dark quiet still night, it was 3:27 a.m., only the three armed guards were left . . . no one said anything. At 3:37 a.m. the landing lights of a plane flicked on, the plane was landing in the direction of the men.

In the quiet of the night Mr. Stanley enjoyed the calm darkness after another epic day. It was surreal to think they started the day in the merciless Sahara on the truck, then the attack, etc., etc., etc., to end up at the end of a runway in Senegal in the calm still night. It was surreal.

And then the plane landed. It was pitch dark and the massive landing lights were blinding. What kind of plane has such bright Xenon lights and there seemed to be seven, but the glare merged all of it into one blinding mass. You couldn't look at it, just a glance and even that could give you a headache. Then the lights went out and the four men, Mr. Stanley and the three guards, were left with no night vision at all. It was black in every direction but the plane was quiet, no roar from the thrust reversers.

Two minutes passed for the four men. Everything was quiet and their vision had been disabled by the lights.

Then Mr. Stanley heard the faint whine of the engines and the whine became louder quickly. The phantom airplane would soon have to show itself.

And show itself it did. Each man regained their night vision in time to see it. If only the Brandon Craig movie team were here.

The silhouette was just visible. It was a dark gray mass moving slowly, menacingly toward the area at the end of the runway. As the plane inched closer, Mr. Stanley could see the red glow in the cockpit from the night lights. For the first time he got a look at the pilots from the red glow. Not surprisingly, they were very lean and very hard looking men. Their job is not one where you go home to play with the kids and watch sports center. There is no telling where these men had been and what they were doing just six hours ago, enough adventure and adrenaline in one week to last a lifetime.

Yes, it was the Apocalypse Plane, Mr. Stanley's overwhelming favorite and this made his day, even given the over-the-top day it had already been. The plane never looked more aggressive, and the still black sky of West Africa was the perfect backdrop.

The plane pivoted around at the end of the runway and the tail stairs dropped, more red night lights. Three armed men descended and Mr. Stanley moved to the stairs. A fingerprint scanner confirmed his identity; it was just too dark to see any features.

As Mr. Stanley got to the top of the stairs, he glanced down across the runway. He could see a further four trucks in guard position. He felt special with all this attention, but they shouldn't have . . . just another day at the office.

Just as Mr. Stanley strapped in, the plane was lined up to take off in the opposite direction of its landing. The guards dispersed quickly, as the Apocalypse Plane lit up the sky with its three afterburners. The plane lurched down the runway and was thrown aggressively into the air at a 50° take off angle.

And just like that it was gone, vanishing into the black ink colored sky. The afterburners were switched off at 5,000 feet, and the Apocalypse Plane glided into the black abyss.

It left a dark, sullen, quiet night behind. The shadowy figures got into their vehicles and also disappeared in the black abyss.

It was 3:57 in Dakar, Senegal, West Africa. Some would remember the noise but would never see the plane, never know why it came, and certainly never know where it was going.

CHAPTER 173

Brandon Craig turned in his bed in the quiet opulence of Nice, France. He and his entire staff slept peacefully, not knowing that the events that transpired in Dakar would have made epic scenes for their movie.

Kelly Grant slept quietly also. She had spent the night in a world of erotic dreams. Her hair was thrown everywhere on her pillow and one leg lay sprawled outside her covers.

Kelly and Abbey Bond had spent another evening dining at harbor side. The exotic, posh setting was becoming part of their everyday life. They had become very involved with the movie. It was a life neither could have imagined just a few months ago.

Kelly still had not told Abbey about the "man from London," maybe she wouldn't now as time had passed.

In Cape Town, South Africa Alex Kagamba was not sleeping as soundly. He had not slept soundly since he had found out about Lisa and her "other" weapon's dealing "boyfriend." It had been too good to be true, and thus it wasn't true. Lisa was far too sexy and exotic not to have other "interests," and the "cash for the Aston Martin" maneuver should have been Alex's sign. But men are relentlessly self-delusional when it comes to women, and Lisa Aswanela was too much for any man. Her looks and her walk made life for her a minefield full of male pursuers. There seemed to be no easy answers for Alex, and it ate at him every day.

And the ultimate nightmare for Alex continued to be General Mosamba – Uganda Western Forces. He knew the General expected Lisa to come with a weapons deal and if General Mosamba knew that Alex also "knew" Lisa, then his nightmare would be complete. Alex, as Farsi Abbas, knew his only hope was to find a replacement for Lisa, but somehow he knew it wouldn't work . . . Lisa was way to exotic and erotic for men to ever forget.

Farsi Abbas also slept poorly. He worried about paying for the private jet, he worried about paying for Lisa, and he also worried about dealing with General Mosamba. He worried about the "wild dogs" nipping at his heels and his business. Losing the MIG-23 deal was unacceptable, and he still didn't know who was behind it. He worried about that too. The only good news was that Said Alawid had been executed. The knowledge that a filthy fat Said was blown away in those miserable slums of Khartoum was all that brought a smile to his face.

Farsi Abbas did not worry about his wife and children. He didn't worry about them, as he actually never thought of them. As Farsi lay awake in Beirut, Lebanon he had lots of issues in his head but no answers.

He only thought of Lisa and she would meet him in Nice in two days' time. He wanted a change of scenery to change his attitude.

As these people lay asleep, the dark gray plane of the Apocalypse was at 47,000 feet over Mauritania. Mr. Stanley had become Kent Benson again, as he had decided where he would "rest" for a few days. And the "new" Kent Benson slept easily in his massive airline seat, he slept from pure exhaustion. There were no thoughts or worries about Lisa, Kelly, Christy Alexander, Eva Escobar, Alex Gomez, etc., etc. All the "girls" in a row, sexy and desirable; but don't worry about them, their survival is in far better shape than any of the men that pursue them.

CHAPTER 174

The Apocalypse Plane slammed into the runway at Gibraltar. It quickly taxied to a remote spot at the airport and dropped its tail stairs.

A lone figure departed the plane and went immediately to a black Range Rover parked nearby. Then the plane's stairs went up and the plane immediately taxied to the runway and was gone to the west. The Range Rover barely had a chance to cover two hundred yards before the plane had vanished. Kent Benson missed the plane already.

It was Friday and the sun had been up for some hours shining brightly on this British colony in Europe.

After that Kent Benson was on British Airways Flight 687, Gibraltar to Nice, France, Seat 6A. Then it was a quick train ride to Monaco, then a suite at the Palms Hotel, then a quick lunch on the veranda overlooking the yacht harbor at Monaco.

Kent Benson then made a quick call to a one Kelly Grant, she was in her office to take the 1:20 p.m. call. Ironically, she was developing another scene with sexual situations when he called.

She was shocked. She was lost for words. The call was surreal, the sound of the voice surreal, and her mind swirled with memories that seemed so long ago but had only been weeks. Yes, she would come to Monaco for the weekend and, yes, she also was looking forward to it.

As she hung up, her mind raced. What to wear? How to act? It was both exciting and awkward. But the exciting part was bigger, a rendezvous, an affair, an affair to remember. She would also be in a creative mood, this set up had great backdrop for the movie. And the sections she had developed for the movie still puzzled everyone. Had she lived those sexual scenes or just dreamed them? So this weekend in Monaco was for business and pleasure. She didn't know how she would explain this to Abbey, but Abbey would surely know this time.

She would meet this Kent Benson in Monaco. The "man from London" had arrived.

CHAPTER 175

Farsi Abbas touched down at Nice International in his chartered private jet at 1:47 p.m., exactly five minutes after Kelly had hung up the phone. He waited two hours in the VIP lounge at the private jet hangar, Lisa was due in on Air France Flight 617 from Paris then. He used his two hours to make a rapid series of phone calls to Sudan, to Beirut, to South Africa, to Uganda and General Mosamba.

He was happy for this little five-day diversion. He was avoiding Beirut, his family was so tiring, and he was avoiding London until he had the money to buy the Dassault 7X. He was especially avoiding anywhere General Mosamba might be, as the General had him pinned in now. He desperately wanted the General's money, as a Dassault 7X doesn't come cheap at $50 million plus. But he also desperately wanted Lisa, and he wanted to keep her away from the General's eyes. In just that five-minute chance meeting in Sandton the General was hooked, he always asked about her, and given the psychotic nature of these generals he would not forget until he had Lisa naked and astride him. Farsi could not stand the thought, and it haunted him. He would like to do the deal, get the money, and then send his "friends" from South Africa to deliver the arms and a bullet to the General's head. Then the next Ugandan general with his side game in the Congo would have his weapons, but he would never see Lisa.

Farsi had just learned the lesson that girls in Lisa's sexy sultry class not only cost a lot in real money, but also a lot in time to keep them away from the ever present males on the hunt. And the animals on the plains of the Serengeti think they have it bad.

Lisa had also been in an epic swirl. There was Alex, a special guy to her, and there was Farsi to deal with. Lisa was planning her exit, but knew it might be dangerous, but never knowing how incredibly dangerous it actually would be.

Lisa had been in such a swirl, and it always came back to these images of Kent on Bayswater Road, Lancaster Gate – London. If the young girl had not been so delicately beautiful, she would not be obsessed with it. So as much as Alex was special, she needed to get Kent and get him naked for about three days, like the old days in Sandton, South Africa.

In all this swirl Lisa had forgotten about another recent dimension to her life, Brandon Craig and the movie and . . . Nice. That's where she was going! It all hit her about thirty minutes before landing. She would have to regroup, she didn't bring his business card. She also had Cannes in her mind, the Cannes Film Festival, she wondered how far from Nice that was. All of this brought her out of her gloom and the four days she must spend with Farsi. Oh well, another $100,000 in her bank account. And now the money meant something, as it was going into her "escape" fund. She would use that nest egg to flee Farsi and have money to hide. At least she thought so. She thought that was where London came in, maybe a place to hide from Farsi, but Lisa had no idea. Just ask Ali Alawid, the Sudanese arms dealer with a bullet in his head. He had collected that bullet courtesy of Farsi Abbas in the very upscale posh safe haven of Knightsbridge – London, and Farsi did that without emotion, it was just business. Lisa was far different, a passionate obsession to have and to hold, even if they rarely had sex. Actually, Farsi was not concerned he didn't have sex with her, but he surely was obsessed that no other man would either. Farsi did not care how long a line of dead bodies he left to keep that sacred mission. And you thought Muslims could be fanatics. Farsi was a Muslim but cared little for it, Lisa was his religion, and he was clearly fanatical about that.

Lisa had no idea what Farsi's plans for them were, but it didn't matter, as she was the driver of this train. She would get to Cannes and she also would try to contact Brandon Craig if she had the chance.

Then her plane landed at Nice.

CHAPTER 176

The next morning Lisa did in fact wake up in Cannes, a brilliant hotel suite on the water at $3,000 per night. She flung open the double doors to let the light crisp sea breeze in. It had been a magical night only because she had seen the Cannes lights and dined at the restaurant for the stars. She was happy to have come and dream her new dream of a movie.

And now Farsi would call the Rolls Royce to take them on a casual journey to a place he wanted to see and be seen . . . Monaco. They would stay at the elegant Palm Harbor hotel, and Farsi could make his entrance at the famous Monte Carlo Casino. They were heading there now for Lisa to shop for her dress and for Farsi to be fitted with his tuxedo. Farsi Abbas would become James Bond in his mind for at least the next three nights. With Lisa on his arm he clearly had a top tier Bond girl, even as he was a far cry from Bond himself. Although Farsi clearly thought he had a license to kill.

On that same morning Kelly Grant had also opened the double doors over Monaco harbor to let the sea breeze in. It had been a slow placed encounter with Kent Benson. The kisses had been long, her clothes had come off slowly, and he had gotten on slowly and taken his time. Then he took his time again slowly. Then they fell into a deep sleep with one of her long thin legs laying on his stomach, just in case he wanted some more. She had taken notes in her mind as she gave into the lust, there would be additional scene descriptions for the movie next week. She had enjoyed this more as she now knew what "it" was all about. She was a delicate quiet girl, so she mostly just gave herself to Kent to do as he pleased, and he knew how to do that.

CHAPTER 177

It was 1:17 p.m. when it happened.

The Rolls Royce had made good progress from Cannes to Monaco, a wonderful drive with the glamour and elegance of Cannes, Nice, and now Monaco as a backdrop.

The Rolls Royce slowly navigated the small curvy streets into the harbor area. Farsi was excited, he would make his entrance tonight at the Monte Carlo Casino with the young long-legged Lisa. She needed to get something in a low-slung dress to show those dimples above that ass.

As the Rolls Royce made one last sweeping ninety degree left turn before easing along the harbor, Lisa glanced to her left and saw the profile in the distance, maybe two hundred yards. She locked on immediately and her heart pumped heavily.

He was alone and that seemed so natural. His being alone seemed to be his natural state . . . always alone, never lonely.

As Farsi was transfixed by the massive gleaming yachts to his right, Lisa never broke her gaze. The Rolls Royce was moving at 15 mph, perfect for viewing and being viewed. The Rolls Royce was a deep silver.

Lisa quickly thought that Kent being alone would allow her to see him and get out of her skimpy panties. Everything was coming together, she could not believe her luck. Four days of endless boredom with Farsi would be broken.

Lisa smiled to herself on seeing Kent about seventy-five yards away casually reading and looking around, all alone. Then, coming from the left, she was clearly visible if only for her radiant long blonde hair. The sun shone off it like a beacon.

The rest seemed to be in slow motion. The wind hit the girl's face and blew her hair away from her face and neck. What was this, a Vogue front cover? The girl was a delicate haunting beauty, her skin so light and wafer thin, and her eyes a light crystal blue. The sweater fit her tightly, and it was clear she wasn't wearing a bra or needed to wear a bra. The breasts were perky and the cool breeze made her little nipples stand up; or was it the cool breeze. Her pants hugged her tiny waist.

It just got worse for Lisa. Lisa had recognized this girl immediately from Bayswater Road – London, and now here she was in Monaco.

The girl went straight to Kent and coming from behind, put her arms around him and nuzzled his neck. She then gave him a quick full kiss and stood beside him. As the Rolls Royce eased by them, this haunting beauty was still standing talking to Kent with her hand on his neck. It couldn't get any worse for Lisa. There goes the chance to get with Kent, and now her brooding manner returned. Who is this girl anyway, she certainly doesn't look like Monaco material, far too innocent, too quiet, too young, and too humble. Lisa hoped she could find out soon. She would keep her eyes open for Kent the whole time, she didn't need to for the girl. The blonde clearly stopped traffic also, but just not in the raw aggressive powerful sexual way Lisa Aswanela did. Lisa was nineteen years old, but right now she just felt old period.

CHAPTER 178

The elegant sexually charged and glamorous Monaco of yachts, Aston Martins, Rolls Royce's and seaside Villas were relegated to another planet. This was the opposite to all of that, this was the Eastern Congo. About 120 miles northwest of the tortured town of Goma were General Mosamba's band of militia. Every general needed a private militia to extract the side revenue needed for the VIP's, it was getting so difficult just to steal the money from the government.

General Mosamba had just started his, and this was his first visit to his new private army. The goal was to take over the mines currently held by another self-styled general, General Simbas. All General Simbas had going for him was he knew Winston Burton, the Winston Burton of London. General Simbas was in charge of keeping the rare earth mine under control so that the tantalum could be moved. General Simbas was a proxy guard for Winston Burton, Winston Burton in turn had a contract to hold and protect the mine. And that was the name of the game in the Eastern Congo, and that is why the ground is always littered with dead bodies. Today would likely be no different.

General Mosamba had come by private helicopter as far as he could. That got him within seventy miles of his guys and a three-hour 4 x 4 ride got him to the camp. It was a standard Congo camp.

The camp was muddy and littered with beer bottles. The beer took a tortuous two-day trip from Goma, but General Mosamba paid them well to make the delivery.

The head of the camp, a General Asamba, only had a hundred fighters and lacked the firepower to take over the mines, so General Mosamba was coming to analyze the situation.

But before he did he spent the first two days raping a collection of young girls captured from one village or another. Oh the spoils of war. War is likely to grandiose, more like a series of low-level savage encounters by drugged-up teenagers who run on a two day stampede of random killings before they become so exhausted and spent they literally fall where they are. If enough of their comrades are around, they get loaded into trucks to return to a base or set up a base. Should they not be found in their coma within a day or so, they become so sick from one jungle fever or another, or snake bites, that the only real alternative is to shoot them in the head. Great job if you can get one.

General Mosamba didn't really care, he needed more boys and more weapons and the mine would be his. And another page would be turned on the militia wars, all for a villa in Goma and shopping trips to Johannesburg. But the pages in this book were all the same, violent dysfunctional drug-fueled boys killing other drug-fueled boys to take a mine or territory for a year or so, only to be killed or taken over by the next gang of jungle boys. The airport at Goma had its hands full delivering all the bullets and booze needed to keep all this going. General Mosamba was just the latest character.

After General Mosamba's two day foray into booze and girls he decided that somehow with a hundred and fifty more boys and assorted weapons he would be able to take the mine. To get the hundred and fifty boys he hoped to capture fifty or so from other ragtag units, recruit fifty and then just take fifty from surrounding villages.

To keep all this going he had brought a supply of local beer for the boys, some Chivas Regal for General Asamba, as well as $3,000 in crisp U.S. dollars to keep the General's spirits up.

General Asamba was most grateful and wanted to ask General Mosamba a question. They sat down just as General Mosamba was ready to leave.

General Asamba wanted to use $600 of the money to pay six of his better soldiers on an assassination mission for General Simbas. General Mosamba was impressed, here was $3,000 bonus money and this guy wants to use it to get the mission done. Mosamba liked that very much, he slapped Asamba on the back and said please keep him informed. A brilliant idea had come forth in the wet overcast death-drenched landscape. Men come here to slowly rot into insanity, but this guy was still clever. Mosamba definitely took note.

CHAPTER 179

Speaking of movie scenes, as Kent rested in bed he had a view of Kelly standing at the balcony doors, just thong panties and a short t-shirt. Right out of a teen porn video.

But that was not the movie scene in Kent's mind. His was his entrance into the Monte Carlo Casino with the young, elegant, willowy Kelly Grant in some flowing pale blue dress to match her eyes. Now that should open the next James Bond movie, but he would leave that for another time. In two nights Kelly would go back to work and Kent Benson would become Jason Stoner, Upper East Side – New York City. And Kelly Grant looked sixteen years old and no amount of money under the table would get her into the casino.

They would do a simple dinner, a stroll along the harbor and then back to the suite to watch life cruise by from their balcony, maybe a light wine to sip.

Farsi Abbas did not have that problem. Lisa was only nineteen but with those hips, the breasts, the hair, she could pass for twenty-one should the right amount of money be made available. For Farsi a $300 tip at the door was just polite, what got Lisa in on his arm was a $700,000 credit line just for tonight and another $700,000 for tomorrow night.

The hotel butler had collected the tuxedo and Lisa's dress from the tailor. The Rolls Royce had dropped them off and was to be at the ready for the entire evening. Farsi and Lisa were to have a light snack, then go to the casino floor by 9 p.m.

At just after 9 p.m. Kent and Kelly were strolling fifty yards away from the Monte Carlo Casino when the dark silver Rolls Royce rolled up.

Out stepped a well-dressed Middle-Eastern man followed by a girl in an over-the-top gold gown. Kent was twenty yards away when Lisa emerged.

Kelly grabbed Kent's arm and looked in awe. If ever there was a movie scene, this was it. The tuxedo, the Rolls Royce, the Monte Carlo Casino and now this extremely exotic . . . and erotic young woman, breathtaking, and Kelly took mental notes for their movie project.

Kent also was in shock but he had to regain it quickly, and he was off balance. How did Lisa get here and who was the man? He would have to think about that.

Lisa was beyond sexy, an overpowering sexual presence. The dress dropped in the front and it really dropped in the back, all the way past those hip dimples. There was a slit up the left side that also stopped at the hip. The dress flowed and it showed. And what it showed was a firm sultry long-legged goddess. And Kent couldn't help the flashbacks when he was all over and between her legs. He would have to think about that also. Maybe his movie scene would have him with Lisa and Kelly for the entrance. That might be James Bond times two. His mind was racing with possibilities, Kelly with her British accent, Lisa with her South African accent, charming, sexy and deadly.

However, no one would know that the man slowly walking toward the casino entrance had not only been with the magnificent beauty walking with him, but also the sex goddess that was currently making the grandest of entrances into one of the most fabled and elegant casinos in the world. No one would know because the only other person to know had not seen him, and he would keep it that way for now. But where had Kent seen this man before? He would have to think about it.

Kent watched as Lisa was escorted into the casino, the men were in sexual awe, the women just wanted to kill her right there, right now. And the animals on the Serengeti Plain think they have it bad.

CHAPTER 180

The six men deployed from General Asamba's camp at 8 p.m. The driver had night vision goggles, courtesy of General Mosamba. The 4 x 4 would creep through the night to within ten miles of the mine and General Simbas' camp. They would hide in the jungle all day tomorrow and then assess the camp.

The men were heavily armed and the 4 x 4 was powerful and rugged. They would likely have to make a hasty retreat but they were prepared for that. The .50 caliber machine gun was mounted facing the rear, and they had twenty land mines they could deploy to slow any counterattack.

At around 5 a.m. the 4 x 4 pulled off the trail into the dense jungle. They put camouflage net over the entire vehicle. Everyone ate and rested with two men always on guard.

The next night they only traveled seven miles and stopped again deep in the jungle. The next morning at 5 a.m. three of the men set off on foot to get close to the camp. This was an extremely dangerous mission, as none of them knew the area and any encounter with the mine camp would send the bullets flying at random. The jungle would be filled with random fire, of which one or two of the bullets would likely hit home. At that point a slow torturous death would entail. It would be slow and tortuous if the wounded men were found and slow and tortuous if the men weren't found.

They proceeded quietly and got next to the camp. At that point one soldier broke off to the left and got some twenty-five yards away from the other two. That was five yards to far.

The lone man literally stumbled over three drunk and sleeping militia men in the bush. He shot one right away, but then was shot in the leg by one of the other roused soldiers. Wanting credit for their find and great guard duty, the remaining two started firing in the air, and ten young men ran from the camp only fifty yards away, also firing in the air. The two hiding soldiers of General Asamba's group then witnessed the ultimate apocalypse, the capture alive of one militia of another's fighters. It would now become an orgy of savage torture. At least six men had part of the poor captured soldier, and they were running through the jungle to their camp clearing dragging the man through the mud, branches and slime.

The remaining two men were in shock but remained in hiding long enough to witness the gathering mob. There were now some fifty bodies in the camp clearing shouting, dancing and firing randomly in the air. Most were drugged up but it didn't matter, it was torture time.

The man they had captured had already been tied to a post for the brutal festivities to begin.

One of the hidden soldiers did have the presence to scan the assembling soldiers. In the fifteen seconds he delayed to do that, it paid off. He spotted General Simbas and four of his top men in the clearing. The men then beat a quick and quiet retreat in shock, shaken to the very core of their being. Welcome to the Eastern Congo. It was now 6:17 a.m.

CHAPTER 181

By 8:27 a.m. of the same morning the Congo torture rituals were on, a sleepy and happy Kelly wrapped her arms and legs around Kent. They kissed deeply for a minute, with Kent bringing her dress up to her waist. No more innocent Kelly, it seems.

He then put her down and went down with her to get her a taxi to the train station, then back to Nice. It had been a powerful sexy weekend and things would never be the same. But Kelly was excited not only for the memories but also the entire weekend, which was the basis for the movie. The locations, the scenes, the sex, the yachts, the Rolls Royce's, her life could not be more alive and interesting and glamorous. She kissed Kent one last time and then she actually skipped to the taxi, her magnificent blonde hair flying everywhere. Oh, to be twenty again.

Kent watched her leave, a final wave as the cab pulled away. Well, that was incredibly memorable, even seeing Lisa in what had to be a James Bond movie at the Monte Carlo Casino.

Kent decided to go straight to the sidewalk café overlooking the harbor and enjoy a quiet breakfast, read the Financial Times, be alone and think about things. It was 8:41 a.m.

At 9:21 a.m. a Rolls Royce was approaching from Kent's back. It was going slowly because at all hours in Monaco it is "see and be seen" time. And Lisa saw, she knew the profile so well, but there was a sadness this time. Even though he was alone she knew the young haunting beauty must be nearby. She gazed back as they passed and saw him immersed in his paper. But she would not know that this time he really was alone, but it was too late anyway, as the Rolls Royce was heading to Nice International Airport. She wanted to go to Cape Town to see Alex and feel wanted again. Loads of money from Farsi left her an empty shell, be careful who you sell your soul to.

On the train Kelly was in a quiet mood. Also having had such a swirl of a weekend it would take some time to digest all that went on, but in a day or two she would be feverishly at work to capture the magic, the scenes and the drama. She felt like she had been in a movie. As Kelly gazed sleepily out the train window a beautiful dark silver Rolls Royce glided by on the road below. She was happy to know Kent, and the sexy magnificent girl in the Rolls Royce was also happy to know Kent but she couldn't be happy right now. For Lisa it had been a world class weekend, but sandwiched between were two very ironic and sad sightings. And life goes on.

CHAPTER 182

In the camp clearing the torture and brutality were reaching an ever escalating peak. A fire had been built, the roar of the AK-47's into the air continued and nothing could be heard. The senior officers were powerless to stop it, it just was the culture of the raw ragged violence of the Congo and drugged-up boy soldiers. Another fire was started and the boys started a parade dance around both fires.

What they couldn't hear also was a 4 x 4 slowly backing up to within sight of the clearing. The bush partially hid them, but mostly the energy of the entire camp was on the mutilation of this one poor soul strapped to the post. So far he was relatively untouched, but that would change. At some point they would slit his stomach so he could watch his intestines fall out . . . while he was still alive. That was Congo culture, and then the dancing would really begin. Some would also eat.

The 4 x 4 backed up ten more yards, just because no one even noticed and ten more yards would be that much more deadly.

The five men were set. Two on the .50 caliber machine gun, three with RPG's. Then the driver and his assistant came from each side of the 4 x 4 laying down a close line of landmines. Ten on the front line, ten staggered on the back line. It seemed a couple of the camp fighters saw this movement but it was all too late, all so very late.

The machinegun opened up full blast, starting in the middle where the senior guys were and then sweeping right to left, left to right. They paused once and changed ammo belts, as they had just put 200 rounds into the crowd in less than thirty seconds. As they changed belts the RPG's were sent in, one to the left, one to the center, one to the right, and they then reloaded. By this time the machine gun was ripping again, ripping and smoking. The smoke completely enveloped the 4 x 4 and was drifting into the camp center. It did not matter, there were no targets left as three more RPG's let loose.

Now they were moving away. The damage was massive, certainly fifty plus guys were hit, and being grazed by a .50 caliber bullet is being dead. They were firing the machine gun into the campground, just a signature farewell gesture. Then they drove off.

Five minutes later they heard some of the land mines go off as some fighters had been outside the clearing and apparently had run up the road in raw anger.

They radioed General Asamba and told him to bring all one hundred of his men in right now. The mines and camp were his.

General Asamba got the word and did exactly that. In the space of two hours five men had taken over what General Mosamba thought would take three hundred men.

General Asamba had his mine. Mr. Winston Burton of London would not know of this for five days and he would be shocked to his core. His man in the Congo, General Simbas, had been ripped apart by a bullet and then buried under five more falling bodies.

The smoke still had thin layers hovering over a mass of dead and dying men, and one very large pile of rotting bodies. And the man strapped to the post had been lucky, a machinegun bullet had ripped him apart, also before the boys could cut him open. In the Congo that was a victory indeed.

And in Monaco Kent continued to read the Financial Times and enjoy the morning. Things were quiet and settled and he knew how to enjoy the simple quiet time. "They" would find him soon enough, they always did.

CHAPTER 183

Winston Burton was having a nice lunch with his son Trent at Lloyd's, a small elegant restaurant off Berkley Square, Mayfair – London, actually just behind the Rolls Royce dealership on Berkley Square. Farsi Abbas often shopped there.

He had things under control for his myriad of worldwide interests. It was one of those days that seemed to be taking care of itself. No hurried phone calls, no special meetings, just a quiet lunch with his son. It had been three days since his camp had been leveled. As he enjoyed his filet mignon he had no idea that General Mosamba had already shipped twenty tons of "his" tantalum to the Uganda border and that the buyer had already sent the cash to General Mosamba, not to clients of Winston Burton. And when the money doesn't flow, then there will be frantic phone calls and rushed meetings. Those days were coming because it is "about the money," always "about the money," and the money was not flowing to Winston Burton's clients as the contract specified. Enjoy your day Winston, it will be quiet, then not so quiet.

It was a quiet day for Jason Stoner as well. Quiet because he was in his own world, even as the traffic hustled by on Fifth Avenue, Upper East Side, New York City. He had followed up the last quiet day in Monaco with two quiet days at his place on East 67th Street. Christy Alexander had spotted him yesterday, and so she was to come by at 5 p.m. for a little evening wine. She would arrive in her usual black town car and, as usual, not be wearing any panties. They had become regular lovers, Christy had been married for seven months.

Jason had also visited his offices on Avenue of the Americas for two hours to catch up on the business there. He didn't know how long he would be in New York, he didn't really care, he was just enjoying another quiet day as the world rushed by.

In Nice the latest meeting with Javier Henri and Brandon Craig had gone very well. The locations, scripts, costume designs and production details were in a set of binders that now exceeded seven hundred pages and counting. Javier Henri was very pleased that his small team had been so productive and so creative. He would have never imagined these kids were so motivated and clever. Javier Henri had always thought of a production with a $20 million-dollar budget that he would independently produce. But now this project seemed worthy of more like a $70 million-dollar production budget to do it justice, which means he would take on some finance partners and gave him an excuse to socialize and court the big money. Cannes was just down the road where the "big boys" come each year, so why not. It also gave him an excuse to go to Beverly Hills and New York. This team had become too good to short change on production. Javier Henri said as much to Brandon Craig as they ended their meeting. Brandon was ecstatic, a rookie but going to the big time. Javier Henri told Brandon to keep developing every detail with the staff, that he would find the money and set the business arrangements. Now Javier Henri had a specific role that was crucial to the project. He would start the contacts and networking in the next two weeks.

The movie project would get an unexpected boost when Kelly input her next script notes on the sexual content of the movie. And the staff would be shocked at the detail she provided and began thinking this sweet innocent girl was either living a well-concealed double life or had a vivid sexual imagination. One member of the staff knew, Abbey Bond. Kelly and Abbey Bond had spent three intense evenings discussing Kelly's exploits with both writing extensive notes as Kelly recalled the "Monaco nights."

Abbey Bond also made a note to start her own affair. She thought Kelly had been brilliant by choosing a stranger, and then to the event. No drama the first time, just enjoy the sex without the follow on baggage . . . and Abbey had the pouting lips and svelte figure to pull it off at her choosing. But she would ask Kelly's advice along the way. She was excited.

Within a week Kelly and Abbey would again provide more notes to include Monaco locations to blend with the sexual script. Again, this was well received to the point that Kelly's three day sexual escapade in Monaco would likely be in the movie scene by scene. And that means the "Lisa/Rolls Royce" entrance into the Monte Carlo Casino would be there. In ironies of ironies, Brandon Craig was already recruiting the actual Lisa to play such a role in the movie. But no one knew the serendipity of all of this.

In fact, as Lisa returned from Monaco to South Africa, Brandon contacted her. Within five weeks Brandon wanted Lisa to come to Nice to meet the staff and go over the details of the project. It was the spark Lisa needed, as the Monaco trip still wore her down, it was the "other girl" syndrome. Now she was up and would see Alex Kagamba in three hours in Sandton. She couldn't wait to tell him about the movie.

By the time Lisa would get to Nice the movie project details would exceed 1,000 pages. And her "Farsi escape fund" was growing. She would leave just as this project started, she had decided. And that was even more reason to celebrate.

CHAPTER 184

On the seventh day in New York Jason Stoner made his own arrangements. He would be in South Beach, Miami for a series of investment research meetings. He phoned a quick goodbye to "his" staff on Avenue of the Americas, as the black town car took him to the 34th Street heliport.

He had chartered a small Phenom 100 business jet to Miami. He showed up at the plane at the Teterboro Airport in New Jersey and told the crew he was it, ready to go. No assistants, no big boys, no girlfriend with a French poodle, just him and one seventeen-pound duffle bag. The flight crew was elated, no prima donnas today.

Within two hours of landing the old Jason Stoner became Conrad LaSalle at the News Café on Ocean Drive. He liked that name, but maybe it was a little too clever, whose name is actually Conrad LaSalle. Well, it would do for now, as this was just a whimsical side trip, no special plans, just see what happens. His "investment research meetings" were likely to be in the form of a Porsche 911 turbo down to Key Largo. Who knows, he might just keep going to Key West. No plans, any plans were likely to be worked out on an hour by hour basis.

If Key Largo turned into Key West, then maybe Key West would turn into Havana. He had a British friend in Key West with a Cigarette powerboat, and an hour and a half later it could be Mojitos at the Floridita Bar – Havana with that special girl named Eva, in a life that seemed to have been lived a hundred years ago. But he had not ever forgotten Eva Escobar, the olive skin, the hazel eyes, the long firm legs, the teenage innocence.

This time Conrad used his own small condo on Ocean Drive, as his Porsche 911 turbo was parked there and he intended to use that every day. To keep the car in perfect shape Conrad had a very skilled man, by way of Istanbul, who took care of the Ferrari's and Aston Martin's on Star Island and Hibiscus Island, so Conrad had him tend to his Porsche on South Beach.

The first two days were spent sitting at the News café, exercising on the beach, walking up and down Ocean Drive and ripping the Porsche up and down MacArthur Causeway.

On the third day he let the Porsche rip down to Key Largo for a Florida Keys sunset. On the fourth day the Porsche ripped down to Key West. On the sixth day a British man with a British passport turned the Cigarette boat out of Key West harbor to Havana. Underneath a pile of boat equipment in the lower hull was a guy with the clever name, Conrad LaSalle. What border agent is going to believe that name? With luck they would not have to answer that question.

Two nights in Havana with Eva rekindled Conrad's faith in life. She was as quiet, dignified, and as sexy as ever. They spent two nights together and Conrad gave her enough money to last one year in Havana, and that would be $400.

Then the British man gunned the 870 hp Cigarette boat north, and in one and a half hours spanned two cultures that were one and a half light years apart; Miami to Havana, Bangkok to Phnom Penh, Bangkok to Rangoon, three trips where a one hour plane trip leads you into a surreal time warp from another existence.

CHAPTER 185

Conrad LaSalle spent two days in Key West upon his return from Havana. He was strolling along Duval Street, the main commercial street of Key West, when he saw him. It's not that he looked out of place, it's just that Conrad knew this man was coming to see him. But nobody would know, as the man just strolled along.

Conrad decided to make it easy, so he stopped at the corner of Fleming and Duval Street in the shade of a store called Fast Buck Freddies. As he waited, the man got closer but at a leisurely pace. The man even stopped to look into two stores on the way.

The man approached Conrad, even gave him a slight smile as he shook his hand. A minute or so passed in conversation, and then both men walked down Fleming Street toward the Key West Post Office. They continued to talk as they walked the one block to Whitehead Street and, ironically, the famous Mile 0 of U.S. Route 1. Ironic because as the man turned to the right to leave Conrad at the Mile 0 sign on Route 1, Conrad was at Mile 0 for the next contract. The irony did not escape Conrad, maybe all his contracts should start here. Mile 0 in Key West and it starts over.

Conrad stood there for a few moments. In addition to the contract, Conrad also thought that if Key West could charge $1.00 for every picture someone took of a single sign that said Mile 0, all budget problems would be solved. All towns should have at least one sign that simply says Mile 0. Even Omaha, Nebraska could have one.

CHAPTER 186

Conrad left Key West the next day, guiding the Porsche up Route 1. Conrad even went out of his way to actually go to the Mile 0 sign to start this journey. After all, that's what the sign is for.

He headed to his condo on Ocean Drive, South Beach, Miami. And at only one hundred and seventy miles apart, the cultures of Key West and South Beach are also as starkly different as the one-hour flight from Bangkok to Rangoon. South Beach is sleek, sexy, and super cars. Key West is flip flops, a cold beer and Jimmy Buffet in a hammock.

And South Beach did not disappoint. As Conrad strolled Ocean Drive, three Ferrari's, one Lamborghini and two Maserati's inched along the Drive. And if to prove the point of South Beach being the land of long firm legs, as Conrad turned to stroll along Lincoln Road he saw a fashion shoot going on. It was a shorts and halter top fashion shoot. Currently in the photo arena was none other than Alexus Gomez, that Alexus Gomez from Bogota, Colombia. And she was as ravishing as ever. The thick blonde hair was over the top and the legs as long and sleek as ever.

Conrad decided to just sit across the walkway from the shoot. He knew he could be gone at any minute, so he was not going to disrupt the flow of events. But it was so good to see Alexus again. She was special to him and he so enjoyed just seeing her again. The next time he was in town . . . or in Bogota she would not get off so lightly.

He spent the evening sitting on his veranda, as the endless spectacle of Ocean Drive paraded by. If not the girls, then the cars, then back to the girls, an endless parade until about 2 a.m.

The next day Conrad took a dip in the crystal waters of South Beach, Miami. As he was walking back to Ocean Drive, the second meeting occurred. The man came from the right and walked with Conrad until they got to Ocean Drive, then he disappeared. Apparently there were to be three "meetings," as the contracts were complex. Conrad was going to do what he wanted to do, they would find him. And that they would, they always found him.

CHAPTER 187

British Airways Flight 117, Miami to London, touched down at Heathrow at 8:31 a.m. By 10 a.m. Conrad was in his condo on Bayswater Road. He would sleep for thirteen hours.

At that same time a Mr. Farsi Abbas was in the spartan offices of Lt. General Abdul, Sudan Armed Forces. Mr. Abbas was glad to be here because the bare concrete walls, a single light bulb, and a single squeaky ceiling fan reminded Farsi Abbas how superior he was to these dolts. He had contracted the assassination of Lt. General Abdul's predecessor because he did not like the cash flow. Now he would see what Lt. General Abdul could do.

Farsi Abbas did not know anything about General Abdul, but it didn't matter. The money mattered and if he actually knew General Abdul, he might delay by two to three months his execution. This way, if the results did not come, General Abdul would be efficiently eliminated.

General Abdul was off to a good start, he talked of a $21 million-dollar arms deal with more to follow. He hoped to get the money moving within two months. Farsi liked that and thought to himself that two months, maybe three months, was all the General would get from him, he had a private jet to pay for.

And by the way, Farsi asked, what about those two MIG-23's? Farsi said he had hoped to do that deal. The General swallowed hard and said they had been stolen out of inventory, a Brigadier General was being investigated. Mr. Abbas could not tell if the General was sweating because of this hellhole of an office or because of the question. Farsi reminded the General he would follow-up on that question with the Sudanese President and others . . . if it was okay with the General. General Abdul again swallowed hard and said he understood and would welcome Mr. Abbas helping them solve this.

Farsi Abbas rose to leave, he had tolerated enough of these spartan miserable conditions with a replaceable general. General Abdul should be quite thankful that Mr. Abbas even stopped by. General Abdul saw him to the door and even walked him to his car. Mr. Abbas noticed the General still sweating and was happy. This time Mr. Abbas knew it was his visit and not the weather that had him sweating. Good, he liked that, it always helped business.

Farsi Abbas got into his chauffeured tan Bentley and slowly left the military compound. Twenty minutes after Mr. Abbas left, General Abdul left driving his own military jeep. He drove to a small hotel, changed to civilian clothes and drove into Khartoum.

If you had followed General Abdul, you would have seen him enter an internet café and make a call. The call lasted ten minutes, and then the General left. He retraced his route to the hotel, then back to the military base. He had placed a call to London, an unofficial call, he had paid for it himself and the total bill for ten minutes was $7.57. The internet is not cheap in Khartoum.

CHAPTER 188

General Mosamba had his first chance to visit "his" military camp and rare earth mines inside the DRC-Congo. He was very happy. The fifty or so dead bodies of the massacre had long since been dumped in the jungle to join the literally millions of other last souls of the Congo. Soldiers of General Simbas who had survived were taken as slave workers for the new camp. General Mosamba then did something few expected, he actually paid the poor miners who dug the rare earth by hand in the miserable pits. He paid them and then he gave them a ten percent cash bonus for their efforts. Everyone was happy and peace settled on the camp . . . until the next savage militia war. Well of course the ex-boy soldiers, now slaves, were not joining the dancing, but they had before when they killed the previous group. And so it goes in the dark wet savage Eastern Congo.

General Mosamba had a nice cash flow now. He had sent $17 million to his South African bank and would get a further $8 million from recent rare earth shipments. In less than two weeks he had become "the man" in the Congo. The mine was flowing, the money was flowing, now General Mosamba was in the mood to get the weapons flowing, followed quickly with the wine flowing and Lisa on his lap. General Mosamba called Farsi Abbas, it was 9:21 a.m.

Mr. Abbas was still in Khartoum but was an hour from getting on his chartered Gulfstream. He was tired of charters, he wanted his own private jet. General Mosamba said he was ready to sign on for at least $17 million to start. Mr. Abbas was not happy. No, the money was wonderful, it's just Mr. Abbas knew what was coming next, and it came. "And how is my Lisa," General Mosamba asked.

And with that Mr. Abbas very nearly lost it. The term "my Lisa" had clearly gone overboard, and it took all of Mr. Abbas' considerable charm to get by that phrase. Mr. Abbas thought quickly. His schedule was packed, but he could come to Kampala in the next day or so to set up the deal. General Mosamba wanted to go to Sandton, South Africa to get close to Lisa. Mr. Abbas said Kampala now and certainly Sandton in a few weeks, along with Lisa. A "few weeks" was a long time to wait for Lisa. But in the short-term Mr. Abbas prevailed and they agreed on a meeting in Kampala in three days, $17 million up front. General Mosamba agreed.

Mr. Abbas would deliver the arms to General Mosamba, as well as a bullet to the General's head. The term "My Lisa" would forever haunt Mr. Abbas. His rage increased every time he thought of it. Definitely a bullet for the General, maybe one to the knee first so his assassin could deliver the message . . . and then one to the head. Farsi Abbas did not know who would take over for the dead General, some ragtag bush general would, but Mr. Abbas was ready to lose a new customer immediately, just over his use of the term "My Lisa." Lisa was all that trumped money. His obsession and devotion had become complete.

CHAPTER 189

As General Mosamba and Mr. Abbas had settled on their Kampala meeting, Lisa woke up and stretched her long beautiful legs . . . in Alex Kagamba's bed in Cape Town, South Africa. It turns out Lisa belongs to other men, and that fact would get a bullet to her head by the same Mr. Abbas. She would only belong to him or no one. He would give her a beautiful funeral.

As she turned over to display a tight firm ass, the phone rang. Alex Kagamba reached over Lisa to take the call. He talked for ten minutes, then hung up.

Then Alex Kagamba rolled slightly on to Lisa and slowly put his hands between her legs. The "celebration" he was about to enjoy would have driven Mr. Abbas and General Mosamba into a violent frenzy. Lisa turned on her stomach and spread her legs slightly.

The call had been from General Mosamba, he had a $3 million sweetener deal for Alex. The General would come to Cape Town in seven to ten days to set up the contract. General Mosamba needed to keep an alternate source should Mr. Abbas prove difficult. General Mosamba had detected a slight aversion from Mr. Abbas to providing Lisa. Slight aversion would not even begin to tell the story, Mr. Abbas raged on every day over the term, "My Lisa."

Right now Lisa clearly belonged to only one man, and he was on her as he took her from the back. He was clearly on top, and on top of the world. Lisa enjoyed the "company" of a simpler young man.

She clearly needed this after the blonde in London and Monaco. She clearly needed this, and she was getting it, and Alex could have all he wanted right now, this afternoon, tomorrow morning. Each time helped ease the memories of London and Monaco. It was 10:21 a.m. in Cape Town, a light breeze coming through the patio doors, gently caressing Lisa's very naked and very busy body.

Should Mr. Abbas or General Mosamba have known of this scene, both would have been equally violent, Mr. Abbas for obvious reasons, and General Mosamba because his arms dealer was enjoying Lisa when he should be delivering Lisa to his customer to enjoy. The General would let Mr. Kagamba watch if he wanted. If the General knew of this, he would make Alex Kagamba watch as the General's men held a gun to his head. In fact, the General would make him watch for several days. Lisa not want to do this? No problem, put a gun to her head as well, off with her clothes, let the party begin.

After all, this was not only General Mosamba of Uganda Western Forces, this was General Mosamba of the Congo rare earth mines, and General Mosamba of the Congo Kivu Private Army, and General Mosamba an excellent customer of South African and Swiss banks. His time was now and he was taking it.

CHAPTER 190

The bedroom was a busy place. The next call came in, this time for Lisa. It was Brandon Craig.

Things were progressing on the movie project at a rapid pace. In fact, Brandon told Lisa, the movie had just tripled its production budget, so this was not to be some side project. It was to be a full blown movie. Brandon just wanted to stay in touch, he still wanted her to come to Nice soon, just not sure when, maybe within three to four weeks. Brandon said he had just come from a meeting with the head guy, so all this was official.

Lisa was excited. She told Brandon just to let her know, she would love to come. She hung up.

And for the first time she told Alex the whole story about meeting Brandon and the movie. This was going to happen, not just a dream.

Alex was shocked, but then excited for Lisa . . . and then himself. Within a few minutes they were talking about the premiere, walking the red carpet in New York, or London, or Cannes, or Monaco. They could arrive in Lisa's Aston Martin, Alex in a custom Ralph Lauren tuxedo, Lisa in a flowing and revealing gown, maybe this time a blood red versus the gold from the recent Monte Carlo Casino entrance.

They laughed and talked as Alex enjoyed touching Lisa's body. They laughed and talked some more, wondering what part she would have, maybe she would become a "Bond" girl, they laughed some more.

Then they became quiet, as all of this had been very stimulating. And Alex kissed Lisa, as she rolled on her back and slowly spread her legs. Yes, Alex could have all he wanted and she was happy he was young and strong enough to take it.

CHAPTER 191

In all this swirl Alex had briefly forgotten about General Mosamba's discussion of Lisa with him, the "other" arms dealer, and Lisa's shadowy life. It did hit Alex now, but he was not as traumatized now, maybe because Lisa was now sleeping quietly next to him. She did have a shadow life, but then he did too. She did not know he was a budding arms dealer. She had shadows, he had shadows. Lisa's shadows included South African and French Intelligence, but that was too much to give Alex now. But after the last two days, and particularly the last two hours, Alex let all his personal anguish before slowly ebb away. This special time with Lisa had put all of that down in significance. He was happy she was with him and he hoped she became a "Bond" girl. Alex smiled to himself as he watched Lisa sleep. What a great start to the day, they would hit the harbor for lunch.

Alex Kagamba was in the shower when the call came. It woke Lisa up and she answered quietly. It was Farsi Abbas.

He was to be in Sandton in two days, where was she. "Cape Town," she said.

"Why always Cape Town," he asked her.

"I just have a project here," she answered softly.

"Great," Farsi said, "Should I come to Cape Town to hear about it?"

"No, I will return to Sandton in two days," Lisa said, and then she hung up.

Well that didn't last long, she thought. She was glad she and Alex had had their fun and laughs, now it was back to the dark world of managing a one Mr. Farsi Abbas. It was 11:21 a.m. in Cape Town, and she had a big appetite, and the real world had returned.

CHAPTER 192

Conrad LaSalle had become Kent Weston of Bayswater Road – London. He had "done" Monaco, New York, South Beach – Miami and now it was London. He knew there was to be a third meeting when they decided it was time, so Kent would rest here in London until the third meeting. Hyde Park was across the street and was so soothing. He would spend his days reading at the bench made famous by one Kelly Grant. On rainy days he could sit at his large circular window overlooking Hyde Park. This location equaled the bay window on East 67ᵗʰ Street, New York, which had its pleasant view of Central Park.

Lisa had left the "honeymoon" world of Alex Kagamba and Cape Town to return to Sandton. Farsi Abbas was quite neurotic in his suite at the Michelangelo. It seemed to be more than just business to Lisa. Farsi always had lots of deals in the air but it seemed more than just business, and of course it was. There was the overhanging drag on Farsi's mind, the General Mosamba and "my Lisa" situation.

They spent three days together at the Michelangelo, and Farsi was preoccupied the entire time. Lisa was just a fixture in the room. That was fine with her, her bill would top $100,000 again, just more for her Farsi Abbas escape fund.

In those same three days Kent Weston just rested and read with the occasional stroll up Bond Street and Regent Street.

In Nice Brandon Craig was having regular meetings with Javier Henri LeCirac on the movie. Now that Javier Henri had decided on a big budget of some $70 million, things had become more intense. Javier Henri would have to work to get the extra $50 million, but that was what he was good at.

Brandon had finally introduced the subject of Lisa to Javier Henri and he was very excited. Part of that excitement was the photo of Lisa Brandon had shown him. The other part was the introduction of the South African accent to the picture and even the inclusion of Cape Town as a setting in the movie.

Javier Henri definitely thought Lisa should come to Nice soon, as the script and movie treatment were maturing fast. She also should come because Javier Henri wanted to see if she was as sexy and sultry in person as in that photo.

It was only on the fourth day that Farsi Abbas brought up the subject of Lisa's "project." Lisa had dreamed that up to cover for the moment, then she thought of the movie. She told Farsi the story and he became happy and excited. His attitude took a major turn to the upside.

He loved the idea, as with Alex Kagamba he pictured himself escorting her to the premier. Maybe they would recreate the Monte Carlo Casino entrance scene. Farsi was ready to do this, why didn't he think of this. He wanted to fund it so he could control it. Who were the "money" people?

Lisa only said she knew the creative guy, but not the money people. Actually, she only knew the one person but was to meet the others shortly. Farsi thought all of this was beyond great.

"Where, where are you to meet these people? I will take you there," Farsi said.

Lisa was not sure, but it was likely to be within two weeks. At that time the entire movie project would be outlined, maybe even the money.

"Where, where are you to meet these people?" Farsi asked again.

"In Nice, France," Lisa replied.

CHAPTER 193

Kelly Grant was not in Nice, France. She had returned to London for a two day visit with her parents. She was taking a cab along Bayswater Road specifically to remember the memories there. She only spotted him by chance. But just inside the gate to Hyde Park she saw him. The man who was talking to him was the real sight. The man was tall, lean and unusually hard looking. The man looked professional, and he looked ominous. As Kelly's taxi slowly rolled by, she looked intently at the two men. It was good to see Kent Weston, but the other man being present led to an air of serious danger. With this man present Kelly would not dare say hello. She did not know Kent was in London, actually she realized she never knew where he was unless he was right with her.

Then the taxi moved past the two men and Kelly felt relief. The scene had been short and intense for Kelly. Then she realized it, another scene for the movie. Well, we might as well make the whole movie about this guy.

In another irony of ironies Kelly was making a movie based on notes to a book called "The 4th Mercenary," and she was literally by the side of the man central to each. She did not know that . . . and it was likely she would never know.

And Kent Weston had just completed the "third" meeting.

And one mile away in Mayfair – London off of Berkley Square, Winston Burton took a short phone call. He received the information and hung up. And in Hyde Park a tall, lean unusually hard looking man put the cell phone back in his pocket. A slight drizzle had started to fall in Hyde Park and along Bayswater Road – Lancaster Gate – London. It was 2:38 p.m.

CHAPTER 194

Two days later the man called Kent Weston stood in the drizzling rain on the tarmac at RAF Northolt. He was the only man standing outside, three other lean hard men stood inside a hanger. Inside the hanger were two British Aerospace 146-200 aircraft used for military and royal duties as needed, no one would be using those planes tonight. It was 8:47 p.m.

A plane had landed in the drizzle and had thrown up a massive rainstorm of its own. The rain and wind had muffled its landing noise. Then the piercing whine of its engines could be heard, and they were familiar to Kent Weston, who now was merely referred to as Code 011. The last time he heard that whine was in the pitch black stillness of the runway at Dakar, Senegal. That time Code 011 was straight on to the plane, and it seemed an introduction to a nightmare. This time the plane taxied from the right and came out from behind some building and was again an introduction to a nightmare, the same dark brooding gray color, the ominous whine of the engines, the various antennas sticking out and like Dakar, a blood red glow coming from the cockpit.

This is why Code 011 was standing outside in the rain, to again get a glimpse of what had to be the most ominous and experienced flight crew on the face of the planet. And the two pilots he caught a glimpse of were lean and hard looking, just like the Dakar pilots, but these were two different guys. They all look to be recruited off the poster of the "Marlboro Man." Then the plane swung around and threw up a hurricane of wind and rain. Then the engines shut down.

Six men in all black descended the tail stairs and took up security positions around the aircraft. At least twelve men came out of an adjoining hanger and started servicing the plane. Two black Range Rovers pulled up to the tail stairs and five hard lean men descended the stairs and went directly into the SUV's.

But it was enough, after all this time Code 011 finally caught a glimpse of the flight crew. He only knew that because they all wore black flight suits. Curiously, each carried their own Uzi automatic; there was nothing about this plane that was not ominous.

As soon as those two Range Rovers left, two more arrived at the base of the stairs and five new flight crew members went up the stairs rapidly.

It wasn't much, but Code 011 had finally gotten a glimpse of the air crew. He slowly walked backwards, then along the side of the hangar into the room with the three men. Then something strange happened.

"Where were you?" one man asked sternly.

"Outside for a smoke," Code 011 replied tentatively.

"But you don't smoke," the man said sternly.

"After seeing that plane, I've decided to start," Code 011 replied. And that was the last time any of the four men spoke. But how did that man know Code 011 did not smoke. It was 9:15 p.m.

CHAPTER 195

Brandon Craig completed the movie meeting with Kelly Grant and Abbey Bond. It was 11:37 a.m., and they decided to go to lunch together on the harbor.

As they strolled toward a sidewalk café, Javier Henri shouted hello from another restaurant. He was sitting with two well-dressed men, maybe money for the movie. All three turned to wave, but only two were noticed. Yes, that's right, Kelly and Abbey were the laser focus of the two men. And this is why they had made their way to Nice, to see the good life and catch a glimpse of the beautiful people.

The two men were Didier Francois and Patrice Guiot of French Intelligence. They had come to see Javier Henri to update him on the Dassault crash in Angola. But mostly they had come to have a chance to spot something special. The mission was complete as of now, as just seeing Abbey Bond with her sexy legs would have been enough, but then there was Kelly Grant and the long blonde hair, long legs, and light blue eyes. They felt like two French James Bonds. The girls continued to walk, but Brandon stopped. Javier Henri wanted a meeting at 5 p.m. on the status of the movie.

And on a hard-baked clay runway Code 011 sat. It was Mauritania and they had a one hour stop. The three men had gotten off and had disappeared into the desert on some kind of 700 hp dune buggy with armaments, provisions, and not the least, a giant rack of five night lights. They roared off to leave the Apocalypse Plane baking on the runway in 107° heat.

It didn't last too long. Another powerful dune buggy roared up and four dirty, weary and drained men got out and crawled up the stairs.

The Apocalypse Plane started its engines and the air conditioning came on. Code 011 could hear the planes inside showers going, but no one was likely to tell these hard men to sit down and buckle up. The plane ripped into the air and headed due south. Which didn't mean much, it could be going anywhere.

And in Sandton, South Africa Lisa once again told Farsi Abbas about the movie project, and now she was locked into including Farsi in the deal. He asked her every day.

Lisa did catch a break when General Mosamba called wanting to meet in Sandton to do the deal. Farsi was thrown off and delayed the General, saying he would get back to him.

Back in Nice the two agents of French Intelligence were concluding their lunch meeting with Javier Henri. They both had come all the way from Paris to tell Javier Henri they didn't have any new information. They did have a source and if anything changed, she would relay it. Did they say "she"?

At that time Abbey Bond and Kelly Grant returned from lunch and French Intelligence had completed their mission, plus some, as they watched the girls stroll by.

CHAPTER 196

Brandon Craig had his meeting with Javier Henri at 5 p.m., and then some. The meeting extended to 8 p.m. with both men back on the harbor side for dinner.

The movie planning document now extended to 1,300 pages, and both men thought they could move forward with more concrete steps. Kelly Grant had just added some fifty pages of locations and script of clandestine meetings, shadowy locations, and lean hard men. Both men talked about Kelly. She either had a great imagination or she was living a double life and including it in the movie. Either way the movie project had proven to be much more in-depth and creative than Javier Henri had ever thought possible on a first try by his young rookie team.

Brandon had interviewed two young male Italian actors whose English was good and whose Italian accent would add the needed international flavor desired. Brandon had also interviewed a nineteen-year-old French girl who was also just right for a part. And then there was Lisa, she was to be the "wow" factor and being South African it would add the dimension they needed.

Javier Henri liked all the cast Brandon had to date. He wanted Brandon to set up a meeting with the European "locals" and then set Lisa to come to Nice the week after, if possible.

As Brandon Craig and Javier Henri finished their evening, Kelly Grant was busy detailing the Monaco sexual nights for the movie. She was ready to live them again.

And deep in the Congo a small group of hardened mercenaries had finally arrived close to a remote militia base. It was the newly acquired base for General Mosamba being run by General Asamba.

There were only four mercenaries and even though heavily armed, this was a most difficult mission. They were on their own on a spy mission that could see them slaughtered by any of the very numerous militias roaming the Eastern Congo. They would stay the night and into tomorrow morning and then try to retrace their route back to the professional mercenary base. As a last resort they could call in an airstrike to save themselves, if found. It was not a good alternative, but it was better than nothing.

As the night wore on the lead mercenary, a man named Peter Hunt, made a satellite phone call. It wasn't to the main base; it was to Mayfair – London. And while Peter Hunt sat in the damp rotting Congo in pitch darkness and the ever present rain, the man he called was sitting in a warm wood-paneled library enjoying a Davidoff cigar and Drambuie cognac. Peter Hunt spoke for three minutes and hung up. And in Mayfair – London Winston Burton hung up as well.

CHAPTER 197

The Apocalypse Plane had headed straight for that remote base in northeast Namibia, or so it seemed. Code 011 had fallen into a deep sleep from the general exhaustion of the preceding month. He only knew two things, the plane had slammed into the runway hard enough to wake him up, and it was as dark as he had ever seen anyplace. The runway lights had been turned out.

Code 011 was still in a stupor when the armed flight attendant came by. Code 011 took his duffle bag and departed down the stairs in the rear of the airplane. On the tarmac things were so pitch black he could not even see the old hangars, which he thought should be fifty yards away. But they weren't because the plane was at a holding area at the end of the long runway.

In the distance Code 011 saw a vehicle coming their way, the headlights being the only light at all. The lights looked suspended, as there was no sense of up or down, just pitch black.

As the vehicle approached, Code 011 realized he had been standing next to a man all along. A crew member from the plane spoke briefly to the driver and then went back up the stairs, no goodbyes, no handshakes, no best wishes. Code 011 would complain about the service, definitely.

The driver helped Code 011 and this other guy get their stuff in the Land Rover Defender 4 x 4. They then headed back down the runway. Code 011 turned to look back and again saw the blood red glow from the cockpit. As always, it looked surreal, but with the pitch black night it was even more so. The red glow just looked suspended in midair.

The truck was back at the hangars when the engines finally started. And as they did at Dakar, they just lit the afterburners and took off in the opposite direction from which they had landed. It left the runway with a massive roar, and then one minute later everyone on the ground was left with a complete vacuum of silence.

Code 011 went to his quarters behind the hangars and slept for another thirteen hours. When he did wake, he went to the small dining room where a cook was always on duty to fix whatever you wanted, steak and eggs, no problem, cream beef with toast, no problem, Frosted Flakes, no problem.

Code 011 had the steak, eggs, and hash browns and returned to his quarters.

Three hours later he sat in a briefing room with the other man from the plane. The man looked Russian but was actually from the Ukraine. The briefing lasted two hours, some of that time being spent in translation to the Ukrainian pilot.

The translator was of note only because it was a she. She looked to be twenty-five years old, classic blonde hair and fair skin, an attractive young woman but not in the category of a Lisa, Kelly Grant, Alexus Gomez or Christina Martinez. But sexy, if only because she wore her hair up and also wore tiny little wire framed glasses, kind of the librarian look out of a good porn movie. She was from Russia and likely some kind of KGB agent out of Luanda, Angola and with the Russian embassy, or used to be with the Russian Embassy, who knows.

Then Code 011 and the man left the room for the hangar.

And there it was, a reunion for Code 011, the old MIG-23 that he had stolen from the Sudan Air Force was parked front and center in the hangar. The plane had five guys servicing it, all Russian or Ukrainian, Code 011 assumed. The Ukrainian pilot spoke some limited English, so he explained some of the finer features of the plane.

They were joined an hour later by the blonde translator who helped the pilot again go over the plane in some detail. The girl's name was Natasha Terashova, can't get any more Russian than that, and she had managed to get into a flight suit that did accent her girlish curves. As it turned out part of her charm, and being the only young woman for three hundred plus miles in any direction, she had gotten herself a brief ride in the MIG-23 and they were going now. It's just as well, as Code 011 did not feel like pulling any G's today.

Code 011 was heading back to his quarters, as the practice missions would come at 6 p.m. this evening for him. They were practice missions it seemed but who knows, real missions, practice missions, it all merges together.

But Code 011 did take time to stop and watch Natasha get into the jet. She was lean and did have a very nice firm little ass. Code 011 was feeling better already.

CHAPTER 198

General Mosamba was dining at Cape Town harbor with Alex Kagamba. Alex was quite happy at the moment, as General Mosamba had just given him $3 million up front to deliver some small arms, machine guns, ammunition and some military trucks. General Mosamba needed the supplies as soon as possible. Alex was ecstatic and would have to make some calls to associates in Rwanda and Uganda to meet these deadlines. It's likely some of these supplies would actually have to be stolen from General Mosamba's own command to fill the order, stealing and looting being what it is in that part of the world . . . well, any part of the world actually.

Alex Kagamba was very happy, and then General Mosamba had to launch into another story about Lisa and what he would do with her when he "finally got his hands on her!" Alex barely kept it together. Now, like Farsi Abbas, he had his own nightmare phrase. For Farsi it was the expression, "my Lisa," for Alex it was the more graphic, "finally get my hands on her!"

Two arms dealers with the same girlfriend and the same customer. And for the most part the arms dealers could not give up either the customer or the girl. And really no one involved knew completely about the other. Both Alex and Farsi hoped to divert General Mosamba to some other girl, but that did not seem likely. Both understand, as they were obsessed also, the "Lisa disease." Code 011 knew about and appreciated the "Lisa disease," he had just never contracted it. And Lisa knew that, which made Code 011, or Kent to her, the man she thought about most.

There had been uncountable men who had also caught the Alexus Gomez disease, the Christina Martinez disease, the Ashley Summerall disease, the Christy Alexander disease, and soon to be many men who would catch the Kelly Grant and Abbey Bond disease. It's just that Code 011, Kent Weston, Conrad LaSalle, or whoever he would be tomorrow, would not be among them . . . always alone, never lonely.

Alex took the money and decided to ship the weapons quickly. Maybe with weapons to organize General Mosamba would have to get busy back in Uganda and the Congo. Alex also took note to at all times keep Lisa away from the General.

CHAPTER 199

The next seven days in Namibia's northeast wasteland and in eastern Angola's highlands saw Code 011 and his Russian pilot "turning and burning" in the MIG-23. For the most part it was the same flight plan. First, it was a full afterburner takeoff and maximum climb to 40,000 feet, then there were some turns and dives, some more climbs, turns, rolls, and then back to the base to refuel. The MIG-23 did go through the aviation fuel. It went through so much fuel that on a nightly stroll just to look at the incredible star-filled sky in the Namibian outback Code 011 happened to hear some men in front of the hanger. He casually walked some more into the bush and was able to see a C-130 cargo plane offloading a major supply of fuel. He was not sure when the plane had come.

On the way back to his quarters he passed the pool, and there was Natasha wearing a thong swimsuit bottom . . . and that's all. Not that she needed more, she was built like a boy upstairs. She came out of the pool to talk to Code 011 and did so as if she were fully clothed, very relaxed and cordial, so Code 011 was as well. Code 011 said he had to fly early but maybe they could meet tomorrow.

Natasha said, "No need to wait, I wouldn't keep you up late." She followed him back to his quarters. She didn't keep him up late, and when he woke at 5 a.m. she had already slipped out.

Three more days of "turning and burning" and the Russian and Code 011 were comfortable with each other and the airplane. And on the 11ᵗʰ day they rested. At least the Ukrainian did, Natasha came by after her swim wearing just the thong again . . . and then not even wearing that. It was 2:48 p.m. in the middle of a vast wasteland along the border of Namibia and Angola.

Nothing going on, the satellites would only see an old runway and some old beat up dilapidated hangers, one of which just happened to contain a fit, powerful and ready MIG-23 jetfighter.

CHAPTER 200

During those eleven days training in the middle of nowhere the rest of the world was busy also.

Lisa, that Lisa of General Mosamba's desire, had spent three days with Farsi telling him about the movie project as she knew it. Farsi wanted to talk to Brandon Craig, so as to push himself into the project. If Farsi did that, she would never be free. Lisa told Farsi to let her talk to Brandon first. If Farsi was too aggressive, he would ruin it for her. Farsi did as she asked.

General Mosamba had returned to Uganda for a short stay. Seven days after signing with Alex Kagamba the ordered arms were moving across the border into northeastern Congo. General Mosamba decided to visit.

As the General arrived at his new camp, a new shipment of ore was heading to Uganda. Things were clicking for General Mosamba.

The only problem in his camp was a minor one. His militia had captured five rebels from yet another militia, and the five were tied to posts. General Mosamba's troops had consumed most of the hard liquor in the camp, had some drugs also, and were busy building a fire and chanting, working themselves into a froth that would end in the mutilation of the five poor souls on the stakes.

This noise made it hard for General Mosamba to hear his camp general, General Asamba, on the details of the camp and the mining. But they kept at it, as it was important.

The roar outside their tent continued. After forty minutes more General Mosamba was satisfied. He then used his satellite phone to call Farsi Abbas. Farsi was sitting with Lisa, having been in yet another discussion on the movie. Now Farsi was obsessed with Lisa <u>and</u> the movie, the perfect train wreck of events for Lisa who now only dreamed of her escape from Farsi.

General Mosamba wanted Farsi to start his shipments tomorrow into an airfield in Western Uganda that the General controlled. Ironically, the general also had five MIG-23's at that airfield as of this week, so the next time he had trouble at his camp in the Congo he would send those guys in. General Mosamba had tried to sell the MIG-23's just to get the cash, but the Sudan buyers only took two, he had heard.

Farsi said he would get right on it. The General asked for timelines and Farsi said within a week or so.

Then General Mosamba asked where Farsi was, "I'm in Sandton and my suppliers are here on this one," Farsi replied.

"And how's my Lisa," the General ambushed Farsi.

Farsi flushed with anger but controlled himself. "I haven't seen her," Farsi replied and lied.

"Are you sure?" the General teased.

"Not yet, but she is on the list," Farsi replied.

"Good, I will come to see you soon . . . and see her," the General continued.

"Good, General Mosamba, see you soon, thank you," Farsi ended the call.

He was shaken to his core, Lisa sitting beside him, could she see it? It was touching for about fifteen seconds, then she didn't care. She did pretend to, touching Farsi's shoulder. Farsi, still shaken, put his right hand up her pants between her legs. Lisa let him, but that was as far as he could get today . . . or tomorrow.

Lisa smiled to herself, she liked to see Farsi cornered. He deserved it more than anyone she had known. She, of course, had no interest in General Mosamba at all. He actually would be her worst nightmare, but she was confident Farsi would keep him at bay. But General Mosamba was clever. If he did try to get to Lisa, it likely would turn messy. Farsi had his assassins, General Mosamba had his bodyguards. Lisa did not want to think about it, so she let Farsi play with her and she pretended it was Alex.

The other boys playing were not so gentle. Two of the staked soldiers had been split open, their stomachs and intestines all the way to the ground . . . and they still had two minutes to live.

The other three men were in shock and barely conscious. The young boys, who must have numbered seventy or more, continued to dance around the bonfire and fire into the air. Well, fire into the air for the most part; there was one boy dead from a stray bullet, but he lay face down outside the dancing circle so no one noticed or cared.

Outside the seventy dancing boys were twenty or so "professionals." Should this celebration get out of hand, they were there to restore order typically by shooting a few of the boys who refused to stop shooting.

To be safe General Mosamba left by the rear exit to keep clear of the stray bullets. He managed to get his 4 x 4 and his four escort vehicles on the road without taking fire. As his convoy left the camp, the third soldier had been slit open . . . another day in the Congo.

After one mile the convoy was clear of the mayhem behind. It slowly made its way along the jungle road, actually a jungle trail. As it slowly passed there was one miserable mercenary mired in the mud only twenty yards from the trail. It was Peter Hunt again. As the convoy passed he quietly called London again. Winston Burton was comfortably in his office; he got the information and hung up. His assistant served him a nice hot cup of coffee; it was a Rwandan blend, quite good.

CHAPTER 201

General Mosamba returned to his base in western Uganda. As he crossed the border into Uganda from DRC Congo, he was quite happy to see seven large unmarked trucks heading into DRC Congo, and he was sure Farsi Abbas was already filling his order. Everything was in order.

As he returned to his base he saw the five MIG-23s, his luck just kept getting better. He had wanted to sell these even before the planes were under his command. Now that they were his he would start looking again for buyers. Though the planes had been sent to protect the border and even go into DRC Congo if the rebel militia acted up, General Mosamba just saw dollar signs. Of course, should Uganda actually need the MIG-23's and found out the General had sold them, then it would be the General's turn to be tied to a post and executed.

General Mosamba made a note to call General Abdul of Sudan to see what he knew about the price.

The General saw all of the planes being worked on as he reached his offices across the runway from the five MIG-23s. He stopped just to gaze at them, he had never been in command of real jetfighters . . . and these were real jetfighters. All was in alignment with the General's life, the new private army, the new rare earth mines, the money flowing in, his new command, and now his very own MIG-23s. If he had Lisa naked and sitting on him, his life would be complete. Farsi Abbas owed him a call on her location, and he owed Lisa to him . . . at least he thought so.

CHAPTER 202

In the days Code 011 was burning the sky in the MIG-23 Brandon Craig was burning the airwaves, as the movie project shifted into the "reality" gear, meaning Brandon Craig and Javier Henri were talking to "real" people about parts, costume design, and actual filming locations.

Brandon had it under control. A skilled French director was to join the project in one month, and Brandon wanted a base set for the director to evaluate. He had even set up five actors and actresses to be in the movie, so now he was ready for the interesting part . . . bringing Lisa onboard.

Brandon called her. He got her and they chatted. He wanted her to come to Nice soon, how did her schedule look? Lisa said it should be okay, but she would call him tomorrow to get a definite timeline. That was great, Brandon would wait.

As Lisa hung up, Farsi was standing over her. He was excited too, what did she need?

Lisa said she would need to go to Nice, France in the next three days or so. She actually wanted to see Alex first, but she just said something to throw off Farsi.

Farsi took over from there, and she was cornered with no clear way out. Farsi jumped for joy and reached over from behind the couch to slip his hand down her shorts.

His great news is he would join her. His great news was her nightmare.

He told her after all their private jet shopping he had decided and had the money, thanks to General Mosamba. They could fly to London first class on British Airways or South African Airways, shop and relax for three or four days, do the paperwork, pick the plane up in London, and use it to make a grand entrance in Nice. Farsi maybe could help finance the movie, but for sure Farsi would treat the entire movie project team to a dinner at the Monte Carlo Casino, Monaco. That way Farsi could repeat that very grand entrance he and Lisa had conducted not so long ago. Life would look like the movies once again.

After that Farsi could treat the key movie project team to scout a location or two.

That was Farsi's plan, and he had been thinking of it for a while. It seemed that Lisa was stuck, but she did not want to miss this opportunity, and she would still plan her escape.

The next day Lisa did call Brandon back and basically repeated Farsi's story to him, except she did substitute that she would bring Farsi as a source of finance should the project need it. And, of course, it did. But she did not want anyone to think he was anything other than a finance man and while she would accompany him, she must sleep in her own quarters to keep her professional prospects clean and viable. Farsi understood in a way, he was just so excited about the whole series of events that it was a small gesture to him. For Lisa it was everything, she had managed in the swirl of events to distance herself from him. She might do the Monte Carlo night with him. But before and after that she would be very hard to locate. And the thought of meeting some new young men added to her excitement.

CHAPTER 203

It was not nearly as exciting in the barren base of outback Namibia. Code 011 had started new training. The Ukrainian pilot said goodbye after his rest days and sadly, Natasha Terashova left with him. They might return later, who knows.

His training now was mostly in the time around sunset with a newly arrived British pilot and the dark and sinister looking British Hunter jetfighter designated RF/F-07.

While the MIG-23 training was high altitude, the Hunter training was "on the deck" at one hundred feet or lower every mission. The missions did not last long because flying 500 mph at one hundred feet simply guzzles the fuel in massive quantities. After three days of the training missions, the pilots took three days off. The low level missions in the dark were particularly draining. It was of note that on the last day of training before their day of rest in the barren wasteland of Southwest Africa as their jet touched down, British Airways 719, Johannesburg – Nairobi – London touched down. Lisa was in Seat 5A, Farsi in 5B. They were in the upper level, first class section and were escorted to a VIP lounge, and then a dark green Rolls Royce limousine took them straight to the Ritz Hotel on Green Park – London.

By chance the route to the hotel took them up Bayswater Road, and even at night Lisa relived those tortuous days when she saw her Kent with the magnificent blonde. As they passed again, she swore she saw him in the shadows of Hyde Park. Was it him? It seemed to be but it was rather dark, and the thought haunted her.

CHAPTER 204

In Kampala, Uganda the High Commander of Ugandan Defense Forces hung up the phone. He had just gotten privileged intelligence of the most valuable kind, an intelligence source of impeccable accuracy. Of course he had to pay for it, but it was so worth it. Of course he had to pay for it . . . after all, the man he got it from was a . . . no not a source from some national agency . . . it was from . . . a mercenary . . . a Congo mercenary.

The High Commander, Bamamin, was a silent partner with General Mosamba on the Congo mines. His job was too busy and visible for him to get into the details of the private army and the mines. But he was the "main" man; he had even sold his own weapons to Farsi Abbas to get to his camp in the Congo. He took his cut of the arms sale to his private army, and he would take a cut of the next national deal to replace the weapons. Money was always flowing to him.

And his crucial asset was none other than Peter Hunt, the most powerful mercenary at the covert mercenary camp in the Congo. After Peter Hunt phoned Winston Burton, he would also phone the High Commander. He was a double agent, which meant he got paid twice, which always beats just getting paid once.

While Peter Hunt would verify that the camp had been overrun and was with General Mosamba now, he would also tell the High Commander what his "General on the ground" was doing.

What was developing was of material interest to the High Commander. Peter Hunt had insight into the planning of a raid on General Mosamba's camp and mine by Winston Burton, so that Winston Burton could return the mine's control to his clients. The recent planning from the mercenary camp indicated a covert air raid followed by an attack by a mercenary-led rebel group, which would be used to retake the camp and mine.

Upon hearing this, the Ugandan High Commander, Bamamin, positioned the five MIG-23 fighters at General Mosamba's base. From that Ugandan base to the mine's area was less than fifteen minutes with afterburners. Five MIG-23's waiting for one covert jetfighter were good numbers, particularly good when someone can tell you when the one jetfighter is coming, and Peter Hunt would do just that. When the raiding jetfighter lifted off from the mercenary base, three MIG-23's would be there to greet the lone fighter with two more in reserve, just in case. The lone jetfighter would be flying right into an overwhelming ambush.

Peter Hunt would step away from the two teams. If the fighter got through and completed the raid, Winston Burton would give him a bonus. If the MIG-23s annihilated the lone jetfighter (unlikely), then Peter Hunt got a bonus from the High Commander.

Peter Hunt did not know all the specifics. He did not believe the fighter pilots for the mission were at the base now. He had been the lead professional mercenary at this very sophisticated camp for seven years, and he was still sane or seemed to be. So he knew a lot, even when the covert operations came and went. It was likely that the mercenary pilots would be brought in at some period before the actual mission. He would know about that and then monitor the runway.

A black British Hunter RF/F-07 jetfighter had been used in the past, and it was presently on the base in a very secure covert hanger. Peter Hunt could not get near the plane, but he did not need to as its departure from the base was not quiet, it was roaring.

Also, if Winston Burton sent his son Trent Burton to the base, that was a sign of something major as Trent was there to observe the activities. So Trent Burton was a spy and Peter Hunt was a double spy. Who else at this mercenary camp is a spy? Peter Hunt did not know, but he knew this base was "party" central for covert mercenary actions, so there were likely layer upon layer of mystery and intrigue.

CHAPTER 205

Brandon Craig called Lisa in London. She briefed him on the tentative schedule. Farsi, "her money man," was to conclude his deal in two days. On the third day they would head to Nice, maybe arrive about 4 to 5 p.m. at Nice International. Brandon was excited, Lisa was excited, and Farsi was much more excited.

Farsi would get his brand new baby Dassault Falcon 7X and then proceed to show it off to "movie people" in Nice and Monaco. Then there was the Monte Carlo Casino.

Farsi had Lisa phone Brandon Craig back. He wanted to have an informal dinner with Brandon Craig and Brandon's boss the first night in Monaco. Farsi would arrange a helicopter to take all four to Monaco and then return Brandon and his boss back to Nice. Brandon said he would check the schedule.

Brandon did check the schedule and asked if Farsi could drop by the LeCirac Industries helipad in Nice and pick up himself and Javier Henri LeCirac, then to Monaco. Lisa and Farsi said perfect, and it would be done.

It was all coming together, the movie, the people, and hopefully the money. Yes, there is the money. Nothing is going to happen without that.

Kelly Grant and Abbey Bond just continued to work and enjoy their young lives and with a perfect job in a perfect setting, not much to complain about.

But visitors were coming.

And in the deserted desolate African wasteland two men waited for transportation, the mission was a go.

And in the lush dark green highlands of western Uganda, General Mosamba was preparing to head to his new camp and base. When he started moving, then these two men in all black flight suits to the far southwest of Africa would also move. The dance had begun.

Trent Burton arrived at the mercenary base via a MI-17 helicopter from Rwanda that evening.

CHAPTER 206

Peter Hunt called Winston Burton in London. Winston Burton was getting a personal shave in his opulent office when the call came through.

"They have arrived," Peter Hunt said, then hung up.

Winston Burton sighed and sipped his coffee, an Ethiopian blend, I believe, then settled back for the shave to be completed.

Peter Hunt called the High Commander in Uganda and said, "They have arrived."

The High Commander called the base. General Mosamba was there but heading to "their" camp in the Congo. Good, the High Commander told him, but the MIG-23s must do a light training run, the High Commander would tell him exactly when.

And Trent Burton at the Congo camp called his father to confirm Peter Hunt's message. You can never have too many spies.

And indeed "they" had arrived. They slammed into the runway on that wonderful and ominous plane, the dark gray brooding Apocalypse Plane. The plane threw up a storm of wind and mist as it roared to a stop.

The mercenary camp always gathered for this spectacle. But the plane parked and then was pushed inside its covert home. No one knew if any "hired guns" got off or if there were even any on board. And if to emphasize the point, a 4 x 4 with a .50 caliber machine gun mounted on it parked in front of the hanger with three guys on it. After that three more guys patrolled on foot, all were in black jungle gear, all were very stern looking. There would be no "open houses," no come "meet the troops" scheduled here, no picnics, no balloons, no kids riding on dad's shoulders, that world did not exist here . . . it never would.

There were many compartments to this base, each compartment did its business, and clearly the other compartments were none of its business. Every day was a grim stern and steely-eyed day. Some of the men could relax in their compartments, others had missions.

On the far side of the runway, if you had been looking closely, you would have spotted in the gray mist a lone 4 x 4 heading west along the runway. That 4 x 4 stopped at the last section of four tents and, if you had been looking, you would have seen two figures dash to each of two tents. The 4 x 4 returned in the gray and the mist and the fog that was the weather in the Eastern Congo and the mood which was the surrounding events in the Eastern Congo. The weather always seemed to match the mood.

CHAPTER 207

Finally, it happened. Farsi Abbas was the more than proud new owner of a Dassault 7X private jet. The jet had been flown in on its delivery flight last night from France and had landed at the exclusive private jet base at Northolt, thirty minutes west of London.

The call came to Farsi's elegant suite overlooking Green Park, and he clearly was beyond happy. He excitedly told the flight staff to service the plane today, as they would use it today at 4 p.m.

Lisa then called Brandon to set the timelines. The plane would be at Nice around 5:30 p.m., and they would take the helicopter to the LeCirac helipad, then on to Monaco for an informal dinner. Tomorrow night Farsi wanted to host a proper dinner at the Hotel de Paris – Monaco for the movie project team.

Brandon was excited too and said his boss, Javier Henri LeCirac, would come with him to Monaco tonight for a get acquainted chat and then more key staff would join tomorrow night. Lisa said great, all was set.

In the mercenary camp in the Congo all was quiet. At least all was quiet in the four tent area where the two pilots stayed. Trent Burton kept a keen eye on any activity.

However, last night had not been quiet. Peter Hunt was told to marshal ten large military trucks with full supplies and arms to the same area where he had conducted his spy missions. There were some forty of the most hardened mercenaries onboard, and they were traveling non-stop to the area of General Mosamba's camp. So Peter Hunt knew it was on. Peter had briefed the men on the location. Do not stop for anyone, any miscellaneous rebel groups were just to be killed. These trucks needed to be in place by 3 p.m. tomorrow. And they had left in the soggy drizzle into the pitch darkness. Mercenaries live for adventure more than money, and this was it. A nasty, dangerous and difficult journey, the stuff of legends it would be.

Only one hour after the first five trucks left the second five left, again fully loaded with provisions. The mission was on. Trent Burton watched all of this from the shadows, it wasn't hard, the shadows were everywhere.

Peter Hunt reported the movements to Winston Burton, and Trent Burton verified the reports independently to his father. Mercenaries are a hard breed, and the top level are amazing professionals. However, Winston Burton was an old military hand who never quite trusted even the most hardened and professional mercenary. Peter Hunt was a top man, but who knows.

And a lone 4 x 4 left the camp after the second wave of trucks. It melted into the intense liquid darkness. It was gone for only fifteen minutes and returned. It had gone up on the ridge just east of the base, a location near Bryan Norton's grave. The call lasted one minute.

The caller merely said, "Whatever you need, be ready in two days. I will tell you later."

Trent Burton was still in the shadows when the 4 x 4 came back into the base.

CHAPTER 208

The second column of five trucks came into the jungle at 6 p.m. They had encountered ten wandering rebel fighters and had to spend some time chasing them and then killing them. The second group buried itself into the jungle. It was now 7:30 p.m., the mercenaries settled in for a quiet but tense night.

General Mosamba was quite comfortable in his camp, not knowing the immense danger just two miles away.

Things were festive in Nice and why not, it was 6:30 p.m. The brilliant peach Dassault 7X was startlingly beautiful in the late afternoon sun. Lisa was first off the jet in a tailored short skirt with a slit up the left side, the legs on display were simply beyond sexy, and the plane as a backdrop as she waited for Farsi to come down. The plane had performed beautifully and had equally been beautifully turned out inside. Most noteworthy were the full wide light peach leather seats. It created a very elegant and extremely lush look. Lisa loved the new plane. Quite a step up for a nineteen-year-old, it could be difficult to keep this lifestyle pace since none of the money was hers.

They quickly boarded the helicopter to head downtown to the LeCirac helipad. When it arrived Brandon Craig and Javier Henri LeCirac were waiting. They walked to the helicopter and Lisa noticed Javier Henri. As the wind swirled, his suit flew and she saw the body of a French swimmer and the handsome elegance that goes with a business executive. She felt a surge of sexuality. She could take him as a lover, she was ready right now.

They got onboard and, of course, Javier Henri paid a lot of attention to Farsi Abbas so he could smoothly take in Lisa. She was much more dramatic in person. Her outfit was sexy and elegant, but she still looked like a very sexy teenager. And that's what she was.

Kelly Grant and Abbey Bond were doing a light dinner at the harbor side café across from their LeCirac movie production offices. The girls were so young, but living such grand lifestyles it was hard to imagine how they would keep this up as the years went by. That's, of course, nothing you would think about at twenty years old. They remained innocent and unspoiled. They sat at the back of the café, at harbor side, to keep the cruising Ferrari's from honking. It didn't totally work, a thirty-year-old in the "usual" red Ferrari just honked and waved, they continued talking.

They took note of the helicopter landing. What they particularly took note of was, as it left a few minutes later, it went not to the Nice airport but east toward Monaco.

As the helicopter lifted off, if Lisa had just glanced to her right and down, she would not only have seen the harbor but also that haunting blond beauty from London. It is so much better she didn't, such an experience would truly unnerve her and in fact destroy the absolute magic that this day had become. Magic even before she met Javier Henri less than ten minutes ago. Because Lisa did not look, this day would be forever magic. As the helicopter disappeared, Kelly and Abbey continued their light dinner.

The helicopter took only ten minutes to get to the Monaco helipad. They exited to get in Javier Henri's Bentley that was waiting, having been sent ahead by his staff. The arrival at the Hotel de Paris was equally opulent and grand.

And in the Congo the mercenaries were mired in the mud deep in the jungle, the rains were starting again. Their weapons were loaded and ready to let loose on a moment's notice. All was quiet; however, the night was total darkness and rain became steady. The life of a mercenary can be very hard .

. . and then you die. Peter Hunt was one of the very few core mercenary professionals, and his seven years at the Congo mercenary camp was stuff of legend. And he was still sane and extremely effective . . . still sane being the more impressive of the two.

CHAPTER 209

As Brandon Craig surveyed the surroundings and the backdrop, he thought of the movie. The hotel restaurant was beyond spectacular. The ceiling was twenty-one feet high and the drapes that extended the length of the wall had a light gold sheen. The other gold accents in the room and on the chairs left the room dazzling and fit for royalty, which it was, since the Royal family of Monaco often dined there.

And that Lisa as the centerpiece of the four people was right. She was beyond ravishing in her outfit, conservative enough, but still showing the long legs and a hint of midriff.

Javier Henri and Farsi got along well. Farsi was very impressed with the LeCirac building, the helipad, Javier Henri's suit, and the company Bentley. Farsi was glad to know these people.

The dinner went smoothly because the service and food were impeccable and the company was happy. Javier Henri clearly noticed Lisa, who wouldn't, but Lisa noticed Javier Henri too.

The group discussed tomorrow. Brandon was going to sit down with Lisa and go over the "book" of the movie, and then meet some of the staff. Javier Henri and Farsi were going to meet and talk about the movie and the other "m" word . . . money. Farsi brought his checkbook, but thank God for General Mosamba and his $17 million order. That order was complete, so his $5 million cut meant he could put $5 million into the movie tomorrow as a show of faith. Farsi could tell Javier Henri was used to the big money, but such a nice fellow, no arrogance. Farsi tried not to let his show.

Javier Henri excused himself to go to the restroom. Two minutes later Lisa left. She was in the hall, by design, when he came out. She casually thanked him for his generosity for including her in the movie. They chatted briefly, then Lisa leaned forward, touched his forearm and gave him a light kiss on the cheek, then moving over to give him a light kiss on the lips, saying softly, "I am so happy to meet you." Javier Henri was startled but recovered, "I am so glad you came. I look forward to tomorrow." They returned to the table, Lisa's walk now more a stride, a provocative confident stride.

As the dinner broke up, Lisa had a short soft private talk with Javier Henri . . . just to say she was on her own in Suite 714, should he have movie questions.

It wasn't late, but it had been a long day for everyone. Tomorrow would be a big day, so at 9:11 p.m. Javier Henri called the Bentley. They all walked to the waiting Bentley under the hotel foyer. Brandon thought it would be a perfect scene for the movie, rich charming well-dressed people of the world, and among them one deeply sultry and sexual girl.

Farsi said he insisted on hosting a dinner for Javier Henri and his staff tomorrow night. He would send a Rolls Royce to pick up Javier Henri and Brandon. Javier Henri thanked him graciously and said he would include only three more of the movie staff and he would take care of their transportation.

Farsi was ecstatic. It was set for 8:30 p.m., dinner at the Monte Carlo Casino, party of seven for the LeCirac movie studio staff. In his mind Javier Henri would invite Kelly, Abbey and the young Italian actor they had recently signed. With the odd mix of males and females, it would be clear to all there were no couples. Javier Henri certainly was not bringing his "sometime" girl, not after seeing Lisa.

The night in the Congo had turned miserable. For every elegant beautiful moment in Monaco, there were likely ten dirty, muddy, grim moments in the mercenary field camp of ten trucks and eighty men.

And at the base the two pilots slept soundly, not knowing when the mission would begin. And they certainly did not know five MIG-23s were set to meet them and certain to blow them out of the sky. Five jetfighters with a total of twenty air-to-air missiles against one totally unsuspecting jetfighter with zero air-to-air missiles. This was simply a sacrifice at the altar, an aerial execution. There is no viable way the two pilots and the single Hunter RF/F-07 fighter could manage to get through this. It surely was to be a dramatic and explosive assassination of a lone unsuspecting jetfighter.

So the evening in Monaco was a classic time for the beautiful people, the evening in the Congo was as grim as the Monaco evening was clean, crisp and elegant. Tomorrow could be a big day for each of the locations.

CHAPTER 210

The epic day in Monaco started beautifully. A light crisp breeze came off the Mediterranean Sea. By 9 a.m. the helicopter with Farsi and Lisa had arrived.

Lisa was so refreshed, her own suite with no doting Farsi. And to finish the magical evening last night, Javier Henri had managed to call Suite 714 at 10:30 p.m. to say good night. She was ecstatic and told him she hoped she could meet him tomorrow to get his take on her and his movie. By getting his take on her she hoped he would take a new lover, she was certainly ready.

Brandon had planned the day in general. Brandon would spend from 9 a.m. to 11:30 a.m. with Lisa. Brandon fully recognized the sexual powers of Lisa, but he also knew his league and the movie was his main focus, his pride, his passion. He would never jeopardize the movie project for a shot at something he knew would end very badly and be embarrassing for both parties. Lisa, besides being sultry and sexy, was a smart and nice girl around guys like him. He would let the alpha males chase her, and they did. But he and Lisa were comfortable with each other, and the movie would benefit from her being in it. The meeting was about the movie and with a project book exceeding 1,300 pages, their time together focused on the movie. It was fun and stimulating for both.

Brandon had also arranged for Javier Henri and Farsi to meet from 9 a.m. on. They could decide their own schedule after that. Javier Henri had his own copy of the project files to show Farsi this was a legitimate project. Farsi would actually be overwhelmed; the details and the creativity were impressive. He knew little about the movie industry, but he knew this was a detailed professional project. And the project with the backdrop of Javier Henri's massive opulent office and conference room complex was overwhelming to Farsi. He realized that his new jet was fairly shallow, there were no office buildings or mansions behind it, just one very, very modest apartment in Beirut, Lebanon with a wife and four kids stuffed in it. All the apartment furniture was used.

But Javier Henri was so gracious, so unassuming and polite, that Farsi felt so at home. After two hours Farsi told Javier Henri he would be glad to add some money to the project if Javier Henri was looking for some. Javier Henri knew by now that Lisa was everything to Farsi, but for her it was just business. That was fine. The entire economy of the French Riviera and Monaco existed because of these relationships.

Javier Henri said the movie had expanded due to its quality and that he was looking to add investors. The project seemed to be too good to be limited by what Javier Henri could invest.

They decided to go to lunch, and Javier Henri picked an elegant private restaurant. He and Farsi could get into the numbers one on one. Farsi really did like Javier Henri and Brandon, most unusual for a hard-bitten greedy arms dealer whose number one assassin stayed busy and spoke in the same South African accent as his number one woman.

Likewise, Brandon and Lisa went to lunch. Brandon invited Pierre Bodit along with them. Pierre was a twenty-four-year old actor just signed on. He was a mature twenty-four years old, but Lisa still rocked his world. And when Pierre met Lisa he was polite and gracious, and he also remembered why he had become an actor, to meet the Lisa's of the world. Good career choice, Pierre.

CHAPTER 211

The day started in the Congo much as it had finished yesterday, dark brooding low hanging gray clouds. Not a day to be flying, at least not flying below the clouds. The camp of rebel soldiers was beaten down by the weather, they all stayed in their huts and mostly slept and smoked. Given their twenty-four/seven junkie ride of drugs and mayhem, a day to do nothing was a treasure.

General Mosamba was in his tent with his camp commanders. They had a productive day because there was nothing else to distract them, the weather was just miserable.

The same was true of the mercenary camp. Activity was at a minimum, although Trent Burton kept tabs on movements in general. And it seemed the Apocalypse Plane was still in the hanger, it had been over two days now. Unusual in that it often just came and went, rarely staying even one hour, such a mysterious and ominous plane. Trent never got used to seeing it, it just looked so serious and deadly.

The pilot compound had no movement. If the two pilots were there, no one saw them, and no one was allowed near their tents.

So at 2 p.m. all was quiet. And at 3 p.m. all was quiet in the Congo. In Nice the prime day's activities had been very productive. Brandon and Lisa had really gotten into it, and with Pierre in the afternoon had had some wonderful insights and additions to the project. Brandon was ecstatic getting to work with these "beautiful" people, who were also creative. Kelly and Abbey had been working hard too, but unseen, Pierre had actually never seen them before. Brandon and his group met Farsi and Javier Henri at 3:05 p.m. in Javier Henri's office. They said some concluding remarks, Pierre was told to be ready at the office for a 7:30 p.m. pick up to Monaco.

As things were breaking up, Lisa spoke to Farsi privately for just a moment. Lisa said goodbye to Javier Henri privately to also ask for a moment of his time in just a few minutes, Javier Henri said yes.

Lisa followed Brandon and Pierre back to Brandon's office just long enough for Farsi to see her, and then he departed. Lisa stalled for five minutes in Brandon's office. Then she heard her cue, just like in the movies.

With the sound of the helicopter on top of the building, Lisa excused herself saying she wanted to briefly talk contracts with Javier Henri, then she would see them tonight at the Monte Carlo. Brandon called Javier Henri's staff to arrange the Bentley to take Lisa back to Monaco when she needed it. She then left for Javier Henri's office. It was only 3:15 p.m.

CHAPTER 212

At 3:17 p.m. in the Congo base there was only one thing moving. A 4 x 4 driven by Peter Hunt left the gate and disappeared up the ridge above the base. He made a short call . . . to the High Commander in Uganda. He said simply, "Be sure to be ready by 5 p.m.," he then hung up.

If Trent Burton had been looking, he would have seen Peter Hunt return after only fifteen minutes, nothing too unusual. After all, Peter Hunt did what he wanted. He was the number one alpha male in a whole camp of alpha males. By the way, Trent Burton had been looking.

By the time Peter Hunt had re-entered the mercenary base the Ugandan High Commander had radioed the airbase in Western Uganda. No more than five minutes later the pilots were climbing into the MIG-23's.

The High Commander wanted a last minute check on these powerful but also delicate machines. That's why he wanted all five to be ready. He only had five MIG-23s, if he had had more he would have sent them.

The High Commander insisted they do a fifteen to twenty minute flight to retest all systems. Nothing had flown since the men had been doing service work on them the last four days. Strangely, it seems these very men had left the base yesterday and had not come back.

The MIG-23 jets lined up on the runway. The first MIG-23 lit the afterburners and scalded down the runway. MIG-23 number two and MIG-23 number three lined up in staggered position and lit the afterburners. Then number four and number five followed with afterburners. The noise and thunder shook the onlookers to their very core. Nothing is more humbling and awe inspiring than a powerful jetfighter roaring down the runway and then leaping into the air. The MIG-23's did that and more, a thoroughly frightening and exhilarating moment.

After thirty minutes the powerful MIG-23's had done their system checks successfully and were lining up for their touchdowns. All was well. They would be refueled and ready for the mission in thirty minutes or less, then they would just wait for the signal to get their prey.

It was now 3:47 p.m. at the mercenary base and there was slight movement in the mercenary pilots' compound. Trent Burton saw it.

CHAPTER 213

In Nice Brandon had told Kelly and Abbey about the evening, a dinner treat at the Monte Carlo Casino. The girls were excited. Then Kelly Grant had a flash back, the same Monte Carlo Casino where she and Kent had witnessed an epic real life movie scene. Kelly was pretty sure it would be in the movie, as she wrote it. She still saw the glittering Monte Carlo Casino, the Rolls Royce, the man in the tuxedo, and finally a seductive and sexual young woman as she had ever seen. Kelly remembers grabbing Kent's arm in shock at the power, elegance and sexual presence of the spontaneous event. She smiled to herself now, as she remembered it led to her own sex filled scenes later that night. This would be great even if she was part of the backdrop herself tonight.

One floor down from where Brandon was outlining the night's activities, Javier Henri was firmly between Lisa's legs and Lisa could not get enough. She had started it all by basically letting Javier Henri review the package under her outfit. She took her panties off first. They now were in his apartment off his opulent office. Afterwards Javier Henri played with Lisa and she played with him.

She then got up, took a chair to the window, put her knees on the chair, and looked out over the harbor. She then looked back at him and she was not smiling, just a serene look. She used to use the routine with Kent a long time ago in Sandton, when she was eighteen.

As Javier Henri was getting on Lisa again, Kent, now Code 011, was getting into the flat black jetfighter at the Congo mercenary base. It seemed a suicide mission awaited.

CHAPTER 214

The MIG-23s were returning to base in Western Uganda. The first MIG-23 flew deep into the runway to give extra space for the timed landings behind him. It was good he did.

As he touched down, all was fine . . . very smooth, very fine. Then the nose gear touched down and for seven seconds all was fine . . . very fine. After seven seconds the nose landing gear collapsed and the nose of the MIG-23 hit the concrete runway with a sickening crush, and then a sickening scrape, sparks flying, pieces of metal flaking off. The plane stopped fifty yards from the end of the runway. But it was too late in the timed landings. MIG-23 number two touched down, deployed the parachute to stop the plane, and then eased the nose gear down. And in slower motion the second nose gear collapsed with more crunching, scrapping and metal flying. So they were lucky . . . no fire had started.

It was also too late for the third MIG-23. His problem was on touchdown he had less places to go because the two previous MIG-23s were stacked on the runway. So he deployed his parachute and gently sat the nose down, but to no avail, the nose gear collapsed. But he did manage to get a 10° deflection of the plane before the nose wheel collapsed, and thus he plowed into the ground on the side of the runway rather than the MIG grounded on the runway in front of him.

The fourth and fifth jets were able to go around. The air controller had no option, the jets should divert to Kampala, Uganda only twenty minutes away. The same air controller notified the High Commander of the incredible events he had just witnessed. Damn Soviet planes, the High Commander cursed.

But the High Commander recalculated. He would have two left. In twenty-five minutes the planes would be in Kampala and refueled.

With more aviation fuel the same mission could be done, he would just have to have the time the jet at the mercenary base was taxiing on the runway. The MIG-23s would scramble then and given their superior speed to the Hunter RF/F-07, they could still intercept it. Their advantage is the prey had no idea that there were predators out there. The MIG-23s would go supersonic out of Kampala. The sonic booms would lead to heart attacks among the elephants and gorillas, not to speak of the population. So be it, the High Commander and General Mosamba had money to make.

Eventually being a double agent ceases to be a double payoff. Peter Hunt got the call from the High Commander. If Peter sides with the General, he calls the taxi in time. If he chooses the mercenary pilots, he "forgets" to call it in or the radio went "dead." He didn't have time to go to his career counselor. If he had, they probably would have advised him to just choose another profession, but too late for that.

Code 011 had started the engines, and the sleek flat black plane slowly taxied out to the runway. The engine whine was the only noise in the camp. Code 011 and his co-pilot went through the checklist as they slowly taxied out. The jet engine whine sounded more ominous since it was the only noise on base. It was 4:37 p.m.

Peter Hunt had a decision to make, and right now. He made it.

He called the High Commander and said, "It's rolling, mark time at 4:47 p.m." Which meant the MIG-23s should be fueled and ready to launch in about fifteen minutes . . . then the execution of the poor lonely jetfighter.

The High Commander is beyond intelligent. He had rushed to the Kampala airport to see his last two MIG-23s land and give them Plan B, as they sat in their jets. All could be fine after all.

But it wasn't fine. MIG-23 number four touched down, deployed the parachute, avoided putting the nose wheel down at all costs until his speed forced him to, then seven seconds of hope, then no hope. More scrapping, more crunching, more sparks, more flying metal, and then the General knew something or somebody is operating at a higher plane than he or his team. And they had won.

MIG-23 number five landed and by then everyone knew what would happen next . . . and it did. Number five went the way of the previous four and all was lost.

Could Peter Hunt be part of this? The General was ninety percent sure he must be a double agent. However it works, it had been slick and professional.

CHAPTER 215

The flat black Hunter RF/F-07 was roaring down the runway. Trent Burton called his father, Peter Hunt called no one. Let the best side win, even as he had personally stacked the deck against his own. Peter Hunt knew Code 011, but not as a comrade-in-arms, as the mercenaries from his camp were known to him. He only knew this guy as a "hired gun," the guy "from out of town," the "consultant," whatever you can put a spin on what Peter Hunt did, but it is not a case of turning on your own. He actually resented Code 011, as he was operating at the highest level and Peter Hunt was stuck in the Eastern Congo.

Either way it would soon be over, and Peter Hunt could continue to do some deals. He did not know that the MIG-23s had been "disabled" or even that they existed. Maybe that would save him.

CHAPTER 216

Lisa took a shower at Javier Henri's apartment and rushed to get dressed. The Bentley awaited her, then to Monaco and the epic dinner date.

She left her panties behind, she said she wanted to remember this on the way home. She just hoped to heavens Farsi did not come to inspect her. He didn't.

Kelly and Abbey were in a frantic swirl, excited about the evening but what to wear. It was 5:11 p.m. along the glamorous seaside with its beautiful people. It was a bit later in the Eastern Congo.

The flat black jet flew through the darkening sky. At twenty minutes northeast of the base it took a slow shallow turn, then it dropped into the clouds, and Code 011 started obeying his flat screen computer. It told him everything he needed to know flying through the rain clouds.

He came out of the clouds at only two hundred feet, but the computer knew that and gave him speed, altitude and bomb release point. He flipped the missile switch cover up, one minute away to target. Maybe not too late but closing fast on too late. He flipped the second missile switch cover.

Switch one up, count to three seconds, switch two up. Then it was all too late, so very late.

The two 500 lb. napalm bombs slowly headed for the target. They began wobbling but it didn't matter, they had only fifty feet of altitude left.

The napalm hit, exploded and created immense heat, immense flames and an immense fireball. There would be no cries for help. Everything and everybody were simply vaporized.

The intense heat expanded so rapidly it created a furnace-like blast of air. The shock wave did not last long, as the dense soggy jungle absorbed it. Then the hot air reversed and came storming back in, thus creating a majestic, if deadly, mushroom cloud. But the artwork was lost, the jungle too thick and the clouds too low. The drizzle started to dampen any fires immediately. Within an hour or so the wet would cause a horrible charcoal infused smell, a pungent, miserable, disgusting smell of burned flesh; wet, soggy burned flesh.

The mercenaries slowly came out of the jungle in their trucks. They went less than a mile and stopped. The camp was just too unbearable to occupy, they would set up their own camp in this clearing.

The head mercenary called Peter Hunt. He said, "It's been done, the camp is annihilated, the mines secure." Peter Hunt hung up in silence. So the jet he had sent to its assassination had made it.

And it was true, for as Peter Hunt hung up, the jetfighter came roaring overhead and slammed into the runway, throwing up a mist to the point the plane disappeared in it. The plane was like a black ghost.

As the jet was slowing, the hangar housing the Apocalypse Plane opened and the plane towed out.

With the gray day came the gray shadowy evening. Peter Hunt was in a daze. He watched the flat black jetfighter slowly taxi in, mirage-like picture of a lone black assassin. He didn't think he would see that sight, but now seeing it sent a chill up his spine. It was taxiing toward him as if it was coming after him. It wasn't pale, not on a day like today, but it sure looked like one of the Four Horsemen of the Apocalypse, the one death rode on. Today anyone of the other Three Horsemen of the Apocalypse would have been fine. Give me War, Pestilence, Famine, but don't give me Death.

Peter Hunt did not want to talk to the High Commander, so he didn't, he destroyed his phone to him. It didn't matter, the General knew what had happened; it was not Peter Hunt's fault. There clearly was a higher, more mysterious, more powerful player at work. And it wasn't Winston Burton, his was just lucky. Winston knew nothing of the MIG-23s or their mission.

CHAPTER 217

As Code 011 was extracting himself from the jetfighter, the High Commander was on the runway at Kampala. He was beside one of the MIG-23s and one of his technical men was looking at the landing gear. The general was not upset; he was haunted.

By the time Code 011 had cleared the jet and the fighter was being pushed into the covert hangar, the technical man in Kampala had made some startling findings. He told the General a lot could have happened, but one thing clearly stood out that was mysterious and out of order.

The MIG-23s were from Ukraine, all parts from the Ukraine, except the nose landing gear. For some reason the nose landing gear had the stamp from . . . the Cuban Air Force. How could that be. Ask Eva Escobar of Havana, she knew the man.

As the world turns, the man who had bought and smuggled those landing gears out of Cuba had been directly saved by their ultimate sabotage and use. Sometimes in this murky shadowy world luck is your only friend. To Code 011 those Havana nights seemed to have occurred seventeen lifetimes ago. He would never know this story. The charred flesh in the Congo was supposed to be his.

CHAPTER 218

The original four had arrived at the Monte Carlo Casino. The grand entrance was indeed repeated. The men in their tuxedos were dazzling, and then came Lisa, absolutely stunning, radiant and with a clear sexual presence. Farsi Abbas had hired two photographers to capture the moment and the evening.

Javier Henri and Lisa did a superb job of acting in their own right. They barely spoke to each other, except Lisa softly told Javier Henri she still would like some more of him. Then she went back to her role of giving attention to Farsi and Brandon.

The last three had been detained by traffic, the driver had called ahead to tell everyone. Kelly had missed the entrance scene, but it had been good and the pictures would show that.

CHAPTER 219

Then through the casino, moving modestly but still capturing attention, came the three. There was Pierre turned out in a tuxedo and looking like a young Brad Pitt, then came Abbey, and then quietly and modestly came Kelly Grant. Kelly wore an all-black gown, very conservative, but she did show a neckline with a black choker. The neck showed off a skin so delicate it didn't seem real. The hair and pale blue eyes were beyond captivating.

The three came from Lisa's back side, so all of a sudden there she was. Lisa froze as she gazed upon the blonde Kelly, the haunting beauty of Bayswater.

Thank God she was among the last in the introductions. The girl's delicate refined beauty was much, much stronger in person. And without Kelly doing anything, Lisa became truly haunted by this slender mysterious girl.

Thank God with seven people no one noticed Lisa losing her edge. She purposely did not look at Kelly much. Kelly's presence was so calm and beautiful to Lisa as to be eerie, yes eerie, that's the word. Who was this girl anyway, and why was she here?

The evening did not answer those questions, too much chit chat for Lisa. She only wanted to know about this girl. And where was Kent? Was he nearby?

As the evening wore down, Farsi and Javier Henri talked away from the table. Brandon and Lisa talked, and the other three talked.

Then it was over. Without getting any more insight, Lisa knew the evening was ending. She was still in a bit of a trance.

Then coming from behind Lisa, Kelly gently said goodnight to Lisa. Lisa turned and got the full impact of the face, the eyes, the hair. One very understated but dazzling display. Lisa said goodnight, now not only haunted by this girl, but now by her delicate soft but crisp British accent. Kelly Grant seemed to be from another dimension to Lisa, another plane, another world. She seemed beyond beautiful and sexy, from another world.

As Kelly walked away, Lisa felt an immense sense of relief. She needed to talk to Javier Henri desperately. Wow, what a crackling super charged evening.

CHAPTER 220

Code 011 was exhausted, a drenching wet, part from sweat, part from the rain. A jeep was bringing him straight from his mission to the Apocalypse Plane. The mercenary crowd gathered to look at the plane in the rain, and then they parted to let Code 011's 4 x 4 through.

They had seen him before, and they knew when he came something was going to die. They did not dislike him, it's just that he came only for a three or four day period and was seen by no one most of the time.

Trent Burton was watching. Lisa has her haunting Kelly baggage, and Trent Burton has Code 011. He swallowed hard looking at this man slowly pass through the crowd. From a distance Peter Hunt was also watching, and he now had also become haunted by this man.

There were no handshakes, good job, see you next time, nothing. Code 011 simply got out of the 4 x 4 and went up the tail stairs of the gray monster. As he walked up the stairs, he did glance at the crowd. No smiles, no waves.

Trent Burton felt a chill. It looked like Code 011 had looked right at him. Peter Hunt felt a chill, had this man singled him out? Actually, Code 011 saw no one in particular; he was just climbing the stairs. Trent Burton was haunted by him, now Peter Hunt was haunted by him. But Code 011 knew of nothing, they had clearly done it to themselves.

Peter Hunt called Winston Burton to tell him of the success. He was late. Trent Burton had called his father with the message as soon as the jetfighter slammed into the runway.

It was now into the evening and the taxi and take off were of a giant lumbering monster. The plane roared down the runway with afterburners like God's blowtorch. The plane leaped into the thick wet night and was gone. It was a powerful moment, and then that silence. It was clear to Trent Burton that the biblical saying of centuries might have it wrong, death may in fact ride on a dark gray horse, not a pale one. The plane turned to the southwest, but no one could see that.

CHAPTER 221

The day after the Monte Carlo night was busy. Brandon spent more time with Lisa, then they again rejoined Farsi and Javier Henri for lunch. Lisa looked for Kelly but never saw her.

At lunch Brandon mentioned going to Cape Town to scout locations, and Farsi Abbas jumped on it.

Farsi insisted Brandon come with he and Lisa. Lisa was puzzled and did not want to go to Cape Town because Alex Kagamba was there. But just like that, Farsi had set a schedule that did not exist three minutes ago. Lisa had to go along with it. And Brandon was leaving tomorrow, so there goes more time with Javier Henri. Was this Kelly coming along? Maybe.

Farsi would have his pilots set a flight plan right now. And so it was, it would be Monaco/Nice to Cape Town via Dakar, Senegal for fuel. Let the good times roll, the new private jet in its svelte light peach color would get a proper shake down.

The day wound down, everybody was happy. Lisa was still off balance but no one noticed. And Kelly was not to be found.

Lisa did manage to visit Javier Henri in his apartment for a short time. She gave him a long kiss as she left. She would be back, and she looked forward to that.

As she opened the door to leave, she turned and smiled at Javier Henri, "See you in the movies." Javier Henri smiled and said, "See you soon!" The movies and real life seemed to have become the same once again.

The day in a remote airstrip on the Angola/Namibia border had started at 2 a.m. when the Apocalypse Plane landed. Only one lone man stepped down, and then the plane once again departed with a roar on its relentless journey to some other clandestine existence and operation.

Then the "day" ended for Code 011 at 3:30 a.m. when he went into a coma. He would wake up at 6:15 p.m.

CHAPTER 222

The helicopter lifted off from Monaco with Lisa and Farsi onboard. The helicopter landed on the helipad of LeCirac Industries to pick up Brandon Craig. Standing with Brandon to see him off and wave to Farsi and Lisa were Javier Henri . . . as well as Kelly Grant, Abbey Bond, Pierre Bodit. Lisa waved as she looked at Kelly and there she was, young, radiant with wind blowing her magnificent blonde hair as if it was a Vogue shoot. Lisa then looked at Javier Henri and gave him a special wave and look. Then the helicopter lifted off for Nice Airport. It was 1:21 p.m.

Lisa had spent her last night in Monaco enjoying her peace and freedom. She sat on her balcony full of hope for this new life. She would try to keep Cape Town, Nice and London on her schedule. The real challenge was to lose Farsi, and she knew it would be difficult. He owed her $300,000, which meant she was financially free now but that was not the challenge. She would find a way . . . maybe there was some South African assassin for hire. Maybe South African intelligence could help, then she smiled, maybe that was not the way to go.

CHAPTER 223

The magnificent new Dassault 7X touched down at Dakar, Senegal 7:37 p.m. It's too bad it was dark, as the sun off the light peach colored plane was so startling elegant.

They would spend the night for crew rest. Since it was a new and expensive plane, Dassault had even sent a mechanic to be available for such a long trip. The mechanic stayed with the plane as the rest of the team went to the hotel to rest. Tomorrow was another long flight to Cape Town.

At the dilapidated airbase in Africa's no man's land Code 011 had opened his door to the pool. It seems the Ukrainian pilot had come back and little Natasha Terashova had conned her way along. She was swimming but popped out of the pool with just her thong, ran to Code 011, and fully wet threw her arms around him. Code 011 put his hands between her legs in the front and back, picked her up and brought her inside. She stayed the night.

CHAPTER 224

The next day was not a rush day in Dakar, Senegal. Lisa even went for a swim and lounged by the pool. Brandon and Farsi talked about the movie, particularly the location scouting. Brandon was excited about getting to shop for exotic locales and backdrops in Africa. It all made sense since he had his South African connection now with Lisa. She was as smart as she was ultra-sexual.

At 2 p.m. on the tarmac at Dakar, Senegal all was set. The crew was onboard and Farsi, Lisa and Brandon went up the steps. The engines started their whine and the plane taxied out.

At 4 p.m. everyone onboard enjoyed a light dinner. Farsi had commissioned the hotel chef to prepare dinner, as well as snacks for the eight-hour flight. The flight would go to Dakar, over Luanda, Angola, jog inland over Angola, then into Cape Town. The plane was magnificent and performing flawlessly. It was a marvel of engineering, as well as a work of art. The afternoon African sun highlighted the sleek lines and the gentle glow of the peach color. Its registration number was Zu-171 registered in South Africa because Farsi expected to spend a lot of time there now. Lisa's life's dream was exactly the opposite.

CHAPTER 225

At 7:13 p.m. over Africa everyone was content. The pilots were enjoying a cold fruit juice, the mechanic dozed, Farsi was writing notes, Lisa was in a light sleep and Brandon was buried as usual in his movie project book. He already had eleven things for Kelly and Abbey to do for him. He would call them tomorrow with the list. He smiled, they were two great young girls. He knew they were gorgeous but he worked with them, so they were like two younger sisters. They were part of what made his job so much fun and stimulating.

It was now 7:21 p.m. There was no way the Dassault 7X could have known it was coming. There was no checklist the pilots could have used to see it. And there certainly was no way they could have avoided it and to know how quickly it was closing in on them.

At a distance of only 1,700 yards behind the Dassault the powerful MIG-23 slowed down. A final command was radioed, the safety switch cover flipped up, the air-to-air missile switch switched on. A red light in the cockpit came on, the missile had gone.

The missile slammed so ferociously into the Dassault 7X that explosives were not even needed. Likely Lisa's and Brandon's necks were snapped some milliseconds before the entire crew and Farsi were vaporized.

The MIG had fired the heat-seeking missile some 500 feet below the Dassault and then broke and dived 1,500 feet to the left to avoid the heat and debris. The massive white glare that came through the right side of the canopy was all they needed to see. They dove in stages from 41,000 feet to 100 feet, then raged across the African wasteland to that dilapidated airstrip. They landed twenty-one minutes later. Code 011 climbed out exhausted and covered in sweat.

The Code 011 mission was complete, which meant the young lives of Lisa Aswanela and Brandon Craig, along with their dreams, had vanished forever. They had been in the wrong place at the wrong time with the wrong man.

The smoldering wreckage of the Dassault 7X hit the African floor not one mile from the previous aviation carnage; the wreckage would lay silent this time, only the harsh wind and the raw countryside of the Angolan highlands to keep it company.

CHAPTER 226

Life is neither fair nor just . . . then you die. All the hopes and dreams for the young people, those still living and those now dead, had of course evaporated. Kelly and Abbey lost their innocence in those seconds over desolate Africa. Their lives would go on, but there would always be a hint of sadness. Even the worldly Javier Henri would be affected, if only because of that one afternoon with Lisa having made this all so personal. And Brandon Craig had become a very special friend.

Alex Kagamba would never find out what really happened, nor would Farsi's family, nor General Abdul. Farsi Abbas and General Mosamba had just started their lucrative deals when in the space of two to three days they were both reduced to carbon molecules. General Mosamba's dream of touching Lisa had vanished, as both he and Lisa had vanished. Two missions, one man, two jetfighters, one man. And that's the way it went that day on the continent of Africa.

Farsi Abbas in his self-absorbed arrogance had never realized the first downed plane of his was meant for him. This time "they" got it right. A hard, tall, lean, extremely dangerous looking man had been at the Dakar Airport. If Lisa had spotted him, she would have recognized him as the man she saw that night she drove by Hyde Park. It was the same man, she just did not see him this time in Dakar. Lisa never knew the danger.

Code 011, or the next name would go on, never knowing or wanting to know the carnage he left behind. It wasn't personal. The delightful Alexus Gomez would still have a father, except for Code 011. Of course other young girls would not have a father because of Pedro Gomez. So it goes.

Lisa was special to Kent (Code 011), she had always been special. Likely, as the next year unwound, he would realize she was gone but he would not think how she disappeared or if he was the direct cause. He would think she had selected someone and now was living in her own house. Maybe it was the young man she walked with along harbor side in Cape Town. They would make an excellent couple.

CHAPTER 227

And now Todd Blake and Javier Henri LeCirac shared a very special bond. Both knew enough about the "4ᵗʰ Mercenary" story only to be mystified by it. It was a haunting story that seemed destined to never be told. Javier had called Todd Blake after the plane had disappeared, and both knew the trend that was being set here. Javier Henri did not want to give up on the project, but he would clearly take his time before moving forward.

And now there was only one man who had actually seen the "4ᵗʰ Mercenary," a one Trent Burton. But he knew nothing about a "4ᵗʰ Mercenary" or its connection to this man. If he did, he would surely be in a mental ward; he was almost there without knowing.

And surely the French Intelligence agents would be in touch with Javier Henri again. The cycle of events was beyond their understanding. They would likely plod along like good bureaucrats . . . understanding little except the day they got paid and the day the mortgage payment was due.

CHAPTER 228

In the Eastern Congo life went on, if it can be called that. At the Congo mercenary camp, a 4 x 4 left the base gates. Fifteen minutes later Peter Hunt parked the 4 x 4 up on the ridge overlooking the base. He got out and walked to the front of the vehicle.

He was leaning on the front of the vehicle and had just begun to talk when the bullet from an AR-15 assault rifle ripped through his chest. The shot had come from the brush in front of him. There had been only a slight sound.

Peter Hunt slowly slumped on the front bumper and then slowly fell face down, slow motion death. Three mercenaries came from the brush fifty yards behind the 4 x 4. A single man came from the bush in front of the 4 x 4.

The man carrying the AR-15 handed it to one of the mercenaries; he had already screwed the silencer off.

Another 4 x 4 appeared and stopped by the first 4 x 4. The assassin said a few words to the mercenaries and got in the 4 x 4 to go to the Rwanda border, then to Kigali, then to Johannesburg. The assassin had spoken in a South African accent.

CHAPTER 229

The three mercenaries carefully wrapped Peter Hunt's body and carried it to a prepared grave. They had dug it yesterday. They gently laid him in and covered the grave with several large slabs of stone . . . also brought up yesterday. They paid a silent respect. He had been a hard professional mercenary, a legend among legends. That's all they knew or wanted to know. All men die, few ever live. Peter Hunt had lived, that was good enough for them.

The men got in their 4 x 4. As they did, the Apocalypse Plane came roaring overhead toward the runway and they got out to watch. It slammed into the runway and threw up vortexes of smoking rubber, then began roaring to a stop. For a brief moment the sun's angle on the gray paint turned it to a pale white shade. It was the Apocalypse Plane, and it seems Death still Rides on a Pale Horse.

And in Seat 7A, British Airways Flight 081, Cape Town to London, a man sat in a black outfit. It seemed to be some kind of custom designed expedition clothing, it was hard to tell. He read the Financial Times; he was drinking a pineapple juice on ice. His Bell & Ross watch showed it was 3:21 p.m.

All Men **Die** . . .
       Few Ever Live. . . . . . .

THE CREST OF THE 4TH MERCENARY

Made in the USA
Coppell, TX
29 July 2021